IF WE HAD
NO WINTER

IF WE HAD NO WINTER

◆ ◆ ◆

A Billie Dixon Novel
Book One

D. L. Pitchford

Straight on till Morningside Prints

First published in 2017 in the United States
by Straight on till Morningside Prints

Cover Design by Sarah Anderson of No Synonym Book Covers

ISBN   978 0 9987 9456 3

Straight on till Morningside Prints
11923 NE Sumner St., STE 709378
Portland, OR 97220

www.DLPitchford.com

For my mother and father,
who were always there for me,
no matter how stupidly I behaved.

If we had no winter, the spring would not be so pleasant: if we did not sometimes taste of adversity, prosperity would not be so welcome.

Anne Bradstreet

One

"Don't you ever spend time in your own room, Dixon?"
The words are out of his mouth before he's even inside the
door.

Leaning against the headboard, Jimmy offers me an apologetic smile and runs a hand through his messy brown hair.
He only defends me from his asshole roommate as a last
resort.

But I can hold my own.

When I look over, ready to retort, Xander's unloading
his textbooks onto his unkempt bed. He's waiting for me to
take the bait. He knows I can't ignore his jibes.

Jimmy pokes my ribs and nods toward my *Norton
Anthology*. "Focus, Billie. Walt Whitman. American Lit."
Per usual, he wants to prevent any conflict.

I scoff but tug the book closer. "If I have to read one
more section of this poem, I'm going to hurl."

He laughs good-naturedly. "They're call cantos. If
you're going to pass the final, you should know the proper
terminology."

Despite my irritation, I smile.

On the desk, Jimmy's phone buzzes, and he reads the

text with a little smile. "You need to check your phone more often."

I shift to pull my phone from my pocket. Two messages, both from Imogene. "Oh."

Across the room, Xander drops his textbooks on top of the mini-fridge and shoves his backpack under his bed. It takes me hours to unwind at the end of the day, but he pushes everything out of sight and moves on without a second thought.

Jimmy's phone goes off again, and he releases a little laugh and responds. His freckled cheeks are pink with amusement when he relaxes, the device clutched firmly to his chest.

"I don't know what she wants from me." I let my screen fade to black. This is the third text of the day.

He almost laughs. "Maybe you should've gone home over break. How many other people were on campus for Thanksgiving?"

Aside from our RA and two foreign exchange students, it was only me and Xander in Lincoln Hall. With Jimmy away, we weren't forced to spend time together. No heated arguments. No angry compromises. I didn't even have to acknowledge his existence.

"It was a short break." I heave a sigh. "You know I can't afford to fly home for every short break." Even if it means disappointing my little sister.

The headboard squeaks as he shifts. "My parents don't mind contributing if it means they get to see you."

"I'm not a charity case, Jimmy."

"You could've at least told Imogene you were staying on campus. Sounds a lot better coming from your sister instead of your neighbor." He pushes his black-rimmed glasses up. "She gets her feelings hurt whether you see it or not."

He's right, of course, but I have my reasons for staying in a tiny-ass town in Vermont for the holiday. Imogene is the only real reason to go home.

Xander powers up his PS2 and massive 55-inch TV, then makes a detour for the bathroom they share with the boys next door. Of course. He's going to play his stupid video games, completely ignoring the fact that we're studying.

"Do you need a break?"

Or maybe we're not studying.

I offer Jimmy a small smile. "Sorry. I'm distracted."

He gestures for me to explain.

I push up into a sitting position and brush a section of auburn corkscrew curls over my shoulder. It's up in a ponytail, but it's still in the way. "I have a thing at five, and I haven't mentally prepared for it." I don't know how else to explain, how to make him understand.

Jimmy's face transforms into a wide smile. "Are you finally getting together with your dad? He is the reason you're at Bradford—you should at least pay him back by spending time with him. You've put this off for too long."

I open my mouth, but Xander walks out, and his loose black hair shimmers in the light from outside. His t-shirt and jeans are tucked under one arm, and drops the dirty clothes in his hamper.

All I can do is gape.

It's barely four o'clock on a Thursday, but he has no qualms walking around in Wolverine boxers.

Jimmy clears his throat.

I straighten my glasses and focus on the discussion. "My

3

father's a professor here. That doesn't mean I'm indebted to him. He doesn't pay my tuition. His job just makes it cheaper."

"The divorce papers went through over three years ago. Being here at Bradford is the first you've seen him."

"That was his decision, not mine. I'm not the one who stopped calling."

"People make mistakes."

I roll my eyes. This isn't the first time I've heard this spiel. "He's made the same mistake for three years straight."

With a sigh, he closes his textbook. His phone, now on the mattress, lights up. The bed vibrates. Is he still texting Imogene? "I'm not making excuses for him." He pauses to read the text. "But he probably thought you wanted to reconnect with him since you're attending his school and majoring in his department. You've avoided him since we arrived."

I frown. "He hasn't taken the time to contact me either."

Jimmy pushes the phone away without responding. "Which is why I'm glad you finally made plans, Billie. I know better than anyone how upset you were when your parents separated."

My gaze shifts to my textbook, still open to Whitman's "Song of Myself." How can I tell him I haven't? Especially when he's so happy for me. How can I say I haven't spoken to my father since we arrived in August? How can I say I have no intention to talk to that man ever again?

From the floor, Xander releases a derisive laugh.

Apparently, I don't have to.

I grit my teeth. "Do you have something to say?"

He doesn't look over as he navigates the game menu.

"There's no world in which you reached out to your dad."

"You don't know that."

He casts a lazy glance over his shoulder. "Go on then. Tell me I'm wrong."

But I can't.

He knows I can't.

His intense blue eyes study me, but when I don't speak, he sends me his patented smirk and turns up the volume. The game's starting.

When I turn to Jimmy, his face has fallen. "You're not meeting your dad, are you?"

I shake my head. Somehow, he manages to make me feel guilty even when he's the one who misinterpreted.

His disappointment is obvious, but Jimmy moves on quickly. "Then what are your plans at five?"

I close my *Norton* textbook and lay my notes on top. "I'm meeting someone for tutoring."

Xander snorts. Apparently, he can still hear us over the Japanese music. "You suddenly failing Western Civ? Or are you so anal you can't stand anything less than an A?"

I force myself to ignore him. "I put an ad on the school website last week, and someone took me up on it."

Jimmy's bushy eyebrows bunch together. "You're tutoring someone?"

On the floor, Xander bursts into laughter.

"I can be professional, and I'm good enough at math to tutor someone in calculus."

Finally, Jimmy's face shifts to a smile. "I'm not skeptical of your ability, trust me. You're the reason I passed high school math."

"But?"

He averts his eyes. "It's just, your social skills—"

Xander pauses the game and twists to face us, a smirk on his tawny face. "Who's the unlucky moron?"

Jimmy's curious frown is the only reason I answer. "All I have is a name. Nelson something. I don't remember."

"And what in the world makes you think you'll be a good teacher?"

I square my shoulders. "Definitely not you."

When Xander sprawls across the floor, his muscles stretch, his abdomen taut. It always surprises me how fit he is when he never gets off his ass. "Is this your first job? How cute."

"I got a job the second I turned sixteen, thank you. What would you know? You've never worked a day in your life, rich boy." I don't give him a chance to counter. "A blow-off job at the Eyrie doesn't count. All you do is flirt with the female customers."

Xander releases a humorless laugh and directs an enormous calligraphy brush across the screen.

I'm still glaring when Jimmy speaks. "I'm sure tutoring will be fine. I mean, you're good at everything you do—math, computers, coding, art. You'll be great." He's trying to placate me.

My phone says I have forty-five minutes, but I want to be as far away from Xander as possible. "I should get ready. We can study more tonight."

From the floor, Xander laughs again. "Make sure to take your Midol before you meet him."

I gather my things, jaw clenched, and Jimmy follows me across the hall. He pauses while I unlock my door. "I didn't mean to screw with your confidence."

Thankfully, the room is empty.

I shake my head. "It's fine. I'll be fine."

Let's be honest, though. As much as I try to ignore the ache behind my eyes and tension in my neck, I'm anxious about the meeting.

"Sorry we have to postpone our study session." I drop my things on my desk and pile up my calculus textbook and notes. I cannot forget anything. I need to be a professional.

He leans against my door. "It happens."

"At least you have Xander." I may not like the guy, but they've become quite close.

"That might be a comfort if he weren't going to play *Okami* for the next five hours."

I drag my backpack from my desk chair and yank it open. The textbooks from my morning classes are still inside. "He never does anything useful."

"He's most productive in the morning, I think. You'd know if you weren't almost late for class every morning."

I cock an eyebrow. "You think?"

Jimmy shrugs. "He gets up before me—except on Saturdays."

On Saturdays, Xander's too hung over to get up early.

"Why in the world were we stuck with awful roommates? Those compatibility forms were supposed to room you with someone you get along with."

But this is where I lose him.

"Don't say that." His tone is reproachful. "I can't vouch for Val, but you're the only person who doesn't like Xander."

I purse my lips. "Well, I'm the only person who sees reason."

Jimmy laughs.

"What? He's an ass."

He shakes his head. "He's not a terrible person, Billie. And it works both ways. He's not the only one who could be a little kinder."

"Whatever." I shove all the calc supplies into the bag, trying to keep my irritation in check. "I'm glad he's a dick to me. That makes me the one girl he has no interest in boning, and that sounds perfect to me."

Jimmy smiles conspiratorially. "Like you'd notice if he were into you." He's definitely not conspiring with me.

I glare. "What does that mean?"

He laughs. "We've been best friends for ten years, and you're the most clueless person I've ever met."

"Right, because you're great at understanding our fellow humans, strange creatures that they are."

"All I'm saying is, you should get to know him instead of making assumptions. Not everyone fits inside your perfect bubbles. I don't."

I frown and look away.

Of course he doesn't. Jimmy's special. He's my best friend and the only person who stayed by my side when my dad left. He never pressured me, never judged me when I retreated into the background, never stopped caring— unlike everyone else.

"I need to get ready. We'll talk later."

I don't know why he still puts up with me.

◆

By the time I reach the library, the small pain behind my eyes is a full-blown headache, but I set up at the agreed-upon table a full ten minutes before five.

Beneath large fluorescent lights, the second story of Chapman Library is divided into three sections. At the top of the stairs, where I sit, an area is cordoned off for study tables, each with its own lamp, and the other two sections spread across each side with rows upon rows of books.

Across the table, I spread my calculus book, spiral notebook, and one-inch binder. On my right side, I line up the bottom edges of a black gel pen and a green highlighter. And when everything is organized, I cast my gaze around the library.

The top floor is nearly empty. Even two weeks before finals, it's quiet at dinnertime.

He arrives seven minutes after five. Under the harsh fluorescents, his white skin looks translucent, especially beneath his jet-black hair. Sharp jawline, angular features, and he's slim and tall, visible on the stairs long before he reaches the top—he's at least six foot. He strolls up the stairs, one arm wrapped around a binder, the other hand inside the pocket of his Bradford hoody, and upon discovering me, stops at the table's edge, looming. "Uh, Wilhelmina?" He glances at the sticky note on his notebook.

I grimace. "Billie."

"You're in my calculus class, right?" He tilts his head. "Eight a.m. with Hodges?"

I've never noticed him, but I nod. I'm usually too engrossed in the classwork to pay attention to my peers.

"I'm Zane." He leans over to offer his hand. "Zane Nelson."

For a moment, I stare at the hand. It's pale like the rest of him, smooth and unused, but his nails are down to the quick. He's never done hard labor, and he possibly has an oral fixation. But more importantly, I don't like people touching me.

"Then you're in the right place," I say instead. I turn my attention to the books, push my thick-rimmed glasses up my nose, and move a large section of coiled hair behind my shoulder. "Let's get started."

Zane pauses before pulling his hand back, then he lays his things down and sits opposite me. "Hold on. Aren't you a little young to teach me calculus?" He eyes me skeptically, eyebrows furrowed.

I frown. I knew this was coming, of course, especially after Jimmy's morale-boosting speech earlier, but the head-ache behind my eyes flares up. I push my fingers beneath my glasses and pinch the bridge of my nose. "Yes, I'm eighteen, and yes, I'm a freshman." I pull back my hand and clasp my fingers together on the table. "That makes me no less capable than anyone else here."

"How good are you at math? Because I'm a senior and—"

"And you're only now taking Calculus. If you were good at it, you would've taken it sooner. This isn't an instance where you should save the best for last."

Unconvinced, he shrugs.

I focus on the edge of my notebook. This is easier if I don't look at him. "I took every possible math class in high school, five of which weren't required. I intend to major in Mathematics. This calculus class is going to be a cinch for me. If you don't want me to teach you, leave. You don't have to be here."

We sit in silence as he digests my words.

"Wait." He leans forward to get a closer look at me.

"You're Wilhelmina Dixon. Are you related to Dr. Dixon?"

I purse my lips. My father is the last thing I want to talk about. "No."

"You are!" A smile spreads across his face. "He's the Head of the Math Department. You must be good. Let's get down to it, Wilhelmina."

"Billie," I correct again, but he turns his attention to his notepad. "We need to discuss terms."

Zane raises an eyebrow. "I thought we agreed on ten bucks an hour? Do you want more?" I shake my head and open my mouth, but he laughs. "Alright, you can have eleven, and hell, if I get a good grade on the final, I'll give you a bonus. We have a lot of stuff to go over in the next two weeks."

"A bonus?"

"Yeah, whatever you want. Within reason."

We sit in silence for a moment, our eyes locked. I doubt my skills as a teacher warrant that much, but would refusing imply I'm unprofessional or unqualified? I need this job. It's December now, and I haven't worked since arriving at Bradford mid-August. If I don't find something soon, I won't have the money for next semester's books.

Finally, I turn to my textbook. "We should get started then."

"Where do we begin?"

I take a deep breath. "How did you score on the midterm?"

With a small smile, Zane flips through his textbook until he finds one of the many papers sticking out. He shoves the stapled sheets toward me.

C-. It could be worse.

11

My phone chimes, and I reach into my bag to retrieve it. A text from Imogene: *When are you free? We should talk soon.* I frown and push the phone aside. Right now, my sister can wait. That conversation will require my full attention.

I thumb through the four sheets of paper, glancing over Mr. Hodges's corrections and notations. Zane has a good understanding of limits, but difficulty with derivatives. Differentiation needs a lot of work. No idea how he's processing integrals, since we started that Monday, but it probably needs improvement as well.

I clear my throat and lay his test down. "What's the definition of a derivative?"

Apparently, he expected more of a preamble. He flounders for a minute before flipping through the book again, searching for the chapter. He's taking too long.

"This shouldn't be something you have to look up. It's an easy formula to remember, and it's essential to solving for the derivative of any function. Of course, as you should remember, we have plenty of shortcuts, but if you can't remember those, you need the definition to solve the problem."

"Um, it's f of x equals...something."

"If by 'f of x,' you mean 'f prime of x,' so far so good."

Finally, he gives up and stares at me helplessly. "Okay, what is it?"

"Chapter 2.1, Zane. It should be on the first page. Let's look at it together."

He furrows his brow before turning back to the book for the pertinent information, and I scoot closer and swallow down the nausea in my nervous stomach.

Two

DESPITE THE THICK CONCRETE WALLS, VAL'S SHOWER IN THE en suite bathroom is still discernible. I glance at the clock on my phone. She's been in there for twenty minutes, and there's no end in sight.

On her bed, she's already laid out her clothes for the evening—a tight, plum-colored dress and a pair of gold hooker heels. Several pairs of earrings and an Egyptian-style pendant that reaches down to her navel sit on her desk. She's going out tonight.

I glance through one of the later chapters in my textbook. Partial derivatives. We won't study it in this class—probably not in Calc II either—but I already know all this. The class is a refresher.

With a sigh, I skip ahead to the next chapter and thumb through sections on relative and absolute extrema. I flip another page, and a knock sounds on the door.

I don't want to get up, but I'm not studying—not really. I'm already caught up on all my classes.

I force myself to my feet, leaving my calc textbook behind, and march to the door. "Yeah?"

Ugh. Xander.

"What do you want?"

He forces a smile. "Hello to you too."

The sight of him makes me pause. Button-up shirt, shiny shoes, and sleek dark jeans. Aside from the leather jacket slung over his left shoulder, this is quite a change from his typical Batman and *Legend of Zelda* t-shirts and Vans. Nevertheless, he looks good in everything he wears—and he's well aware of that fact.

I raise an eyebrow. "Sure, hi." I return to my bed, but for some reason, he doesn't go away. I glance at my phone again. "The cafeteria closes in twenty minutes. Isn't it a little late for all of us to go to dinner?"

Xander laughs and collapses on my giant beanbag, letting his jacket fall beside him. "I'm so not here for you."

"Then why are you here?"

A smug grin envelops his face. "I have a date."

"Why would I care?" I push a few loose strands of hair out of my eyes. Where was I?

Right, relative extrema.

Xander interrupts before I can immerse myself. "You wouldn't."

Huffing, I look up at his stupid face. "Give me a straight answer or get out. Seriously."

He laughs again. "I'm not here for you, Dixon. I'm waiting for Val."

Nausea wells in my stomach, and I don't bother hiding my disgust. "You two are perfect for each other. Congratulations."

Another smug grin. "You know, now that you say that, I'm having serious second thoughts. Maybe I should go."

"Please. You're a distraction."

"I'll be quiet." He leans back in the beanbag, the picture of relaxation, and zips his mouth shut.

I roll my eyes and return to my book.

There's barely any difference between working with one variable and two. This is easy. It's the only thing in life that is.

"What're you doing?"

I glance up. Xander's eyes are on me, and he leans forward curiously, but he's too far away to catch a glimpse. When I don't answer, he cocks an eyebrow expectantly.

Frowning, I look back to the book. "I'm reading about relative extrema."

He snorts. "What the hell's that?"

"You wouldn't understand."

He scoffs. "Do you have a test over it?"

"No."

A small laugh bursts from his lips, and he scoots the beanbag closer, past the footboard. "Is your Saturday night so boring you have to resort to reading about some stupid mathematical principle that's not covered in your class?" He leans against the bed, smirking.

"I like math." I shake my head. I don't know why I bother talking to him. "You wouldn't understand."

Xander snatches the book from my bed. "*A function,* f *of* (x, y), *has a relative minimum at the point of* (a, b) *if* f *of*—okay, seriously, you read this shit for fun?"

I glare. "Give it back."

"Gladly." He pushes the book, open to my current page, across the bed. "I learned enough about functions in high school to last a lifetime."

"I'm impressed you know how to read it."

"That's not the only impressive thing I can do." I don't have to look to know he's smirking.

"I'm sure you'll tell my roommate all about your talents tonight."

Once she manages to get out of the shower. How much of her body does she need to shave in preparation for their date?

Xander rests an arm unnecessarily close to me. "How long has she been in there? I told her eight, and it's ten after."

I grit my teeth. I'm tired of this conversation. I really have no interest in their evening activities, especially considering it's no secret how often Xander's dates end in sex.

"Dixon, are you ignoring me?"

My eyes move down to critical points, and Xander groans.

"It's boring to make fun of you when you're ignoring me, Dixon. But I know you can't do it for long. You have to retaliate."

I narrow my eyes at the page. The words are insulting—mostly because they're true—and despite my better judgment, I shift my gaze to look at his irritated face. "What more could you possibly make fun of? You've already mocked my entire evening."

His face transforms into a grin, and he leans closer. "There's always more I can make fun of. You make it so easy—and tempting."

I'm saved from responding by the water finally shutting off.

Val exits the bathroom and waltzes into the room wrapped in a towel to retrieve her clothes. She barely contains a shriek at the sight of Xander. "Go away!" He's probably never seen her without makeup before.

Unfazed by her outburst, he places his hands over his eyes with a dramatic flourish. "I can close my eyes."

I return to my notes as Val snatches the clothes off her bed and hurries back to the bathroom. When the blow-dryer starts a few minutes later, Xander gives up on covering his eyes to check his watch. "How much longer is this going to last?"

I send him a glare and keep reading.

"Forever, apparently." He leans his head against his arm and shuts his eyes.

At last, Val returns, her hands on her hips. Her attempt to play it cool isn't very convincing with a quivering lower lip. "Okay, you can look now."

Between the dress, the makeup, and her styled hair, she's trying too hard, and Xander isn't easily impressed. He barely gives her a once-over before standing and pulling on his jacket in one fluid motion. "Let's go." He leads her by the shoulders, and Val scrambles to grab her purse.

As he closes the door, Xander calls over his shoulder, "Don't wait up," and waggles his eyebrows suggestively. The latch clicks into place behind them.

Silence.

Beautiful silence. They can stay out as long as they like.

By the time I finish the chapter on maximum extrema, I'm exhausted. It's only 9:30, but I'm always tired—one of the side effects of never sleeping enough.

I close the textbook and push it aside. I need something, anything, a distraction.

On my desk, my phone lights up, vibrating and blasting the opening bars of Weezer's "Troublemaker." Not exactly the distraction I was looking for.

I stand and grab the phone. Imogene.

My finger hovers over the 'Reject' button before sliding over to 'Accept.' She's talking before I have the phone to my ear.

"You didn't come home for Thanksgiving, Billie." Her normally bubbly tone is a cross between sadness and accusation. I knew this conversation was coming. "You didn't call."

"You knew I wasn't coming, Mo," I say in a small voice. "Jimmy told you."

"Yeah, when he arrived Wednesday afternoon."

"I should've called, I know."

"Yes, you should have." But her tone quickly loses its bite. "I miss you."

My chest tightens. I want to tell her I miss her too, sorry I didn't call, but all that comes out is, "How's Mom?"

On the other side of the line, a ball bearing clinks as she shakes up a tiny glass bottle. She's applying nail polish. "She's getting out of the house more." Imogene chooses her words carefully. "Doing a Latin dance class to try to keep her mind off things. I'm sure she'll tell you all about it at Christmas. It's all she talks about right now. She says the instructor is amazingly talented." She pauses. "You are coming home for Christmas, right?"

I nod, though she can't see me. "They do kick us out of the dorms over winter break."

"Good, good," she says absentmindedly. "How're your classes? Not failing anything, are you?"

I let out a small hollow laugh. "Won't find out till the end

18

of the semester, but my midterm grades were fine. Jimmy is in my American Literature class, and we work on our papers together. Not that he's any better with English than I am."

She leans away from the mouthpiece to blow. "Yeah, he mentioned something like that."

I grab my wallet and head for the door, pausing when I open it. "Wait, what? Since when do you talk to Jimmy about that?"

Imogene huffs. "Since you barely communicate, Billie. I have to get news about your life from somewhere, and if that happens to be from our next-door neighbor and your only friend, so be it."

My grip tightens on my wallet. "You can talk to me, you know. You're just better at communicating than me."

The short trek into the hallway to find the Coke machine is cold in a t-shirt and gym shorts. The vending machines are located at the end of the hallway, near the elevators and laundry room. Most of the rooms are closed, including Jimmy's. With Xander out, Jimmy's usually studying or working a shift at the Eyrie. He's always been a shut-in like me—until Xander came into the picture.

On the left, across from the laundry room, David's door is open, and he glances up from his bed as I pass. He lifts a hand to wave and smiles. Our RA.

"Everyone is better at communicating than you, sis." Imogene sighs. "Except maybe Dad."

And there's the segue.

The carpet in front of the vending machines is worn down from heavy foot traffic. I push my quarters into the soda machine, and the *clink clink* echoes in the enclave as it collects my change.

19

Out of Sprite. I settle for orange soda.

"Speaking of him," she says, her voice slow and unsteady, "what's it like being around him? It can't be easy."

No, the meticulous effort to avoid him at all costs hasn't been easy.

"We don't see each other often."

The bottle is dispensed at the bottom, and I retrieve it before taking a glance at the snack machines. I don't remember the last time I ate.

"Billie, what's he like?"

I move closer and pick out a bag of chips. "What, you don't remember?" I grab it from the dispenser and turn back toward my room.

"There'd have to be something for me to remember. Someone had to keep Mom company while the two of you were gallivanting at the university and exchanging your secret codes."

I purse my lips as I walk down the hallway again. "We did not gallivant."

She doesn't respond.

"He's the same as he always was. Rides his bike to campus every day. I don't know. We don't see each other often. I've got loads of homework, and he, you know, has to grade loads of homework."

"Yeah, I know." Disappointment laces her voice. "When does your break start? When will you come home?"

"It's a couple weeks away. I think my last final is on Thursday; I'll fly out after that."

I haven't even thought about travel back to Missouri yet. Jimmy booked his flight, and Xander's flying out around the same time. They're driving up to the Burlington

International Airport that Friday afternoon since their flights are the following morning. Jimmy's been nagging me to book mine so I can go with them, but I'm not particularly keen on an hour-drive with Xander.

"Okay." Imogene sounds skeptical.

I pause at the door of my room. "I'll let you know when to pick me up at the airport, alright?"

"Yeah. Mom and I'll be there for you. Give us a little heads-up, though. I don't want to rush over there because you forgot to tell us your arrival time."

"Of course. I have to go, Mo."

"Do you have plans?" Her voice bubbles again.

I almost laugh. "Does studying count?"

She scoffs. "Alright, fine. I'll let you go."

"Yeah, bye." I end the call and reach for the doorknob.

To my right, the door to Room 421 opens, and the happy face of Prudence Marlowe peeks out. "Hi, Billie." Her flowing brown hair bounces as she exits her room and locks the door.

I nod and turn the knob.

"Can you believe how long Val's showers last?" Prudence laughs. "I don't think I've ever known someone who needs that much time to bathe." She and her roommate Cynthia—otherwise known as the love of Jimmy's life—share the bathroom with us; we see each other on a daily basis.

I shrug. "I wasn't paying attention." Or at least trying not to.

"Did I hear she's going on a date tonight?" Her face lights up with curiosity, then she glances at the chips in my hand. "How do you eat that junk and stay so skinny?"

I raise an eyebrow. "Yeah, she has a date." I push open

21

the door and gaze at my bed before looking Prudence's way.

"Really? With who?"

I don't bother keeping the sneer off my face. "Xander, of course." Honestly, I should've expected it sooner with the way Val's thrown herself at him during our seminar class.

I turn back to the room and step inside. "I'm going to turn in." She's still sending me warm wishes when I lock the door behind me.

I take a quick drink and open up my laptop to play the soft mellow sounds of the Foo Fighters. With Val gone, I can listen to whatever I want without complaint.

From beneath the stacks of textbooks on my desk, I withdraw my most recent sketchbook, pages torn and faded, ragged edges, nearly full. Maybe the flow of ink can help me sleep tonight.

Three

WHEN MR. HODGES FINISHES HIS LESSON, I PACK AWAY MY books.

On the other side of the classroom, Zane shoulders his bag and stands, ready to leave, but he pauses. Per usual, his straight black hair falls in his eyes. He approaches and stops next to my desk as I zip my backpack.

"I might be late tonight," he says as we exit the classroom. "I have a meeting with my adviser, and he usually runs late. But it's in Mercier Hall, so that's close."

"That's fine." We head upstairs to the first floor of Stanley Hall. The math classes are in the basement. "We can start later if that's easier."

Zane shrugs and pauses at the top landing. "Oh, hey, I have something for you." He rifles through his bag, and I stop beside him, glancing around the foyer as the other students pass. He pulls out a tattered envelope, overflowing with cash. "We've done six sessions already, and I figured you'd like to get paid."

He offers the envelope, and I cock an eyebrow. I didn't realize we've spent that much time together. I accept the envelope and flip through the contents. "Uh, thanks." I pocket it. Why does this feel like a drug deal?

"It is the deal, Wilhelmina."

"Why do you call me that?"

Zane sends me a skeptical glance. "We exchanged emails and text messages for several days before meeting. How was I supposed to know you go by a nickname?"

I suppose that would be my fault for not clarifying.

"Right." I turn away from him, ready to move on. "I have class. I'm sure you do too."

"Yeah, whatever."

He follows me, but my fingers fight with my hoody zipper. The bottom pins won't fit together. Finally, they catch, and I slide the zipper upward and collide with someone in front of me.

"Mina?"

I look up.

The man in front of me has wavy deep-brown hair, smooth dark-brown skin, wire-rimmed glasses, a five o'clock shadow—and hazel eyes to match mine. He looks professional with his navy dress shirt, khakis, and a bright-blue bow-tie, but he stammers at the sight of me.

"Dad."

Behind me, Zane comes to a stumbling halt, nearly running into me.

My father clears his throat. "You look, uh, well."

"Thanks. You too." I slide the zipper up to my neck and glance toward the door. "I have class...in Cameron Hall."

"Of course." A rueful smile spreads across his face. "You're always welcome to stop by my office. Room 311 on the top floor."

"Sure thing." The forced excitement in my voice probably sounds like sarcasm, but I take a step toward the door.

"Mina..."

I look back. He and Zane are both standing awkwardly, watching me. The contrast between their skin tones is unmistakable under the fluorescent lights.

"Yeah?"

Dad takes a couple steps closer, and his lips form a thin line, the mark of determination. "I would like to see you. I have my tea at four o'clock and dinner at seven. Would you join me tonight?"

For a second, I hesitate, but a response stumbles out of my mouth. "I have plans at five, and I don't have the address."

"I can email it to you." For a second, his firm gaze falters. "Could you make dinner?"

No. Of course I can't. It doesn't matter if it's true, say no.

"I should be free then."

"Then I'll see you at seven."

"Yeah." I step toward the door, utter one last, "Goodbye," and leave the building.

The door shuts behind me.

All at once, the wave of nausea hits me full-blast. Under the awning, I clench my eyes shut. Count my breaths, not my heartbeats. Swallow down the lump in my throat.

That wasn't supposed to happen.

In the past four months, all I've seen are glimpses. Him riding down the Lane on his bicycle, walking up the stairs of Stanley Hall, packing a to-go meal in the cafeteria. A million times I've seen him and turned the other way, hidden behind a bush or in the bathroom. Even so, surely he's seen me sometime during these months. But he never pursued me, never contacted me, never showed any interest.

Why now? And worse, why couldn't I think of an excuse?

I tear open my eyes and kick one of the shrubs along the walkway. In the green space between here and the library, a couple students glance my way before continuing the trek to their next class, and I lean against the nearest awning support. "Dammit."

"Are things really that hard with your dad?"

I twist my head.

Zane, standing outside the building doors, stares at me.

"Don't worry about it." I shake my head. "I have class."

He approaches before I can force my legs to move again. "Just curious. I didn't get the impression it was that serious."

Wasn't that the point? My failed relationship with my father has nothing to do with my business arrangement with Zane.

"I have to go to class, Zane. I'll see you at five. When you're done with your adviser?"

He nods. "I'll meet you in the library."

◆

Zane glances up from his notebook. "Don't you need to wrap up? We can finish later." He pulls over his phone and lights up the screen. "It's 6:30."

I square my shoulders and point to one of his homework problems with my pencil. "Make sure you use the chain rule for twenty-one."

"Sure." When I look at him again, he's watching me. "Your dad said seven, didn't he? How long will it take you

26

to get there?"

Eight minutes, according to Google Maps.

"We need to go over more integration techniques."

Despite the serious look on his face, Zane laughs. "Should we meet up tomorrow to catch up? Or do we just want to do one more session before the final?"

My eyes peruse his homework. "Everything else here looks alright. You're getting better."

"No meeting tomorrow, then?" He pulls the notebook closer and closes it. "You ready for the weekend?"

I shrug and glance at my phone. It only makes the tension in my stomach worse.

"My frat's throwing a big blowout Friday night for finals." He grabs his backpack from the far side of the table and shoves his things inside.

"I guess we should call it a night." I pile together my notes and books inside my own bag. "We'll want our pre-finals session to be in-depth. We have to go through everything since midterms."

He continues as if I haven't spoken. "It's the biggest party of the year. Blacklights and beer pong and dancing." He slings his bag over his shoulder. "We hired the Finnick twins to organize it this year."

I frown. "Why would you have a party before knowing whether you pass your classes?"

Zane laughs. "To relax before studying like mad. Besides, everyone leaves campus once they finish their finals."

"I don't see the point." I stand up, push in the chair, and head for the stairs.

He runs to catch up. "You have friends, right?"

"Something like that." I take the stairs two at a time, but

he straggles. "What makes you ask?"

"You could come to the party and find out. Bring your friends, hang out, see if you like it. What d'you think?"

I pause on the landing halfway down to the ground level. "Why?"

He smiles, but the laughter dies in his throat. "It'd be nice to get to know someone I'm spending this much time with, away from the textbooks and classwork. We spent an hour and a half together—and this was a short session—and I know nothing about you. Besides, based on this morning, I'd say you could use a relaxing evening."

I grip my backpack straps. "Friday is tomorrow. I have plans." Another step down the stairs. "Maybe you should've asked sooner."

I still would've said no. An evening in a sea of drunken morons would hardly be relaxing.

Zane catches up. "Really? Because you don't strike me as particularly social. I've never met someone who gives me quite as much cold shoulder. Are you always this tightly wound?"

"Are you always this invasive?"

He huffs. "Is it that strange for someone to want to know you? What do you do in your spare time?"

"I study and I do this. I doubt you'd be interested."

At the bottom of the stairs, we head for the exit. With a furrowed brow and a frown, Zane pushes open the double doors to the courtyard outside and holds the door. "You're making an assumption based on nothing—because you haven't tried to know me."

"Aren't you doing the same thing about me?" I pause on the steps outside, and he stands a few feet away. "I said no, leave it at that."

"Fine. When do you want to study for the final?"

I sigh. "The final's Wednesday at eight a.m. How's Tuesday night?"

Zane nods, but there's a sour look on his face. "Yeah, sure. I'll text you."

We turn our separate ways. He heads for the upperclassmen housing, and I cross the green space behind the library to reach Finchley Avenue.

I'm supposed to head for my father's house now. His email said it's on Cherry, a couple streets over, but I'm unfamiliar with the area beyond Bradford. The only places I've visited off-campus are the local Walmart and Xander's favorite coffee shop downtown. Jimmy has made it his job to force me to socialize, even if my only interactions are with his asshole roommate.

My uneasy stomach wells with nausea, and I pause in the middle of the sidewalk.

The streetlights barely illuminate the walkway.

I swallow down the lump in my throat, trying to calm my quaking stomach. This is a terrible idea. Too soon. I don't belong in that house. I shouldn't go there.

I take a step toward Cherry, then look down Finchley. The back of Lincoln barely sticks out from behind Arthur Hall. It looks particularly inviting right now.

◆

Jimmy's door is open when I return to Lincoln Hall, and I poke my head inside, not bothering to drop my bag off in my own room. Inside, Jimmy lies on his bed and taps away at his keyboard. A smile spreads across his cheeks when he spots me. "Hey, come in."

Otherwise, the room is empty.

"You done tutoring already?"

"Uh, yeah."

Thankfully, I never had the time to tell him about my dad's offer—let alone my acceptance of it. If he doesn't know, he can't be disappointed I chickened out.

"Where's Xander?" I sit at the foot of Jimmy's bed. "It's Wednesday night. He's usually playing some stupid game." I incline my head toward the gaming systems.

Jimmy returns to his laptop. "He's on another date with Val—or whatever you want to call it. Are you going to write your final essay on Whitman or Dickinson or…who are the other options?"

"Thoreau, Frederick Douglass, Louisa May Alcott," I list off. "I'm leaning toward Thoreau."

"I started outlining mine on Whitman, but it all sounds stupid. I don't know what I'm talking about."

I shrug. "Mo continually tells me writing English papers is all about bullshitting. That must be why she's so good at them."

Over the glow of the laptop, Jimmy smiles. "She'll do well in college. I'm pretty sure most papers are all about bullshitting."

I laugh and scoot back.

"Can we study for our American Lit final? I know it's a week away, but we have the test and the essay. If I put it off, I'll forget."

"I'm way ahead of you. I've been studying for the last week. Let me grab my note cards. I'll be right back."

In my room, I drop off my calculus book and grab my notes, *Norton Anthology*, and flashcards for American Lit, only to pause at the door. The calc book sits on the edge of my bed, a solid reminder of my own incompetence. I should at least let him know I'm not coming. It's after seven now.

When I join Jimmy on the bed again, his laptop is away, and he has his notes and *Norton* book in front of him.

"You ready?"

I pull out my phone. "Gimme a sec." I pull up the email from when he sent his address this afternoon and hit 'Reply.'

Sorry I can't make it tonight. Not feeling well. Can we reschedule? Best wishes.

I'm not sure I can manage more than that.

When I put my phone away, Jimmy's watching me curiously. "That looked serious."

I frown.

"To be fair, 'serious' is a pretty normal look for you."

"Don't worry about it." I twist to face him. "Let's get to work."

"How much of Emerson do you think it'll cover? We read 'Self-Reliance' and 'The Divinity School Address' and…others."

I laugh and flip through my book. "I imagine the test will be like the midterm. We need to know author, title, publication year, and a general synopsis of all the pieces we discussed in depth."

"Right…"

Jimmy continues, but I pause at the sight of Xander's empty bed.

"What did you mean?"

Jimmy stops mid-sentence. "Huh?"

31

"You said they're on another date—Xander and Val—or 'whatever you want to call it.' What did you mean?"

He adjusts his position, mouth twisted uncertainly. "He doesn't seem that into her."

I quirk an eyebrow.

"This is their third date, but Xander doesn't stay excited about anyone for long. He has no problem sleeping with them, mind you—or telling me all about it afterward—but he doesn't stay emotionally attached."

I snort. It's hardly surprising. "Why would he when he can fuck them and move on to his next mark?"

But Jimmy shakes his head. "If that were true, he wouldn't try so hard to feel something in the first place."

I roll my eyes. "Whatever. Let's move on. I don't know why I asked."

"Morbid curiosity." He sends me a devious smile before looking back down at his *Norton Anthology*. "Anyway, back to Emerson..."

Four

MY FATHER'S RESPONSE WAS PROMPT AND OPEN-ENDED. HE simply said we could get together when I was feeling better. We settled on tea the following afternoon.

That's the problem, though, isn't it? The thought of being here is nerve-wracking. But here I am.

A couple blocks from campus, the house on Cherry Street is quaint. One of those adorable cottages from the '70s with a white picket fence, golden-yellow siding, and an extra-large rocking chair on the front porch. Three steps lead up to the porch from the main walkway. An intricate design is carved into the dark wood front door.

I've double-checked the address a million times, but honestly, I'm impressed I made it to the front yard this time. Two and a half blocks closer than the previous evening.

I force my feet closer, along the walkway, up the stairs, and pause at the front door. Deep breaths. Swallow down the bile pushing up my throat. Breathe—seriously, breathe—and press the doorbell.

He opens the door immediately, wide enough for me to step inside. "I'm glad you're able to join me." He casts as small smile in my direction as I stumble over the threshold.

"Come this way."

Inside, the cottage has dark wainscoting and intricate wallpapers that contrast with the dark wood. He leads the way past the foyer. We pass a library on the left, a small living room with a hearth on the right, and pause in the middle to point out the half bath. Stairs lead to the second floor, plus a small door to the kitchen, and to the right of the bathroom, an arched doorway leads into a large dining room with a table and six chairs. The furniture is all antique, crafted from cherry-stained wood, and has delicate leaf designs in the legs and support beams.

In my faded Motley Crüe tee, battered jeans, and bright-blue Converse, I do not fit in.

"Have a seat, Mina." Dad gestures to the nearest chair. "I put together a few sandwiches. I hope that's alright." In the dim light, the smile doesn't reach his eyes. He straightens his polka-dot bow-tie and flattens his dress shirt, his hands quivering nervously.

I sit down on one of the green and cream striped dining chairs.

He heads to the adjoining kitchen and returns with a plate of bite-sized sandwiches and a few cookies. An ornate Japanese teapot sits on a trivet at the center of the table. "Help yourself." He places the tray between our chairs and joins me, clasping his hands in his lap.

Uncertain, I pop one in my mouth. Cool and slimy. Cucumber sandwiches.

"How do you like Bradford so far? Are your classes going well?" He nibbles on a cookie. "They're maple cinnamon, by the way."

I force a smile. His topic of choice will always be mathematics. "Calculus is going well. Mr. Hodges is direct and explains the principles well. He focuses mostly on equations, though, but it is an introductory class. I'm actually tutoring another student."

He nods, seeming to relax. "You're doing well then?"

"I've gotten high marks on every exam."

"And you're tutoring. A student in your class?" He finishes his cookie and pours some tea into two cups.

"Yes." I accept the cup and saucer he pushes toward me. "It helps me stay focused."

His bow-tie jostles as he nods, and his wire-framed glasses slide down the bridge of his nose. "What about your other classes?"

"I'm mostly taking gen ed. First-Year Seminar of course, Western Civ, American Lit." The tea is too hot to drink. "I joined the Honors Program. I'll have that seminar class with Dr. Lewis in the spring."

My father smiles. "Henry is a fantastic teacher and a great friend. We've gone fishing together, you know."

I lift my teacup to my mouth and blow before taking a small sip. The steam fogs up my glasses.

I can't imagine him with a rod in hand.

"How was your holiday?" He picks up a cucumber sandwich and takes a bite. "How's your sister? And your, um, mother?"

"Fine, I guess."

"Good." He pauses to take another sip of tea.

And I fill the silence. "Imogene asks about you sometimes."

"Oh, does she?" He tries to sound nonchalant, but his voice quivers. "Does she still dance?"

Mo quit ballet when she started cheerleading as a freshman last year. "Not anymore, but she's still doing gymnastics."

"She's a brilliant dancer."

"I guess." I eat another sandwich, straining to remember.

He clears his throat, drawing my attention. "And you? What have you been doing?"

Something tells me wasting away on Jimmy's bed while he studies and Xander screams at his video game isn't an appropriate answer. "I'm majoring in Mathematics, Dad."

"Yes, and you're tutoring." He's fishing for more.

I shove in another cookie.

"Do you really need the money, Mina? You don't have to work if you need money." He hesitates. "I'm sure I could scrounge up something for you. It wouldn't be any trouble."

I swallow quickly to protest. "I'm already doing it, and I'd hate to bail on the guy just because I don't need the money anymore. Besides, today was the last day of classes. All that's left is finals." I gulp down the rest of my tea now that it's cool. "Really, you don't need to do anything."

He turns to his own teacup. "I am willing to offer my services if you ever need assistance, Mina."

I reach for the pot.

"Are you thinking of taking on any other students?" He's staring at his cup.

"I'm sure I'll figure something out next semester." The golden liquid trickles into my cup, and I determine to change the subject. "What are your plans for winter break?" The pot slides silently onto the trivet.

He glances at me before taking another drink. "Oh, I never do anything of consequence for the holidays."

I nod.

"What about you, Mina? When are you returning to Springfield?"

I frown. "Actually, I still haven't booked my flight."

For a moment, my father meets my gaze. "Are you not intending to return? Surely your mother wants you home for Christmas."

I barely hold back a snort. "I'm not sure Mom cares either way."

A frown spreads across his drawn features, and then, his hazel eyes look away. "If it's not too presumptuous, perhaps you might consider staying here for the holidays. I would enjoy your company."

I cast my gaze downward. What can I say to that?

This is exactly the moment I waited for, what I dreamed of the second he left.

But that was a long time ago now, and I no longer have the same fantasies. I'm no longer a little girl.

How to let him down easily?

"I'm sure you'd rather spend the time with your mother and Imogene, though."

When I meet his gaze, all excuses disappear. "Let me think about it."

"Of course. You don't need to make a decision now." He sounds uncertain but hopeful. A small smile tugs at his lips.

I look away.

◆

In the dark, the path back to Lincoln Hall eludes me. The streetlights cast strange shadows along the sidewalk, but my feet follow the roads toward Bradford without difficulty.

I cross Olive and pass more houses.

In the dark, the walk is bearable. My breath billows out as a cloud of fog. In the cold, everything is numb.

I reach Finchley. On the opposite side is campus.

No cars are on the road. No night classes on a Friday night. There are no resident parking lots nearby. I step onto the road, and my pocket vibrates.

I pull out my phone, pausing at the edge of the sidewalk. Imogene. The only person who calls.

"How's it going, Mo?"

"Billie." Her voice is exasperated. "Please tell me you've booked your flight to Springfield. Seriously."

I frown. The conversation is still fresh. "Actually, something happened."

"What?" She's immediately alarmed. "Is something wrong? Are you okay?"

"I'm fine. Calm down."

"You can't say that and not expect me to assume something terrible happened. What's going on, Billie? You promise you're okay?"

I laugh. That's not a promise I can make. "I was talking to Dad. He wants me to stay here for Christmas." My voice shakes, and my body trembles as I cross the street. "I don't know what to do."

For a moment, Imogene doesn't speak, then her words come in a hesitant voice. "What do you mean? This is what you've always wanted."

I take the sidewalk along Finchley, then follow the curve toward the dorms. "It is, isn't it?"

The excitement is apparent in her voice. "You have to do

it, Billie. This is the perfect opportunity. You have to take advantage of it. I'll let Mom know you're staying. I mean, trust me, we wish you'd come home for Christmas, but I'm happy for you, Billie."

My grip on the phone tightens. How can I say no to that? To her? She's always believes in me, even when I don't believe in myself.

"Right."

The dorms loom above, and I turn to Lincoln Hall.

"Um, Mo, I need to go. I'll talk to you soon."

"Okay." She's so happy for me she's not irritated that I end the conversation early.

Upstairs, I barge into Jimmy's room, disgruntled and clutching my phone to my chest. The door pushes open to a poorly lit room before banging against a chair oddly situated behind the doorway.

Inside, Jimmy is working on his laptop in a t-shirt and flannel pajama bottoms at the desk. He glances over with a smile.

On the far side, Xander reclines on his bed in a pair of Rupee-encrusted boxers, wireless headphones on, a bowl of popcorn tucked between his arm and torso, his enormous gaming laptop in front of him. His giggling is interrupted by my entrance. He nearly screams. "Close the door, jeez!"

God forbid someone see him in his underwear.

But closer inspection reveals he's watching *Gilmore Girls*. When I shut the door, he happily returns to his show, shoving a fistful of popcorn in his mouth.

"You look like you've had a day." Jimmy rolls his chair closer to get a better look at me.

I collapse on his bed, dropping my phone to grab his pillow so I can smother myself. "You know—"

"I can't understand you through a mass of feathers, Billie."

I groan and push the pillow past my mouth. "You know how I still haven't bought my plane tickets?"

"Right."

"Well, apparently, I'm not going to."

"What?"

I shove the pillow away and sit up on my elbows. "My dad asked me to stay with him for the holidays."

Jimmy's eyebrows rise dangerously close to his hairline. "And you agreed?"

I collapse again and stare at the popcorn ceiling. "Not technically."

"But?"

My eyes close. "But I'm going to."

For a moment, Jimmy doesn't say anything. He probably doesn't believe me. "Why?"

"Because Imogene—she called, and we talked about it…"

"And you don't want to disappoint her."

It's true. I don't have to say anything to confirm it. Jimmy understands me better than anyone.

"Are you sure you're ready? Winter break is three and a half weeks long, Billie. That's a long time to spend with a man you haven't talked to in as many years."

"I don't know." I blink a couple times, trying to focus. "I have no reason to celebrate Christmas with him. He left. He walked out on me. I don't want to see him. That's exactly why I've avoided him for so long. We were never supposed to talk in the first place."

But Jimmy spins in the swivel chair. "You're being melo-dramatic again. If you don't want to do it, tell him so."

I frown. "I can't. You have to help me."

He stops to raise a bushy eyebrow. "How am I supposed to do that? Just tell him you don't want to. Your sister will get over it."

"No. Help me break the ice."

His other eyebrow shoots up. "Again, how?"

"My last final's Thursday, but I don't have to go over there till Friday night, and your flight isn't till the next morning. Have dinner with us."

"That kind of screws up our plans…" He glances in Xander's direction. "But it wouldn't be too difficult to rear-range stuff."

I sit up and catch his eyes. "I would appreciate you forever."

He laughs. "You don't already? I'm insulted."

I quirk a smile. "Seriously, thank you."

But Jimmy shakes his head. "Don't go thanking me yet. You know, it'd look a lot like you want to introduce your boyfriend to your father, right?"

"Don't be ridiculous." I brush away his words. "Your heart belongs to Cynthia Allen, and it's not the first time you've met him. It's not a date."

"But that's not what it looks like." He leans back in the chair and grabs the pencil off his desk. "Can you imagine the fit your mom would have? Or if my parents heard?"

Mr. and Mrs. Powell always hoped we'd wind up together. Then I'd actually be their daughter instead of the weird neighbor girl they pseudo-adopted after my parents divorced.

"Okay, then what do you propose?"

When I look back, Jimmy's smiling. "Very simple solution. We do dinner at your dad's, get to know each other again, break the ice for you—and to prevent any awkward assumptions, we bring Xander."

The last three words rush out of his mouth faster than the IBM Roadrunner.

Gritting my teeth, I glance over at Xander, who's too busy dropping popcorn kernels on his lean chest to notice the turn in conversation. "That's the worst idea I've ever heard." I keep my eyes trained on the half-naked imbecile across the room.

"Maybe, but I won't come otherwise. You'll have to break the ice on your own."

It's a fair point, though. They were supposed to drive to Burlington that afternoon. This would set back both their plans. What would Xander do while we have dinner with my father?

Jimmy tosses his pencil up. "See?" He tries to swipe it from the air, but it clatters to the linoleum floor. He laughs it off before leaning down to retrieve it. "I'm being helpful."

"I'm not sure I'd consider this helpful." My gaze shifts between his fumbling fingers and Xander's laughing face. "And I'm definitely not sure I want to spend dinner with you, my dad, and Xander."

"It's a good thing I've already made the decision then."

I roll my eyes. "With you acting this cocky, I worry you're spending too much time with dickface over there."

Jimmy laughs, his pale freckles crinkling with his cheeks, and scoots the chair closer. "Come on, Billie, relax, will you?

You stay this stressed and you'll fail your finals." He nods his head toward the television. "Wanna drag Xander away from his girly show and watch a movie?"

"Aren't you going out tonight? It's Friday. Shouldn't you be at some frat party getting trashed?"

One particular party springs to mind.

But Jimmy dismounts the chair. "I'll have you know, I don't drink at those parties." He crosses the room and powers up the PlayStation and flat-screen.

"Right." I head over to Xander's bed. "It's your job to make sure this moron comes back alive." He doesn't notice me until I snatch the headphones off his head and hold them captive.

Xander turns to me, fuming. "What the fuck are you doing, Dixon? He's about to push Jess in the lake."

"I so don't care." I nod toward the TV, but he glares. "We're watching a movie. If I don't have a choice, neither do you."

From behind me, Jimmy calls out, "Okay, guys, *Jaws* or *Big Trouble in Little China*?"

Xander's narrow eyes don't leave mine as we say, "*Big Trouble*," at the same time.

Grumbling, Xander pauses his show and closes his laptop. "Why're we watching a movie? And why don't I have a choice?"

I shrug and turn back toward Jimmy, who selects our choice with the controller. "Pillows?"

"Yes, please," Jimmy says. "Billie's having a paranoid moment and needs to relax."

I roll my eyes as I cross the room to toss a couple pillows from Jimmy's bed to the floor. "Not paranoid."

"And why do I care?" But Xander moves his laptop and grabs his own pillows for our nest. Irritated, he chucks one at Jimmy's head before joining us.

"You don't," I say, "but that doesn't stop him from trying."

Jimmy fixes his glasses. "Play nice, you two."

On the flat-screen, the movie starts with a short introduction with Victor Wong, and Jimmy sits, dragging me down beside him. Xander grudgingly sits on my other side.

"Cozy." Jimmy sends both of us a grin.

Xander rolls his eyes. "Whatever."

"No." I shake my head.

Jimmy pouts. "You guys are jerks."

"Shut up." Xander reaches his arm around me and snatches the TV remote from the floor behind Jimmy. His arm brushes my back on the recoil, and I shiver at the contact. "Either we watch this movie or I go back to my show." He turns up the volume.

I snort. "Yes, you should definitely go back to *Gilmore Girls*. I need to take pictures so I can show Val who you really are."

He nudges me in the ribs and sends me his patented Xander Theroux smirk. "Trust me, she's far more aware of who I really am than you are."

I pull a face. "That's disgusting."

On my other side, Jimmy gags. "Seriously, I already know too much about your sex life."

Kurt Russell's narration begins, and I look at the door. "This is a waste of time. I need to write that essay for American Lit."

Jimmy turns to me with narrow eyes. "Everyone else on

campus is out getting trashed before finals, and you're going to complain about a relaxing movie night? That essay isn't due till Thursday."

"It's ten pages," I say.

"And I'll bet you're already half done."

"Seriously, guys?" Xander grumbles. "Shut up."

Five

For the first time, Zane is waiting at the library when I arrive. He's been notoriously late for every previous session, but today, he's already hunched over his textbook.

I take my regular seat across from him and examine the area before unpacking. The surrounding tables are all full, even though it's dinnertime. Inside my bag, I nudge a sketchbook aside and pull out my calculus book, notebook, and folder of tests and quizzes.

Zane plugs along with his current problem until he at last finds his solution and circles it. He looks up and smiles. "Hey. How was your weekend?"

"Fine, thanks." I stretch over the table to peek at his work. "Doing the study worksheet?"

He checks the time on his phone. "Actually, I could use a break."

"A break?"

"I've been here for over an hour. My last final finished around 3:30."

For a moment, I can't decide whether to be surprised he's dedicated that much time to studying for the Calc final or because it's taken him nearly an hour and a half to finish the suggested practice problems. "Well, I don't need a break. Let me look over your work."

He pushes the papers toward me and heads for the stairs.

Everything appears to be in order. I circle a few problems for him to look over and redo, but the majority of the work is accurate, though definitely less organized than my own.

Zane returns with an energy drink from the vending machines in the basement and leans his chair back on two legs while he waits. "What did you do this weekend?"

"I told you before." My eyes flit across the page. "I was busy."

"Right, you had plans." He pauses. "You were studying, though, right?"

I stop in the middle of circling a problem. The ink pools on the paper. "None of your business."

"Of course." He takes a drink, and I continue.

The quiet of the library is only interrupted by the soft roll of my pen as it moves across the page, circling every misstep.

"Why don't you want to tell me?" He leans forward. His chair bangs against the hardwood floor as it lands.

A few heads turn our way, but they quickly return to their studies. Zane doesn't notice the disturbance.

"Do you have a secret boyfriend or a secret identity? Are you a bank robber? A vigilante?"

At last, I turn to him with narrow eyes. "You know how completely ridiculous you sound, right?"

He shrugs.

"This is work. That means I have no obligation to tell you about my personal life or spend any time with you outside of this library. I don't have to have a secret identity or a secret boyfriend or a secret anything in order for me to tell you no."

He studies me. "So you're not seeing anyone then?"

I raise my voice as I speak. "Are you deaf?"

But he smiles. That's all the answer he needs.

I turn back to the offending worksheet. There's one problem left, but I don't want to look it over. I circle it like the others and shove the paper under his nose. "Rework these please. That has to be enough of a break for you."

His smile widens as he accepts the paper and begins to look over the problems.

"Did you bring all your notes and tests to go over?"

"Yeah, of course." He nods toward his textbook and a barely used notebook. I've certainly never seen him with it. It's wide-ruled.

I grab the books and scoff as I thumb through the pages. "I don't know how we haven't gone over this, but you'd probably do a lot better in class if you took notes—real notes."

He doesn't look up. "It's a bit late for that, isn't it?"

I move on. "When you're done, we need to go over each chapter. We covered eight this semester, so I figure fifteen to thirty minutes each. We want to be as in-depth as possible. For your sake."

Despite the jibe, Zane glances up with a smile.

I return to the table of contents in my textbook. "Let me know when you're ready to start. We'll begin with functions and limits before making our way to integration."

"I'm mostly done." He's already worked through most of the problems I circled. "I'm having trouble figuring out what's wrong with this last one."

I quirk my mouth to the side. "It's fine. Let's get to work

with functions." I flip a couple pages to the introduction of the chapter and go over the definition of a mathematical function.

"I'm getting hungry," Zane announces as we flip through the chapter. "Can we eat something while we do this?"

"I don't think that's a good idea."

He taps the table with his index finger. "Come on, you've got to be hungry too. I'll pay."

I shake my head and turn the page to look at limits. "That's definitely not a good idea. Let's work."

"Fine."

But I can hear his stomach grumble.

◆

By the time we arrive at the Eyrie, I already regret my decision.

Zane leads the way inside the campus restaurant and heads for the register, but I push past him to buy a drink and find a table. I lay my bag on the chair beside me and unpack before prying open my bottle of water. Hopefully Jimmy isn't on the clock—or worse, Xander. But there's no sign of either around the restaurant.

Zane joins me with a receipt and a soda and takes out his materials.

"Alright, we've gone over functions, limits, and derivatives. We need to focus on integrals now. We're not even halfway through the semester's work; we're a little behind."

He brushes my words aside. "Relax. Can't we talk while we wait for my food?"

I clasp my fingers together atop the table. "We need to

focus. This final determines half our grade."

Zane leans forward and smiles. "Where are you from?"

"A boring town in the middle of the Bible Belt. We need to talk about indefinite integrals."

He ignores me. "I was born out in California, L.A. area. I lived there with my mom for about fifteen years before moving to upstate New York with my dad."

I pause. "Your parents are divorced?"

He nods. "It wasn't a big deal. It was mutual, and I was so little it didn't affect me much."

I raise an eyebrow.

"Yours are divorced too, right? Or separated?"

"Yeah."

One of the student workers in the kitchen rings the bell and calls out a number, and Zane hops up to grab his sandwich.

When he returns, I dive right in. "What's an indefinite integral?"

"Isn't it the anti-derivative or something like that?" He picks up his sandwich and takes a bite. "You stayed with your mom?"

I heave a sigh. "Yes, it is a differentiable function whose derivative is equal to the original function, which is why we have to solve for it using an operation that is the opposite of differentiation."

He takes another couple bites of his sandwich. "Right. I'm just saying you staying with your mom would explain all the weirdness with your dad last week. Why are you majoring in Math?"

I raise an eyebrow. "Am I not good at it?"

He sips his soda. "You've definitely improved my work."

"Then let's keep improving it." I turn back to the book. "Let's start with a simple problem, okay?"

"I mean," he continues as if I didn't say anything, one hand cupped around his drink, "you seem kinda upset with him, so why're you studying math?"

I grind my teeth and glare at the paper. "Zane, you need to focus. I don't imagine you want to fail your final, and I definitely don't."

We sit in an awkward silence. I pull out our last chapter test and look over the two answers I got wrong while waiting for him to get his head in the game.

"Look," he says finally, but I refuse. "I was a little insensitive at the library. I want to apologize."

I stop in the middle of taking a drink.

"You've been a big help, Wilhelmina, and we're spending a lot of time together. I'd like to know you better. That's why I was asking you all those questions. I'd like for us to be friends."

The paper in front of me is white, crisp, clean. Even my own notes on the page are precise and organized—exactly how I want my life. I glance over at Zane's test, sticking out from under his food basket. His work is anything but organized. Honestly, I don't know how the professor follows it.

"I accept your apology, Zane, but this is a business relationship, and that's how it should stay."

"Come on." He places his hand over mine. "You have to be more underneath that cold exterior. Give me a chance."

I roll my eyes. "You're setting yourself up for disappointment. I'm not a hard shell with a soft gooey center. I'm just me."

"Then show me."

I pull away. "I want to be at my best for the test tomorrow, and I'm sure you do too. We can discuss this later."

◆

By the time Zane and I finish at the Eyrie, it's late, and with the final at eight, I want nothing more than to collapse on my bed and fall asleep. Holding a conversation with Zane is exhausting—both from the number of hours we've spent studying and from his unwavering attempts to hijack the conversation.

I kick off my shoes and drop my backpack at the foot of my bed before slipping into pajamas.

Thankfully, Val is elsewhere.

I lay my glasses on my desk and curl up under the covers.

Someone shoves a key in the door lock.

With a groan, I turn toward the wall and bury my head under the blanket, preparing for the bright fluorescent light that's sure to follow.

"Hush," Val says as the door creaks open, "I think she's sleeping. That's a first." She shuffles inside the room, trying to avoid making noise, and opens her closet. "I'm going to grab a new shirt. This one has deodorant on it. Am I spending the night in your room or not?"

Her companion snorts, probably at her concern over deodorant. Xander—not that I'm surprised. "Who're you trying to impress? We're literally going across the hallway to have sex."

She rifles through her closet, metal scraping against metal as she pushes hangers aside. "Should I wear this one? Or this one?"

There's no sound for a moment.

"Well, your tits look great in the lacy one."

"Xander! If I stay the night in your room, I might not have the time to come back for my stuff in the morning. I need to dress normally."

"Right," he says, sarcasm eating away at his voice, "we wouldn't want you to do the two-doors-away walk of shame."

Val huffs. "Which shirt?"

The mattress squeaks as he sits on her bed. "How the hell am I supposed to know? If you want a girl's opinion, ask a fucking girl. Wake up Dixon and ask her."

Dear God, no.

Val releases a low growl and returns to flipping through her closet. "Billie? Please! That bitch wouldn't know fashion if it walked up to her naked and bit her on the ass."

My grip tightens on the sheets, and for a while, the only sound is the scraping of hangers against the metal rod as she continues her quest for the perfect outfit, no longer concerned about the noise she's making.

The bed squeaks again.

"Don't call her that." Xander's words are so quiet I strain to hear them.

I frown.

Val pauses, then resumes rifling through her clothes. "She's such a snob—and what the hell does she have to feel superior about? Doesn't she know everyone hates her?"

"That's not true."

She releases a mirthless laugh. "Fine, she has one friend— and she's as much of a bitch to him as she is to everyone else." She pulls out another hanger. "I'm wearing this one."

53

"Then you don't get their friendship. You don't get her."

"Are you seriously defending her right now? You have to deal with her bullshit more than anyone else because your roommate is the only one who can stand her. All she does is play on her laptop and draw in that stupid sketchbook anyway. She's not so special."

"Have you seen it?"

"Seen what? The sketchbook?" The empty hanger clatters to the hard floor. "Like she'd show me what's inside." Val's voice is muffled. "It's probably a bunch of stick figures, and she won't show anyone because she wants people to think she's amazing."

"You never know," Xander says noncommittally, "maybe she is amazing. I bet she's too nervous to show anyone. She's probably really good."

"I highly doubt that. Now, how do I look?"

He groans. "Why does it matter if we're just going to bed? Can we go now? Jimmy's studying till they close the library. I told him to make himself scarce for a while."

"Fine, let's go."

Their footsteps lead to the door, but they stop as Val fumbles in her purse.

"Oh, come on, I just had them." She laughs triumphantly as she yanks her jingling keys free, and the door opens.

"Seriously, can we go already?"

Val scoffs, and her keys jingle again.

The door shuts behind them, and Val locks the deadbolt from outside.

I push the covers away to breathe and stretch across the mattress. Above me, the dark ceiling plays back the discussion. I can picture it all in my head down to the irritated crinkle between Xander's eyebrows at her high-maintenance apparel needs. He's sent me that same look often. But the way his voice sounded when he spoke about me: soft, pensive, kind—that's new.

Six

My eyes wander across the dorm room. While Val's side is pristine, my half of the room is cluttered with clothes and sketchbooks. My bed is disheveled, shoes shoved under the edge, and the wall above it has two posters, one of Batman and Robin from *The Dark Knight Returns* and one of Ryuk holding an apple. On my desk, the surface is covered in textbooks and nearly a dozen sketchbooks, well-worn with frayed edges.

Most of the time, I can't bring myself to clean my mess.

"Billie, are you sure this is a good idea?"

No, not even remotely.

Jimmy watches from my beanbag, hunched forward, his elbows resting on his knees. There's a skeptical look on his pink face.

"No, packing sounds like a perfect idea." I pull the duffel bag from the bottom of my closet. "I don't know what to bring, though. Three and a half weeks is a long time."

"Yes, it is." He's not talking about my packing, though.

I toss the duffel bag to my bed and pull a couple handfuls of t-shirts from the closet. "You're really not helping, you know that?" The shirts land on the bed haphazardly, several of them sliding down to the floor, and I move to the dresser. I need jeans, socks, underwear, pajamas, headwraps.

On the beanbag, Jimmy sighs. "Well, one of us is being realistic, and it's obviously not you."

I walk back to the bed, arms full of clothes, and stuff everything inside my bag. "This is a perfectly realistic amount of clothes." I move toward my desk to grab my laptop, a few sketchbooks, and my charcoal and Conte crayons.

"You know that's not what I'm talking about. You don't have to do this because Imogene wants you to. She just wants you to be happy anyway."

My jaw tightens, but I wrap my laptop in a couple shirts before pushing everything inside my bag. "What else do I need?"

"Hairbrush?" Jimmy suggests.

Right.

I open the door to the bathroom and grab my toiletries from the closet shelf. They go in the side pocket.

"You're really going to do this?"

"I already said I would." I zip the pocket and examine the room to make sure I'm not missing anything. I pause a moment, then grab my calc book from the desk and shove it in to. "Seriously, Jimmy, I cannot have this conversation right now. I have to go."

He heaves a sigh. "Do you need a ride?"

I raise an eyebrow. "Did you miraculously obtain a car in the last twenty-four hours? Because I don't see any other way you could give me a ride."

"Xander…"

But I shake my head. "I don't need a ride from Xander."

Jimmy rolls his eyes. "We're going over there in a couple hours anyway. Why does it matter? Wouldn't it be better if we went over together?"

Behind him, a shadow blocks the light from the hallway. "Will you stop offering me up like that?" Xander leans against the door frame and crosses his arms over his chest. "I'm not a chauffeur."

"Trust me," I say, "no one's asking you to be."

"Good. You can get a cab if you can't handle carrying that thing a few blocks."

"I'll be fine."

Jimmy glances between us before turning his attention to me. "Really?"

The concern on his face says he isn't talking about the walk over. It's the whole idea. Three and a half weeks with my father, who I've spoken to twice since my arrival here. Jimmy isn't the only one who's unsure I can handle it.

I look around the room again. What have I forgotten?

My closet is still open. A full-length mirror hangs on the inside of the door. I'm several feet away, but my reflection is gaunt, exhausted. I'm hardly presentable, but I force a smile on my haggard features when I turn to Jimmy. "Yes, I'll be fine. I promise."

From the doorway, Xander snorts. "Don't make promises you can't keep, Dixon. You lie enough for everyone in this room."

I glance at the mirror again, frowning, and step closer to push the door shut. I don't want to look at that anymore.

"Really?" Jimmy turns to his roommate. "Can't you lay off it for two seconds?"

Xander shrugs. "You're making me go to some stupid

dinner so your crazy friend can postpone admitting she's terrified. I have to entertain myself somehow."

I narrow my eyes. "You don't have to come."

His blue eyes meet mine, and he cocks his head. "The idea's growing on me. I want to meet him—maybe then I can figure out why you're fucked up."

Shaking my head, I look away. "I'm really not in the mood, Theroux."

Jimmy rises from the beanbag. "Seriously, Xander, she doesn't need wound up right now."

Xander shrugs again and turns to the hallway.

I pull the duffel bag over my shoulder, then check my pockets to make sure I have everything. "Okay, get out."

They move into the hallway, pausing outside the door, and I follow, locking the deadbolt behind me, and push past them toward the exit.

◆

When my father opens the door, there's a nervous smile on his face. "Come in." He steps to the side. "You can hang your coat here." He gestures to a row of hooks on the wall awaiting use.

He motions me down the hallway, and we pause in the open space in front of the bathroom and stairs. "I have a spare bedroom made up for you." He nods toward the stairs. "Would you like to put your stuff down? Maybe relax before your friends get here?"

I glance around the house. From this vantage point, I can see into the four main rooms on the ground floor. He organized and decorated everything for the holidays. For our guests later. For me.

He watches me expectantly.

"Um, sure."

He carries my bag up the stairs, and I follow.

The second floor consists of a master bedroom, two small guest bedrooms, a hall closet, and a large bathroom. I don't imagine he's had much use for the guest rooms before, but he stops at the room nearest the stairs, places the duffel bag inside, and steps out of the way.

He stands awkwardly to the side. "I'll let you settle in. I'm working on dinner. Come down whenever you're ready." He sends me a quick smile before heading downstairs, and I turn back to the room.

The bedroom is minimally decorated. The bed is a full with a plush comforter and down pillows, and nightstands sit on either side of the bed. A matching dresser with a large attached mirror is on the opposite wall. Aside from that, the room has one small wall ornament—a generic print of an Henri Matisse still life. The only other objects in the room are an alarm clock and a picture frame on the dresser.

I pause in the doorway before stepping inside. Slowly, I shut the door behind me and unzip the duffel bag, but I can't bring myself to take anything out.

Instead, I sit on the edge of the mattress, heels resting on the bed frame, head in my hands, and wait.

I hate waiting.

Two hours till Jimmy is here. Before I have some sort of buffer. How long can I hide in this room before my father becomes suspicious? Will he realize what a terrible idea this is? Doesn't he know I don't belong here? Can't he see that?

I swallow to wet my dry throat, but my muscles are constricted. My chest tightens. My legs shake.

This really is the worst idea. Jimmy was right—I should've told my father I couldn't come, that I need to be at home with Mo, with Mom, with Jimmy and the Powells.

I rub my temples, push my fingers under my glasses to massage my eyes, and they clatter to the floor. There's another headache coming on, and a well of nausea builds in my stomach.

Breathing exercises don't help with this.

Everything is blurry now.

Dear God, how did I let Imogene talk me into this?

Seven

A LITTLE BEFORE SIX, I HEAD DOWNSTAIRS. MY FATHER IS in the kitchen, mashing potatoes in a pot on the stove, and I poke my head through the doorway.

Does he make every meal? He's obviously the one who prepared those cucumber sandwiches last week. No store in tiny St. Clare would sell them, and he seems particularly conscientious in the kitchen.

I watch from the doorway as he adds butter, cream, and herbs before working the potatoes with his masher. Two other pots sit on the stove, one simmering. Below, something's in the oven. The light is on, and the temp is set to 425. A timer with two minutes left counts down on the backguard.

When the potatoes are smooth, he pulls out several large serving bowls from a cupboard to his right.

I tug my phone from my pocket. It's only a few minutes till six, food is almost ready, and they're still not here, but I have no messages. As soon as I put it away, the device vibrates, and I withdraw it to find a text from Jimmy: *Running late. Be there soon.*

My father is looking at me.

62

"They'll be a little late."

He nods and returns to his work. "Most everything will be ready soon. The duck will need to rest for twenty minutes before we can eat, though."

I look at my phone again.

"How are you settling in? Is everything in your room alright?" He leans close to the stove to turn off the timer a few seconds before it beeps. "Do you need anything?"

I flip through my email but pause. I didn't manage to unpack before coming down. I don't think I'm ready for that. But I say, "Everything's great. It's a nice room."

"Would you like anything to drink?" He places the duck, fresh out of the oven, on a thick wood cutting board and nods toward the island, where several bottles of sparkling juice and one bottle of dark red wine sit on the counter.

"No, I'm fine."

"Could you pour a few glasses and take them into the living room?" He gestures toward the hallway. "There's a record player in there. Put something on."

When I reach the living room, I pause at the entrance, three flutes of sparkling cider in my hands.

I never expected to see my father's house this festive. The room is covered in tiny holiday lights, which glitter against the stone mantle and entwine with holly and garlands on the walls. Cream-colored candles sit above the fireplace, and one lone stocking hangs by the flickering hearth. Even the coffee table has a small display of red and green decorative spheres.

On the far wall behind a green Victorian-style couch, there's a small turntable and a shelf of vinyl records. After placing the flutes on the coffee table, I flip through the options. It starts with classical music—Vivaldi, Beethoven, Bach, Chopin, Tchaikovsky, Gershwin—but then it transitions to Benny Goodman, Glenn Miller, Judy Garland, the Andrew Sisters, a few members of the Rat Pack, and a wide array of jazz musicians—Miles Davis, Duke Ellington, Thelonius Monk, and of course, Louis Armstrong. Finally, it switches to some of the milder classic rock—Chicago, the Beatles, Van Morrison, Huey Lewis.

Nothing fits my taste.

On a whim, I grab *Abbey Road* and place it on the turntable. It takes a moment to find the switch and start the needle, and the speakers crackle to life with the opening chords of "Come Together." I crank the volume to drown out the sounds from the kitchen.

I sit on one of the green armchairs and read the track list on the back of the case. Way more songs on the B side than I thought possible on vinyl.

Midway through the song, a chime sounds throughout the house. That must be the doorbell.

I stand, still carrying the case, and move toward the hallway.

"Mina, can you get that?"

Jimmy, a nervous smile on his face, stands on the other side of the door. Khakis, green dress shirt, sweater-vest. Jimmy is one of the few people born after 1990 who willingly wears sweater-vests. His thick wool coat is unbuttoned.

Beside him, Xander leans against the wall, the last half of a cigarette sticking out of his mouth. His dark hair is slicked back and loosely spiked. Beneath his gray full-length trench coat, he has a silver dress shirt, fitted gray slacks, a silk tie, and the same shiny shoes he wore for his first date with Val. Even for her, he never dresses this formally. I suppose I should feel honored.

I look down at my own clothes at the sight of them. In jeans and a multi-colored harlequin sweater, I'm completely underdressed.

"Come in, I guess." I step to the side.

Jimmy walks inside slowly, his eyes wandering the entryway. "This is nice."

I roll my eyes. He's being kind, of course. It's nothing compared to his parents' house back home, but it's certainly enough for my father's quiet life.

He turns back and smiles again. "How're you doing?"

"It's been two hours since I saw you." I point out the hooks for their coats. "How different do you really think I could be?"

He lets out a short mirthless laugh. "I'll interpret that as 'could be better.'"

"Really, though, I'm glad you're here." I take a step closer and pull him into a hug, which he returns, his warm arms wrapping around me momentarily.

"Where is he?" He steps away to get a better look.

"Kitchen. Have a seat in the living room, I guess." I nod my head in that direction.

Jimmy hangs up his coat and walks into the living room, but beyond the door, Xander takes a long drag off his cigarette before lazily shifting his gaze to me. "Where's my hug and thank you for coming, Dixon?" A smirk tugs at his mouth.

I purse my lips. "Are you coming inside or not?"

He drops the cigarette butt on the porch and smashes it

with his foot. "Well, I'm definitely not staying out here. It's fucking freezing." He sheds his trench coat.

"That is a requirement for snow."

As he walks past me, he snatches the record sleeve from my hand and replaces it with his coat. He reads the back of the case as he follows Jimmy into the living room. "The Beatles—your choice? I'm impressed. Far better than your usual whiny 'alternative' rock." He makes little air quotes as he walks.

I shut the front door, hang his coat on the rack, and follow him. The second song, slower than the first, is winding down.

Jimmy and Xander sit on the green couch and make themselves comfortable. Xander is still looking at the album, but his hand reaches out to the coffee table to grab a flute. I almost laugh at the following grimace—he was probably hoping for alcohol.

I sit on my chair again.

After a moment, Xander lays the album on the coffee table and downs the rest of his sparkling cider. He's already bored.

Jimmy catches my eyes and smiles, but I can't return it. "Have you talked to him at all?" He inclines his head in the direction of the kitchen noise.

I shrug. "He's been in there the whole time."

"And what have you been doing, Dixon?" Xander leans forward, hands clasped. "Having a panic attack?"

"I have a room upstairs," I tell Jimmy. "Mostly, I've been settling in."

Xander snorts. "Sure you have."

But Jimmy turns on him with a glare. "I told you, if you

came, you had to be nice. This isn't being nice."

I grab a flute off the coffee table. "It's fine, really." The sweet flavor is overpowering. I set it down again.

On the couch, Jimmy fidgets, flakes of snow melting in his hair, and takes a drink from the third and final glass.

"Mina." My father enters the room, wiping his hands with a green kitchen towel. "Why don't you introduce us?"

I glance between him and the two guys on his fancy sofa. "Uh, right. Dad, you remember our neighbor Jimmy, right?"

Jimmy stands to greet my father. "Hello, sir." He reaches across the coffee table to shake before pocketing his hand again. "It's good to see you again, Dr. Dixon."

"Yes, it is, Jimmy." Dad nods. "How are your parents? Is your mom still working with the local theater crowd?"

Jimmy nods. "She's the assistant director of the holiday production. We'll see it as soon as I'm back in Missouri."

"And you're leaving in the morning, correct?"

"Yes. We're going to stay the night in Burlington before heading out." He inclines his head toward Xander, and my father turns to Jimmy's roommate, who has never been this quiet before.

"And this is his roommate, Xander." I flinch as Xander turns to meet my father's gaze.

In one fluid motion, he stands, accepts my father's outstretched hand, and shakes it firmly. "It's good to meet you, Dr. Dixon. Alexander Theroux. I'm in your daughter's seminar class."

My father nods. "Elijah Dixon. It's wonderful to meet you, Xander."

"Thank you, sir." Xander releases his hand. "And thank

you for inviting us. We're happy to be here."

My father gives a small awkward smile and looks back to the dining room. "Food will be ready soon. You're welcome to stay in here while I finish, or you can take a seat at the table."

He excuses himself to the kitchen, and Xander plops on the couch again.

When he's gone, Jimmy turns his eyes on me. "He seems…exactly the same."

I turn my attention to my hands. He certainly seems to be. He has the same eyes, the same coarse dark hair, though it's thinning and receding now. He's tall—much taller than me—and he's quiet, unsure. His confidence when doing mathematics never spread to other areas.

"You know," Xander says, "I'm not sure what I was expecting, but that was incredibly anti-climactic. Is the entire night going to be this awkward?"

I snort. Probably.

The final song on the record comes to a close, and I stand to flip it over, but Xander moves first. He stretches over the back of the couch, his knees on the cushions, and removes the needle from the LP, but instead of switching sides, he runs his finger over the spines of my dad's collection.

He laughs and withdraws a case. "Now this is a good album."

I grab the case for *Abbey Road* and walk to the turntable as he switches the records. The music starts slowly, but the pressure quickly builds, and I pause next to the player and trade cases with him so he can put the Beatles album away.

I look at the front cover—primarily white background with a circular design at the center. Queen's *A Night at the*

Opera. The song: "Death on Two Legs."

"This song is perfect for you," I tell Xander as the lyrics start, and he laughs as he slides the Beatles album into place.

When he looks over, he's still smiling, and I avert my eyes, my stomach tight. He's never smiled at me. Not a real smile.

I place the cover on the shelf atop the other albums and walk back around.

In the dining room, my father places the dishes and platters on the table. The duck isn't out yet, though.

"Time to eat?" Jimmy asks from behind me.

"I guess."

My father returns to the kitchen, and Xander ambles over, pausing beside me. "Are you actually going to eat something tonight?" His arms cross over his chest. "I imagine you're trying to hide all your shortcomings from Daddy Dearest."

Without waiting for an answer, he heads into the dining room, but instead of sitting, he walks around the corner into the kitchen.

Jimmy gives me a reassuring smile. "This will be fine." He stands from the couch, and we take our seats at the dining room table.

The six-person table is set for four, two on each side. With Jimmy beside me, that means my father will be seated next to Xander. This really is a terrible idea.

In the kitchen, there are voices. What are they talking about? Then, a door opening and closing.

My dad enters a moment later, carrying a white china platter with the oven-roasted duck, garnished with sprigs of parsley and thyme. "Your friend said to start without him."

He casts a small smile in my direction. He sets the platter at the table edge and begins slicing, but the meat falls apart as he cuts. When finished, he takes a few small pieces for himself, moves the dish to the center of the table, and signals us to serve ourselves.

We pass around serving dishes of mashed potatoes, brown gravy, peas and leeks, and stuffing. No one speaks. The soft clanking of silverware against the china is the only sound.

As my father strikes up a conversation with Jimmy, catching up, I push the food around my plate. The more I stare at the greasy dark meat, the less I want to eat. The nausea wells in my stomach.

I take a drink of water, but it doesn't help.

My father's asking about Jimmy's parents, about Imogene—he'll get better information on her from Jimmy than me—and I'm going to be sick.

I push away from the table and retreat into the kitchen to find the back door. I need air.

Outside, the backyard is dark and vacant. There's a covered area with a porch swing, and beyond that, I can't see much. A couple trees. A privacy fence in the distance.

The cold night air is immediately refreshing. I perch on the porch swing, eyes closed, and nudge it into motion.

"What're you doing out here?"

I jump, my eyes flashing open to find Xander, cigarette in hand, moseying around the corner of the house. "I could ask you the same thing." But my voice is shaking.

"You could, but I don't know why you would." He takes another drag of the cigarette and approaches. "Even you're not that stupid."

I glare before averting my attention to the concrete.

"So, again, what're you doing out here, Dixon?" He sits beside me, his weight upsetting the swing's rhythm. "Shouldn't you be inside bonding with beloved Daddy? Or are you seriously this overwhelmed?"

I shake my head. "I needed some air."

He snorts. "You're joking, right? It's dinner, and you're out here just waiting for it to be over. At some point, you have to suck it up and deal with your problems instead of hiding from them." He takes another drag. "Cowardice doesn't look good on anyone."

I grit my teeth and stare out into the darkness. "Xander, I don't want to talk about this—especially with you. Leave me alone."

Laughter bursts from his mouth. "Where's the fun in that?"

I purse my lips. "I don't exist purely so you can mess with me. Go screw with someone else."

A smirk spreads across his lips, and he drops the cigarette to the concrete and stands to step on it. "Come on." He drags me up by my arm. "Time to suck it up and go back inside." He nudges me toward the door, but I tear away from him.

"Don't touch me."

Does he have to treat me like a child?

Behind me, Xander scoffs, and I stiffen as he leans close. "You can resent me as much as you want, but you got yourself into this mess. Now, you have to deal with the consequences." His breath tickles my ear—I can barely suppress the shiver.

When he pushes me toward the door again, I let him touch me.

Inside, we take our seats, and Jimmy sends me a curious glance. I take a drink of water, and my father asks Xander to join the conversation:

"What do your parents do?"

Xander responds with all the geniality and respect of a well-bred gentleman. "My parents are business owners down in the Miami area. My mother runs a clothing franchise—or maybe it's two now—and my father is the presiding CEO of the Royal Alaskan Suites luxury hotel chain. You probably haven't heard of it. They only have locations in large metropolitan areas, New York, L.A., Miami of course, and the like."

It sounds like a brochure. He's probably recited this a thousand times.

My mouth pools with saliva, and I swallow to keep the bile down. My little chat with Xander didn't help with the uneasy stomach.

"Alaskan?"

"It started out in Juneau, Anchorage, and Fairbanks, but I think the original hotel is the only one left in the state. Not a lot of big cities there, you know?" Xander pauses to take a sip of his water. "My father is looking into going international—London, Paris, Tokyo, the works."

"And what are you looking into? What are your plans after graduation?" My dad's voice quivers with interest.

"I'm leaving myself open to possibilities. It's three and a half years away."

"But you're studying?"

"Business Management."

"And you, Jimmy?"

I grab the large water glass beside my sparkling cider and take a long drink. But after nearly half the drink is gone, my stomach is still queasy.

On my right, Jimmy tugs at his collar. "Oh, uh, Music, sir."

"You still play?" Dad sounds impressed.

"Mostly guitar now. Though I have to play the piano every holiday for Mom. She insists."

"You were fantastic at fourteen. I can only imagine your expertise now."

I finish my water and stare at the empty glass, willing it to refill. With only a few drops inside, it taunts me, but for the life of me, I can't take my eyes off the crystal glinting in the low lights.

"Imogene always loved to dance when you played."

I shut my eyes and wipe the sweat from my forehead. Brow creased, I take my fork and stab blindly at the poultry on the white plate.

"Billie?"

My head shoots up.

They're all staring. Xander is the only one who looks amused.

"Yeah?"

My dad clears his throat and looks down before venturing to speak. "Mina, you talked with your mother, correct?"

Jimmy and Xander dutifully turn their attention to their meals to give us some semblance of privacy.

"Not yet, but I'm sure I'll talk to her soon." Most of our conversations take place through my sister, though.

He reaches for another helping of mashed potatoes. "When you talk to them, would you kindly wish your mother and sister a happy Christmas for me?"

I frown. "Why would I do that?"

My father pauses, his eyes stuck on the serving spoon in his hand, and Jimmy freezes mid-bite. "It was only an idea." He lets out a puff of anxious laughter and replaces the spoon in the bowl.

"I didn't mean it like that." Despite the nausea building in my abdomen, my voice is steady. "Nothing's holding you back from calling Mo yourself."

He takes hold of the gravy boat and pours the dark liquid on his potatoes. "I'd probably call at an inconvenient time." I strain to hear him. "I wouldn't want to be a bother."

The irritation expands in my chest, and I grit my teeth. "Is that why you didn't call for years? You didn't want to 'bother' us?"

He drives his fork into his mashed potatoes and brings the bite to his mouth. He swallows without chewing. He's not going to respond.

"Do you have any idea how long I waited for you? A phone call, a letter—anything." I take in a shaky breath. "Three years. I waited three years. You didn't come to my graduation. You didn't even send a card."

Jimmy's hand shoots out to grab my clenched fist. "Billie…"

My entire body is shaking

I know what he's thinking—that I'm overreacting. But he doesn't understand. He never has, and he never will.

I stand, tearing my hand away from his, and on the other side of the table, my father stops, his fork and knife resting in his hands on either side of his plate. The room is silent, but I'm shaking, holding back the tears welling in my eyes.

"You know, Imogene never lost faith in you. But that's not enough for you to call her and talk to her. I'm not going to relay half-hearted attempts at making amends. You have your own phone for that." I clench my fists at my sides. "But I'm done waiting, I'm done hoping, I'm just done. Coming here—to Vermont, to Bradford—was a terrible idea. I don't know why I thought it'd be okay. This is the worst decision I ever made."

Across the table, my father releases his utensils and lifts his gaze to meet mine, and I can no longer talk. When he speaks, his words are painstaking, forced. "Then you should leave."

I stop, unable to move.

"If that's how you feel, there's nothing I can say to change your mind. You should leave."

I grit my teeth. "Fine. I never wanted to be here anyway."

Eight

I PULL MY COAT TIGHTER AND HUG MY ARMS AROUND MY torso.

I'm not sure where I'm going. Campus dorms are probably locked. I have nowhere else to go. Only half the sidewalks have been salted or shoveled, and I trudge through the snow on my walk to nowhere.

There's no one around. No one to see, no cars to avoid, nothing in sight.

The sidewalk comes to a stop at the edge of Olive, but I keep walking, and on the other side, it resumes. Cherry Street is particularly long, the cracks deeper, the gradation higher. Ahead looms Finchley, and I step onto the street, my eyes following the uneven sections of the road.

Beeeeeeep.

I stop, my head twisting around.

There's a car right next to me. Not just any car. A faded red car. Xander's car.

The driver's side window rolls down, and he sticks his head out. "Want a ride?" He nods toward the passenger side. "Or do you intend to freeze to death?"

I pause. He's stopped in the middle of the intersection,

blocking all traffic—if there were traffic.

"I'm not driving until you get in the car, Dixon."

But I don't move.

"Get in the fucking car."

I take a deep breath and force my legs to move again, walking around to climb into the passenger seat. I don't bother buckling my seatbelt.

Xander directs the car left onto Finchley and drives right past Bradford. The campus is dead and lonely with no one there. I don't know much beyond campus—and I'm not sure Xander does either—but we're heading toward the edge of the small town.

"Where are you taking me?"

He doesn't look at me. "Does it matter?"

I lean my head against the glass and watch the streetlights pass. No, not really.

"I figured you could use getting away for a little while—and maybe a drink."

"Where do you plan to get this drink? You're not old enough to buy alcohol, and you're too smart to regularly keep a bottle in your car."

Xander laughs. "I may have swiped a bottle of wine from your dad's house." He pauses. "Relax, I'll pay him back."

"I really don't care if you steal booze from my father."

He scoffs. "Well, maybe you should."

Outside, Finchley ends at Highland Road, and we turn right, heading farther out of town. The area is mostly trees with a few homes, but the farther we drive, the more the road winds and the fewer houses there are. A few minutes past the city limits, there's a clearing on the right and a gravel area on the side of the road where Xander parks the car.

"Come on, Dixon, time to get out." He leans into the back seat and withdraws a bottle of red wine—the same kind my father was drinking during dinner.

I follow Xander but pause when we reach a barbed wire fence. Beyond is a small pond, the water shimmering in the moonlight. The edges are iced over, and the snow here is pristine.

"This is someone's property."

He steps on the bottom row of barbed wire, carefully lifts the next one up, and nods me through.

But I don't move. "This is trespassing. It's illegal."

Xander rolls his eyes. "So?" He holds the bottle of wine aloft and dangles it in front of me. "So's this, but you have no problem with that."

I frown but crouch down and step through the opening he made for me. I wait for him, and he climbs through, then leads the way to the edge of the pond and sits on the bank.

I pause beside him. "We're going to sit here in the cold and the snow and drink alcohol?" I purse my lips. "My butt's going to be numb and wet, and this is a terrible idea."

"Shut up and sit down."

Grudgingly, I join him. The cold permeates my jeans.

He sets the bottle in the snow between us before leaning back and withdrawing a waiter's corkscrew from his front pocket. I watch in fascination as he removes the cork expertly—*pop*. He's probably had a lot of practice, though, I admit, I never pictured him getting drunk on a bottle of wine.

"Do you always carry a corkscrew with you?"

He lets out a short laugh. "This is your dad's too. I'll

return it." He lifts the bottle to his lips and takes a drink before offering it to me. "You know, this was the cheapest thing I could find in his liquor cabinet." I swallow down a gulp of the dark bitter wine, and he adds, "Only seventy-five bucks."

I gag and pull the bottle back before examining the label. Cabernet Sauvignon, 15.5 percent.

Beside me, Xander laughs. "How does it taste?"

"It's perfect." I swallow down another gulp before allowing him to take the bottle from my hand. "Where's Jimmy? Shouldn't he be here?"

After a swig from the bottle, he places it in the snow between us. "Nah, he's consoling your dad. He was really upset by your outburst."

I snatch up the bottle and glare at my clenched hands. "He was upset? He could've said something instead of sitting there."

Xander snorts. "I think he did say something, Dixon, or have you wiped that from your memory?"

How could I possibly forget? After years of utter silence, my father—meek, shy, the ultimate pushover—kicked me out of his house.

I take a long drink from the bottle, ignoring the bitter taste.

"No," Xander says, and he pauses to laugh, "what you mean is, he could've said what you wanted him to say. Were you expecting him to apologize? While you were screaming at him?"

"I don't know."

He scoffs. "You haven't exactly given him a reason to apologize."

79

I swallow down more wine and hold the bottle close to my chest. "What the hell does that mean? Why should I give him a reason? He's the one that left, the one that didn't have anything to say to me for the three years before I came here." I take another drink.

Xander rolls his eyes. "Sounds pretty nice to me. I'd love to not talk to you for three years. That'd be a fucking dream."

"Agreed," and I continue to drown my sorrows. "I'd be totally happy if I'd never met you, Xander."

For a moment, he smiles. "Same here." He nudges me with an elbow, and I scoot farther away in an attempt to alleviate the unease at his close proximity. "You know, when I said cowardice doesn't look good on you, I didn't mean you should freak out on your dad over one word."

I frown. "It's not a word, it's the whole concept—and what part of 'I don't want to talk to you about this' do you not understand?" I take another long drink before looking at the bottle again. Half of it's gone, and most of that's in my stomach.

"My comprehension's perfectly fine." He pulls out his cigarettes and lights up a smoke. In the cold night air, the scent is sharp and strong.

"How many of those do you have a day?" I take another drink.

He shrugs. "More than any doctor recommends."

"You're going to die."

Xander releases a low laugh and takes a drag from the cig. "Everyone dies."

In the silence, I take another sip of wine, then pause to the consider the bottle. When is it supposed to kick in?

I don't feel any different, but I know I've had a lot. How much is in here? It's hard to focus on the label.

Beside me, Xander leans closer, cigarette dangling from the side of his mouth, to examine the surface level of the wine inside the dark bottle. "At some point, I'm gonna have to cut you off."

"What? No."

He removes the smoke from his mouth and holds it away. "You've probably already had more than enough. You've never been drunk before, right? And you weigh, what, a hundred pounds?" He snatches the wine from my hands. "You're going to die if you drink this whole bottle."

I grit my teeth and level him with a glare. "What the fuck do you know? Give it back."

He releases a short laugh. "Trust me, it's already affecting your judgment."

I lean toward him, grabbing for the bottle, but he drops the cigarette in the snow and holds me at bay with his hand. I press closer, and my fingers graze the bottle, but he moves it farther away, out of reach.

"Stop treating me like a child. You're six months older than me."

He scoots farther away, and I stagger after him.

The movement's too much, too fast. I grab his pant leg to steady myself, fingers digging into the smooth fabric. My other hand finds the snowy bank, and I bite my tongue.

Xander grabs my shoulder, abandoning the alcohol behind him, and I hunch down, my forehead brushing against his thigh, and breathe. When did everything start spinning?

"I'll stop treating you like a child when you stop acting

like one. I know way more about alcohol than you do, and as annoying as you may be, I have no intention of killing you."

I lift my head, nostrils flaring, and stutter my words. "Why don't I believe you?"

He smells like patchouli and sandalwood—and cigarettes of course. But he always smells like cigarettes. A wicked grin spreads across his face, and I focus on that smile even after it's gone. "There's a long list of reasons why you're too fucked up to believe me when I say I don't want you to die."

"You're disgusting." I push away from him and lie back on the snow.

The cold spreads throughout my body, but my ass and hand are already numb. Above us, the moon is bright.

"You're actually pretty funny when you're drunk, Dixon." The grin plastered on his face says he's unmoved by my bitter words.

I almost laugh, but then, I remember I hate him—really hate him—and I swallow. "I'm always this hilarious, Theroux." I struggle into a sitting position. "You're too much of an asshole to notice."

His smile fades. "Seriously, though, you should play a little nicer with your dad—"

"I thought we were done talking about that."

"—I think he's a bit of a sentimental spirit, not like us."

My words catch in my throat. "I'm nothing like you."

Xander snorts. "Oh, please, drunk-ass." He laughs and leans down to find his dropped cigarette, put out and damp from the snow. "You and I both know we're far more alike than we'd admit, and I'm only saying this because you won't remember anything in the morning with how quickly you drank that."

I shake my head. "I'll have you know I have a fantastic memory."

"Of course you do."

I grit my teeth but pull my phone from my pocket. Better to ignore his stupid words. He doesn't know anything. We're nothing alike—he's a selfish, conceited asshole, and I'm...I don't know what I am.

The screen lights up. No notifications. Not even a text from Jimmy asking how I am. Does he know where I am or what I'm doing? Or who I'm with? I could be lost or dead, and he'd have no idea.

But now, he cares more about my father than me.

I turn off the screen, hug the phone to my chest, and clench my eyes shut. "This really was the worst idea. How did I talk myself into this?"

Snow crunches as Xander shifts. "Winter break with your dad? Or coming to Bradford in the first place?"

"Either. Both." I take in a deep breath and force my eyes open to look at the starry sky. Out here, the stars are brighter than I'm used to. You never see a sky this clear in Springfield.

Xander sighs. "You need to lighten up with your dad. They got divorced, and your mom got to keep the kids, which is pretty typical. If she didn't want him around or if he didn't want to be around her, that doesn't mean either of them loved you any less. Cut him some slack. He's doing what he can."

I twist to look at him, but it's too fast. The world spins with every movement.

He cocks an eyebrow. "Careful."

"I'm fine." I sit up slowly to glare at him. "If he wanted to talk to me, he could've at least written. I doubt my mom was so bitter she would've refused his calls or burned his letters."

"It's not always that black and white."

My jaw tightens. "And why not? When it's your own children, it should be that fucking black and white."

Xander rolls his eyes and sneaks a drink from the bottle of wine he's hiding. "Look, here's the thing, you're being completely idiotic and unreasonable. He's your father. No matter what shit he pulls, he's still your father. You should be fucking grateful he wants to be a part of your life now, even if he didn't before, because not everyone is that lucky. Don't squander what you have because you're as stubborn as a mule."

My eyes narrow. "I'm the one being unreasonable? You wanna see fucking unreasonable?" I pull up my phone again and flip through my apps. "I don't need to be here. My mom's house is one fucking flight away, and I can go there and never come back—and never see your stupid face again."

Xander groans. "Right, because running away again is the perfect way to deal with this. God, just go back to his house and tell him you're fucking sorry."

I pause halfway through filling out my flier information to glare at him. "I'm not the one who should apologize. I didn't move halfway across the country to get away from him. I'm not the one who never called, never wrote, never contacted, period."

A muscle in his jaw trembles. "As moving as your life story may be, get over yourself, Dixon. You're not the only person in the world with an absentee parent, and that's not justification for how much you hate people—and it's definitely not justification for how much you hate yourself. Nobody, not even Jimmy, wants to listen to you bitch about your dad all the time. Yeah, he left. Get the fuck over it. He's here now, and you're the one abandoning him." He takes another swig from the wine before dropping it in the snow again. "Alright, seriously, fuck it. I'm done. I'm going for a walk."

He pushes himself into a standing position and storms down the bank into the trees.

My fist tightens around my phone, but I scream after him. "Go fuck yourself, Xander!"

His footfalls stop, and he turns back halfway. "You know what, Dixon? Have the whole fucking bottle—it's right there for you—and when the alcohol poisoning sets in as it most certainly will in the next twenty minutes or so, I sincerely hope you asphyxiate on your own vomit."

Without another word, he turns, and slowly, his figure recedes into the darkness.

Tears of anger welling in my eyes, I unlock my phone and finish filling out the form. Confirm my seating. Add a carry-on. Select my debit card for payment.

What does he know anyway? He's never had a hard day in his life. His wealthy parents could give him anything he wanted. He leads an incredibly privileged life.

The card processes, and I sit for a moment, staring at the confirmation email. The tiny words are hard to read. My head is spinning, my stomach churns, but I switch to my text messenger and start a new message to Imogene:

This isn't working out. My flight lands at 6:10 tomorrow night. Pick me up?

I close the phone and look around. He's nowhere to be seen. Who knows when he'll be back. But my eyes land on the bottle a few feet to my left, and I reach out with an unsteady hand.

Nine

I DON'T KNOW WHERE I AM.

The room is dark, black. The one window has black-out curtains. The floor is hardwood, cool against my skin. There's a rug, a bed, other furniture, but they're just dark blobs. Where are my glasses? A trash bin sits next to me, reeking of vomit and alcohol.

I push up on my hands and knees, but another bout of nausea hits before I can sit up. I clutch the trash bin and pull it closer, resting my cheek against the edge.

Somewhere nearby, my phone buzzes. Text message.

I glance around, searching. My head is pounding. The device is glowing in the darkness from a nightstand. Are my glasses there too? The light fades.

I rub my forehead and sit up as the nausea subsides, my hands behind me for support.

There's a glint of light shining from a crack between the curtains. What time is it?

I take a deep breath and crawl across the floor to the nightstand. My fingers grip the edge, and I pull up on my knees to grope around for the phone. Alarm clock. Notepad. Glasses. Phone. I pull on my glasses, and the room comes into focus.

My dad's house. The guest bedroom. The bed's a mess—I must've slept there until I needed to throw up. My duffel bag is sitting on the floor, unzipped as I left it yesterday.

Shit. How did I get back here?

I drag my phone closer and unlock it. Five text messages, most of them from Imogene, but the most recent one is from Jimmy. I open his first:

Just got back. Hope you're feeling better. Call me.

Talking sounds like the worst idea—partially because I don't know what to say, but also because my throat hurts.

I turn my attention to Mo's texts. The first three are from last night:

Wait, what happened? Are you okay?

Yes, we can pick you up. It's not a problem. You're flying into the Springfield airport, right?

Seriously, are you okay?

But the last one is from early this morning: *Billie, I'm worried. Please call me.*

I turn off the screen and push the phone away.

What the hell am I supposed to say if I do call her? Am I supposed to explain everything—the way I freaked out, the way I screamed at our dad, the way I got trashed after years of watching Mom destroy her life with alcohol, the way I booked a flight on a whim instead of talking about my feelings, the way I fuck everything up?

Because the truth is, I don't know how to talk about my feelings—not without getting mad at someone, or everyone, especially myself.

Everything I do is wrong.

Fuck. The flight. What time is it? Almost eleven. My

flight's at 12:30, and it's an hour drive to Burlington. I have to go. Now.

I stumble to my feet, pocket my phone, tighten my hair tie, and search the room. My shoes are by the door, and the only other thing here that's mine is the bag. I slip on my Converse, not bothering to retie them, grab my duffel bag from the floor, and leave the room.

Downstairs, it's quiet.

My father is sitting in the dining room with the newspaper spread across table. He's doing the crossword puzzle. He glances up as I come into view but promptly returns his attention to the paper.

I hesitate at the doorway. "I have a flight back to Missouri. I'll get out of your hair as soon as I call a cab."

He squares his shoulders, but he doesn't look at me again. "You're going to pay for a cab to Burlington?" His voice is empty.

"I don't have any other way to get there."

He heaves a sigh and pushes his chair away from the table. "When do you need to leave?"

I purse my lips and glance toward the front door. "Now."

"Then let's go."

He walks around the table and retrieves his keys from the sideboard. He brushes past me and walks toward the door beyond the stairs—it must lead into the garage.

Hesitantly, I follow.

◆

The Burlington International Airport glows with holiday lights as I pass the lines and rows of people, dressed in

Christmas red and green, waiting for their respective flights. Over the speakers, Dean Martin does a cheery rendition of "Let It Snow," and in the foyer stands a ten-foot tree, decked out in strings of extra-large bulbs, gold and silver globes, and burlap ribbon. Like most public settings, they're overdoing it.

By the time I reach my gate, the flight back to Springfield is arriving.

I watch through enormous floor-to-ceiling windows as the plane hooks up to the jetway, and minutes later, the passengers disembark from the gate. As soon as they're out of the way, the woman at the computer by the gate entrance calls the first group to line up at the door.

I check the ticket on my phone. No, I'm in section three.

I take a seat near the gate and wait, tapping my foot against the floor, my phone at the ready.

The trip to the airport was unbearable. My father didn't speak, but I learned an hour's worth of information about an up-and-coming folk rock band whose name I don't remember.

Not to mention the light. The light was more unbearable than the drive. And unfortunately, I don't have prescription sunglasses. Or ibuprofen on me.

"Section two," calls out the attendant from her station, and I tap the screen of my phone again to keep it lit.

Everyone is scanning through the gate quickly now, and halfway through section two, she requests section three as well. I force myself to my feet and shoulder the duffel bag as I join the crowd. I have to turn up the brightness on my phone for it to scan and head past the checkpoint down the ramp.

Probably not a great idea to take a bumpy, five-and-a-half-hour flight while hung over, but I'm already buckling my seatbelt. I don't have another option.

I clench my hands around the armrests as the plane takes off twenty minutes later, forcing my eyes shut, trying not to focus on the motion of the aircraft. The nausea hasn't fully abated, and it swells up inside me as we lift into the air.

I'm never drinking again.

◆

The flight lands in Springfield, Missouri five minutes after the ETA. The airport is small; it's simple to navigate to the lobby, my eyes focusing on the purple and green floor as I trudge to the exit.

"Billie!"

That squeal has to be Imogene.

I search the sea of faces to discover most of the others from my flight have already left or are waiting at baggage claim, and near the front doors stands Imogene. She wears a fluffy mauve sweater and skinny jeans, her dark blond hair in pigtails, her bright eyes glistening with excitement.

I force a smile before approaching. "Hey."

Imogene is already rolling her eyes. "Hey yourself, silly." She wraps her arms around me in a big hug. "You're alive!" Then, she pauses and pulls back, her brow furrowed.

I scoff. "Of course I'm alive. Why wouldn't I be?"

But we both know why. My only text to her today was simple: *Yes, the Springfield airport.*

Imogene's face transforms from curious and confused to irritated. "Billie, have you been drinking? The night before

91

coming home? How could you?"

I frown and look to the duffel bag at my feet. "I know, it was—"

"Incredibly stupid." She turns and heads toward the automatic doors. "How could you be so insensitive?"

"I'm sorry." My voice quivers, and I follow her out of the building.

"You need to keep your distance from Mom right now— or at least have the decency to stay downwind."

I nod, even though she can't see.

My sister releases a sigh and moves on, her voice still annoyed. "What happened? Or are you not going to tell me like usual? You know you don't have to keep everything to yourself."

"We can talk about that later." I rub my eyes. I bought some pain relief when the flight landed, but it won't kick in for another twenty minutes. My head is still pounding.

Our mother is waiting inside the car when we arrive, and she opens the door to greet me. When she stands, clutching the car door, her long hair blows in the breeze. Imogene inherited her blond hair from Mom—and her classically beautiful facial structure—but I wasn't that lucky.

Beside the car, Mom hesitates, then smiles. "Welcome home." Her normally boisterous voice is quiet and reserved.

"Hi, Mom."

"Pop the trunk, Mom." Imogene takes my duffel bag and stows it in the back before beginning her interrogation. "Okay, you don't have to talk about that, but at least tell me everything else. What's Bradford like? Have you made friends? A boyfriend?"

Huffing, I climb into the back seat. "Give it a rest, Mo."

I buckle my seatbelt, and she climbs in beside me. "At least let me take a breath first."

Imogene rolls her eyes. "You've been breathing for the past several months all by yourself. Now you have to deal with me for three weeks. I hardly think that's unfair."

"I'm not in the mood."

In the front seat, my mother belts herself in and shifts the car into gear to back up and exit the parking lot. "What do you want for dinner, Billie?" She uses the rear-view mirror to meet my eyes. "Chinese food?"

I haven't had good cashew chicken in ages. "Yeah."

"Jimmy said he was bringing back a surprise." Imogene belts herself. "I think he got in today, but I haven't seen him yet. What'd he bring?"

I raise an eyebrow. "It wouldn't be a surprise if I told you."

She's not amused. "You have no idea what I'm talking about, do you?"

I send her an apologetic smile. "I've been a little distracted lately, so no, I really don't."

Her face falls. "Are you going to tell me about what happened with Dad?"

I never expected her to bring him up in front of Mom, but surprisingly, our mother doesn't notice. She turns east down Sunshine to reach our usual Chinese takeout restaurant on the opposite side of town.

I shake my head. "Uh, it was just a bad idea. We agreed it was…jumping in too quickly. He hopes we have a good Christmas." And he probably never wants to see me again.

Imogene's face lights up, and I want to tell her everything, but I can only imagine how disappointed she would be.

"Will he call over the holidays? I mean, he has your phone number, right? D'you think he'll call to wish us a happy Christmas?"

No, I really don't.

"Maybe." I try to sound hopeful for her.

Apparently, Imogene is satisfied with that answer. "How'd you do in your classes? Have you heard yet?"

"Grades aren't posted till Monday." I look at the streets and shops as we pass. "Mr. Hodges said I got an A in Calculus."

She laughs. "What about the grades that actually matter? I mean, no one thought you'd get less than an A in Calculus, right?"

I had my doubts.

"What have you been doing besides classes?"

There isn't much to say there either. I'm sure my number of extra-curricular activities would be an enormous disappointment to Mo. I'm too intimidated to check out Bradford's art club, and the mathematics society consisted of no more than five members when I attended the first couple meetings.

In the end, all I can come up with is, "I've been tutoring another student."

"Cool." She doesn't seem interested. "What about friends? Do you hang out with anyone? What about a boyfriend?"

"I don't have time for any of that." I turn my attention to the window again.

"But you do hang out with Jimmy, right? And he has friends."

"That doesn't mean I'm friends with his friends."

We pull into the drive-thru, and I read the menu with my mom as she decides what to eat. The intercom crackles to life, and a woman requests our order and tallies up the bill. Mom pulls up to the window to pay.

While she's distracted, I turn to Imogene again. "Is Mom okay?"

Mo glances to where Mom sits in the front of the car and keeps her voice low. "Most days. Seriously, Billie, she's doing really well."

"She's so quiet right now." I can't picture the last time she's been this reserved.

"This is what she's like most of the time now." She shrugs. Apparently, it's not a big deal.

I swallow again and stare at my mom's smiling face via the rear-view mirror as she talks to the Asian woman through the window.

"I'll take your word for it."

Ten

THE BED IS TOO COMFORTABLE TO GET UP, AND MY HEAD is still fuzzy.

The Chinese food helped settle my stomach, but the alcohol remains in my system. I must have reeked of it yesterday. There's no way Mom didn't notice.

A cold shower and a new pair of underwear later, and I feel better than I have in days. I tug on a fresh t-shirt and glance around the bedroom where I spent most of my life before Bradford. The walls are bare, aside from the Nine Inch Nails poster hanging above my bed, and the corner bookshelf holds my collection of alt-rock CDs and the set of porcelain dolls my mom got for my eleventh birthday. The closet is packed from floor to ceiling with boxes and old clothes. There's nothing here for me.

What am I supposed to do over break? Every previous winter, I simply requested more hours at the cupcakery, but getting a job for three weeks isn't an option.

I pat my auburn coils dry and run a few fingers through it in an attempt to prevent the inevitable frizz. I drop the towel at the foot of my bed and examine the room again. I have to do something. I can't sit here.

From inside my desk, I pull out an assortment of papers and notebooks. Looks like math homework. Is that an essay about *Wuthering Heights* from junior year? That book with those selfish, depressing people, none of whom are remotely likable. The essay's covered in red marker. I wasn't exactly top of my class in the subject, and like most people in the room, I wasn't horribly interested in the undeniable, irrevocable love of Catherine and Heathcliff.

Outside, a car pulls into the driveway, honking twice.

I climb off my bed to reach the window and glance between the curtains. No car in our driveway, but Charlie Powell's navy-blue Impala has pulled into the driveway next door. They're probably still celebrating Jimmy's return.

Under the essays and notebooks, I extract a well-worn, leather-bound sketchbook and flip through the pages in the dim morning light, but the drawings are difficult to see.

With a sigh, I push the sketchbook aside and move to the window again. I push open the curtains to let in more light, and across the way, over the porch awning, there's a silhouette in Jimmy's bedroom. I lift a hand to wave when he flips on the light, but it's not him.

What the hell is Xander doing here?

He pauses at the door, and his eyes search the room. When his gaze passes the window, it lands directly on me, and I fully expect him to blow me off. After a moment, he raises an eyebrow and smirks.

Right. Not wearing pants.

I turn away and lie on the bed with my old sketchbook again. With more light, the images are more discernible. Sketches of my high school and the houses in the neighborhood, most from memory. I couldn't get up the nerve to carry the thing around and draw in front of people.

I pause at a self-portrait I did with a mirror.

A few feet away, my phone chimes.

I scramble over, reaching across the papers and notebooks on the edge of my bed, and grab it off my bedside table. No surprise, it's Xander.

Nice ass, it reads. Wow. So eloquent.

I'm not justifying that with a response. I return the phone to the table and examine the final pages of the sketchbook. Why didn't he go home for the holidays anyway? Surely, he wants to spend Christmas with his rich family.

The phone goes off again.

I'm not looking at it. It's just Xander being a dick again—as if he wasn't enough of one the other night.

At the bottom of the desk drawer is another notebook. It's barely used, only a few pages at the beginning with numbers and letters. Transposition ciphers, Caesar shifts, pigpen ciphers, Morse code, and only half are in my unrefined scrawl. The codes, once exciting, bring back distant memories—ones I have no interest in reliving.

But the last pages are different. It's been three and a half years since I've read these words. They still sting, even though they're mine.

Dear Dad,

Imogene wanted me to say her opening dance received many raving reviews. You should've imparted how deeply and overwhelmingly you needed her to see—know—that no matter obvious impediments, what you wanted wasn't hiding.

Don't ask us to believe in miracles. Don't—and if you do, know we don't require it—offer what no one gathered as possible. You left, and everyone knows acceptance is specially important.

Every single chance, Mom offers for me to explore therapy. Hopefully, her "offer" isn't more. Mom especially asked if we— Mo and I—are sure you said that you'd call or write. Unknown currently.

Mina

I push the letter away with its frayed edges and smudged ink. I wasn't particularly good at coding at the time. My father was the talented one in that department, and I wanted to do exactly what he did.

Like everything else, I didn't have the nerve to send it. As if he would've responded anyway. I was incredibly naive.

Another chime, and I take a shaky breath before grabbing my phone off the bed. Xander's snarky texts aren't allowed to be ignored.

No. It's Zane.

Honestly, I forgot about him in the tumult with my father and the alcohol. I unlock it to read the texts. What does he want? He doesn't need to study for Calculus again.

Mr. Hodges posted grades this morning, and I got a B. You are amazing.

How can I repay you?

How am I supposed to answer that? With money obviously—but that's not what he means. Uncertain, I let my phone fade to black and shove the notebooks and papers into the wastebasket. I don't want to look at them anymore.

◆

That evening, I take my chair for the first true family meal since I got home. The dining table is decked out with a white linen tablecloth, white china with painted silver edges, and utensils actually made of silver. What are we celebrating?

Imogene sits next to me with a big smile, and Mom carries in a pot roast with veggies. Has she recently relearned how to cook?

"We wanted to make a big to-do of you being home, Billie." A reserved smile tugs at my mother's lips. "You like my pot roast, right?"

I nod, even though I don't remember.

We pass around the serving dishes and fill our plates, and for the first time in years, my mother doesn't say a word. Not that that stops Imogene from hogging the conversation.

"Jimmy texted me," she says happily. "He wants us to come over tomorrow night. They're going to Mrs. P's show at the Little Theatre. You don't mind, do you?"

Brow furrowed, I shake my head. "What show is it this year?"

"*A Christmas Carol.*"

Why didn't he text me? Maybe he hasn't cleared it with Xander—I can't picture him being particularly keen on seeing me after our drunken argument, even if he was fine through the window.

"And did you notice there's someone at the Powells' with him?" Imogene doesn't stop to blink, but somehow, she's stuffing her face.

"Yeah, that's his roommate from Bradford. Xander." I pick at my food.

"That must be the surprise, though I don't know why he'd keep it a secret."

Neither do I.

My phone, sitting on the sideboard against the far wall,

chimes twice, signaling two consecutive texts. I ignore it.

"What's his roommate like?" Imogene asks.

For a moment, I don't know how to answer. "He's, uh, really into comics and video games and stuff," I say lamely. "He drives a classic car."

She rolls her eyes. "Wow, you really paint a picture there, Billie." She pauses to consider me. "Comics and video games, huh? You two must get along well."

I shake my head. "Not exactly."

On the other side of the room, my phone blares the Weezer ringtone. I heave a sigh and push away from the table to look at it. Zane again. The texts probably were too.

"I'm gonna take this really quick," and I slip into the living room.

"Yes?" I say after answering the call.

"Wilhelmina?" Zane's voice seems particularly foreign now, far away and unfamiliar. We've never spoken on the phone before, only texted.

I don't have the patience for his mind games right now. "What do you want, Zane?"

"I was worried when I didn't hear from you all day. You got my texts, right?"

All five of them. Or is that seven now?

"I did."

"Why didn't you text me back?"

"I've been busy." Not technically true.

He pauses. "Are you alright, Billie?"

I lean against the living room wall and shut my eyes, clutching the phone close. "I'm just fine, Zane. I'm glad you did well on the final."

"Really?" He sounds skeptical. "Because the way you say

'just fine' isn't very reassuring."

"I don't like the holidays." Maybe that will satisfy him.

Zane lets out a quiet laugh. "Yeah, well, it's not even Christmas yet, and then, there's New Year's. How's the beautiful family reunion?"

I snort. "Hardly beautiful."

His curiosity is incorrigible. "Are you spending the holidays with your mom or your dad?"

I hesitate. He never knew about my plans to stay in St. Clare—let alone how they fell through. "I can't imagine staying in St. Clare with my father for Christmas."

"Do you get along better with your mom then?"

I glance back toward the dining room. Too close. They can probably hear me. I cross the living room to the scarcely decorated tree and sit on the couch. "Is it unreasonable to be mad at my dad for leaving?"

The other line is silent. "No, not unreasonable. Being angry is understandable and, you know, normal."

"You know, when I was little, my dad was my idol. He went to these symposiums once a week, and he took me every single time and explained it all to me. I learned about Platonism and Boolean algebra long before most people my age. I lived for every Thursday."

"If you were close," Zane says, voice hushed, "all the more reason to be angry. I went through the same thing with my parents, even though I was little when they separated."

"But?" I suggest. His tone says he isn't finished.

Instead, he relaxes. "But nothing. You have every right to be angry—you should be angry. He wasn't fulfilling his duty as your father if he left and didn't contact you."

I nod, but my stomach twists. "How do I stop being

angry? This isn't sustainable."

"Hey," Zane says, suddenly flippant, "I'm not here for some big philosophical debate. All I wanted was to make sure you're alive."

"Right." I heave a sigh and push up from the couch. "I need to get back to dinner."

"Oh, I'm sorry, I didn't realize I was interrupting. You're in a different time zone, right?"

He's still talking as I pull the phone away and end the call without a response.

Eleven

ALL THAT SEPARATES OUR SIDE-LAWN FROM THE POWELLS' house is a long narrow driveway that leads to the Powells' detached garage and pool shed. Beneath a canopy of barren branches, we walk across our lawn, the driveway, and the Powells' paving stone path to the front door.

In this older neighborhood, the difference between the Powells' well-kept house and our poorly maintained residence is normal. Beside the sleek, gray, minimalist style of the Powells' residence, our house is a two-story disaster. The white paint is chipping away, the roof is far past its prime, and the single-pane windows freeze over in winter, but the house next door has been continually updated and renovated. They have a larger lot with room for a small circular pool, an ambitious garden, and a tennis court—not that I've seen any of the family play tennis. Jimmy tried once, but it was never repeated.

I press the doorbell, and Thea Powell, wearing a long red dress with a cashmere scarf hanging from her neck, answers a moment later, her smile an exact copy of Jimmy's toothy grin. "Wonderful to see you, Billie." She pulls me into a hug. "I'm glad you two are home."

When she releases me, she pulls Imogene into a quick hug as well. "The boys are up in Jimmy's room getting ready. Go ahead if you like."

We head for the stairs across the foyer, and as we ascend to the second floor, my phone chimes. With an irritated huff, I reach into my coat pocket to drag out the device.

Zane again.

I slip it back into my pocket without reading it. He can wait.

At the top landing, the soft twangs of guitar strings filter through the air. Jimmy's room must be open. Imogene and I listen at the door as he murmurs the soft melodic words of Simon and Garfunkel's "Homeward Bound" and strums along. On the bed, Xander is tossing and catching a mini basketball. They're wearing t-shirts and jeans.

Imogene pokes her head inside. "I forgot how well you play."

The music stops, and they turn to the door, Jimmy's eyes wide.

"This doesn't look like getting ready," I say. "You know your mom wants you to dress up, right?"

Jimmy relaxes. "I'm going to change. I was finishing up." He places his guitar on its stand and rifles through his walk-in closet for more appropriate attire.

I lean against the wall, waiting, and Imogene follows. My phone goes off again. I don't bother looking at it.

Xander quirks an eyebrow as he sits up. "Do you suddenly have a habit of not responding to your texts?"

"Not yours." I shrug. "Besides, it's been four seconds. He can wait."

"Dad?" Imogene asks, but I shake my head, and across

the room, Xander snorts.

"He doesn't text, Mo." And even if he did, I'm the last person he'd contact.

But Xander won't let it go. "What guy would possibly be texting you who isn't in this room?"

"It's nobody."

"Why, Dixon, have you started seeing someone?" He chucks the tiny basketball at me.

I duck and try to catch it, but it sputters out of control and falls to the floor. Grumbling, I reach down to pick it up. "Definitely not." I toss the ball back to him and try to distract him. "Shouldn't you be getting ready too? I don't think Mrs. P would be too pleased to see you wearing a Charmander shirt to her show."

Xander rolls his eyes but tosses the basketball into the hoop across the room and strips off his shirt. "Anything for Mrs. P." Since he's prone to walking around without a shirt, his bare chest—lean muscles, a hint of curly black chest hair—isn't any less tan than the rest of him.

I avert my eyes as he pulls on a new shirt from his bag.

"Speaking of dressing up…" When I glance up, he's tucking in a gray dress shirt, a black and silver tie slung around his neck. "Do you own a skirt?"

"No."

"Shame, really." He shrugs.

I narrow my eyes. "What?"

"I would pay ridiculous amounts of money to see that."

I pause, oddly tense. "Why?"

He sends me a smirk. "Because right now I'm picturing this pained look on your face, and I want to see how accurate my imagination is."

"Asshole."

Jimmy exits the closet, pulling on his favorite plaid sweater-vest. "She hasn't worn a skirt since fifth grade when her dad told her she didn't have to if she didn't want to."

"Nearly broke Mom's heart," Imogene says, finally drawing attention to herself.

Xander pauses in the middle of tying his tie to study her.

"This is my sister Imogene. Mo, meet Xander."

She sends him a small wave, and he smiles.

"If you so much as look at her, I will kill you."

He lets out a short bark of laughter. "I guess we'll never be able to be friends if I can't look at you."

I cross my arms. "You know exactly what I mean, Theroux. No leching on my little sister."

Xander cocks an eyebrow. "Your flesh and blood? No, thanks." He reaches for his leather jacket, hanging from a bedpost.

I huff and divert my attention to Jimmy, who crosses the room to stand beside me. "How are you doing?"

Imogene and Xander exchange guarded greetings.

I send him a small smile and keep my voice low. "I'm sober and I intend to stay that way if that's what you're asking." I clear my throat. "Everyone's sober actually."

He nods. "Yeah, my parents mentioned something about how your mom's been in better spirits."

That's the nice way of saying she's actually attending AA and taking medication.

"I doubt I'd call it that. She's so quiet it's unnerving."

"I'm surprised she didn't come tonight," Jimmy says. "Mom said she was at the opening."

I shrug. "I've spent the last four years living at your

house. I have no idea what's going on with my mother. Mo said she had other plans and she'd make it up to us." I snort. "Go figure."

Jimmy opens his mouth, but he doesn't get the chance to speak.

"Knock, knock." Thea Powell raps her knuckles on the open door. Her coat is now buttoned, and the scarf is tied around her neck. "You lot ready to go?"

◆

The theater is already quite full when we arrive, Xander leading the way to a row midway down the aisle. He files in, Imogene behind him, and Jimmy and I hold up the rear. Charlie Powell was unable to join us, and Thea, of course, is up in the sound booth. We can barely see her from our position, but Jimmy sends her a quick wave before we sit down.

"Who's playing Scrooge?" I take the end seat.

Jimmy glances through the program. "Jonathan Levy. Never heard of him." He turns to me, holding his place in the pamphlet with a finger. "You don't have to feign interest, Billie. I know you don't want to be here."

"I'm here for your mom."

Around the auditorium, an array of people find their seats. On the stage, the black curtains remain closed, but every once in a while, the dark cloth rustles.

"Yeah, that's the only reason you're here. You hate Christmas."

"What, a deep passionate hatred for the holidays isn't normal?"

He lets out a fake laugh. "You can be sarcastic all you

want, but don't deny your feelings."

I shift in my seat. That doesn't need justified with a response. Jimmy turns his attention back to the program, and in my pocket, my phone buzzes. Yet another text from Zane.

Finally, I unlock the phone to read the messages he's sent throughout the day.

Jimmy leans over my shoulder as I craft my response. "Speaking of feelings…"

I pause to look at him. "What?"

"You've been getting a lot of texts from this Zane guy." He turns back to the program with a shrug. "Why are you ignoring him? He sent you, what, four texts in the last half hour, and you didn't respond to any of them."

"I'm responding now." I send the text and switch my phone to silent.

I lean forward to look at Imogene and Xander, chatting amicably. Xander has shrugged off his leather jacket and loosened his tie already. Beside him, Mo laughs.

The lights dim, and I lean back, frowning.

"Four texts seems pretty determined." Jimmy rests the program on his lap. "He must like you an awful lot to not be bothered by your lack of interest."

I freeze. "He doesn't like me. That's ridiculous."

The curtains open.

Jimmy lowers his voice to a whisper. "Why ridiculous? You guys spent a lot of time together in the last two weeks. It's pretty obvious he's into you." He considers me a moment. "Is that such a bad thing?"

I turn with a glare. "He's not into me, and if he were, I have no interest in a relationship. I have actual goals."

He nods, but there's a twitch at the side of his mouth. "Right, because those of us who want the warm fuzzies don't have real goals."

I sigh. "You know that's not what I meant. I need to focus to get into a good Master's program. Having a boyfriend would get in the way."

"Becoming a cryptographer and having a boyfriend aren't mutually exclusive, Billie. Why can't you have both?"

"Shut up." I nudge him in the side. "The play's started. Aren't we supposed to pay attention?"

Jimmy shrugs. "There are at least three more showings before Christmas. It's not the end of the world if I miss it." He leans his head closer. "Answer the question, Billie. Why can't you have both?"

I shake my head, and he sighs.

"Just because you don't think there's anything special about you doesn't mean no one else does. Obviously Zane Nelson thinks you're special, and he's not the only one. I happen to agree with him."

"You're my best friend. You're supposed to at least find me tolerable."

He rolls his eyes. "You'd be a lot more tolerable if you talked to me. That's what friends are for, remember?"

I let out a long sigh, ignoring the play as it unfolds on the stage in front of us. "I'm not sure what I'm supposed to talk about, Jimmy. I tutor the guy, and I'm happy to keep that relationship professional."

"You don't tutor him anymore. The semester's over."

"Okay, sure, we spent a lot of time together while I was helping him, but that doesn't mean he developed feelings for me. That sounds so…Stockholm syndrome."

Jimmy cocks an eyebrow. "If anything, he was imprisoned by math, not you."

I lay my head in my hand. "I don't understand him. We barely talked for the first sessions, and then out of nowhere, he started telling me all about himself and asking me questions. I barely respond, but he continues to text me, expecting me to care."

He laughs. "He's been blinded by love. He wants you to care."

I send him a skeptical glance.

"I'm serious, Billie. He likes you."

"No." I shake my head. "Don't give me any of this love-at-first-sight mumbo jumbo. We've known each other for three weeks, and he isn't you. He didn't fall for me the way you fell for Cynthia—hard and in a matter of seconds."

Jimmy smiles wistfully at the mention of her name. "You'd understand if you got to know her."

I roll my eyes. "I know her better than you do, Jim. We share a bathroom. All you do is stare at her like she moves the heavens and earth. She's not that great."

"You don't know what you're talking about."

"Oh, yes, I do." I glare. "This is the one thing Xander and I agree on. All Cynthia Allen's interested in is science—not you."

"She doesn't know me yet."

"Speaking of Xander," I say, eager to change the subject, "why did you bring that idiot here? Didn't he want to spend Christmas with his parents?"

"They're on a business trip for the holidays, so I invited him. You weren't going to be here anyway."

Xander and Imogene are watching the show and whispering back and forth, and my jaw clenches. "I don't know why you're friends with him. He's a complete dick. He only cares about himself."

"That's not true, and you know it." Jimmy's voice is tired. We've had this conversation too many times. "He's been a good friend to me, and he'd be a good friend to you too if you'd let him."

I shake my head. "That ship set sail months ago, and I waved happily as it passed."

"That's your fault. Why do you have this obsessive need to see the bad in everyone? You never gave Xander a chance."

I frown. That's not true.

"I know he made fun of you when you guys first met, but that's how he jokes. He didn't mean it. Not like you think."

"And you only see the good parts of people, Jimmy. I'm not like you."

"You could try."

I raise an eyebrow.

"You need to open up to someone. I'm not saying it should be Zane—he's not the only guy who'll be interested, trust me—but you can't keep everything to yourself."

"What's the point?"

"You'll never know unless you try, Billie. I won't always be around for you to talk to."

"Right, you're going to marry Cynthia and have eight children." I let out a long sigh.

On the stage, Scrooge is already meeting the Ghost of Christmas Past.

"You guys coming to the Christmas Eve party? Or New Year's Eve?"

I shoot him a quizzical look. "I haven't heard anything

to the contrary. Why?"

"I mean, is your mom feeling up to a celebration with alcohol. She's only been sober for a couple months, right?"

I shrug. "I'm sure it'll be fine. Everybody loves Christmas, right?"

◆

The night air blows into the room when I open the window. The curtains billow to the side, and I yank out my hair tie to let my massive hair hang free. The cold breeze hits my face.

It's nearly eleven now. Thea Powell took us home an hour ago after she finished up. The wait was unbearable with Xander constantly complaining about the weather, but I relish the cold. It's the only thing that feels real. Mom still isn't home, but Imogene went straight to bed, and I returned to my bedroom to sleep as well.

But per usual, sleep didn't come.

I squish inside the window frame and rest my foot on the opposite side to keep balanced. Zane continued to text me throughout the play—no surprise, especially after I responded. *How's the acting? Is the play any good? Oh, that's one of my favorite Christmas stories.* Text doesn't communicate sarcasm well, and Zane can barely pick up on that syntax in person.

Across the driveway, a window opens, and Jimmy presses his face against the screen. "Don't fall!"

I look over as he removes the screen from the window frame. "Don't be ridiculous. You of all people know how many times I've snuck out this window. I could literally stand on this roof right here." I put one foot on the flat roof that covers the side-porch to prove my point.

Jimmy laughs and nods his head toward his bedroom. "Then why don't you sneak out and come over? We're not going to bed anytime soon."

"What? No!" Xander pushes Jimmy aside and pokes his head out as well. "This isn't a dorm room."

"Which means we don't have to worry about David finding her." Jimmy laughs.

I hold back a smile. If the last five months have taught me anything, it's that our RA couldn't care less about my sleeping in their room.

"No," Xander counters, "that means there's one bed. It may be a queen instead of a twin, but it's only one. I have literally zero intention of getting into bed with her."

Jimmy snorts.

I laugh. "What? You don't want to be that close to your arch nemesis?"

Xander scoffs. "Don't flatter yourself."

"Relax," I say, rolling my eyes, "no one is asking you to tarnish your good name. Thanks for the offer, Jimmy, but I'm not in the mood to socialize."

Jimmy smiles, but beside him, Xander scoffs again. "Like always." He turns to Jimmy with a grin. "Oh, you know what we should do? Break into your parents' liquor cabinet and get drunk."

Jimmy and I laugh, and I retrieve my sketchbook from my nightstand while he explains they don't need to break into anything to get booze. Charlie and Thea have the unique perspective of willingly giving their children alcohol to prevent them from seeking it in an unsafe environment. It worked. As many parties as Jimmy has attended with

Xander, he's never had more than a drink, and I—well, I ruined that with the drinking fiasco the other night.

I settle onto the window sill again just in time to see Xander's skeptical face. "Doesn't that ruin the fun, though?"

Jimmy turns to me again, and I flip through my sketchbook to find a blank page. "You sure, Billie? You can draw here too. You don't have to do it alone."

"I like being alone."

I return to the sketchbook, not wanting to see Jimmy's sad face, but a loud shout of laughter echoes between the houses. I glance up as Xander says, "Right. That's exactly why you spend every evening in our dorm room."

Jimmy elbows him in the side, and I inhale the cold winter air to steady myself.

Rubbing his ribs, Xander pulls inside slightly. "Whatever. Can we close the fucking window? It's freezing."

Jimmy sends me an apologetic smile. "Have a good night." He and Xander retreat, and he pops the screen back into place and closes the window.

I watch a moment as they move toward the bed, the bright light in the room illuminating their forms while they laugh. I return to the sketchbook on my lap and pull out a pencil to draw.

My phone buzzes again. Let's see what Zane has to say this time.

You going to sleep now? It's getting late.

I sigh. *I rarely get to sleep when I want to.*

Not a minute later, another text.

So you're up?

Yeah.

I push the phone aside and try to focus, but the white

page glares at me. As I press my pencil to the thick-toothed paper, the window sill begins to vibrate.

I drop the sketchbook on the carpet and grab the phone again. "Hello?"

"Hey," Zane says on the other line. "I'm not bothering you, am I? You seemed a little down."

"It's fine. I'm just ready to leave Missouri."

"Is being home that bad?"

I rest my head against the window frame. "It hasn't been home in a long time. I feel like I'm stuck here."

"I get that. You don't belong anymore." He pauses, and I listen to his breathing. "Why don't you like Christmas?"

I scoot my legs over the window sill and press my bare feet onto the porch roof. I can barely feel them anymore. "When I was a kid, it was my favorite part of the school year. Finally, after months of following him around like a lost puppy, my dad would be home for the holidays. No classes to teach; it could be just me and him."

Unconsciously, my eyes drift back to the wastebasket near my desk, a few feet away, where the unsent letter rests. I spent years waiting for him to call. So many Christmases hoping for a present or a card. Christmas was when I missed him most.

"But in the end, it was Christmas four years ago he stopped coming home."

"I'm sorry. I wish there was something—"

"I need to go."

I push myself the rest of the way through the window, leaving the phone on the sill, and slide down to sit on the roof. Surely that's enough opening up to last a lifetime.

Twelve

Like most winters in Springfield, the ground is bare come Christmas Eve, and it's an easy walk to the Powells' house. No snow, but it's below freezing.

My mother rings the bell, and Thea Powell answers the door with a smile on her wrinkled face. "Come in, come in." She hugs my mother, then Mo, and wraps her arms around me last in an enormous embrace. "The boys are in the library."

I nod Imogene toward the library, and Mrs. P and our mom head in the opposite direction to the adjoined living and dining rooms.

Like most rooms here, the library is twice the size it needs to be. The hardwood floor is pale, and the walls are lined with floor-to-ceiling shelves, full of classic literature—plus an entire wall of Jimmy's fantasy and sci-fi books, the only wall not covered in dust. On the far side, Jimmy and Xander sit in a couple armchairs by the gas fireplace, a small rust-colored rug beneath their feet.

The light of the flames reflects off Jimmy's glasses. "You're on time."

I lie on the rug directly in front of the hearth and rest an

117

arm over my forehead. "There's a first time for everything. I'm as shocked as you are."

Imogene settles into the third armchair.

Xander clears his throat. "Am I missing something? You're never late. What's different here?"

"Mom's doing a lot of things differently these days," Mo says. "It's better this way."

She's right, of course.

"That doesn't stop it from being weird," I say. "Is there a reason we're hiding?"

Normally, we'd be with everyone else in the living room, even though we're the youngest. Jimmy doesn't have any family in the area; the party typically consists of work colleagues and friends.

Jimmy hesitates. "There's a lot of people out there."

I raise an eyebrow. "You're not usually quite this anti-social. What gives?" I glance around before returning my attention to Jimmy. "Xander can't be that embarrassing."

Xander leans forward with a smile. "I'm not sure whether I should resent that or laugh."

Imogene furrows her brow. "Embarrassing?"

"He's not embarrassing," Jimmy says, shaking his head. "He's…charismatic."

I snort. "That's the nice way of putting it."

"How would you put it?" Xander raises an eyebrow.

I look him straight in the eye. "Manipulative." I turn to Jimmy without waiting for a response. "You don't want people to like him more than you."

He flushes.

"I don't know why you care." I shrug. "Your parents already think you're perfect."

Mrs. Powell raps her knuckles against the door and waltzes in, her sparkling blue evening dress shimmering in the firelight. "Hot cocoa?" She brandishes a silver platter with four mugs of hot chocolate and hands them out before returning to the party. "Dinner will be ready in fifteen."

In the golden firelight, the melting marshmallows swirl around the mug as I turn it lazily. It's almost too hot to hold.

My phone buzzes in my pocket. It's obvious who it is, but I glance at the new text anyway. *Hope you're having a good time at your party. Happy Christmas Eve, Wilhelmina.* I grimace at Zane's affectionate wording. Since when did we become friends? I must've missed the memo.

I set my mug on the edge of the hearth to write a response, but no words come.

"Who're you texting?"

I glance up. The three of them are watching me over their hot chocolate.

"Are you texting that guy again?" Imogene asks, reiterating Xander's initial question.

"Don't worry about it." I return to my phone, but Xander snatches it from my grasp to read the long line of texts from Zane.

"You don't make a very convincing argument, Dixon." His eyes flit across the screen.

I scramble to my feet and dive at Xander, who's smirking and laughing at the texts. Reaching for the phone, I wrestle against his arms, but he pushes me away. His mug of hot chocolate falls to the floor in the struggle, breaking and spilling on the rug. My fingers close around his fist, but his rough fingers hold the phone firmly. "Give it back, asshole." I dig my fingers into his skin.

Xander holds me back with his free arm. "Why do you care so much? You're obviously not that into this guy. Have you seen the things you've texted him? If girls talked like that to me, I'd be a virgin."

Laughing, he loosens his hand, and I manage to pull the phone out of his grasp. I stumble back and open the conversation with Zane again.

"What, are you worried I told your boyfriend to leave you alone?" He lets out a low howl of laughter. "Trust me, you need to get laid more than anyone I know."

"He's not my boyfriend."

The library door pushes open, and my mother enters, a champagne flute in her hand.

I glance between her and Imogene, whose face is suddenly pale, and let my hands fall.

Mom smiles and leans against the back of Imogene's armchair. "It's time for dinner, kids. Come along to the dining room."

The liquid in the crystal flute is golden and bubbling.

"Mom, what's that?"

Jimmy looks down at his half-gone mug of cocoa. Imogene takes in a deep breath—mentally preparing herself to deal with this. But Xander watches curiously.

She doesn't bother answering. "Is everyone having fun?" She glances between us, ignoring the broken mug on the floor.

"Mom," I say again, and I set my phone down beside me, "what are you drinking?"

When no one else speaks, she at last turns to me. "What are you saying, Billie?"

"You're holding a drink in your hand. What is it?"

120

She looks to her left hand and sighs. "It's a drink, Billie. What are you worried about?"

As if she doesn't know.

Xander leans toward my mother, putting on his most charming smile, and offers his hand. "Alexander Theroux." When she places her fingers in his grasp, he presses a kiss to her knuckles. "It's an honor to meet Billie's mother."

The sound of my name in his voice turns my stomach.

A grin spreads across my mother's face. "Such a gentleman. How did you fall in with these troublemakers?"

He laughs and side-steps the question. "I believe you said dinner is ready. Can I walk you to the table?"

She nods, and he stands, holding her hand, and directs her toward the kitchen. "Alexander, is it? You're very sweet. Sit next to me, won't you?"

"I'd love to."

Then, they're gone.

I think I'm going to throw up.

"What the fuck was that?"

Jimmy shrugs, and Imogene grabs her mug of hot chocolate and follows them.

I lean over the broken mug, where cocoa is soaking into the rug, and begin to pick up the pieces. The rug needs washed.

"Hey." Jimmy nudges my shoulder, and I look up. "Don't worry about that. I'll have Xander take care of it later. Let's get some dinner." His soothing voice helps me focus, and I take his hand to stand.

In the dining room, Imogene has a seat two chairs down from Mom, and a couple chairs are open on her left. I pause beside my sister and watch as Xander pushes in my mother's chair and subtly lifts her champagne flute from the table while she isn't looking. He tosses back his head to drink the remainder of the liquid, places the flute on the far end of the elaborately decorated sideboard, and takes his seat beside her.

After dinner, Jimmy, Imogene, and I sit in the front parlor, sipping champagne. Mine rests, full, on the bench beside me.

In the living room, Xander's telling jokes and chatting up my mother and the other women in their thirties and forties. My stomach still churns.

"You didn't eat anything." Imogene pokes me until I look at her.

"I'm not hungry."

"Or thirsty." She nods to my glass.

I shake my head. "Alcohol isn't exactly the drink of choice for someone who's thirsty."

"Tell that to your mother." I glance up at the sound of his voice, and Xander grabs my drink and squeezes his way between me and Jimmy, pushing me into Imogene. He downs the champagne and spins the flute between his fingers. "Can it be someone else's turn to keep the booze away from the crazy lady? I need a break from babysitting."

This bench was not made to fit four people.

I finagle my way out from between them. "I need air."

Outside, the air is cold and crisp. The wood patio is cool to the touch. Beyond the railing, the small swimming pool is empty and covered with a tarp, and the typically beautiful garden space looks barren in the moonlight.

I lie down on the patio, my back pressing against the cold wood, and pull out my phone. I never responded to Zane's text, and now there's a second one.

You're not answering, so I guess you're having a great time. :)

Ugh, a smiley face.

I hold my hands at the ready to craft a response, but I don't know what to say. Instead, I lift my thumb and press the 'Call' button. It doesn't ring more than twice.

"Hey." His voice is warm and kind. "I didn't think I'd hear from you."

"I needed a distraction."

"What's wrong, Wilhelmina?" He's instantly concerned.

"Please don't call me that." I sigh and stare at the partly cloudy sky as I listen to the silence on the other end of the line. "What're you doing? It's Christmas Eve."

Zane lets out a small laugh. "I'm at my dad's, but my mom is visiting, so it's a bit tense. I'm glad you called."

I force a smile. "You needed a distraction too."

"What's going on there, Billie?"

I take a shaky breath and close my eyes, and curiosity gets the better of me. "What are your parents like?"

"It's been weird since I moved to my dad's, but that was six years ago; things are better now. I guess I'm not sure what you're asking." He laughs slightly. "My mom's excited to be here, but she gets nervous when she's excited, which makes Dad uncomfortable."

At least they talk to each other. I can't imagine my parents being in the same room.

"Why did you move to your dad's?"

He responds more promptly than I expected. "Things with my mom weren't going well. Money problems. Taking care of me was getting harder, so I moved. It was weird—I'd barely seen him since I was seven—but we settled into a rhythm after a couple months."

I close my eyes and listen. Focus on his foreign life. Anything to distract from my own.

"Is everything alright there?"

I open my mouth to speak, but the back door opens and closes. "I need to go." I hang up before setting the phone beside me.

Footsteps echo across the wood, heading toward the edge but not too close to me. The clicking of a lighter reverberates off the side of the house. I crack an eye.

"What're you doing out here?"

Xander glances over and quirks an eyebrow. "What does it look like?" He raises the now-lit cigarette to his mouth and takes a deep breath. His pack is in his other hand, and he lifts it toward me, offering, but I shake my head. "Sure? You look like you could use one."

"I'm fine." I lay a clenched fist on my chest.

"I'm trying to decide," Xander says, staring out into the darkness, "which parent you dislike more." His voice is cool and casual, but the words dig at me.

I don't have anything to say to him. I shouldn't even look at him right now.

"I really thought it'd be your dad, what with the aban-donment issues and all that. I mean, I've heard plenty from Jimmy about your life—his attempts to rein me in—but I was sure it'd be your dad." He takes another puff. "Then, I meet your mother, and now I can't decide."

I give in. "It's none of your business."

"Of course not." He shrugs. "You know, if you'd told me

your mom was an alcoholic, I wouldn't have given you a bottle of wine. But Jimmy says she's getting better. Is tonight too high a stress for her? Suicide rates go up around the holidays." He turns to me, but I look away. "You really want to live here instead of going back to Bradford?"

I glance back, brow furrowed. "What?"

He laughs. "Your drunk self thinks dropping out is a great idea." He takes another drag. "You said you never want to see me again. I like to think it's because you can't handle how attracted you are to me."

"Right, because that would happen." I roll my eyes.

For a moment, he's quiet. "Tell me, was it the alcoholism that destroyed their marriage, or did that come after your dad bailed? Why'd they get married? I can't imagine them being in love." He lifts the cigarette to his mouth and releases a cloud of smoke into the air. "Your mom's young, though. Did your dad get her pregnant and marry her out of the goodness of his heart?" He snorts.

I frown. That's exactly what happened.

In the silence, Xander takes a few more drags before dropping the cigarette to the patio and smashing it with his foot. "In any event, you need to get your shit together, Dixon. I'm tired of having these little chats."

When at last I open my mouth, ready to retort, he's already inside the house. The door closes quietly, and I fume.

In the front parlor, Jimmy, Xander, and Imogene are sitting together on the bench, laughing. I pause in the doorway, standing on the foyer's side of the threshold. My seat has officially been usurped.

Why am I here?

I glance around to the living room, where my mother is sitting with Thea Powell and chatting. She sends Mrs. P a simpering smile and stands to grab a glass of wine from the oak buffet. Mrs. P calls after her, but Mom waves her comment away and looks toward the foyer where I stand. Our eyes meet, and her hand quivers.

I inhale a shaky breath, grab my coat from the ornate freestanding rack, and walk out the front door.

The trek back to the house is cold but easy, despite the fog. The ground crunches underfoot, frozen but it gives, and I pull out my keys to unlock the side door into the kitchen. I move past the kitchen, into the hallway, up the stairs, and to my room, not bothering to turn on any lights.

I prefer the darkness.

I bolt the door behind me, drop my coat on the floor, and head straight for the window. The frame moves easily at my touch, and I climb onto the awning. The roof is slick with ice, but I sit and pull my knees to my chest. The cold permeates my clothes. My breath only adds to the fog.

On the other side of the drive, the Powells' house is alight with life and holiday decorations. Beneath Jimmy's bedroom, Charlie and Thea's friends are enjoying their evening in the family's artfully adorned living room.

I close my eyes for a moment, until I hear voices.

Two figures exit the front door and cross toward our house, barely visible through the fog. Imogene leads our mother by the hand. They were in too much of a hurry to button their coats. They follow the edge of the road to our front door, and soon, they're out of sight. The front door opens and closes, and I lean against the sill and listen.

"This way, Mom."

They're on the stairs now. Imogene takes her to the master bedroom, and a moment later, the door closes. Footsteps approaching. A knock on my bedroom door.

"Billie?" She knocks again. "Billie, are you in there? I couldn't find you before we left." She heaves a sigh, and the door creaks as she slumps against it. "Mom's going to bed, and she'll be in there for a while. She doesn't feel well. She's—well, it could've been worse, and we have Xander and Mrs. P to thank for that." She tries the door, but the knob doesn't budge. "I know how difficult this time of year is for you, but you forget how hard it is for the rest of us. I wish things were different. I wish Mom could get up on her feet. I wish Dad were here. But more than anything, I wish you'd talk to me."

Across the driveway, the light in Jimmy's room comes on, and Xander peeks his head inside, searching. I press my body closer to the roof as he peers outside, and the roof groans. I can't tell whether he spots me, but he turns off the light and returns downstairs.

"Have a good night, Billie," Imogene says at the door. "I'm going to bed."

When she's gone, I clamber back inside and bend over the trash bin. The letter, along with the other codes, sits at the top. I haven't had the heart to empty the trash into the garbage can outside.

I pull out the paper and flatten it, my eyes skimming the faded page. I pause at the final paragraph: *I miss you.*

There was a time I too wished Dad were here. Keeping this stupid, naive letter all these years is telling enough.

Thirteen

WHEN MORNING COMES, IT'S AFTER HOURS OF TOSSING AND turning. As a child, that was in anticipation of the morning's presents. Now, it has far more to do with the sick feeling in my stomach.

I rise with the sun and go through my bag from Bradford, locating my enormous calculus textbook right on top. I flip through the upcoming chapters: parametric equations, polar coordinates, vectors. Numbers. I need numbers. Numbers always make sense.

Halfway through the chapter on polar coordinates, my phone buzzes on the nightstand, then buzzes again. Curious, I unlock the screen to read the texts. From Zane, of course.

I hope your holiday is better. Merry Christmas!

Let me know if there's anything I can do to help.

I furrow my brow and set the phone aside. Our conversation last night ended rather abruptly. He must have a lot of questions. Giving in, I craft a short response. A simple *Merry Christmas* will have to be enough.

It buzzes again as soon as I set it down. *Can you talk right now?*

I guess.

I don't have to wait long.

He breezes right past salutations. "I wanted to make sure everything was okay. You sounded upset last night."

"I'm fine." My eyes wander to the calculus book. "The holidays are stressful. I was overreacting."

"So I was worried over nothing?"

He was worried?

"Don't freak out, Zane. It's not like you need me to tutor you anymore. Besides, I'm not going to die out here in Missouri."

"How am I supposed to know that?" He laughs. "I'm not there to make sure."

I pause, staring at the middle paragraph. "No, that would be incredibly strange."

He laughs. Maybe he thinks I'm joking. "Did you get anything good for Christmas?"

I glance at the clock on my nightstand. It's barely 10:30, and Imogene got out of bed an hour ago. She's probably waiting for me. "My family isn't into giving presents."

"Okay, so what did you get?"

"Nothing special. Why? What did you get?"

I can hear the smile in his voice. "My dad got me a lizard."

"A lizard?"

"Yeah." A little defensive at my tone. "You know, you can't have any dogs or whatever on campus, but you can have an aquarium or terrarium. So my dad got me a lizard." There's movement on his end of the line. "A long-tailed lizard. You know their tails are three times the length of their bodies?"

"No, I didn't." I close my textbook and set it aside.

129

"I named it Jack."

"I should go." I swing my legs over the edge of the bed and walk to the door.

"Oh, already? Um, I'll talk to you later then."

"Yeah, sure." After hanging up, I toss the phone onto my bed and open my bedroom door, careful not to make too much noise.

I guess it's time for damage control.

Downstairs, the living room is minimally decorated. An eight-foot tinsel tree, covered in a standard set of gold and silver ornaments from Hobby Lobby, stands beside the worn couch, but that is the only sign of the holidays. The room glows from the white lights, and Imogene sits on the couch, her hands clasped together, waiting.

She looks up when I walk in, a glass of water in my hand. "I almost didn't think you'd come downstairs."

I approach and sit on the couch a foot away. "It's Christmas."

"Mom isn't feeling well." I'm not sure why—she was barely drunk. "She said to open presents without her." Mo nods to where half a dozen silver and gold-wrapped boxes sit under the tinsel tree. "Do you want to open them?"

"It's up to you."

Slowly, she picks up a couple boxes. There are two or three presents for us each and one addressed to Mom. It must be from Imogene. She probably wrote my name on the tag too like she always does. I never bothered with presents, but she always covered for me.

She passes me a box, and we open ours at the same time. Inside, I find a sweater: gray, soft, and probably comfortable—with a huge lavender ribbon tied in a bow on the front. My second present is a designer handbag, real leather with brass finishings, but the final present is a new book on mathematical theory and a pocket sketchbook. That one must be from Imogene.

"Thank you." I clutch the books to my chest.

She sends me a small smile as she opens her final box, which contains a green pashmina shawl. "It was nothing. Don't worry about it."

I didn't get her anything.

"Uh, Mo." I look down at my lap. "How would you feel about coming to visit Bradford?" When I look up, her eyebrows have disappeared under her blond bangs. "When is your spring break?"

"The last full week of March."

I nod. "So's mine. Do you think you could come visit then? Spend the week with me."

"Aren't the dorms closed?"

I take a deep breath. "I'd have to ask him, but maybe we could stay with Dad." If he's willing to have me.

For a moment, Imogene doesn't say anything, and I brave a look at her. She sits, her hands wrapped in the shawl, and stares at the monstrous tinsel tree, trying to form words.

"It's just an idea."

She turns to me again. "You're okay with that? Staying at Dad's, I mean. You were there a night before coming back."

The very thought terrifies me, but...

"It'd be worth it for you to come visit." Maybe he'll see that too.

A smile spreads across her olive face, and she pulls me into a hug. "I'm thrilled then," she mumbles into my mass of hair, pressing her head into the recess at my neck. "Merry Christmas."

Upstairs, there's a *thump*, and we both look to the stairs, barely visible from our vantage point.

"Do you think she'd be alright by herself?" I pull away from her embrace.

Imogene's face creases. "I'm not sure. Last night was the first drink she's had since September."

"It's the holidays." I stare down at my hands. "Temptation doesn't help when Charlie and Thea have so much alcohol on hand. Maybe we shouldn't go to New Year's Eve."

Mo rises and heads for the stairs. "I should check on her." She casts a smile over her shoulder before disappearing.

"Yeah."

In the distance, she knocks on Mom's bedroom door.

Back in my bedroom, I settle onto the bed with my new books in hand, ready to delve into the pages of Edward Frankel. Imogene knows me too well.

My phone, sitting on the sheets, flashes to signal there's a message. Well, two messages. One, as predicted, from Zane. But I open the text from Jimmy first.

Hey, sorry about last night. I hope your mom is feeling better. You coming over for our usual Christmas dinner?

I respond, *Probably not this year. I'm going to spend the day with Mo.*

Normally, after Christmas morning, I run off to spend the day with Jimmy and his parents. Anything to avoid spending the day with my mom, who spent the last three Christmases holed up with a bottle of vodka. Xander's presence makes spending the day with Jimmy considerably less appealing.

The text from Zane is simple but to the point: *I miss you.*

I stare at the message until it fades to black. How could he possibly? How can you miss someone you barely know? Uncomfortable, I shift on the bed and return to the book.

Two pages in, a knock sounds on the door, and Imogene pokes her head inside. "Can I come in?"

I nod, and she sits with me. "How's Mom?"

Mo lifts her feet onto the mattress. "Could be better. She's not hung over. Just ashamed."

I set the book aside. "Has she really been doing better?"

"She's been a completely different person, Billie. She's quiet compared to, you know, normal, but the doctor said it could take months to get the right medications." She glances at the book beside me and cocks her head. "Do you like it?"

I snort. "It's a lot better than the bow sweater." I nod my head toward the gray knit I threw on my dresser.

"Hey, Mom spent a long time figuring out what to give you. You're lucky I convinced her to get gray instead of pink."

"Yes, I'm horribly indebted to you." I laugh, and she smiles back. "You're going to come up for spring break then? I'll pay for your flight."

"And pick me up at the airport?"

"Of course."

Imogene's smile widens, and she nods. "Thea and Charlie can check in on Mom. I already talked to her, and she loves the idea—and, you know, I'd love to spend the week with you and Dad."

"I'll ask him when I get back."

Fourteen

IMOGENE PUSHES HER WAY INTO THE ROOM DESPITE MY protests. "Mom said we should go without her." She tears open my bag. "Why do you have all your stuff in here? You've been home for over a week."

I push up from the bed. "I don't want to settle in just to leave again."

She frowns as she spreads my clothing options across the floor. "You should wear something nice. I could do your makeup too."

"I'm not going."

She pauses to look at me. "Why not?" When I don't answer, she continues. "You haven't visited Jimmy since Christmas Eve. You've never gone that long without seeing him before."

"It's not a big deal."

"I talk to him too." She continues her search, but everything is thrown into the pile of "unacceptable" options for a semi-formal evening. "I know you hate dresses, but it would really make these nights easier."

I shake my head. "I don't hate them. I don't understand why anyone would sacrifice comfort for a few leers." She throws another article of clothing on the pile, and I grab the bow sweater from my dresser. "This is always an option."

Excitement crosses her face. "Perfect."

Apparently, we need to talk more so she still understands sarcasm.

"I was joking."

"It's not a dress." She pushes all my clothes back into the duffel bag, a grin on her face. "And that means you have to wear it without complaint."

I roll my eyes. "I would, but like I said, I'm not going."

With everything back inside the bag, she stands up. "You have to. You know how much Jimmy hates these things. He needs support, and he's your best friend. We're going."

I tug the sweater over my camisole, not bothering to grab a bra, and change out of my pajama bottoms. "He doesn't need me. He has Xander now. They're practically married." I zip my jeans and slip into my Converse.

Imogene shakes her head. "I don't know why you have a problem with him." She checks her dark blond hair, ironed into soft curls, in the mirror on my door. "Are you sure you won't let me do your makeup?"

I join her. "With Xander?" I purse my lips. "He's the one who has a problem."

She shrugs. "I don't know, he's kind of cute." She leans closer, wets a finger pad, and runs it across each eyebrow. "You do realize he spent all of Christmas Eve flirting with Mom so she didn't get drunk, right? Why do you think he'd do that?"

To play with my head.

"Is that why you're triple-checking your hair and makeup?"

Imogene turns to me with a laugh. "You must be kidding. He's not remotely interested in me, and I have a boyfriend."

I raise an eyebrow. "You're still dating Will Carson? That's way longer than your usual relationship."

She pulls a stick of lip balm from her purse and tugs the cap off. "No, I dumped him in September." She rubs the stick across her lips, leaving a pink sheen on her already red lips, and recaps it. "His name's Andrew."

"And since this is the first time you've mentioned him, obviously you're very serious. If you have a boyfriend, why are you spending all this time primping?" She looks over, and I raise an eyebrow. "This can't seriously be how much time you spend on your appearance."

"No." She shakes her head. "You missed the hours I spent perfecting my outfit and makeup—all so I can enjoy a few leers at the Powells' intimate party."

I push past her to open the door again. "I'm going to assume you're joking." I step out, only to realize my phone's on my desk. I turn back. "Hey, can you grab my phone?" I nod toward the desk, and she sighs before walking the couple steps to reach it.

Imogene leans over the top of the desk, covered in papers and books, but her hand pauses above the phone when she catches a glimpse of the top paper. She grabs it, and her eyes flit across the page. "Billie, what's this?"

Shit.

I cross the room in an instant and tear the letter out of her hands. "It's nothing."

"Billie."

"Drop it."

She starts to say something but changes her mind. "Fine,

dropping it."

I shove the paper into the top drawer, and it crumples as I push it shut. "Let's go." I snatch the phone off the top and take my sister by the arm. "We're already late, and you're pretty enough all the boys will want to kiss you at midnight."

◆

"Sorry we're late," Imogene says as Charlie Powell closes the door behind us. "Billie couldn't decide what to wear."

I shrug off my coat and hang it on the rack, and Charlie gives me a once-over. "Yes, you've dressed up for us, Billie." He laughs and pulls me into a hug. "I'm honored. Everyone is in the living room."

Imogene hangs her coat as well, and we walk to the right of the foyer to join the group.

For Charlie and Thea, New Year's Eve is a less formal event. Instead of an elaborate party, the gathering consists of the Powells and a few intimate friends. There's only half a dozen people when we enter the living room. Everyone relaxes on the couches and loveseats. Several bottles of wine and champagne sit on the coffee table, and on the far side, Jimmy sits at the piano, playing an upbeat song.

Charlie nudges me into the seat next to his, and Imogene navigates her way to the piano to sit with Jimmy.

"How's your mom?" Charlie leans down to whisper in my ear.

I shrug. "Doing really well, I hear. She sends her apologies, of course—"

But he shakes his head. "Nonsense. She needn't apologize

for anything. Thea intends to take her a few things soon since she's missing the festivities—she'll be awake, right?"

I lean back on the cream-colored loveseat and tug at my neckline. The sweater scratches at my skin. "You should check with Mo. She knows her schedule better."

Charlie nods. "That reminds me. We have a box for you to open since you stayed home for Christmas this year. We'll pull it out when you're ready."

I smile. The Powells go to extraordinary lengths to include me, which means lavish gifts during the holidays. One of their boxes usually contains half a dozen gifts. By the end of high school, I spent so much time in their house I'd become part of the family.

"You didn't have to do that."

He takes a sip of his dark red wine. "We have snacks." He inclines his head toward the coffee table. "You should put some meat on those bones."

"Oh, thanks, but I'm not hungry."

"I'm surprised you bother trying." I spin around to find Xander shedding his leather jacket. He leans over the back of the couch, and a wave of cigarette smoke hits me in the face. "Anyone who's spent more than an hour with Dixon knows she prefers to starve herself." He narrows his eyes. "You're in my seat."

Before I can retort, Charlie rises and offers the vacated seat to Xander. "Take mine. I'll get you kids something to drink. Water, wine, sparkling cider?" He looks to me for an answer.

"I don't need anything."

Charlie claps me on the shoulder. "I'll get you a glass of water and some almonds. Good protein."

When he's gone, Xander settles down beside me and flips through his messages on his phone. He's dressed more casually than on Christmas Eve—a pastel blue dress shirt with the top two buttons undone and the sleeves rolled up, rich dark blue jeans that look like they've been ironed, his black dress shoes, no tie. It's weird—at Bradford, unless he has plans, he's usually down to his boxers by ten.

On his phone, his thumb guides him back to the home screen, and he pauses. His eyebrows crease together when he concentrates. He releases a deep breath. "You're staring, Dixon."

"Uh, no." I shift my gaze to the far wall.

"Are you expecting something interesting to happen?" He drops the phone on his lap and turns to me. "Or are you just enjoying looking?"

Out of nowhere, Charlie leans over to place a large glass of water on the nearby end table, along with a small dish of almonds, before moving toward his wife. I take a long drink in an attempt to dispel any previous conversation, but when I pull the glass away, Xander is staring at my sweater.

"Is that a bow on your shirt?" He grabs one of the tails near the knot and slides his fingers down to the tip. His eyes shift from my chest to meet mine. "I'm impressed someone convinced you to put that on."

I clear my throat and take a sip of water. My glass is almost half gone now, and I am on edge. "It was a Christmas gift." That was way too close to touching my breasts.

He releases the ribbon. "From someone who doesn't know you well." He cocks his head. "With that bow, you look like you're the gift. Who's going to unwrap you later, Dixon?"

Heat rises to my cheeks.

Xander's laughter draws the attention of the others, but they quickly return to their conversations. "Are you seriously that easily embarrassed? I know, I know, you wish your idiot boyfriend were here so he could do it. I'm sure he wishes that too, especially with all the effort he's put into wearing you down. Please tell me he's not a complete moron and realizes you're a virgin."

I take another drink and swish the water around in my mouth to calm my breathing. "Why would that matter?"

He raises an eyebrow. "Most players don't like to sleep with virgins. It makes them feel guilty."

I frown. "And what about you, player?"

"What about me?" He relaxes on the loveseat, his head resting against the back. "I have nothing to feel guilty about. I sleep with women who want to have sex with me, no strings attached. Virginity has nothing to do with it."

My grip tightens around the glass.

"Don't worry, Dixon." He pats me on the shoulder. "I'm sure he'll be super gentle when he's popping your cherry. He might prefer you that way—it'll give him the chance to be sentimental while he's taking advantage of you."

I shrug him off. "I don't need your condescension, Xander. He's not my boyfriend, and I'm not going to sleep with him."

"Oh, right. Because you're too smart for that." He laughs and leans in again. "You're not as smart as you think you are."

He's too close. I can't breathe. I press myself into the armrest and take another sip.

Next to me, Xander relaxes, a proud smirk on his lips.

"If I make you this uncomfortable, how are you going to let someone see you naked?"

I purse my lips. "And what, you've got some special advice to help me?"

"Not so special, no."

"Then what?"

He shrugs. "Things come a lot more naturally when you're not trying to perfect everything—and your ass would be a lot more fuckable if you pulled the big stick out of it."

I grind my teeth. My fingers clench tighter around the glass. The water inside trembles. "What is wrong with you? Do you always have to be this inappropriate and crude?"

A smirk spreads across his face. "As long as you freak out over it, yes. It's nice to see you have emotions instead of being your usual robotic self."

I stand, clutching the water glass to my chest, and glare down at him. His blue eyes challenge me—and I can't resist a challenge. In a swift motion, I raise my glass in the air and dump the contents on his face. "I am not a robot."

But all he does is laugh while wiping water from his eyes.

I turn on my heels to leave.

◆

I check my phone. Ten minutes to midnight.

On the roof, it's quiet. The neighborhood is full of old trees that hide the night sky, but the Powells live on a corner and have a much better view. Jimmy and I climbed up here all the time when we were younger. No matter what was happening, we could sit up here and talk. No interruptions, no worries, no judgments.

141

Nine minutes to midnight.

I push my phone aside and pull my knees to my chin.

"You alright?" Jimmy pokes his head over the edge of the roof, his glasses sitting haphazardly on his nose. "Can I join you?"

I shrug.

He climbs up and sits beside me. "Sorry Xander's an ass."

"Yeah, well, it's nothing new, is it?" I rest my head on my knees. "He ruins everything, and then, he has the nerve to try to convince me it's my fault. A reminder that no matter what I do, no matter how hard I try, I keep sliding backwards. He doesn't get it." I grab a twig from nearby and chuck it off the roof. "I wish he would leave me alone. I wish everyone would leave me alone."

"No, you don't." Jimmy heaves a long sigh. "Have you considered being reminded of that isn't a bad thing? Better to remember than fall into complacency."

I open my mouth to protest.

"I'm not saying Xander isn't an ass, but that doesn't mean you shouldn't listen." Jimmy frowns. "He thinks I enable you, and maybe he's right. I just want you to be happy."

Up in the sky, the most vibrant stars twinkle despite the city lights. Andromeda, Cassiopeia, Aldebaran, Castor and Pollux, Sirius the Dog-Star. They look the same as when I was little, when Jimmy and I used to climb out his bedroom window and talk up here for hours. Even Jimmy looks the same—older, yes, but he has the same smile, the same big eyes, the same kind temperament.

No, I'm the one that's different.

"I don't think I know how to be happy anymore."

He rests a hand on my shoulder and squeezes. "Come

on, Billie, it's cold out here. Time to go inside."

I shake my head. "Can I ask you something?"

"Always."

"What happened after I left?"

Jimmy frowns. "After you left where?"

"My dad's house. What happened?"

"Are you sure you want to talk about this?"

Will I ever get up the nerve again?

"Just tell me."

Beside me, he hesitates. "It was awkward, and Xander wanted to go after you, but I didn't feel comfortable leaving your dad alone, so he went without me. I'm glad he found you. You could've gone anywhere."

I close my eyes and shake my head. "I don't care about Xander. What about my dad?"

For a moment, Jimmy doesn't speak, then in a small voice, he says, "For the longest time, he didn't say anything, but then, Xander brought you back and you were unconscious—freaked me out, by the way—and your dad, he cried."

I hug myself closer. That's worse, much worse than I thought.

"Xander and I got into a bit of a fight after that. I couldn't believe he gave you alcohol."

I sigh. "It's not like I needed encouragement." Which is perhaps the scariest part of the matter.

Jimmy presses a hand on my arm. "You're going to be numb if you stay out here. Why didn't you grab a coat?"

"It's easier to be numb."

"Easier isn't always better." He grabs my hand and tugs lightly toward the eaves.

I grab my phone and light up the screen. Three minutes after midnight, plus a text that arrived right at the birth of the New Year. From Zane, no doubt.

I wish you were here.

I turn off the screen again. I don't have the emotional capacity to deal with that.

"We missed the ball drop."

Jimmy shrugs. "An excuse to make out and drink. Oh well. Now, if you don't come inside, I'll sic Xander on you."

Fifteen

WHEN WE RETURN TO ST. CLARE, THE TOWN IS COVERED in a thin layer of snow. Bradford campus is quiet, as most students haven't returned from winter break. The dorms opened this morning at eight.

I kick my shoes off once inside. I drop my duffel bag on the bed and flip on my desk lamp before glancing around. No sign of Val. Maybe she won't be back until tomorrow. Then I'd have a whole night to myself.

I move to the window and open the blinds to take a peek at campus from the fourth floor. Below me, the trees are bare, plus a dusting of snow. The world outside is cold and dark, but in here, the heater starts up. Warm air blows down on my head. My breath fogs up the window.

With a sigh, I drop my jacket on the desk chair and move to unpack. Clothes, books, laptop, my Christmas gifts from Mo, and that awful sweater are all put away, leaving one thing at the bottom.

My thin fingers grab the wrinkled paper. I don't know why I brought this with me.

A knock brings me out of my reverie, and I turn to the open door, where Jimmy is smiling. "You settling in alright?"

I nod.

"Campus food doesn't open till tomorrow morning. We're going to the coffee shop on Main Street. You wanna come?"

I glance at the chilly scene outside and fold the letter in half. "Are we driving?" I don't want to put my shoes back on—let alone walk all the way to Main Street.

Jimmy laughs. "He complains if it's sixty degrees out. What do you think?"

I smile and drop the letter on my desk to retrieve my Converse. I can deal with that later. "Fair enough." I yank the shoes over my socks, not bothering to tie them, and grab my keys and wallet.

We meet Xander outside the front of the building, where he's wrapped in his large wool coat, hugging the cigarette to his mouth. His normally loose dark hair is covered with a trapper's hat, the furry flaps down to shield his ears. He looks utterly ridiculous.

When he sees us, he snubs the half-smoked cigarette on the stone wall of Lincoln Hall and returns it to his pack. "Ready?"

◆

Downtown, the Jittery Bug is a relatively popular coffee house, but St. Clare is a college town. Most students aren't back yet, and the line is short.

After we have our drinks, we grab a booth near the back, and I watch in amusement as Xander peels off his hat and coat. His hair pokes in every direction, despite his attempts to flatten it. When he finally gives up, his eyes catch mine and narrow. "What?"

I pull a straight face. "Something the matter?"

He rolls his eyes and takes a long drink of his Colombian roast. "When's Val getting back?"

I stir my cappuccino with the tiny black straw. "You should know better than me, right?"

He doesn't answer.

"You're still seeing her, aren't you?"

"Occasionally," is his noncommittal response.

Irritated, I take in the expanse of the room.

Behind the counter, the coffee house combines grinders, mixers, and a host of other machines with a rustic atmosphere. On the far side, behind the counter and kitchen space, they have a colorful pallet wall, where several chalkboards display their menu. There are enormous, floor-to-ceiling shelves for their coffee and tea options and prepackaged bags. The long counter spreads from the ordering station to the pick-up station, and leaning against the counter, taking sips from a to-go cup, stands Zane.

I start at the sight of him and turn back to my cappuccino.

It's been over three weeks since I've seen him, and while his face, his clothes, his demeanor are all the same, he's different. We had over a thousand miles between us, but everything has changed—strange late-night conversations and things I wish I hadn't said.

I take a long drink and try to immerse myself in Jimmy and Xander's conversation, but Jimmy pauses mid-sentence. "Uh, Billie, do you know that guy? He's staring at you."

I don't want to look, but Jimmy and Xander have already caught sight of him—and he's caught sight of me. With a deep breath, I turn back toward the counter and lock eyes with Zane, whose face lights up. "Yeah." I glance back at Jimmy, who has a curious eyebrow raised. "I'll be right back."

Zane smiles when I join him at the pick-up counter. "Hey. It's good to see you, Wilhelmina."

"Billie," I correct, though I don't know why I bother.

"How was the flight? You must've just gotten back."

"It was uneventful." I stand uncomfortably under his gaze, my arms wrapped around my chest, and a strand of coiled hair falls in my eyes. "We got on campus an hour ago."

"'We'?"

I look toward the booth—Jimmy and Xander cast curious glances in my direction while chatting—and turn back to Zane. "How long have you been back?"

He's closer than before. "A few days. Being an upperclassman has its perks." He looks past my shoulder and raises an eyebrow. "Are those the friends you never talk about?"

"Um, yeah."

Zane flashes me a smile. "Are you going to introduce me?"

I frown. "I don't think that's a good idea."

He glances at the booth again. "Why not? We're friends, right?"

When one of the baristas brings over a black to-go box and says, "Hot ham and Swiss," Zane accepts the food with a smile and turns back to me.

Friends? I'm not ready to call us anything beyond acquaintances, but he uses the word liberally. By his reckoning, he probably has hundreds, but I have Jimmy. I can't remember the last time I managed to make a friend—apparently, it's now.

I meet his eyes over the box. "You're ready to go."

He nods toward the coffee station, and I follow so he can refill his cup. "I'm not in any rush. I could hang out. It'd be nice to catch up."

Introducing him is a big step. Almost boyfriend-like.

I tug at my sleeve and look at the cup in his hands. "You should go."

He sticks the lid back on. "If you insist." A smile spreads across his face, and he reaches a hesitant hand toward my cheek. "It's good to talk to you. I guess I'll see you round." He grabs his to-go box from the table and turns to leave.

"Yeah." I give him a short wave and return to the booth. By the time I reach it, the bell dings as he leaves.

Jimmy and Xander quiet down when I sit. My cappuccino is lukewarm.

"Who was that?" Jimmy asks.

They're both watching me.

"Nobody important."

But Jimmy shakes his head. "That was Zane Nelson, wasn't it?"

I take another drink, and Xander nods in realization. "Ah, the elusive senior." He lets out a low laugh. "You did well, Dixon."

I cock my head. "What do you mean?"

"He's way out of your league. How'd you manage that?"

My lips form a tight purse. "How many times do I have to tell you we aren't dating?"

He simply shrugs, a smirk on his smug face.

Sixteen

THE CLASSROOM IS EMPTY WHEN I ARRIVE. I CAME EARLY TO mentally prepare myself.

It's the same basement room as last semester's Calc I with Hodges, but this time, my father will be the one writing notes on the blackboard. The situation was inevitable, of course. As department head of my chosen major, we'd have class together eventually, but he usually teaches the advanced classes. Calc II is hardly advanced.

Slowly, the students file into the room, and at exactly five minutes till, my father enters and heads straight for the chalkboard.

When the room is mostly full, he begins his opening lecture: "My name is Dr. Elijah Dixon, and this is Calculus II, which is MATH 215 for those of you who aren't sure you're in the right class."

His voice is steady and firm. In all the times I've seen him here, few and far between as they've been, he has never held such a strong tone.

The syllabus he then passes out is the shortest I've received. One sheet of paper with two lines on the back side. There's no course schedule, and the syllabus is straight, to-the-point, and firm—much like the face he wears as he addresses the room.

"This course covers everything from integration techniques to vectors, coordinates in a three-dimensional space and polar coordinates. In Calculus I, you should've learned about limits, derivatives, and integrals, all of which is pertinent to this class, so please review your books and notes. We will not start with a lesson over previously covered material or a quiz to see if everyone's on the same page. You should already be on this page."

He places the remaining couple syllabuses on the desk and stands by the board. "This class and how you perform in it, is based on your honesty, quality of work, and work ethic. Tests are at the midterm and the final, which means both tests are comprehensive assessments of half the semester. Otherwise, all work will be a set of fifteen to twenty problems from the book per class. When class begins, you will hand in your problems, and then, we will begin the next lecture. You can take notes—I recommend it—but if you can learn this without notes, by all means, do so. As long as you learn and perform well, you don't have anything else to worry about. Any questions?"

No one raises their hand. No one moves.

"Okay, let's begin."

His mouth twisted in irritation, he grabs a felt-tip pen and a large planner from the desk. "I'm required to take attendance. Please inform me of any nicknames, though I should note discussion doesn't play a large role in this class. I won't be able to connect your name to your face for at least a month." He studies the list in his planner before reading them aloud. "Timothy Caine?"

On the board, he's written the words 'Integration

Techniques,' and I turn to the appropriate chapter in anticipation.

"Wilhelmina Dixon?"

I don't look up. "Present."

He moves on with no more than a pause, and I skim the opening paragraphs to jog my memory.

The class is small—not even a dozen students—but I don't recognize anyone else until my father calls out, "Zane Nelson."

My head shoots up. My eyes dart around the room.

In the front row, Zane flips through his textbook and an spiral notebook. "Here." He turns to a fresh page and jots down the words my father wrote on the board. He either doesn't notice me or doesn't care.

Why the hell is Zane here?

Once he finishes attendance, my father returns the planner to the desk. "We'll cover a couple integration techniques in each class until you've learned them all. You should have a working knowledge of basic integration, so again, if you don't remember, you should refresh before our next class."

He writes out a few other points on the board. "Since you should have a good grasp on definite integrals, we'll work with indefinite integrals for most of the chapter. Please turn to page 513."

Class ends early with a generously short assignment for the next session. My father slips his belongings inside his leather satchel while the students pack up.

I wait until everyone leaves.

Dad turns to his notes and sweeps an eraser across the

blackboard.

"Do you want any help?" I pause beside him, backpack slung over my shoulder.

"If you like."

I drop my bag and grab the second eraser. You'd think Bradford would've updated this old building by now, but I don't mind. Smearing the letters and numbers away in the silent classroom, I'm almost at ease. "Did you have a good break?"

His long arm sweeps to the top of the board, then down again. "It was pleasant enough. How was Springfield?" His voice is softer, more tender, than his professional tone, but he refuses to look at me.

For some reason, the only answer that comes to mind is, "Mild." I pause, then go over my section of the board again. "Imogene asked about you."

"I hope she's well." He doesn't let any emotion escape as he speaks.

"She is." I stop moving. Most of the board is clean now anyway. "That reminds me." I abandon the eraser on the bottom ledge. "I asked Imogene to visit over spring break, and she wants to come, but there's a minor problem."

"Oh?" Intrigued, he pauses and finally turns to me.

"The dorms are closed over break, and we don't have anywhere to stay."

He nods stiffly and looks back at the board, his arm still hovering. "No friends could put you up?"

"No." My only friend, after all, will be gone for break. "Everyone will be gone. We thought it might be nice to stay with you—if you're willing to put up with us."

Dad spins on me, his hazel eyes wide. "If I'm willing?"

"I understand if you don't want to try." I wipe my palms on my jeans, ready for his immediate dismissal.

He clears his throat.

"If it's too much trouble, don't worry about it. We have time to figure something else out."

"I will consider it."

"Okay." I retrieve my backpack from the floor and turn, ready to head to my next class. "I'll see you on Thursday."

He doesn't say anything, and I take that as my cue to leave.

"Mina," he calls after me.

I pause, my hand on the door frame, to look at him.

He sets down the eraser and moves to the desk. "Have a good afternoon."

I stumble back into the room. "Dad, are you—that is, could we do tea again? Friday?"

For a second, he doesn't move. Then, he latches his satchel. "I can't this Friday. I have a meeting."

"Oh, okay."

"Perhaps next week."

"That would be nice." I force a small smile, but he doesn't look at me, and I leave.

Halfway down the hall, I stop at the base of the stairs and slump against the wall, my bun pressing against the concrete. That took way more energy than I have at my disposal.

This was the first time we'd spoken in a month after that awful night. He barely reacted to seeing me. Every word was strained, every movement an effort. In fact, he avoided eye contact during that entire conversation.

I know I overreacted. I said some incredibly hurtful

things. But Dad couldn't look at me.

I take a deep breath and choke down the lump in my throat.

"Fun conversation?"

I blink away the sting in my eyes and look around. Zane sits halfway up the staircase, smiling. I swallow again before attempting to talk. "What are you doing here?"

His smile widens, and he stands. "Surprise."

"Yeah, I'll say." I start up the steps toward him. "What in the world made you think taking Calculus II was a good idea?"

"You know, with your help, I rather enjoyed it. I thought I'd give the sequel a chance." Zane shrugs, but his face falls as I stop beside him. "You okay?"

I force a smile. "Why wouldn't I be?" I don't give him the opportunity to inquire further. "Will I have to babysit you again?"

He lets out a short chuckle and follows me upstairs. "Don't think of it as babysitting. You have an opportunity to spread your knowledge to the less fortunate."

"Are you trying to appeal to my vanity?" I send him a short glare, but he grins.

"Is it working?"

On the first floor of Stanley Hall, he stops me. All around us, students bustle to and fro, heading to their next classes—where I should be going—but we stand still.

"I have class." I nod toward the door, but I don't move.

"Which one?" He shifts the weight of his backpack.

"History of Medieval Europe."

Zane quirks an eyebrow. "Who's that with? Rennold?"

I nod.

"I've got my Senior Seminar."

I catch myself before nodding again—I don't know what Zane is majoring in, if he has a job, where he plans to be in five months, what he hopes to achieve with his life…if anything. I meet his eyes, curious. "Which seminar?"

"Oh." Surprise laces his voice. "Advertising."

I frown. How anti-climactic. "How do you have room for a class you don't need to graduate?"

He shrugs. "I've done an extra semester every summer. I actually needed another class to have a full schedule. Can you believe I'm only taking thirteen credits this semester?"

Sadly, I can believe that, though I don't know why anyone would. I've overloaded both semesters.

The hallways are nearly empty now. A few stragglers rush to their classes. I should be among their number.

I glance to the door again and clear my throat. "I need to head out."

"Yeah, I do too."

Zane turns, and I follow him into the cold morning air. Despite his long legs, he keeps his pace equal with mine.

"When are you free?" He catches me by the wrist before we part ways at the end of the awning. "For tutoring sessions, I mean."

I pause, uncomfortably eyeing where his hand holds me. "Um, anytime. We'd only need to do once a week, right? How are Thursday nights?" He raises an eyebrow, and I add, "We can always increase the sessions if you need more help."

But I hope not. Last semester's rigorous schedule was exhausting.

"Yeah, that should work. Can we start this week? I definitely need a refresher after the break." His fingers slowly

156

release me, and he smiles.

"That's not a problem."

"Great."

With a short wave, he strolls off toward the Communications building a block away. My history class, luckily, is only one building to the left, but I'm already late. I sneak one last glance at Zane before heading toward Beecher Hall.

After every strange and intimate conversation, I don't know what to make of him. I think I underestimated him.

◆

Two hours later, when my Honors Seminar ends, my sketchbook is still open to the drawing I spent most of the class working on instead of joining the discussion.

On the page, Zane is sharp lines, strong jaw. His dark hair half-covers his deep-set, cool gray eyes. His thick lips curve into an affectionate smile. His nose is pointed, wide nostrils. I frown, leaning closer to pinpoint where my line work is off.

When I look up, I am the only student left.

At the front of the room, Dr. Lewis logs out of the desktop and turns off the projector, but his papers and books are scattered across the front table. This is the second time I've met him—the first being when I applied for the program at Mo's urging. It still surprises me he's friends with Dad. They're both shy, quiet, perhaps a little awkward, but I struggle to imagine my father with any friends.

Finally, I close my sketchbook and put it away. It's been an eventful day, and I'm ready to be in bed.

I cross the room, but Dr. Lewis only now starts packing. I pause. "Do you need help carrying anything?"

He brought far too many props, which is probably why he was fifteen minutes late. The short discussion we had was little more than an explanation of how this class works. Every text we read, every assignment we complete, every project we create will focus on our central theme—the idea of truth and how it influences society on a whole and on an individual level.

Lewis offers me a smile. "That's very nice of you, but I can manage." He piles the books into a stack again and shoves the papers inside his laptop carrier. "Billie, right?"

"Yes. You know my father."

He raises an eyebrow. "I do?" He studies me a moment before realization hits. "Billie Dixon. You're Elijah's daughter." He lets out a low chuckle. "It's funny, I never made the connection before. I'm not sure why. He talks about you often."

I furrow my brow. "Why?"

Lewis smiles. "He's quite fond of you." He dons his bag, grabs the stack of books, and haphazardly heads toward the door. He talks over his shoulder as we walk. "We've been friends for three years now. He raves about you."

Dr. Lewis's office is located at the opposite end of the hall, and I hesitate at the doorway when he enters. "You can come in if you like. I have my office hours now, but there aren't many callers on the first day of the semester."

After a steadying breath, I sit in one of the guest chairs.

Behind his desk, Lewis organizes the books and papers. "This is your second semester?"

I nod.

"What do you think of Bradford?"

"You've known him since he moved here then. You're friends?" I fold my hands in my lap. "What's he like?"

Lewis pushes aside his things and sits down to face me. "I imagine you know your father better than I do, Billie. You've been far apart for the past three years, but I wish you could've seen how excited he was when you decided to attend Bradford. I've never seen him so happy before."

I frown. That's not the image I conjured after he left, and in the limited time we've spent together since he doesn't seem happy.

"He's incredibly proud of you."

"I need to get a head start on my studies." I rise and take a step toward the door. "Thank you for your time."

He smiles. "I'll see you Thursday afternoon."

I bite my lip as I descend the stairs of Beecher Hall. Perhaps Zane isn't the only person I underestimated. My father is proud of me. Fond of me.

What have I ever done to garner that pride and goodwill?

Seventeen

HURSDAY AFTERNOON, ZANE MEETS ME AT OUR USUAL SPOT in the library.

At the start of the semester, the upstairs of the library is rarely busy, and as it's almost dinnertime, Zane is the only person in the study area. Good. He gets more work done without an audience.

I pause at the top of the stairs. He's sitting in my seat. The seat I specifically chose because it has the perfect vantage point. I can locate every possible exit.

I unload my bag while he flips through last semester's chapters and drums his fingers against the table. "You comfortable?" I pull out his usual chair.

He meets my eyes and smiles. "I thought it'd be fun to mix it up a bit." He pats the seat beside him. "Why don't you sit next to me?"

Frowning, I circle the table and sit in the open chair. "I suppose this will do." Between us, the top page of his notebook is covered in illegible scribbles. "You took notes."

He shrugs, flipping through the textbook. "I vaguely recall someone saying it was a good idea."

A small smile forms on my face, and I flip to the most

recent chapter. "Have you started the homework yet?"

Zane glances up. "I was about to, but then, I had to look some stuff up. How do we find the second derivative?"

I turn to the earlier chapters. "We went over this not too long ago."

"Which is exactly why I asked to review. My memory isn't as good as yours."

Page 227, 203, 198, 195, 193, 192. There. Page 191.

"Right here." I point to the middle of the page. "It's a simple modification to the first derivative formula—and please tell me you remember that. See, the d and the x are squared. Look at this example." I nudge him to make sure he's paying attention.

He grins and reaches for the book. "Let me take a look." He examines it while I grab his notebook. He lets out a low humming sound as he reads and rereads, then at last he returns the book to me. "Alright, I think I see what's happening."

I roll my eyes. "How in the world did you manage a B last semester?" I turn a few pages in his notebook to find the homework he started. Most of the work looks correct, but he's made so many changes I can barely tell what goes where. "Especially if your tests look as horrible as this."

He snatches the notebook back but smiles. "There's nothing wrong with my work. Besides, we both know you're the reason I passed. I couldn't have done it without you."

I cringe. Please tell me he isn't about to get sentimental.

"Then let me help you now."

He laughs. "You've already pointed me to exactly the right page. What more can you do?"

I start my homework on a blank piece of paper, and

circle the answers as I work. Beside me, Zane hunkers down as well, though his progress is decidedly slower than mine. By the time he pauses to ask another question, I have two problems left.

"Things seemed a little tense the other day with your dad. Are you doing alright?"

I glance between him and my book. "That's not something we should discuss, Zane. We need to keep things professional."

"Oh, please. We had plenty of unprofessional conversations over break. Are you seriously going to close back up?"

"I wasn't your tutor over break."

He scoffs. "So if I drop the class, you'll talk to me again?"

I turn away. "That's not what I meant."

"Well, what do you mean?" He huffs but takes a steadying breath. "I liked talking to you, Billie, and I'd like to keep talking to you. I'd rather do that than take Calculus."

But I shake my head, eyes on my work. "It was a mistake. I'm sorry if I misled you, but—"

Zane places his hand on my wrist, and I turn to him. "I think you're misleading yourself."

What am I supposed to say to that?

"I still owe you."

"What?"

A smile tugs at his mouth. "I didn't think I could get a B last semester, but you managed to make it happen—like magic. What do you want?"

Magic would've been getting him an A, an impossibility.

I shrug. His large hand still covers my wrist. "I don't know."

He squeezes. "You haven't thought about it?"

"I was preoccupied."

At last, he retreats—only to guide me by the chin. "Then do you mind if I choose something for you?" His gray eyes hold me.

I pause, uncertain. "I guess."

I almost look away, tear myself from his grasp, but he returns my gaze with a remarkable intensity and presses his lips hesitantly to mine. His eyes flutter shut, but I can only stare as he pulls me closer. With precision, he nudges his tongue inside my mouth.

I pull back, but he holds on.

"Don't panic," he whispers, mere inches away. "I've wanted to kiss you for months."

Before I can prevent myself, the resounding question "Why?" shoots out of my mouth.

Caught off-guard, he leans back against. "You're beautiful." As if that explains everything.

He's completely serious—his face says as much—but I can't take him seriously. Instead, I do the only thing that makes sense. I laugh.

"What the fuck?" Zane retreats farther away.

It takes a moment to rein myself in, and I can't wipe the smile off my lips. "That's bullshit."

He narrows his eyes. "I tell you you're beautiful and that's automatically bullshit? Who've you been dating that could make you think that?"

I go rigid. My fingers clutch the table edge. "My romantic experiences are my own, Zane, and have nothing to do with you."

His face softens, and he scoots closer. "I'm sorry." He almost sounds like he means it. "But how can you not expect me to be insulted by that?"

I take a deep breath. "Let's be honest, Zane. If you wanted to kiss me because of my physical appearance, our conversations over the phone taught you nothing. Have you even looked at me?"

He leans back and chuckles. "Of course I have." His eyes wander my body now, a smile firmly in place.

I cock my head. "I don't think you have. Because quite frankly, I'm a disaster." I gesture to my bushy hair, my loose clothes, my freckles, my complete lack of feminine wiles. Zane opens his mouth to protest, but I raise a hand. "The point isn't that I'm unattractive—I hardly think I'm the objective opinion on that—but you want to kiss me because I'm beautiful? That's illogical."

Zane's mouth twitches, then morphs into an uncertain smile. "You're misinterpreting me, and you're doing it on purpose. I never said physical beauty. You've fascinated me since we met."

Skeptical, I examine the books and papers. Our study session has been entirely forgotten.

"You don't have to pretend." His fingers brush my arm, sending goosebumps along my skin. "I know you like me."

I frown. How could he possibly know that? I don't know.

"Can I ask you a serious question? I mean, without you biting my head off. One you'll answer."

"Yes," I murmur.

"Billie, have you been with anyone before me?"

I shift uneasily. "What do you mean, before you? We're hardly together."

Zane pulls his hand away. "I mean, have you dated anyone before? Have you been...you know, intimate?"

I steal a glance at him. He too is avoiding eye contact. "What you mean is, have I had sex before?"

His silence is confirmation enough.

Why does that matter? What does Zane want from me? Because it's certainly not help with his math—he made that abundantly clear by offering to drop the course.

"I don't really keep track."

Zane releases a long sigh and beams. "Good." He pulls me into another kiss. "You're beautiful."

"This is a library, Zane. It's inappropriate."

He kisses me again. "No one's here."

"You need to focus. We're in the middle of a study session." I purse my lips. "I don't know why you thought it was a good idea to take this class, but if you want to pass, you'll need help."

He offers me a lopsided smile. "I needed a reason to see you again."

"Well, my father has much higher expectations than Hodges. We need to get back to work."

He leans close again. "Can I kiss you again?"

"No."

"Oh, come on. One last kiss before math has my undivided attention." And he closes the distance between us.

◆

The walk from the library to Lincoln Hall has never been so long before.

Zane and I parted ways outside the library per usual. The upperclassmen housing is on the opposite side of campus. The separation meant I could enjoy the silence. No Zane, no nagging, no kissing.

I don't bother going to my own room. I need to see Jimmy. I need to talk to someone. And if I'm alone right now, I won't be able to stop thinking about it. About him.

Outside Room 418, I take a breath and rap my knuckles against the wood.

After a few seconds, Xander pulls open the door, huffing. He appraises me with pursed lips. "You alright, Dixon?"

I can only nod.

"Jimmy isn't here right now," but he opens the door the rest of the way and lets me in.

Usually, Jimmy has the desk set up for his homework, but in his absence, Xander has his enormous gaming laptop set up in the space. It's the only light in the room.

"He's got his night class, remember?" Xander throws over his shoulder as he plops down on the swivel chair.

No, I didn't remember. I wasn't really thinking.

I drop my backpack on the faded linoleum floor. On Jimmy's bed, where I am usually relaxed, I pull my legs close to minimize myself and stare at Xander's messy bed.

Xander spins around, assessing me. "You sure you're alright?"

"Do you mind if I stay here until he gets back?"

He shrugs and spins back to the laptop. "Don't get your charcoal dust all over everything."

I take off my coat, trying to get more comfortable as he returns to his game. The coat lands next to my backpack, and I lie against the mattress and close my eyes.

Zane's face smiles back.

I can still feel his lips against mine, the way he held me close. Remember the grin on his stupid face—and the way

I lied to him.

I don't really keep track. Could it be more obvious? And yet, he couldn't tell.

The worst part is, Xander was right. Not that he needs to hear that—his head's big enough. The look on Zane's face—complete relief at the prospect of my so-called experience…I cannot shake that look.

Why couldn't I say the truth?

That I'm a virgin. That I've never dated anyone. That I've never seen a reason to.

Xander pounds away at his keyboard and makes swift, succinct clicks with the mouse. In every game he plays, he is adept, skillful, and thinks ten moves ahead. He is always in control of what happens—and nothing can break his concentration.

Fire and debris fly across the screen.

He releases a string of cuss words as his hand maneuvers increase in speed and ferocity.

Of course, sometimes, he too surrenders to his emotions. Our taciturn acquaintanceship is proof of that.

When he dies, the camera pans back and circles his corpse. Large yellow text announces his misfortune and prompts the next game.

Eyes narrow, lips set in a firm line, he shoves away and spins his chair around with a glare. "You ruined my concentration."

Despite my confusion and second-guessing, despite my uncertainty, despite the lie and that kiss, despite Zane—somehow Xander always puts me in a foul mood.

"I didn't do anything."

"You moved." He stands and looms over me.

167

I push up on my elbows. "Since when do you require absolute stillness to play a video game?"

Scoffing, Xander turns on his heel and tears open his mini-fridge.

As frustrating as he is, Xander sees things I don't, things I can't. I've never met anyone more caustic, but everyone wants to be his friend. He'll humor them, sure, but the only person he genuinely trusts is Jimmy—and by extension, me. He could do anything if he put his mind to it, but instead he squanders his intelligence, his dexterity, his charisma, on playing video games and getting trashed every weekend.

Oh, and on fucking every willing girl in the school.

According to Val, that isn't a waste of his talents. I don't think she likes his no-strings-attached attitude, though.

I sit up.

On the other side of the room, Xander lets the fridge door slam shut and pops the tab on his Dr. Pepper.

No strings attached. That's exactly what he said at New Year's Eve: *I have nothing to feel guilty about. I sleep with women who want to have sex with me, no strings attached. Virginity has nothing to do with it.*

"Xander?"

He turns, soda in hand, and quirks an eyebrow.

"Can I ask you something?"

"What?"

I slip off my shoes. "A favor."

He casts me a skeptical glance but shrugs.

"Nothing big."

He takes a big gulp of his soda.

"I want you to have sex with me."

Eighteen

XANDER SPLUTTERS WITH HIS DRINK, CHOKES ON THE CAR-bonation, nearly drops the can. "What?" He's wide-eyed and out of breath.

I clasp my hands together over my lap and stare him down. "I think I would benefit from your experience, and from what I understand, you have a lot of experience."

For a moment, he doesn't say a thing, just stares at me. He clears his throat and takes another sip. "Why would you want to have sex with me?"

"Do we need to go into the details? It's just sex."

He raises an eyebrow. "Don't you want to lose your virginity to your boyfriend? I'm sure he's more than willing."

I purse my lips. Perhaps because he can't tell when I'm lying through my teeth. Perhaps because he was so pleased to hear that lie. "Zane Nelson is a non-issue. He has nothing to do with this."

"What, do you want to make sure you know what you're doing before you fuck him?"

"Stop trying to read between lines that don't exist. My motives are straightforward and clear."

He snorts. "Nothing about you is straightforward or

clear."

My fists clench. "You're making a big deal out of nothing."

Brow furrowed, he approaches. "But it's not nothing. Losing your virginity is life-changing and eye-opening, and you should do it with someone special."

Uncertainly, I study him.

He stops a foot away, one hand loosely holding his soda, the other thrust into his jeans pocket, and for a moment, he looks genuinely concerned.

"Why do you say Zane is special? You don't even like him."

One of his eyebrows arches up. "Why don't you tell me? Because for some asinine reason, you do."

I shake my head. "He has nothing to do with this. I'd rather sleep with you than with someone who might matter. You said you don't care whether I'm a virgin." I sigh. "No strings attached."

"When did I say that?"

"New Year's Eve."

All at once, a grin spreads across his lips, and he leans his face close to mine. "I didn't realize you paid attention to what I say, Dixon. I'm touched."

"Don't flatter yourself, asshole."

He steps back, sets his soda on the edge of the desk, and glances over his shoulder. "Of course, if you have your way, there'll be a lot more touching." I scowl, and he collapses next to me with a smirk. "You really want to lose your virginity to me? I suppose I can take one for the team. I mean, if you have your heart set on me and all."

"Very funny." I scoff. "You're not exactly my first choice."

Xander laughs and nudges my arm. "But I am, aren't I? I mean, you haven't asked anyone else."

I glare. "You're starting to make me regret asking you at all."

"Why?" He grins. "I'm warming up to the idea. It might be fun."

I turn to face him, pulling my legs up. "Fun has nothing to do with it. It's just sex."

He raises an eyebrow, and in an instant, he pushes me down, pinning my wrists to the bed. "I'm not sure you have any idea what you're talking about. Have you ever kissed anyone?" His breath brushes my face.

"Of course I have."

He leans impossibly closer. "Then show me."

I don't know if this is a good idea anymore, but I push forward, and our lips meet for a brief second before I pull back. He's frowning when my eyes find his again.

"That was weak."

I roll my eyes. "Well, I'm not exactly excited about this."

He sends me his patented Xander Theroux smirk. "That's because you haven't seen me naked yet."

I strain against his grip, and he releases me and sits up. "You're disgusting."

Like most of my insults, it slides right off. "And you might look too much like a guy for me to get it up."

"Dick."

"Face it, you're no super model. Average height, not enough makeup, but you've got the anorexia down pat."

I sit up and cross my arms. "I am not anorexic."

"I'll believe that when you eat more than half a meal a day. You're skin and bones." He leans over to poke me in the ribs. "I mean, have you seen how tiny your tits are?"

I purse my lips. "You haven't."

"Whose fault is that? You're the one who hasn't taken off your shirt." He ogles my chest, and I pull my arms tighter.

"Neither have you. I'm surprised you didn't strip down at the first mention of getting laid."

He scoffs. "Right, because that's all I think about."

"Discounting video games and your precious *Gilmore Girls*, yes." I stand and walk to the door.

At last, Xander raises his voice. "What the fuck is your problem, Dixon? If you're going to lecture me, you can leave. Literally nothing is keeping you here." He doesn't pause as I slide the deadbolt to the locked position and face him. "You came here. You walked inside fully aware I was alone. And you asked me for sex, not the other way around. You propositioned me. And you do realize Jimmy has a key—"

He falls silent the moment my shirt hits the floor.

"Are we going to do this, or are you going to keep bitching?" I unclasp my gray bra and drop it next to the shirt.

He stares, mouth agape, but tears his eyes away to read his black wristwatch. "It's almost seven."

"Jimmy's class ends at eight, right?" I undo my jeans and ease them over my butt, and the denim slides to the floor. I step closer, leaving the pants behind, and Xander scoots to the edge of the mattress, uncharacteristically quiet.

I've seen him in his underwear a million times; when he stands and removes his own clothes, it isn't out of the ordinary. His boxers are covered in Batman and Superman logos.

I slide my thumbs under the hem of my underwear but pause. He's blatantly staring, and my body is hot under his intense gaze. "Cat got your tongue?"

His eyes shift upward, and he clears his throat. "I could make so many pussy-related jokes right now."

I bite my lip. "What happens next?"

He closes the distance between us and pulls me flush against his bare chest. His kiss, unlike Zane's tentative one, is firm and demanding. His teeth graze my lip. There's no hesitation, no nervous anticipation, no soft touch. He doesn't wait or ask—and I don't want him to. It takes all my effort to keep up.

I struggle to breathe as he drags me to the bed, stumbling over our clothes. He presses me to the mattress, and I yank him on top of me. Fingers wrap around my hip, and he sucks my lip between his teeth. His mouth—eager and unyielding—mesmerizes me. Enough that when he breaks the kiss, I try to follow.

In the dark room, lit only by his laptop screen, he pulls back and stares.

My body flushes under his gaze. "What's wrong?"

He trails a hand down my chest, pausing to stroke a breast, and stops at the hemline of my underwear. "I'm surprised, that's all."

I prop myself up on my elbows, still panting. "This is a bad idea, isn't it?"

Xander laughs, but he tugs at the panties. A finger slips underneath. "Well, it's certainly not one of your better ideas." He leans forward and places a kiss on my breast, and his finger delves between my folds.

"Do I have good ideas?" I try, unsuccessfully, not to gasp. "According to you."

His shrug is minuscule, but he lifts his head enough to

meet my eyes. "They're few and far between, but yeah, I'd say this is particularly rash and stupid."

I grip his shoulder. I don't know how else to stay steady as he slips another finger inside my entrance. "Then why are you doing it?" When he's too busy pressing open-mouthed kisses to my nipples, I say, "You don't have to feel obligated."

He stops all movement and scowls. "Dixon, I could easily be with a different girl right now. Obligation isn't a factor." He pulls his hand back and clutches my panties. "Do you want me to stop?"

My body is on fire. I want to kiss him again. "No." I'm breathless.

He raises an eyebrow and shifts his weight to yank my underwear down and out of the way.

My chest constricts in anticipation. I grab the flannel sheets. "But I wouldn't be surprised if you wanted to." My eyes clench shut. An increasingly large part of me is mad at myself for continuing the conversation.

"Why?" His mouth trails down to my hip, and he spreads my legs with a gentle hand. "You're not exactly hideous." He kisses me again, and I shiver under his caress.

My free hand clamps in his hair. No one has ever sucked on my clit before—I gasp at the contact, and my fingers tighten in his black locks. "But you hate me."

When he laughs, the vibrations spread through my body, tugging a long moan from my lips. He lifts his head enough to say, "Of course I do," before returning to his task. His hands glide back up my legs and hold me open. When he inserts a finger again, then a second, my legs twitch.

I'm wet. I didn't expect to be wet.

I release a low whimper, then his hair. The last thing I

174

need is someone—anyone—finding out about this. I clench my mouth shut.

Xander slides his tongue along my folds and places a delicate kiss before coming up for air. "You don't have to hold back."

I pant, but I can't catch my breath. "Can we move this along? You've got a condom, right?" I should not enjoy this so much—not with Xander.

He pushes up to look around, and I stare at the popcorn ceiling. "Shit."

I look over with wide eyes. "What? You don't have a condom?"

"Don't be ridiculous." He stands, and my eyes gravitate toward the distinct bulge beneath his superhero boxers. "It's on the other side of the room."

I sit up. "Oh." We're on the wrong bed.

He holds out his arms. "Wrap your legs around me."

"What? No, you're not carrying me."

Jaw tight, he leans down, close enough his irritated huff tickles my damp lips. "I'm not going to drop you. It's not like you weigh anything."

"I can walk ten feet across a room."

When will he kiss me again?

His mouth forms a thin line. "Do you have to control everything?"

"No."

"Then for once in your life, shut up and let me do this." He presses his mouth to mine, wraps his arms around my waist and ass, and lifts me into the air.

I've never so much as sat on Xander's bed before, but he lays me down, head on the pillow, and rifles through his bedside table. The top sheet hangs off the side, barely tucked in at the bottom, and his pillow is firm. The bed smells exactly as I expected—a combination of leather, sweat, and cigarette smoke—and I tighten my ponytail.

He slams the drawer shut and holds a sealed condom aloft.

Our eyes meet for a second, and I tear his boxers down. His erection stretches out, the last barrier now on the floor. The room turns pitch black as his laptop enters hibernation.

In the dark, I don't have to hesitate. I don't have to be self-conscious.

My glasses clatter onto his nightstand, and I run a finger down his shaft. Xander inhales sharply. My hand wraps around his base, and I drag him closer—close enough to press my lips to his cock and sweep my tongue around the head.

"Fuck, Dixon."

I release him. "Did I do something wrong?"

He lets out a strangled laugh. "Hardly."

I shift on the mattress and clear my throat. "Let's move this along."

In an instant, Xander sits between my legs and slides the condom on. "You ready?"

"As ready as I'll ever be." I take a deep breath. "Can we get this over with?"

He lifts my hips, and I grab the edge of the bed.

A shuddering breath escapes my lips as he pushes inside. I can barely see his silhouette as he moves in and out, and the pressure builds in my abdomen. Jaw clenched, eyes clamped shut, hands gripping the sheets, I gasp for air.

"Hey, relax." His voice is soft, and I open my eyes to find

him close. "Trust me, it'll be a lot more enjoyable."

"Slow down."

Xander laughs and runs a hand up my side, sending shivers along my body. "I am going slow, Dixon."

"Then stop, stop." I clutch his chest, and he pauses.

His thumb brushes across my nipple, and he places a kiss above my belly button. "I can pull out. You don't have to do this."

I shake my head, but in the dark room, he can't see. "Don't go." I close my eyes again and focus on my breathing, in and out, in and out. "I just can't breathe. I need to breathe."

"'Can't breathe' like you have a medical issue?" His wet lips trail across my abdomen. "Or like you're actually enjoying this?"

I'm definitely enjoying the attention, but he doesn't need to know that. I take another breath in preparation. "Okay, go ahead."

He starts again, and I pull him down for another kiss. "You know," he says as his lips move to my neck, "there's a point where going slow gets pretty difficult." He nips my neck, sucks the flesh into his mouth. I gasp loudly, and he releases a low, pleased growl in response.

"I'll be fine," I manage between heaving.

I hold tight as he increases his velocity. He kisses me again and forces his tongue into my mouth, and I grip so hard my fingers dig into his back. I push my hips up, and his next thrust drives deep inside me. His forehead leaves a thin layer of sweat against mine.

Between gasps and moans, I draw close to his ear and whisper his name.

His guttural response is barely distinguishable from his other sounds: "What?"

"Thank you." I press my lips to the smooth skin below his ear. "For doing this. I appreciate it."

He laughs, but the sound subsides into a long groan when I tighten around him. He recovers quickly. "Not a problem. It's nice to see you lose control."

I try to scoff, but it comes out as a gasping cry as he thrusts. Does he have to be a dick all the time? "It's dark."

"Huh?"

"You can't see me."

"Figure of speech. You know what I meant." His next plunge leaves me panting, and his hands scrape against my skin, dragging down to grip my ass. His fingers, clenched into the cheeks, yank me against him, and a sob racks my body. "Besides, this must be torture for you."

I grit my teeth and bite down on his earlobe. "You must be enjoying this an awful lot then," I snap as he yelps and spasms to a short stop.

He pulls back, and I can tell, even in the dark, he's glaring. "Well…" He grabs my wrists and pins them above my head. "You know how much I like to torture you." He smashes his mouth to mine in a furious kiss and resumes thrusting. I struggle to keep up.

I hook my legs around his waist, and he pushes deeper. His free hand squeezes my breast, pinches the nipple, and he scrapes his fingers down my side. At last, he releases my swollen lips and trails downward. I gasp for air.

It only takes a moment for him to finish, and he places one final kiss on my lips before releasing me and pulling out. I collapse on the bed beneath him. My legs are shaking,

I'm panting, and I can't focus on anything but the way my body feels right now: hot, unsteady, and strangely empty at his absence.

His weight shifts the bed as he cleans up, and then, he squeezes between me and the wall. "Do you feel any different?" His breath hits my face. He's closer than I realized.

When my breathing settles, I turn away from him and fold my hands close. "No different than normal." My body aches from his touch, but I bite my lip—maybe that tiny prick of pain will distract me.

Fingertips press against my shoulder and slide down toward my hip. He doesn't say anything, and I don't protest, despite the obvious. He already got off. He has no need to touch me. But his hand glides over the roundness of my butt and gently cups the cheek. He rests his forehead on my shoulder. "How do you normally feel, Dixon?"

Sometimes, I'm not sure I feel anything, but that certainly isn't true now. He squeezes, and my body responds: my breath catches in my throat, my pulse races, I lean into him and whisper his name. I'm sore and tired and disgusted by my desire, but I'm desperate to reach climax. "You don't have to do this anymore."

"There isn't much room here." His breath tickles my neck. "Would you rather I cuddle you?"

Definitely not.

That notion is sobering. I hug my knees to my chest in an attempt to quell my arousal, but his naked form stays close. "Can I ask you something?"

Xander chuckles. "Another favor?"

"No. I want to talk."

"To me?" He laughs again and presses a kiss to my shoulder blade. "I can't imagine why."

"You're the only one who will be honest without regards for my feelings."

His hand curves around and up the underside of my thighs, grazing past my heat. I don't bother covering up the desperate moan at the almost-touch. "That's the first time you've said that like it's a good thing." He backtracks and slides a finger inside. "What do you wanna ask?"

I can't focus. I can't think. I don't want to.

My hand grabs the gray sheets, and the other reaches down to steady his movements. "Let me breathe, dammit."

He waits but refuses to withdraw, and his tongue glides along the top edge of my shoulder. "I take it as a compliment that I can leave you breathless." His gruff voice in my ear does as much damage as his fingers, and I writhe in his arms, sweating, panting, whimpering. He needs no more cause to slip in a second finger and rub his thumb across my clit. My subsequent cry echoes through the room.

Xander nips at my neck. "Hush. You'll wake the neighbors."

Sarcastic, but right.

I clamp my mouth shut, but he continues his massage, and I can't hold it in. With his free hand, he spins me round and lifts my leg onto his hip. His lips capture mine in a deep kiss.

My limbs are shaking again, and I latch onto him, chest to chest, my hands holding anything within reach. Breasts heaving, barely able to breathe, bucking against him, trembling, demanding, begging, I succumb in his arms. His kisses cannot keep me quiet.

When I stop moving, he retracts but holds me against his

chest as I come down. His lips slow, but I don't want him to go. He pulls back, but my trembling fingers thread through his hair and drag him into one last kiss.

For the longest time, he kisses me, soft, slow, steady. I cannot remember what it feels like without his mouth on mine—until I have to breathe.

His voice is still husky and deep when I break contact. "I believe you had a question for me, Dixon."

For a brief moment, I let him hold me, and then, I remember. "I really fucked things up with my dad, didn't I?"

Xander clears his throat and loosens his grip. "I'm surprised you'd want to talk to me about that night." His words are quiet now. The only evidence of his arousal is the erection pressing against my thigh, hard once again.

"Like I said, you'll be honest." I take in a shaky breath. My pulse thumps through my ears. "Well?"

"That depends on what you want. Because if you hate him as much as you pretend to, you did a great job of driving a wedge between the two of you. But we both know that's not true. You're angry because you're hurt, not because you hate him." He rests his hand on my shoulder—it smells like me. "The question is, do you think he realizes that?"

I burrow closer. "I've seen him twice for class, and he couldn't look at me. I destroyed our potential. I ruined it, like I ruin everything."

He leans down and nips me on the nose. "Everyone else may put up with that bullshit, but you know I won't. Yes, you fucked up. Now fix it."

He releases me then and climbs off the bed. Cold, I pull the pillow close in his absence.

A few seconds later, the overhead light turns on, and I

grab my glasses off his bedside table and squint around the room. Xander stands by the light switch, naked and hard, his body glistening with sweat, and I can't help but stare, enraptured by the sight of him.

With the light on, I almost can't believe he's naked in front of me—let alone that we had sex.

He looks back, and suddenly uncomfortable, I scramble to cover myself with the top sheet.

Xander approaches and stoops to retrieve his boxers. "You should get dressed." He checks his watch and sighs. "And if I were you, I'd hurry." His eyes follow the curves of my body, barely concealed, and he turns toward the bathroom, boxers in hand. "I'm taking a shower."

The door shuts behind him, and I collapse on the bed.

Above me, the ceiling is the brightest thing in the room, and I rest my hand on my abdomen to calm my contracting muscles. I close my eyes and rub at the tender spot where my neck and shoulder meet, where he bit me—God, I better not have a hickey. My pulse is still racing. My chest aches with the pressure. I don't want to think about how sore I'll be in the morning.

Perhaps this was one of my stupider decisions.

I take in a steadying breath and climb off the bed. All my clothes are on Jimmy's side of the room.

The moment I sit on Jimmy's bed to redo my ponytail, fully dressed, the door opens. Jimmy steps inside the room, and a smile lights up his face when he notices me. I force a smile in return.

"Hey, I didn't expect to see you tonight." He drops his backpack on a chair. "You haven't had to put up with Xander for long, have you?" He glances around. "Where is he?"

"Shower."

Jimmy quirks an eyebrow. "He left you alone?"

I shrug. "Maybe spending time alone with me made him feel unclean."

He rolls his eyes but sits next to me. "Tell me about your day."

Nineteen

THE FROZEN GROUND, BARREN OF SNOW BUT FROZEN ALL the same, crunches underfoot as I cross campus under the naked trees. The trip to my father's house is slow, but especially so when Imogene won't stop badgering me. Even from a thousand miles away, she is relentless.

"Have you talked to him yet?" Her voice is hushed, apprehensive. "What did he say?"

I heave a long sigh and focus on the sidewalk. "Will you calm down."

"Well, what did he say?"

"He hasn't given me an answer yet. He needed to check his calendar. I'm sure he'll agree if he can."

"Really?"

The excitement in her voice is unmistakable, but it only adds to my anxiety.

"Okay, let me know, so I can book my flight."

I zip my coat higher. "I told you not to worry about that, Mo. I'm paying for it."

"With what money? Mom said she could."

"I'm getting paid soon."

I'll talk to Zane at our study session tonight. He still

184

owes me from last semester, and I intend to collect.

"From your tutoring gig?" Mo asks, uncertain. "You need that money, though."

"Yeah, well, Mom can't afford to pay for a plane ticket to Vermont. That's the reason I'm here."

Imogene sighs. She knows I'm right.

I reach the edge of campus and cross to residential housing.

"Fine, but Mom'll have to drop me off and pick me up. We have to plan around her schedule."

"Yeah, I know." I pause at the edge of Finchley Avenue to check for cars and step onto the street. "Weekday prices are cheaper too."

"What, I might have to skip classes?" She laughs. "I'm not averse to the idea—it wouldn't mess with my GPA—but I doubt Mom would like that."

"I'm just saying, don't ignore that option."

I turn down Olive and hesitate, not sure what to say next. How can I voice the only question I want to ask? Is Mom okay? Has she had a drop of alcohol since I left?

"How are your classes?" I ask instead.

"No better or worse than when you left, Billie. You've been gone a total of two weeks. It's pretty boring without you. Mom is busy all the time." Imogene laughs. "Maybe I should join her Latin dance class. She's doing the advanced one now. It started yesterday."

"Yeah, you can show her what real dancing's like."

Mo's quiet chuckle crackles through the phone. "From what I've seen, yeah, she isn't very good, but she should have fun. Besides, don't say that like I'm the creative one and you spend all your time holed away in a math textbook."

"I do, though." I turn left onto Cherry Street. Dad's house is now in view.

"Sure, but you're also a talented artist."

"You exaggerate."

"How would you know? You never let anyone see them. Why don't you show Jimmy? Your best friend should jump at the chance to look."

I stop in front of the yellow cottage. This is the first time I've been here since the fight, and I can't think of any reason he'd want me here. "You only say that because you're my sister. I need to go."

Over the line, Imogene huffs dramatically. "Fine, leave me again."

I roll my eyes. "I'll talk to you again soon, alright?"

"Yeah," she says, more seriously this time. "Take care of yourself, Billie."

I slip the phone into my pocket and walk to the porch. Anxious, my hand hovers in front of the oak door before finally knocking.

Dad answers the door with a tight smile and steps aside. The door closes behind me, and I hang my coat on the rack.

"Watermelon hibiscus?" He leads the way to the dining room.

The table is laid out precisely. A soft linen tablecloth spreads across the large wooden frame, topped with a dainty white china teapot. Steam billows from the spout. A tray of sugar and shortbread cookies sits at the center, and a second tray holds a variety of quiche.

"Uh, yeah." I sit in a chair on the far side.

He pours two cups, and heat radiates from the golden

liquid as he pushes one cup and saucer toward me. Once he has everything organized, he sits across from me and blows on the hot tea.

"How's the beginning of your semester?"

His eyebrows raise to his line-up. I suppose I haven't shown interest in anything he does before. "The spring semester always moves faster." He nibbles a cookie. "Perhaps it's the change of seasons or looking forward to the end of the school year, but everything moves faster."

I nod. "What do you think of the Calculus II class?"

"I know most of the students already. Many have taken my classes. It's nice to see a set of serious students."

Except Zane, of course.

He sips his tea. "But it's far too early to tell how the class will progress."

"Right."

My father forces a smile. "Did you have a good holiday?"

"For the most part." I look down. A couple cookies and a quiche sit atop my daffodil-decorated plate. "Was yours alright?"

I'm surprised he can bring up the holidays without acting the least bit uncomfortable. Besides, after her relapse, my bipolar mother isn't the ideal conversation topic—certainly not with him.

"No different than normal."

I imagine his holidays are usually quite lonely, probably made worse by my explosion.

To fill the silence, I murmur, "Good, good," but I don't know how to move on.

Dad leans back, teacup and saucer in hand. "And how are your friends? Jimmy and the other boy—what was his name again?"

I cock an eyebrow. "Xander. And they're doing fine. Focused on schoolwork right now."

Or so I imagine.

I've been scarce for the last week. I can't stand seeing Xander right now. That smug bastard walks around in his boxers whenever he can, a little smirk on his face every time he catches me staring. Which is often.

Dad sets the cup down more loudly than intended. "Surely you have fun too? The semester has barely begun."

I shift anxiously. "What do you mean?"

Here, he hesitates.

I wouldn't call our little romp fun—surely, proposition-ing Xander is a serious indication I've gone insane—but it wasn't unfun either.

"Earning a degree might be the ultimate goal here," Dad says, "but there are other important endeavors. I'm not unaware of the social aspect of college. You must spend time with them outside of classes and schoolwork; it wouldn't be friendship otherwise."

"Oh." I struggle to eat a shortbread cookie. "I suppose we do."

He nods. "Your friend Xander, he cares about you a lot."

I almost inhale my cookie and choke on the crumbs. Where in the world did Dad get that idea? We fight con-stantly. He's an asshole. The fact that he got me off doesn't change that. It's a ridiculous notion.

When my coughing fit subsides, Dad offers me a small smile. "I'm glad you found such good friends, Mina. It would be nice to see them again—if you're comfortable with that."

Stunned, I can only nod.

"Has your sister booked her flight yet? I know it's six weeks away, but the tickets are cheaper now."

I stare at the crumbs—my mess. He said he'd think about it. Apparently, he's thought about it enough. "It's not a terrible idea, then?"

For a moment, he's silent. "Not terrible, no. I would very much like to see your sister."

Right. He's doing this for Imogene, not me.

I nod. "We have to figure out the timing. Then, it's only a matter of picking her up in Burlington."

Dad's curiosity is piqued. "You don't have a car. Would it be presumptuous to offer my assistance?"

I shake my head. "No, Dad, of course not. But I've already asked someone." And yet, the only person who might be willing is the last person I want to ask. The very person I've been avoiding. "Xander's got a car."

He nods. "You'll let me know when you get into town?"

"Yes."

"I can cook dinner that night if you like."

"That'd be good."

Imogene will be thrilled, and I—I'm trapped.

Twenty

ZANE NUDGES HIS DESK CLOSER, AND A BIG SMILE SPREADS across his face. "Okay, I see we've got to integrate both sides. The left side is really easy, but I'm not sure what to do with the right."

I glance toward the front of the room, where my father grades our worksheets at his desk. No one else in the room speaks. We're supposed to work on our assignments until he returns our homework.

Zane pokes my arm and points to where he's stuck.

I scan the page and return to my own work. "Split it up." I'm already five problems ahead of him.

He nods. "Right. Then what? We use the integration by parts formula, right? Or is it the next one?"

I roll my eyes. "We've only studied the integration by parts formula. What do you think?"

He locks eyes with me, smiling, and I can't help but return it. "Fair enough." He scoots closer.

At the front of the room, my father's hand twitches at every sound. I return to my work, but when I look at Zane a minute later, he's stumped. "It's a hell of a lot easier if you substitute. It'll simplify the problem like we talked about."

With a short nod, he continues. "Okay, then, we get this simplified formula, right?" He jots down the new formula.

"Exactly."

Zane is such a slow learner. He works through the problem, backtracks and erases, then reworks it, with his forehead creased.

I whisper in his ear. "Remember that computing v from that is easy. It's $\int dv$."

"Excellent." He grins appreciatively.

Unamused, I raise an eyebrow. "You do realize that's the introductory problem, right? That's the formula. Now, you need to apply that to every problem in our homework. And when we switch to definite integrals, it's a new formula."

Zane's glare makes him look like a petulant fourteen-year-old. "Don't rain on my parade, Billie."

I hold back a snicker.

He smiles and leans closer. Is he going to kiss me right here in the middle of the classroom? "You look lovely when you smile."

And the moment's gone.

I tap my desk to draw his attention to the homework. "Don't worry. Doing the definite integral is easy after you've done a few of these."

"You'd better not be lying." His shoulder brushes mine as he presses closer and jabs me in the ribs.

A loud squeak escapes my lips, and I clap a hand over my mouth. "Don't do that!"

Zane opens his mouth, but a shadow towers over us.

"You're disrupting your peers." My father's eyes are narrow, unforgiving. "If you don't want to be here, you can leave. This is not the place for flirting." He lays my graded worksheet on my desk, then Zane's, and moves on.

Zane issues a short, "Yes, sir," but my father's gone.

My cheeks flush as I study the graded worksheet. Perfect marks, of course, but that doesn't subdue the nausea in my stomach. He thinks we're flirting.

I didn't realize my father's lanky form and quiet nature could be intimidating.

◆

"Well, that was incredibly awkward." Zane follows me across the green space.

I don't know how to respond. It's the truth, of course, but discussing it only makes it more awkward.

When we reach the Eyrie, a long line of students stretches out the doors. It's almost eleven, and the Eyrie is popular for lunch. Most students are ordering meals, but the line moves quickly. All I want is a cup of coffee.

"What are you getting?" Zane stands next to me, a lazy smile on his face, completely nonchalant. "I'm considering a burger, fries, an energy drink."

"I'm not hungry."

We take a couple steps forward. We're almost inside the doors.

He raises a skeptical eyebrow, and I add, "I need coffee."

"I'm not sure you need any stimulants. You're intense enough already. You must get that from your dad."

The line moves forward slightly, and Zane leans against the door, propping it open.

"That was a joke, Wilhelmina." He squeezes my arm briefly. "Calm down."

"I'm perfectly calm. I'm not in the mood for joking."

He runs a thumb across my skin. "Do you want to talk about it? You know I'm always here to listen." He reaches around my shoulders and pulls me into a tight hug I don't return. "We can talk about anything."

I shake my head. "It's just—my dad." The words catch in my throat.

The line moves without us.

After all our conversations over break, with all the effort I made to talk to him, the words don't come. How can I articulate something he won't understand? I don't think anyone understands.

Besides, the middle of the crowded Eyrie is hardly the place to discuss this.

Zane realizes that when the guy behind us scoffs and tells us to fill the open space ahead. We move forward.

That's all I can do.

After I finally place my order, Zane sidles up to the counter. But I don't wait for him before heading to the drink station and filling up my foam cup with a dark Colombian blend and a couple single-serving containers of cream. As Zane finishes at the register, I pop on my lid and head for the door.

Outside, the cold isn't bad with a hot cup in my hands. *"Billie!"*

I don't bother looking back. He ordered food. He's not going to chase me.

"Dammit, Billie, where are you going?"

Just when I think I'm safe, his footsteps pound on the pavement. His fingers grip my arm, and he spins me around. Bits of hot coffee fly through the air, but I cling to the cup.

"Why are you leaving? We were having a conversation."

I pull away. "You were getting lunch. I have to go back to my dorm and study. I already have a paper due."

Zane purses his lips. "You can't be serious. Don't you want to spend time with me?"

I can't meet his eyes. "That's not—there are more important things."

He doesn't miss a beat. "What could be more important than this right now?" He gestures between the two of us. "It's been three weeks since we first kissed, and you barely acknowledge it—acknowledge me. You barely let me touch you, let alone kiss you. We're only together when we're studying or in class, and even then, you panic the second your dad mentions flirting—as if it weren't obvious. When do I get to kiss you in front of people? Or call you my girlfriend? When do I get to introduce you to my friends?" He pauses for dramatic effect. "Billie, have you told anyone about us?"

"Us"—he says it like it's supposed to mean something.

I turn away. "I can't do this now."

But he latches on to my wrist, his eyes set in a bitter glare. "Fine. You don't wanna talk—you can listen. I'm trying to figure out whether this is something worth getting into. Are you so upset with your dad that you can't tell him about me? You don't want me to meet your friends. Are you ashamed I'm not as smart as you? Am I that embarrassing?"

"Of course not. You're overreacting." I try to shake him off, but his grip is tight. "Please let go."

Zane huffs, but his fingers stay firmly wrapped around me. "You keep sending me mixed signals. We spent all break talking, and we kissed—a few times—but the moment it gets real, you run for the hills." He steps closer, holding on, and drags my face close enough for a short kiss.

I yank away. "Zane, let me go."

At last, his fingers release me.

I stumble backward.

"Do you even like me at all?"

"I have to go. Goodbye."

I don't wait for a response. I need to be away from here. Away from him.

A quick glance behind me reveals him returning to the Eyrie for his food.

◆

The coffee keeps me awake, but I don't want to move. Outside, the light fades as the sun sets, but I don't turn on the lights. I like the dark. The dark is safe and secure and good.

The door bursts open, but I don't flinch.

Val flips on the fluorescent overhead light and storms into the room. Her friends follow at a leisurely pace. She chucks her bag against the wall, and it drops to her sheets. Her face is fury itself. Behind her, Cate and Anna look on anxiously.

No one notices me.

"Can you believe him?"

Anna, the girl with a pixie cut who's in my Honors Seminar, closes the door.

"He has some fucking nerve."

"I doubt he meant anything by it, Val." Anna's voice is calm, reassuring. "You went on four dates. It's not like you were exclusive."

But Val sits down at her desk, fists clenched, and glares at her reflection. "That's bullshit. Four dates has to mean something. He shouldn't sleep around with half the building because we didn't talk over winter break."

The blonde, Cate, sits on the edge of Val's bed. "It was one condom."

Val grits her teeth. "One I found. One he was too idiotic to hide before inviting me inside his room. I'm sure he's screwed plenty of girls since we got back." She tears off her earrings and replaces them with studs. "And that's fine. But then, he has the nerve to ask me out tonight. He must've gotten bored."

Cate shrugs. "Or maybe he realized he likes you."

My roommate sends her a glare and pushes away from the desk. "No." She snatches her purse again and starts toward the door. "If he liked me, he'd apologize for his mistake—he wouldn't try to get me in bed right away. Come on, let's eat dinner."

Without even a glance my way, the three of them file out of the room as quickly as they came and flip off the light as they leave.

Did Val even notice me? Am I that invisible?

At last, I force myself up and toward the bathroom. I haven't peed in hours, not since I got back from the Eyrie.

After using the toilet, I stare at my face in the vanity mirror while the water runs. Under the harsh fluorescents, I look particularly gaunt. Perhaps I am invisible—at least to someone like Val.

The door to Prudence and Cynthia's room opens, and Prue sends me a small smile, leaving her door open. "Hey,

Billie." She pauses at the vanity to brush her hair, and I finally wash my hands.

When I turn off the water, Prudence leans close to the mirror and languorously examines her makeup. As I dry my hands, I realize why.

Voices emanate from her dorm room.

"Hi." A nervous chuckle.

Then, Cynthia's ever-critical voice. "You already said that." She pauses. "Can I help you?"

"Yeah, uh, I was wondering what your plans are this weekend."

I freeze.

That awkward, nervous, incredibly shy voice belongs to the one and only Jimmy Powell. Why didn't he tell me he was planning to ask her out? I could've said something. I doubt she even knows his name.

"I have a biology exam on Monday. I'll be studying all weekend."

The door squeaks, but Jimmy intervenes before she can close it all the way. "What about next weekend? Are you free?"

"I have lab reports and essays. I don't have time for you."

The door closes. She didn't give him a chance to respond.

Prudence casts a sad smile in my direction before returning to her room. Like everyone else in our hallway, Prue has known about Jimmy's crush for a long time. Cynthia Allen herself is the only person unaware—until now.

I leave the bedroom immediately.

When I knock on Jimmy and Xander's room, the door creaks open. The two of them sit on the floor, staring at the television as a blind Roy Mustang is led through the darkness by his loyal Hawkeye. Jimmy didn't manage to close the door all the way.

Neither looks over as I shut the door.

Silently, I squeeze into the narrow space between them. Xander's eyes flit over to me, and he offers some of his blanket. I shake my head.

"Well…" I heave a sigh. "This has been a fun day."

Jimmy grunts.

Xander shrugs. "Could be worse." He isn't fazed by whatever went down with Val earlier.

On my other side, Jimmy groans and slumps forward in resignation.

"Or not." I pat him on the back. I've never been the one who comforts in our relationship.

"Cynthia Allen will never love me." He shoves his hands under his glasses to rub his eyes. "My life is over. I'm going to die a virgin."

Xander lets out a snort. "And I'm supposed to be the melodramatic one."

Despite his moaning, Jimmy sends a deep glare past my head. "Like your day's been any better. You're the idiot who left out a used condom."

But Xander rolls his eyes. "It was in the trash. It's not my fault women are so observant. Besides, Val and I weren't doing anything more than fucking. And that could've easily belonged to you."

Jimmy is not amused, and I take the pause to say, "Wait, what happened?"

"Okay, fine, it was obviously mine." Xander turns to me. "You mean you didn't hear the yelling?"

I shake my head.

"A couple weeks ago, the door was open, and Val stopped by to chat, and there was a condom in the trash." He shrugs. "Like it matters. But apparently, it bothers her. I asked about her weekend plans, and she flipped out."

My stomach drops. "A couple weeks ago?"

"Yeah, that first week back." Xander's eyes meet mine. Confirmation.

Oh, God.

"Which is funny," Jimmy says, "because I don't recall you sleeping with anyone our first week back."

Xander clears his throat. "I don't exactly do it with you in the room."

"No, but you do tell me all about it afterward, and unfortunately, it's so detailed the information is burned into my brain." He pauses, relieved to no longer be the center of attention. "And I never received any sexscapade details the first week of the semester." His mouth twists in concentration. "Although, now I think about it, I do remember Connor and Blayne lodging a noise complaint at me."

Connor and Blayne are the next room over—the ones Jimmy and Xander share their bathroom with.

Beside me, Xander snickers. "I'll be sure to let her know she's too loud." He smirks when he catches my gaze.

Heat rises to my cheeks, but I push it down. Focus on the television. The characters are prepping for the final battle.

Still irritated, Jimmy turns to me. "How's your day been?"

I can't look at him. He'll know. It's so obvious, but I don't want him to know. I don't want anyone to know how often those memories flash before my mind's eye.

I clear my throat. I can't take my eyes off the TV. "I've been holed away in my room, wasting my life away."

Xander laughs. "How's that different from normal?"

With a deep breath, I hug my knees to my chest. I'm not sure I'm ready to admit this aloud, but Zane left me little choice with that stupid kiss today. "I think I got a boyfriend, but I'm not sure how."

Jimmy raises an eyebrow.

On the other side, Xander snorts. "Yeah, your day has definitely been shit." He nudges me, and I gasp at the skin-to-skin contact.

Our eyes lock, and I am instantly red.

I just said I have a boyfriend, but Xander gives me a once-over that makes me wonder why.

Twenty-One

ZANE SITS DOWN AND FLIPS THROUGH HIS BOOK. HE doesn't look at me.

"Where were we?"

"Applications." He locates the chapter.

"Right." I flip to the appropriate chapter and pull out my notes from Tuesday's class. "Do you remember the Mean Value Theorem? Or should we go over that too?"

He tugs out the homework assignment he's already started and pushes the papers toward me. "Check my work, and you tell me."

Our homework is twenty problems over the applications of integration. Of the twenty assigned, Zane has completed eighteen. I read over his work while he taps his pen against the table. So messy it's barely readable, per usual, but most of his work is correct. I make mental notes of the problems to revisit, but otherwise, he only has to finish the assignment.

When I push the notebook across the table, he raises an unamused eyebrow. "Well?"

"Let's talk about parametric equations."

"Okay."

I switch to the next page in my textbook and point out

the first problem that needs some work. "Here, on thirty-five, you're jumping ahead."

He looks at the problem and frowns. "What do you mean?"

"This is one of the first parametric curve problems. They're not looking for you to know the answer right away. You're supposed to come up with a random number for t so we can determine what x and y are and plot them on our graph." I push my own work on the problem across the table, pointing out the chart and graph at the bottom. "It's guesswork."

Zane purses his lips. "That's stupid. We've already talked about eliminating the parameters. Why aren't we supposed to do that?"

I flip to the end-of-the-chapter problems and point to the directions above problems thirty-five through forty, where it specifically says to plot points. "It's inefficient, but like all math classes, you have to learn how to do things the hard way before you get the shortcuts. We eliminate the parameters on the next set of five problems."

He groans and grabs an eraser from his bag. He scrubs away his work with that Pink Pearl so hard the paper tears. Doesn't he realize plugging in numbers and plotting points takes less time?

"Is there anything else you think I'm doing wrong?"

Our eyes meet for a moment, but he looks away. "It's not a question of what I think, Zane. It's a simple matter of following directions."

He scoffs. "Well, apparently, I'm not very good at simple directions."

I frown. That's not what I said—though it is true. If he

had bothered to read the directions, he wouldn't have wasted his time. Or mine.

But that's not the real issue here.

I clear my throat. "You're doing well. I think you misunderstood the Derivative for Parametric Equations. It's dx over dy equals dx over dt all over dy over dt, assuming dy over dt isn't equal to zero. It's not one long string of division signs."

"How is that different than what I've been doing?"

With a short sigh, I lay my hand atop my book. "If we have to go over the Order of Operations, we're seriously backtracking."

Zane rolls his eyes. "Okay, fine, it changes the answer. That's all you have to say." He glances over his homework again. "I'll rework those. Anything else?"

"You're good on the tangent lines?"

"Once I have that formula right, yeah."

I nod. "Then, there's one more thing. The area under a parametric curve."

"What, did I fuck up those formulas too?"

I push a few corkscrew strands behind my ear. He's never been this impatient or abrasive before, and I can't help drawing the obvious conclusion: I know I have trouble connecting with people, but did I really put this much distance between us?

"No, the formulas you used are fine. You keep mixing up sine and cosine for some reason."

His jaw clenches so tightly it twitches. "Are you sure I'm the one getting mixed up?"

"All the answers to the odd-numbered problems are in the back of the book, so yeah, I'm pretty sure."

Before I can say anything else, he snaps his book shut. "If that's all, I have somewhere to be. Thanks for your help." He packs up and heads for the stairs before I can call after him.

What would I say anyway?

I check my phone. It hasn't been a whole twenty minutes since he arrived. Our sessions usually last two hours.

◆

The Eyrie is dead when I enter, despite the fact that I'm here an hour or two earlier than intended. Jimmy is one of two workers on shift tonight. The other student worker is in the back.

I slump against the counter, where Jimmy is reorganizing wrapped cookies, and cover my face with my hands.

He leans over. "You're done early."

"Yeah, well, we didn't have much to go over tonight." I push up and glance around. On the far side, a couple students are sharing a basket of chicken fingers. "Are you normally this empty now?"

He shrugs. "It comes and goes. There aren't any night classes, so most students eat dinner in the cafeteria tonight, I think." He nods toward the back. "I need to clean tables."

I sit on a chair while Jimmy wipes down each table with a spray bottle of sanitizer and a white rag. "Why'd you finish early?" In the empty space, his quiet voice carries farther.

I shift in the seat. These chairs weren't made for comfort. "Our fight last week, I'd imagine. He's pretty upset about it."

"Your first fight as a couple." Jimmy sends me a snarky smile.

I roll my eyes but can't help laughing. "Shut up."

204

He finishes one table and moves on to the next. "What's the problem, Billie? You never told me about the fight, and you certainly didn't say how you felt about it."

I scoff. "Are you Freud now? I was shocked when I told you. There wasn't any more reaction than that."

"Really?" Jimmy raises a skeptical eyebrow. "Because if you two are dating now but you don't know how it happened, there's some stuff you need to talk about."

"I'm trying to talk to you."

"Not to me. To him."

I frown. "I'm not very good at talking to people."

Jimmy laughs. "Alright, fine. You can talk to me about it for a while. It's not like there's much to do around here. We've actually turned off the fryers."

And now the opportunity presents itself, I don't know what to say. Where to begin?

I take a deep breath. "He thinks I'm embarrassed of him—that that's the reason I hesitate. But I don't think he realizes I've never had a boyfriend before. I've always prioritized other things. The fact that I talk to him at all is a big deal."

"It'd be pretty easy to tell him that, you know."

I sigh. "Not so easy. We were at the library for less than twenty minutes, and I'm sitting there talking about math, and he's not. He took everything I said personally, like I found fault in his homework to spite him."

Jimmy clucks his tongue. "He's that mad?"

"He's right, though."

"You were doing it to spite him?"

"No. The second things turn remotely serious, I'm ready to give up."

Jimmy frowns. "Billie, you're one of the most ambitious people I know."

"That's with math and academics, not with people. Zane and I—we were sitting and talking in class, and then, my dad came over to reprimand us for flirting. My dad."

"Ah."

"I panicked, and I couldn't explain it. I guess he assumed I was embarrassed of him? But those two things have nothing to do with each other."

Jimmy pulls up a chair. "Well, if you're not embarrassed of him, why did you panic?"

"My dad…" But the words fail me. I clear my throat and try again. "He would hate it, knowing I'm considering dating Zane. He wouldn't want me to waste time on someone like him. Dad would be so…disappointed."

Jimmy struggles repress a smile. It's as close to an admission as he'll get that I care what my father thinks. Somewhere inside, I'm still that stupid little girl, writing my father coded letters and hoping.

"I don't know, I think he'd be pretty happy to know you value his opinion."

I scoot the chair away and glance around. The sanitizer and cloth sit on the table in front of us. "You're not done cleaning, are you?"

Jimmy lets out a short humorless laugh before standing, and I look around the restaurant again. Not a soul has come in since my arrival.

"Who's the other person on shift tonight?"

"Carla." He shrugs. "She's pretty quiet; we don't talk much when it's the two of us."

I nod, but I can't help asking the question that nags and

tugs at my anxious stomach. "What about Xander?"

Jimmy cocks his head. "What about Xander?"

I try to shrug it off as mild curiosity. "Isn't he supposed to work here? I've seen him on shift once."

He nods. "Well, the students on work study get the most hours."

"You're not on work study, and you're here plenty."

He shrugs. "Xander's already talking about finding a job off-campus, but I don't think he wants to waste anyone's time when he'll have to go back to Florida at the end of the semester."

I snort. Xander is the king of wasting people's time.

"Why do you ask?"

I open my mouth, but I don't know how to answer.

"You know, it was pretty surprising the other day when he told me you asked him to drive you to pick up Imogene at the Burlington airport. You're going to spend an hour alone with him in a tiny car, and you're okay with that?"

I've been trying to avoid thinking about that. I can hardly believe I built up the nerve to ask him, and in pure Xander fashion, he stared me down with the smuggest grin while I stammered the question.

"He has a car," I murmur.

"I'd offer to go with you guys—I'd love to see Imogene—but I'm not willing to skip my classes for that awkward situation."

I turn to him, brow furrowed. "Skip class?"

"Her flight's next Thursday, right?"

"Yeah, but I already talked to Dr. Lewis about it, and Mo said it was alright."

Jimmy laughs. "I wasn't talking about either of you.

Xander's skipping his class to drive you there."

"No." I shake my head. "He said his professor canceled class to give students a longer spring break."

Jimmy shrugs. "Well, what do I know? I'm just his roommate." He finishes the table he's on and moves to the final one, where I'm sitting. "When he first told me he was helping you, I thought he was joking—especially since you two haven't been in the same room for more than a few minutes since winter break. I know you can't stand him, but you could at least pretend for my sake."

I frown. I certainly can't tell him the reason I can't stay in the same room as Xander is because every time I look at him, I picture him naked. Or that the same images haunt me while I fail to fall asleep at night. Or that his every look and touch send an uncomfortable shiver through my body. I hate being near him.

It doesn't help that when his eyes meet mine, Xander sends me that little smirk—the one that says he knows exactly what I'm thinking.

"I'll try harder."

He finishes the table, then walks toward the front counter. "Are you going to order anything while you're here? Or are you skipping dinner again?"

I follow him. "Fine. I'll take a Powerade."

At the register, Jimmy puts in the order and swipes my ID, and I grab an orange Powerade from the refrigerator.

I take a gulp and lean against the counter, twisting the lid on. "I don't understand what's going through his head."

Behind the counter, Jimmy is doing busywork. I stopped caring what. "Xander?"

"No, Zane—though that too."

"Okay. What don't you understand?"

"Everything."

"Well, he probably feels the same way about you. If you like him, you have to actually communicate, and you're not—neither of you—doing that. It's never going to work if you don't talk to each other."

"What am I supposed to say to him?"

"It can't be that difficult. We talk all the time."

"Yeah, but I've known you since I was eight, and you're my best friend. That's totally different. I don't have to put on a show for you."

"You shouldn't have to put on a show for Zane either." He pokes me, and I spin round. "If you really like him, you have to be honest with him. Do you like him?"

I frown. "I don't know. I mean, today really threw me off. It was the first time he wasn't trying to talk to me, asking about my day, complimenting me. He was so different."

"Billie."

I look up. "Yeah?"

"Do you miss him? Do you wonder when he'll text you? Do you wait to hear from him?"

I take another drink and leave the bottle on the counter between us. "I don't see how that's relevant."

"He likes you, and it sounds like you might like him. You need to sort out your feelings."

The orange liquid quivers as I rest my chin on the counter. "I don't know how. I mean, I guess I like him, but I don't know why. He's not smart. He's terrible at math. He has no understanding of sarcasm, so he doesn't get it when I make a joke."

"If you make a joke."

"And he's in a frat. I hate frats. They're misogynistic, elitist, archaic bullshit."

"Fraternities are changing with the times like everything else." He shrugs. "A bunch are open to gays and trans men."

"Is his?"

"How am I supposed to know?"

"But even with all that, he's always been really nice to me. He wants to share with me, to tell me about his day. He thinks I'm brilliant. It's nice to have someone think that, even if it isn't true."

Jimmy coughs uncomfortably. "Alright, two things. One, you're pretty damn brilliant, Billie, and Zane Nelson isn't the only guy who thinks so. And two, I'm going to play devil's advocate here and say none of that has to do with your feelings for him. You don't have to like him because he's nice. You're not obligated."

"That's not what I meant. I guess I meant, what's not to like?"

He heaves a sigh. "Whatever you do, be sure you know what you're getting into."

"Don't be a worrywart, Jimmy. I'm not getting into anything right now." I take in a deep breath and grab my drink. "I've wasted enough of your time tonight. I should get back and work on my essay; it's due Monday." I retrieve my backpack from the chair and pull it on.

"Oh, hey, Billie," Jimmy calls after me. "Xander and I are heading out next Saturday night. You and Imogene doing anything before we leave? I want to see her."

"I don't know what our plans are, honestly." I head for the door. "We have a lot to sort out."

Twenty-Two

THE DRIVE FROM ST. CLARE TO BURLINGTON INTERnational Airport is only an hour long, but Xander knows exactly how to make this unbearable. I was suspicious from the moment he sent me a mischievous smirk and the words, "How will we pass the time?" Even I'm not naive enough to pretend he doesn't want something.

I'm not looking forward to a week in my father's house with only Imogene as a go-between, but it has to be better than this—and it's definitely better than the hours of awkward tutoring sessions and class discussions with Zane. Despite his veiled comments, he refuses to talk about anything other than calculus.

In the driver's seat, Xander directs the car onto northbound US-7, then fiddles with the tape deck. He inserts a cassette.

"How old is this thing? Nothing plays cassettes anymore."

He casts a glare toward me. "That sounds remarkably like you're insulting my car, Dixon. I don't have to drive you to the airport."

I turn to the window. "It was just a question, jeez."

We sit quietly as AC/DC's "Back in Black" crackles to

211

life in the old speakers.

"Seventy-nine. It's a 1979."

I frown at the trees we speed past. I suppose I have to play nice, especially if I don't want him to dump me on the side of the road. "It's a nice car. How long have you had it?"

He hesitates. "Three years. I bought it off a friend's dad. He collects classic cars, fixes them up, does the whole auto show thing."

"How much did you pay for this thing?"

"Well, it wasn't in the best condition. It wasn't running. But still, far less than it was worth."

I let out a short laugh. "That must've made your parents happy. I imagine wealthy businessmen enjoy ripping people off."

Xander snorts. "No, they weren't happy. They wanted to impound it."

I turn on him, but he only has eyes for the road. "But it's a classic car."

"That's what I said." He shrugs. "In the end, my dad had to go on another trip and didn't have time to fight me, so I got to keep it."

I nod, then pause. "Wait, you bought this yourself? With what, your allowance?"

He releases a loud, full-bodied laugh and, instead of answering, says, "It was an investment. So were the hours I spent fixing it and the money for parts." He smiles. "You wouldn't believe how much I know about Chevy Camaros now."

"You did all the repairs yourself."

He shrugs. "No one else was going to do them."

On the stereo, the song changes. It takes me a moment

to recognize—"You Shook Me All Night Long"—and I stare at the tape deck for a long moment. Did he choose this album specifically because we're alone? The last thing I need is another reminder of us having sex.

"Something on your mind, Dixon?" He's staring at me.

"You need to focus on the road."

"I dunno, I've got something on my mind. Makes it hard to focus."

"You have to."

"Why don't we talk about it?"

"Let's not."

"Might make you feel better."

I send him a reproving look. "I'll feel a lot better if you focus on driving, Xander."

Smirking, he glances ahead, then back to me. "Don't you trust me?"

"What in the world gave you that impression?"

He turns his full attention to the road, a smug grin in place. "You let me stick my dick in you—kind of a good indicator."

I blanch. "That had nothing to do with trust. Besides, we agreed never to talk about it."

Xander shrugs. "That conversation only happened in your head. I never made any agreement." A smirk spreads across his stupid, conceited lips. "There's nothing stopping me from telling the whole world."

"You wouldn't."

He laughs it off. "You're right. No point." He pauses. "Did it turn out as seamlessly as you'd hoped?"

"What?"

"The sex."

I roll my eyes. "Nothing ever works out seamlessly when you're involved."

"Then why risk it? Because this whole I-want-to-get-it-over-with thing sounds exactly like bullshit. Or at least, that's half the story."

I heave a sigh and locate the side mirror. It offers a poor view of the scene behind us, but at least it's something to look at. "How old were you when you lost your virginity?"

He thinks a minute. "Fifteen."

"And that's a normal age for a guy to have sex for the first time?"

"Fifteen or sixteen, yeah."

I frown at the mirror. "I'm eighteen, and if I'm with someone three years my senior—someone who's probably been having sex for six years—that's a huge disparity."

"I was right."

"Huh?"

"You don't want to disappoint him." His mouth is quirked to the side in concentration—or irritation—but his eyes don't leave the road. "You must like him then."

"Maybe."

Honestly, I still don't know.

"Why would you be a disappointment? You weren't bad."

"How was I supposed to know that beforehand?"

"I'd have no problem repeating it." Xander shrugs, and his tone is flippant. "It was actually pretty hot."

My mouth gapes.

I never expected him to accept my proposition. It was a whim, a really stupid whim. After he agreed, I didn't expect him to look back on it fondly. I didn't expect attraction. I didn't expect his willingness to repeat the carnal act.

"I don't understand why you didn't ask him. Nelson's wanted in your pants for three months. What's the problem?"

I lean my head against the door and sigh. "I told you. He asked me—just like you said he would—and I didn't lie, but I may have implied I'd had sex before. He was so relieved when I said I wasn't a virgin."

"So sleeping with me was—"

"An easy solution. What I said is no longer a lie, as I'm no longer a virgin, and I don't have to worry about any emotional repercussions."

He shakes his head. "Not everyone is emotionally stunted like you. You said, 'It's just sex,' five times while trying to convince me—did you manage to convince yourself?"

I release a snort in disbelief. "Oh my God. You weren't joking."

"What?"

"Before we had sex, you told me it should be with someone you care about. I thought you were joking—or at least trying to make yourself feel better." I stare at him for a moment, not sure what to think. "You've slept with a lot of girls just since I met you. Why can you have meaningless sex but I can't?"

He scoffs. "That's not the same thing. Ninety-nine percent of people sleep with at least one person they don't love—my parents do it all the time—but losing your virginity is special."

"Your parents have affairs?"

Xander laughs. "Yeah, probably that too."

I furrow my brow but move on. "I don't see why it has to be special."

His forehead creases. His grip tightens on the steering wheel. "It should be. You're young and naive and fragile, and you need someone who appreciates that and is willing to be gentle and slow."

The funny thing is, that's exactly what Xander did. He was slow and patient and more than willing to stop. Even when he wasn't slow or patient, his priority was making sure I was comfortable and enjoyed myself. It was unexpected. Would Zane have been as gentle if I'd asked him?

I clear my throat. "I'm not fragile."

"Bullshit." He shakes his head. "Also, I was speaking generally."

But I turn to him and glare. "No, you weren't. At New Year's Eve, when you wouldn't stop pestering me, you said you don't care if the girl's a virgin. But the second I ask you to have sex with me, you won't stop talking about how it should be special. Why? You don't care about anyone else's virginity."

I'm not sure what I expected, but a simple shrug isn't it. "Yeah, well, I don't have to see any of them on a regular basis, do I? If we had sex and you blamed me for your stupid decision, I'd have to deal with you being ridiculous as long as I'm living with Jimmy, which unfortunately for you, is gonna be a while."

I pause. "What do you mean?"

"We're getting a campus apartment together next year. Jimmy didn't tell you?"

"He probably didn't want to upset me."

"Anyway, the point is, if you're going to regret it, I want you to remember it was your idea." He presses on the gas, and we zoom past a white SUV.

"I don't regret it."

He falls silent.

"I mean, it was a stupid idea, but I stand by it. You didn't do anything I didn't ask you to do."

"Well, good, then." He shifts stiffly in his seat.

But that's not true. I asked for sex, penetration. Not for him to go down on me or finger me. Not for him to devote so much time to making sure I came too. That was entirely his decision.

We sit quietly as the cassette switches sides. Xander turns up the volume, but I'm not in the mood for more AC/DC.

I turn it down and bite my lip. "Out of curiosity, and for the sake of argument, how did you lose your virginity?"

He quirks his mouth to the side. "My girlfriend Em. We dated all of high school."

I frown. It's hard to imagine Xander being with one girl for more than an hour, let alone all of high school. "Did you love her?"

He shrugs. "As much as a fifteen-year-old can love another fifteen-year-old."

"Then why did you break up?"

"I'm not fifteen anymore. I wanted something she wasn't willing to do."

"What, anal?"

Xander laughs but shakes his head. "That definitely wasn't a problem, though sadly she didn't have much of an ass. No, we really weren't that compatible—and there was that time she stabbed me with a pencil."

For a moment, I stare, but he doesn't elaborate and I hesitate to ask.

"Why do you like him?"

217

"Zane?"

He nods.

How am I supposed to answer that when I don't know the answer myself? I already deliberated this with Jimmy, but I know exactly what response my answer would receive here—twenty minutes of a condescending tirade about how stupid and naive I am.

I sigh. "Why does it matter? If anything happens between me and Zane, it's between me and him. You have nothing to do with it."

"Fine." Xander's face hardens. "But answer me this— you're certain of him? Because as far as I can tell, you haven't taken the time to learn who he is. Do you have anything in common?"

I roll my eyes. "Stop trying to get inside my head. You don't know him."

"Neither do you. You're far too busy wrestling with your daddy issues to consider his intentions."

"Not every guy is like you. Some of them want a girl-friend instead of sleeping with anything that moves. Look at Jimmy."

Xander's nostrils flare. "Have you met Jimmy? Because he knows absolutely nothing about women or relationships. He may be the only guy who wants a girlfriend more than he wants to get laid, but his crush on Cynthia is based on, what, the five-second interaction when she moved in. They've had two conversations—and the second one was her rejecting him."

I snort.

"Seriously, don't use him to make a point. He's the exception to the rule." Xander pauses. "Just promise me something, Dixon." His voice is quiet again, almost encouraging. I must be imagining it.

"What?"

"Get to know him before you sleep with him. And be careful."

For a moment, neither of us says anything.

I lean back, mulling over his words. Maybe if he pretends to be concerned, he can ease his conscience. It's not like Xander actually cares what happens to me—not unless it affects him.

Outside the window, barren trees flash by. It will officially be spring in a few days, but the Vermont forests are only starting to bud.

I glance at the clock. We're not even halfway to Burlington. It's going to be a long trip if we keep this up, and I'm already exhausted. "I'm tired."

He raises an eyebrow. "I'm not surprised. Val complained about your sleep schedule all the time."

I shut my eyes, but his words strike a chord. Did Val have anything nice to say about me? No, I don't imagine so. I've never given her a reason to. But I don't suppose I've given Xander a reason either, and yet he defended me to her with no benefit to himself—in fact, it probably hurt his chances of getting laid that night.

"Xander…"

"Yeah?"

I frown. I can't exactly thank him for something I wasn't supposed to hear. "Nothing. Never mind."

"Okay."

But I'm still curious. "You really dated the same girl for that long?"

He lets out a small chuckle. "Three and a half years, yeah. And when I find someone actually worth my time, I'll do it again."

I shift in the seat and cover myself with my hoody.

The car is slowing down. We must be off the highway.

I open my eyes. Outside, the airport is already in view.

To my left, Xander has a hardened expression on his face. "You actually slept."

I sit up and let the jacket fall. "Yeah, I guess."

We drive past the planes on the landing strips, enormous lots of long-term parkers, and finally reach the main pick-up location.

Xander, not sure of the plan, stops near the front door and puts on his hazard lights. "You going to get her?" He lifts his wrist to confirm the time. "Is she here yet?"

I maneuver a hand inside my pocket. My last text from her was right before take-off, saying the flight would land on time. Which should be sometime in the next five minutes.

"Maybe." I unbuckle my seatbelt. "Let me go check for her, alright?"

He nods, and I head inside the airport. With a nervous smile, I wait near baggage claim. She should be here soon.

The airport is huge compared to the one in Springfield, and I almost miss her when she walks away from the gates, heading straight for me. But her bouncing step gives her away—especially restless. She's nervous.

Imogene's blond hair is pulled into two French braids framing her face, each end tied off with a violet ribbon that matches the belt of her coat. She dressed to impress.

When she spots me, her green eyes light up, and she

throws herself into my arms. *"Billie!"* She burrows her face into the crook of my neck. "I'm excited to see you—and Dad."

Despite my own nerves, I smile as we pull apart. "It's good to see you, Mo. Did you bring any luggage?"

She nods and looks to the rotating baggage claim, where suitcases are now coming out of the chute. "Something small."

Thankfully, her bag is easy to locate, and we head for the front of the airport.

"Xander drove me."

Outside the automatic doors, Xander's car is where I left it, dusty and old but waiting for us.

Imogene cocks an eyebrow. "You're on good enough terms he agreed to drive out here on a Thursday afternoon?"

I shrug. "He said he had nothing better to do since his last class of the day was canceled."

Xander pops the trunk, and I toss the suitcase inside. Imogene climbs into the back seat and greets our driver. I inhale deeply before taking my seat in the front and putting on my seatbelt.

"Everybody ready?" After confirmation, Xander takes off the hazards and starts the escape from the airport parking lot.

"What will you do over your break?" Imogene asks.

I frown because I don't know. Jimmy didn't go into detail with their plans.

Xander glances through the rear-view mirror. "I'm taking Jim to Playa del Carmen."

"Where's that?" Mo asks.

"Mexico." He grins at me. "I'm going to get him drunk

221

for the first time, and he can't complain because it'll be totally legal."

I roll my eyes.

"Speaking of which, we're going to a party off-campus tomorrow night. You two wanna come?"

I send him a quick glare. "She's sixteen, asshat. She's not going to any sort of party you're going to."

He shrugs. "Fair enough."

Imogene leans forward curiously. "Why don't you ever go home?"

Xander laughs but side-steps the question. "My parents are on a business trip for the next two weeks. There's not much point going back right now."

I swallow down the uncertainty.

I've known Xander—and been in close proximity with him—for seven months, but I don't know the first thing about him. Video games, drinking, sex, comics and anime, his unhealthy obsession with *Gilmore Girls*. Everything I know, everything I see, is surface-deep.

But there's more to him than meets the eye.

◆

An hour later, Xander drops us off in front of Dad's house and says a short goodbye before driving away. We huddle together on the sidewalk, Imogene's suitcase sitting on the concrete beside us.

"You nervous?"

She nods emphatically.

"You don't have to be. He's been looking forward to seeing you since I first brought it up."

She doesn't move. Neither do I.

After a moment, I take the first uncertain step, and she follows me to the front porch. She doesn't say anything, but she doesn't have to. I know she's scared.

"You ready?" I rap my knuckles against the door, and then, we wait.

It takes him less than a minute to reach us. The handle turns, he pulls the door ajar, and he stares back at us. I give him a small smile as I lead Imogene another step closer.

I don't say anything. I don't want to ruin the moment. Imogene still has a chance to make this right.

At last, Imogene releases me and dives at him, arms open for a long-anticipated embrace. All at once, her face is buried deep in his chest, and he wraps his arms around her petite form, smiling. "I missed you, sweetheart."

I look away. I don't think I'm supposed to witness this.

When their hug ends, Dad leads us inside. We leave our jackets and the suitcase by the front door. "I have a fire going." It isn't that cold outside, but they sit together on the Victorian-style couch. I take a vigilant perch on an armchair.

There's a pot of Earl Grey on the coffee table, and he offers us each a cup. I swirl the brown liquid around the mug while they exchange bated glances and nervous conversation. Lavender wafts through the room. Small talk is hardly the most interesting topic, but Dad hangs onto her every word, encourages every minor articulation.

"Which subject is your favorite?" He's genuinely curious.

"English, actually." Mo smiles. "We've been studying the classics—Jane Austen, *Animal Farm*, *Fahrenheit 451*—but I got bored with the selection."

"Oh, you have?"

"Yeah, now that cheerleading season is over, I've compiled a list of books to read on my own." Imogene glances toward the door, where her suitcase sits. She probably brought a dozen with her. "I'm on *The Autobiography of Malcolm X* right now."

Dad nods. "That's impressive. Aside from the cheerleading, are you otherwise active in school?"

"I'm part of the student government."

I sip my tea and lean back. "Boyfriend?"

Imogene glances my way with pursed lips. "I broke up with Ian two weeks ago."

I raise an eyebrow. "Who's Ian?"

She returns her attention to Dad. "Do you like it here? What's the town like?"

"It's small. There are several advantages to that, but mostly I like the quiet, and Vermont is beautiful, especially in the fall."

"Have you lived here the whole time? It's a nice house." She examines the room and the furnishings.

"I moved in at the beginning of my first semester." He stayed somewhere else that first summer. Dad picks up his cup and takes a long drink. It's probably cold by now. "How's your mother?"

Here, Imogene hesitates. "She's…doing better. I don't know how much Billie told you." She shoots a glance my way. "She wasn't doing very well after—after the divorce, but she's doing better now. She started seeing someone."

I bolt up. "Why didn't you tell me?"

"It just happened."

"Who?"

"Her dance instructor. I haven't met him yet."

I make a face and return to my tea, an uncomfortable weight on my chest. But Dad doesn't care his ex-wife is seeing someone new.

"What about dancing?" he asks.

Outside, it's already dusk. The days are still short, and it's cold enough to snow at night. The flurries now falling from the sky are proof of that.

Silently, I rise and head for the half bath. They don't notice.

The latch clicks into place. I turn the lock on the door, and the darkness of the tiny room surrounds me. I sit on the toilet lid and lift my feet onto the rim. The bathroom air is stale—no vent in here. I wrap my arms around my legs and rest my head on a knee.

Everything comes easily for Imogene. She can talk to people. She can talk to him, to Dad. She's been here for fifteen minutes, and they can talk about anything.

Meanwhile, I've been here for seven months, and I still can't manage a normal conversation with him.

Twenty-Three

THE ROOM IS DARK. VAL LEFT FOR BREAK THIS AFTERNOON, so it's pleasantly empty for once.

I dump my textbooks on my bed and examine the room. I need clothes, my laptop, my Aristotle for Honors, toiletries, and my sketchbooks if I'm to survive the week. I postponed packing for too long.

Someone's in the bathroom when I raid the vanity area for toiletries—toothbrush, hair ties, deodorant, a wide-toothed comb. I take a moment to check myself in the mirror before heading back to my room, and in the bathroom, the toilet flushes.

Prudence emerges as I'm leaving, and a big smile spreads across her rosy face. "Hey, Billie." She washes her hands in the sink. "You heading out now?"

I leave the door open and shout a reply. "Yeah. When are you leaving? Doing anything special for spring break?" I drop the stuff on my bed.

She pokes her head into the room. "A couple hours. My dad's driving up to get me. Can I come in?"

I glance back and shrug, and she sits on the edge of my bed with a hesitant smile. I return to packing.

226

"My parents are going to meet Ruby," she says happily. "Things are getting serious."

"Who's Ruby?"

Prudence lets out a small huff. "She lives a couple doors down." She pauses. "She's my girlfriend."

I shrug it off. "I don't remember her."

"You missed Honors yesterday," she says instead of continuing. "Dr. Lewis announced our project for the second half of the semester. It's our final."

"I had to pick up my sister at the airport." I shove the toiletries into the bag, then freeze. "Wait, new project?"

She smiles. "Yeah, he called it a creative project."

But I drop the sketchbook on the bed. "Lewis didn't tell me anything about a project when I asked him about missing yesterday's class. It's our final? How am I supposed to do this if I missed the class? Tell me everything."

Prudence cocks her head to the side, frowning. "It's nothing to worry about, Billie. He hasn't passed out the rubric yet. It was an announcement, nothing more."

I push the sketchbook inside my bag and zip it shut. "I'm sorry, Prudence." I don my hoody and the backpack. "I really have to go. Have a good break."

"Uh, you too," she calls after me as I head for the door.

That stupid flight was more of an inconvenience than I realized. How could I have missed this? Why didn't Lewis tell me when I saw him last week?

◆

Fifteen minutes later, I knock on my dad's front door and enter the house, dropping my backpack in the foyer. Dad and Imogene are sitting in the dining room, working on a thousand-piece puzzle of some European flower garden. They look up and smile when I join them.

"Do you want to help?" Imogene gestures toward me with the lid of the puzzle box. "We're not that far yet."

I shake my head but sit down beside her. "I'm exhausted."

"Long day of classes?"

"Not really. I only had one, but I learned Dr. Lewis announced our next project while I was out of class yesterday."

Across the table, Dad pauses in the middle of fitting the horizon together. "Have you talked to Henry about it?" He plugs his new section into the edge pieces.

"No, I haven't had the chance. He'll go over the project in full when we get back from break. We turned in a huge research paper last week; this one is a creative project."

"What kind of creative project?" Imogene leans forward eagerly.

"I don't know, but it'll be the same focus as the rest of the semester—truth and lies, the human condition, blah, blah, blah." I rest my chin on my hand.

"That sounds fascinating."

I laugh.

"What kind of options do you have for the project? You can do anything you want?"

"I don't know the parameters yet."

"Maybe you can draw something." Mo's voice bubbles with excitement on my behalf.

I frown. "What does that have to do with the subject matter?"

She opens her mouth to reply, but my phone buzzes.

It's Zane.

When are you leaving campus? I'm here till noon tomorrow. Would you be able to do any studying tonight since you missed yesterday's?

I purse my lips. God forbid I cancel on him once during a week when we don't need to study. I craft a short reply—*It's spring break*—and push the phone away. "Sorry."

Imogene has returned to the puzzle and shrugs. "It's nice to see you have friends."

Not the term I'd use to describe Zane. And the term "boyfriend" isn't applicable when we barely talk.

His next response is prompt: *Let me know if you have time.* Apparently, he's going to stay aloof.

Dad steps out to the use the toilet, and Imogene turns to me. "Are you sure you want to come tonight? I know you don't care for the ballet. You don't have to if you don't want to."

Ah, yes. I'd almost forgotten.

Last night, Dad brought out three tickets to the Spring Memorial Ballet Recital in Montpelier—something he "happened" to have. Imogene accepted without hesitation, and I nodded along. The recital's at 7:30; we probably need to get ready.

I shake my head. "He got the tickets for us—even if he said otherwise. He didn't want to look too eager. It'd be rude to stay home."

"Billie." She sighs. "You don't have to go to make him happy. If you don't want to, don't go. You can stay here or go back to the dorms one last night before they lock everything up."

I nod, but it doesn't sit right. Sure, I don't want to go,

but Dad's probably been planning this for weeks.

"Besides, that's Zane texting you, right?" Her face breaks into a grin. "You probably want to see him before he leaves campus."

Heat rises to my cheeks at the implication. I can't say anything. She'd see through any lie.

"Go see him while you can. I'll cover for you."

◆

Zane's response was slow when I told him I had time—Imogene basically threw me out of the house. But eventually, he let me know where his apartment is and to come over when available.

He lives on the far south side of campus in University Park, part of the upperclassmen housing. Although a senior and a prominent member in his fraternity, he doesn't live on Frat Row. That surprises me.

Zane answers the door with a blank face and allows me to enter. He motions me past the minimalist Bradford College decor toward his bedroom. He sits at the desk, where his notepad and calc textbook are already open.

I sit on the bed, hugging my textbook and notes to my chest, but he refuses to look at me. "I'm not sure why I'm here." My eyes wander the room.

The space is small, but the contents are minimal. The bed is opposite the door, and his desk, with shelving and a chair, is pushed against the wall nearby. On the opposite wall is the closet and a small table with a terrarium and heat lamp. That must hold the lizard he got for Christmas.

I turn back to him, but he hasn't moved. "We finished

parametric equations and polar coordinates before the break. We had our test yesterday morning. What more is there to do before classes start again?"

"I thought maybe you could clear up a few things." His voice is low and quiet. He won't look at me. "Some things on the test confused me."

I sigh. "Does it matter? The final won't be cumulative."

Zane clenches his jaw. "What do you care? You're just here to get paid, aren't you?"

My stomach churns, and despite my better judgment, I lean forward. "No, I'm not."

At last, he turns to me. "Then why are you here, Billie?"

"I wanted to see you."

Zane shifts his attention to the objects on his desk and clears his throat, but his previously stiff body relaxes.

I lay down my textbook and notes. "What do you want to look over?"

He clears his throat again and flips through his book. "Uh, it was polar coordinates. I got stuck on a few parts."

I find the chapter in question. "Do you want to work a few problems with me? We can go from there."

With a short nod, Zane grabs his book and notebook and joins me on the bed. He picks out a problem to work on so I can watch his progress.

"You're leaving for home tomorrow?" I'm not very good at waiting.

He nods.

"Driving? How far is it?"

"Four and a half hours," he says, hunched over the page. "I'm good if I remember the formula for parametric equations, right?"

"Yeah." I lean against the headboard and watch from afar. He's slow-going, as always, and his scrawl is hard to read, but he's slowly improving. He hasn't made a mistake yet. "I'm not actually leaving town this week."

His hand stops. "They won't let you stay in the dorms."

"My sister came here for break. We're staying with my dad."

Zane looks up. His pencil drops to the bed. "Wow."

I almost laugh.

"I mean, that's a big step. I'm surprised. How's your sister taking to it? Is she in from Missouri yet?"

"Flew in yesterday afternoon. She's nervous, but she adjusts easily. They're, um, really getting along, happy to catch up." I stare at the ceiling. "I don't really get it."

"Awkward third wheel? Is that why your time magically freed up?"

I shrug. "They're going to the ballet in Montpelier tonight."

He moves the books aside and stretches out beside me. "It'll get easier."

I swallow, but I can't look at him. Mostly because I don't believe him. "This week is going to be the longest week of my life, and it hasn't started yet. How can I live in his house? Even for a week." My last attempt didn't last twenty-four hours.

He shakes his head. "Don't think of it as living there. You're a guest."

With a tentative hand, he directs my face to look at him. I'm conscious of his every movement. Every nervous twitch, the undulation of his breathing, each muscle tremor as he leans closer, the gentle caress of his lips against mine. I'm not surprised, but I watch, unable to move, as he closes his eyes and presses closer.

I pull away slightly and try to lock eyes with him, but I can't go far. The headboard keeps me in place. His every breath reverberates through my eardrums, seeming oddly, unnecessarily loud. At this distance, it's hard to breathe.

He kisses me again and releases my jaw to trail his hand down to my arm. His fingers scrape against my skin, down to my wrist, and he rubs his thumb across my pulse point. He shifts his weight, and his chest falls closer to mine. His body heat radiates through our clothes.

This time, I kiss him back.

It's all the permission he needs. His hand moves to my abdomen and tugs up the hem of my t-shirt, fingers brushing against my bare skin, now revealed. He pulls back from the kiss then, only to trail his mouth down to my neckline, nipping at my collarbone.

I try to keep my breath steady. "We shouldn't do this," I mumble, but I don't stop him when his hand slips up my shirt.

He lifts his face level with mine. "It's whatever you want." But his lips are fierce when he kisses me again.

This is moving too fast.

I hold him by shoulders to slow him down, but he yanks the hem of my shirt over my head and tosses it to the floor.

He pauses to get a good look at me. "We're not in the library right now." One hand gropes my breast over the sports bra, but the other plays with the button of my jeans.

I swallow. Hard. "That doesn't mean we should."

Way too fast. Why is this moving so fast?

He stops moving, his fingers curled around the waist

of my jeans, and leans back. "You're right." But Zane grips and stares at my jeans as if willing them to undo themselves. "We should stop."

When I don't speak—I cannot speak—he pulls me into another kiss, and his fingers yank the button undone.

Weezer's "Troublemaker" blares into the room.

I jump, nearly slamming in the headboard.

"What the hell is that?" Zane's eyes search the room.

"My phone." My voice is hoarse.

I scramble up in search of it. It must've fallen in the tussle. It's on the floor upside-down. I stand with my back to the bed and look at it. I've never been so grateful for a call from Xander before in my life.

Still, it's barely after ten. What does he want?

"What is it?"

"Hello to you too, Dixon." In the background, there are about a million voices, screaming and laughing and yelling, and music blasting. The party.

"What do you need?"

"Are you with your family?" He giggles.

"Are you drunk?"

He snorts. "Of course I'm fucking drunk. It's Friday night and it's spring break. What're you doing?"

"Nothing."

Over the phone, Xander laughs. "You're sober, right?" Then he announces loudly, "Stupid bitch doesn't drink!" He laughs hysterically for a moment before returning to me. "Come on, Dixon, come hang out with us. You should see how wasted Jimmy is. He got drunk all on his own, he's trying to get laid, and I'm alone. Keep me company. I wanna see you. Oh, and can you drive us back to campus? We're on Flint. House party!"

"What makes you think I'm available right now?" I'm only vaguely annoyed.

"Oh, are you, ahem, with someone? Because if you're getting laid, I think you owe me."

I narrow my eyes at the corner near the door. "You have some nerve."

"Whatever you say, Dixon. It's at 1236 E. Flint. You'll need to come for us anyway. You might as well hang out beforehand." I open my mouth, but he says, "Oh, shit. Jim, let's get you to the bathroom."

The call ends.

And then, I remember I'm not alone.

Zane watches curiously as I snatch my shirt off the floor. "I'm sorry, but I have to go." I reach for my jacket next. "Xander and Jimmy need someone to pick them up."

"You don't have a car."

"Yeah, I noticed. I have to go before they decide to drive and kill themselves."

On the bed, Zane sits up and flattens out his shirt. "D'you want me to drive you?"

No, that's the last thing I want right now.

"Don't worry about it." I slip my shoes on, not bothering to tighten the laces, and grab my books off the bed. "Really, it's fine."

He starts to stand, but I'm already halfway out the door.

Twenty-Four

THE HOUSE PARTY ON FLINT IS EASY TO LOCATE, AND IT'S almost eleven when I arrive. I hoped they would be out front, but that wasn't realistic.

Instead, I leave my books on the hood of Xander's car along the street and walk up to the house. The house itself is a small, pale blue, two-story building with a peaked roof. Paint is chipping away in large sections, and most of the windows are single-pane. An old rental house, probably leased to a pair of beer-savvy seniors Xander befriended.

The door swings open at the slightest touch. The music, already loud outside, bursts to life. I step over the threshold, and the crowd surrounds me.

In the living room, all the tattered furniture is pushed to the walls to make room for the guests. A small group sits on one corner of a couch, singing along with the music, while a couple makes out on the other half. Plenty of people are dancing, grinding against each other. At the bottom of the stairs, people take shots from a clear bottle, and in the distance, someone's doing a keg stand. Several strobe lights flash in sync, and I rub my temple. I'm going to have a headache, and I'm not even drunk.

236

But Xander and Jimmy are nowhere in sight.

I weave from room to room, in and out and between people, but no one looks familiar. Then, I remember Xander's words as he hung up on me: *Jim, let's get you to the bathroom.*

Where the hell is the bathroom?

In an off-shoot of the kitchen, by the back door, a small door leads to the tiniest of bathrooms. I knock several times without answer before pushing it open.

Xander's face shifts from concern to excitement when he sees me. "You're here." His grin spreads from ear to ear, and he nudges Jimmy with his elbow. "See, I told you she wouldn't bail on us."

Face pressed against the seat of the toilet, Jimmy squints up at me, trying to see anything beyond my general form. His glasses quiver on the edge of the pedestal sink. He doesn't say anything, but his beet-red face is moist with sweat.

"I'm glad you didn't run off somewhere." I hold my hand out for Xander's keys. "I'd have to stay and get drunk to not make it a wasted trip."

Xander sifts through his pockets before tossing the keys at me. His aim is normally impeccable, but he misses by over a foot.

"Can we go?"

Jimmy pushes his head off the seat and vomits into the bowl, and Xander pats him more forcefully than necessary. "I don't want him ralphing in my car."

I lean against the door frame, clutching the keys in my fist. "Jesus, how much did you let him drink?"

Jimmy finishes and leans back to pull the lever. He wipes

his mouth on his wrist and, with the other hand, grabs his glasses. "Let's go." The words are barely understandable, but he pushes himself to his feet and stumbles toward me.

Xander and I guide him through the house and to the car.

◆

"Hey, you didn't stop at Taco Bell."

I turn away from Jimmy's half-conscious form slumped against the elevator wall to find Xander pouting by the button panel. He pushes the large number four with his thumb, and the doors close. Jimmy slides as the elevator car starts to move, and I grab him by the collar before he hits the floor. Xander cackles in the opposite corner.

"You said you wanted to get back to campus fast," I remind him, and his laughter stops.

"But I'm hungry." His pout returns. "Come on, Dixon, don't you have anything I can eat?"

I raise an eyebrow. "Do you always turn twelve years old when you're drunk?"

He scowls, and the elevator stops at the fourth floor. "Better than being a ball of anger and hatred and woe-is-me."

When the doors open, I hook my arm under Jimmy and drag him toward their room. Xander's attempts to help are more of a hindrance than anything else. He takes hold of Jimmy's arm and leads the way with a bounce in his step, but it takes him five attempts to unlock the door.

Inside, I lay Jimmy on his bed and remove his shoes. He barely looks at me as I tuck him in, and by the time I return with Xander's popcorn bowl and a glass of water, he's asleep.

"Well," I say, turning around, "I guess I'll let you get to sleep."

But Xander is too busy raiding the mini-fridge to hear me. "Dammit." He pulls back. "All we have is Coke. I don't even like Coke." He slams the door shut and crosses his arms over his chest. "Why's there no fucking food in this place?"

I roll my eyes. "Perhaps because it's spring break. There's no point in having food in a dorm you won't be in for eight days."

He spins round and bounds toward me, a grin on his face. "Dixon, you'll take me to get food! Let's go to the store." He grabs my hands and holds them to his heart. "Please."

With a laugh, I tug away. "Yeah, let's definitely take the openly drunk, underage moron to the store to buy munchies."

He frowns but steps closer, pulling his wallet from his back pocket. "Okay, then you go." He offers me a ten-dollar bill. "Get me something yummy."

I snort. "If I leave, I'm not coming back."

The pout is back. "Fine." He shoves the bill back inside and deposits the wallet on his nightstand, then collapses on his bed. For a moment, he lies there, arms stretched out in both directions, one leg over the edge, and stares at the ceiling. "Then stay."

I bite my lip but take a few steps closer. "Why would I do that?"

He pushes up into a sitting position and yanks his shirt over his head. I'm too busy staring to complain as it grazes me on the way to the floor. "Because, I don't want you to leave."

239

"Since when do I do anything because you want me to?" But I sit down and drop my jacket on the mini-fridge.

Xander grins. "You're staying." He jumps off and drops to his hands and knees. One arm extends under the recesses of his bed and withdraws a half-empty bottle of whiskey. "Let's have fun."

"You can't be serious."

He shakes the bottle in front of my nose as if to entice me and sits again, this time dragging me up against the wall beside him. "Come on, Dixon." He uncaps the bottle. "When was the last time you had a drink? You never drink with us."

I glance across the room, where Jimmy is starting to snore. This hardly constitutes as an "us."

"You're already drunk. You don't need more."

Defiantly, Xander takes a big slurp, staring at me. He's paying so much attention to me half his drink dribbles down his bare chest, and I stifle a laugh.

I take the bottle from his grasp, chuckling. "You're too drunk for this, idiot."

"Only if you drink too."

I sniff the bottle suspiciously.

"Otherwise, I'm taking it back."

With a roll of my eyes, I sip the foul-smelling liquid. When the whiskey hits the back of my throat, I gag and shove the bottle into his hands, coughing. "Oh, God, that burns." My voice is raw.

Beside me, Xander collapses in hysterical laughter before taking another drink. "But it's a good burn."

I'm more prepared for my second drink.

Xander holds the bottle on his lap, one hand loosely

gripping the neck, the other resting on his leg. "What'd we interrupt tonight? You said you weren't with your family. What were you doing?"

Zane—and where that make-out session was heading—is the last thing I want to discuss.

"Nothing special."

He pouts again and takes another drink. "Then why didn't you come with us? You never party with us. I wish you came out once in a while."

I raise an eyebrow. "I didn't think you'd want me there."

He releases a long sigh, and his head slides down to rest on my shoulder. "Maybe if you had fun, spending time with you wouldn't be exhausting."

I shrug him off, and he bumps his head against the wall and grumbles. "So sorry I'm such an inconvenience." I snatch the bottle from his hands and take a gulp, ignoring the burning sensation in my throat. "Would you prefer I pretend everything is perfect just for you?"

He leans close. "Yeah, putting up another barrier between yourself and reality is definitely the solution. Besides, since when do you care what I think?" The alcohol on his breath is overpowering, but there are other enticing things about his mouth.

I look down. "I don't. Do you not understand sarcasm when you're trashed?"

"I do. I also understand you use sarcasm to say the truth with plausible deniability. I can only assume you do care what I think."

I frown. My grip tightens on the whiskey. That's not true.

Xander presses his fingers over mine—he wants the bottle back. "It's nice to know you care about something,

Dixon," he says in that stupid smug voice of his.

I pull away. "I care about a lot of things, thank you."

When he laughs, his hold on the bottle loosens, and his hand falls to rest on my leg. "What do you care about then? Grades, being in control, looking like you know everything?" His thumb rubs a small circle on my thigh.

Goosebumps spread across my skin. My breath is short. I can't focus.

"None of that matters."

I push him away. "What does matter, since you know everything?" He's too close.

He grabs the bottle again and takes a long drink. "That's different for everyone."

"Then how can you sit there and preach at me? How can you tell me everything I do is wrong?" My voice rises, and on the other side of the room, Jimmy twitches.

Xander narrows his eyes. "Because it makes you miserable." He shoves the bottle into my hands and pulls his legs up. "You don't do anything for yourself. You do things because it's what you think other people want, what you're supposed to do. If you never do anything for yourself, you're going to be unhappy for the rest of your life. No one deserves that." He scoffs. "Not even you, Dixon."

The muscle in my jaw quivers. "How would you know? You never do anything for anyone else. You're independent to a fault—selfish." I cast my gaze toward Jimmy, who's blissfully unaware and snoring. "He defends you constantly, but you don't care about anyone but yourself."

"God, you're an idiot." He turns away.

I drink deep from the bottle. It's probably too much, but I don't care. I need something—anything—to distract me. I don't want to think about this conversation. Or what almost happened with Zane tonight. And I definitely don't want to think about the drunk, half-naked, and oddly affectionate man on this bed with me. The last time we were here, we had sex.

Yeah, I definitely shouldn't think about that.

My stomach churns, and I press my bun against the wall and shut my eyes. This is definitely too much.

Xander shifts closer to me. Our arms brush, bare skin to bare skin. When he speaks, his voice has lost its edge. "You know I don't hate you, right?" He clears his throat. "Don't get me wrong, you aggravate me plenty. You're angry and frustrating and you always think you're right, but I've never hated you."

God, I do not want to have this conversation.

"You're incredibly blind. You miss so much because you're caught up in your problems. You've lost a lot of opportunities because of that." His hand finds mine, and he threads our fingers together. "I wish you could see what everyone else sees."

I swallow, but my throat is dry. "What does everyone else see?"

"You're more than math and analytics. You're more than computations and codes. You're more than your parents' divorce. You're more than this anger festering inside you."

Finally, I open my eyes. He stares at me with a striking intensity. Will he kiss me? Do I want him to kiss me?

"Then what am I?" I whisper.

He squeezes my hand and smiles. "That's for you to decide, Dixon. Choose wisely."

I snort and slip my hand free. "What is this, a *Choose*

243

Your Own Adventure book?"

He grins.

"Well, for the record, I don't hate you either." I take another drink.

His smile acquires a certain smugness unique to Xander. "I know. I mean, how could you? No one hates me. I'm incredibly lovable."

I shove him, rolling my eyes, and he falls on the pillow. "I don't think 'lovable' is the way I'd describe you, asshat."

"Nonsense." He yanks me down on top of him, and I struggle not to spill the whiskey. When I roll off, his arm hooks underneath me, and the whiskey settles in the space between us. He rests his free hand on my hip in a position that's all too familiar. "You know I'm plotting against you, right?"

My breath hitches. "You are?"

He smirks. "When I get my hands on your sketchbooks, I'm going to look at every last drawing. I've wanted to see them for months."

That's not what I thought he would say. I'm almost disappointed.

I scoot away, and his hand grazes my abdomen as it falls between us. I understand now why he lost his shirt earlier—I'm melting from the heat. "That's personal."

"Is that why you keep them secret? I thought it had more to do with your subject matter." His face transforms with glee. "Seriously, when I find those naked drawings of me, you're never going to live it down."

I roll my eyes. "You're so conceited. You're never seeing my sketchbooks."

"Never say never. Words to live by." He grabs the bottle

from my grip and takes down several big gulps in a row.

"Don't chug it, you moron!" I snatch it away. "You're drunk enough. I don't want to deal with you like that." I point my thumb over my shoulder toward Jimmy's bed.

Xander giggles. "I'm not a complete amateur."

I twist round to look at the sleeping figure in the other bed. "Why did you let him get drunk? I thought you were saving that for Mexico."

Xander pushes up on one elbow, giving me the perfect view. For a moment, he sounds sober. "He was really upset about something all day. Maybe Cynthia. I turned around, and he was drunk already."

"Well, you're not the best example. Why do you have to drink all the time?"

He raises an eyebrow. "And why do you never drink?"

"You might recall how bad it was the one time I got drunk." I don't want to admit it, but I was a mess that night.

He shrugs. "It could've been worse. Sometimes, you need to vent."

I try not to laugh. "'Could've been worse'? If I recall correctly, you basically told me I should die."

For a moment, he won't look at me. Then, he scoots closer. The bottle presses between our stomachs, and he meets my eyes. "Obviously, that was a stupid thing to say, and I didn't mean it."

A shaky breath, and I fan myself. I'm overheating.

"I know I give you a lot of shit, and if any of it made you see a new perspective, I'm glad—but some of it was downright awful. Honestly, I think you're pretty great." He lets out a long sigh and lies back, staring at the ceiling again. "Seriously, Dixon, I want to see your artwork. You're really good, I know you are. In that ridiculously realistic and precise sort of way. I don't think you know how to let go even with the one thing that lets you let go."

The compliment, silly and rambling, turns my stomach, and I take a drink—for nerves. "I'm not as drunk as I need to be for this conversation." I take another gulp.

He shifts his gaze to me again. "Maybe you should slow down, Dixon."

"I'm fine." But I grope around the bed for the lid and set the bottle on his nightstand, fully capped.

He snakes his arm around me and pulls me against his bare chest. Everything moves too fast. I close my eyes in an attempt to slow things down, but my head spins. Xander's arm, draped casually around my shoulder, is constricting. I should've slowed down.

"Where are my cigs?" He finds the pack inside the jeans pocket closest to me and makes a few failed attempts to retrieve them. At last, he turns to me with puppy-dog eyes. "Can you get them?" His breath brushes my lips.

My thin fingers slip inside his pocket and pull out the pack, then the Zippo lighter beneath them. I drop them on his chest.

"You want one?" He offers me the open-top pack, a cigarette already dangling from his mouth.

With a second's hesitation, I snatch a stick from within, and he tosses the box toward our feet before grabbing the Zippo. He lights his cigarette, then mine, and I take a small puff. Shouldn't we crack the window? There's a smoke alarm in here.

"You have to inhale if you want anything out of it." He demonstrates by inhaling deeply, his lungs expanding next to me, ribs pressing flush against my side. A cloud of smoke hovers above us when he exhales, and it dissipates. This is definitely against the rules.

"I don't think I'm ready for that." I take another tiny puff.

"I'm going to have to finish that for you, aren't I?"

I don't have to say anything; we both know it's true.

"So, Dixon," he says conversationally, "how often do you draw me? You spend most of your evenings in this room, and there isn't much to look at. Unless you're drawing from your imagination. Or maybe your memory." He pauses for effect. "I know you think about me naked. There's no way you haven't put it to paper."

My snort transforms into a full laugh, and I elbow him in the side. "I'd have to want to put that image to paper. I'm trying to forget what you look like naked—I don't want to immortalize it."

He smiles. "I like hearing you laugh. It doesn't happen often enough."

I am hot everywhere. I'm blushing. My body pulses with energy.

Then, I clear my throat, trying to get a hold on myself again. "Why don't you think I have fun? I laugh all the time."

Xander snorts and takes another drag. "You really don't. I'm not sure you know how to have fun."

I purse my lips. "Yeah, well, we don't exactly think the same things are fun. Should I get drunk every weekend? Play video games instead of studying? Sleep with all the guys in our hallway? Would that convince you I know how to have fun?"

"That's not fair." He pokes me in the ribs. "I haven't slept with every girl in our hallway—Ruby Prescott's a lesbian, and Jimmy would die if I slept with Cynthia."

I almost laugh. That means he's slept with three-quarters of our section of Lincoln Hall—and a number of other students.

"Besides, doing those things isn't what makes it fun. You only spend time with me and Jimmy because you're scared to be alone. You barely talk to us, and good luck getting you to hang out outside this building. You have to have friends for any of those things to be fun."

I have an intense urge to put the cigarette out on his chest. Instead, I sit up and face the expanse of the room. It takes a moment to make sure I'm not going to fall over.

But Xander continues. "Seriously, have you made any friends in the last seven months? The only person you willingly spend time with is that slob over there, but you already knew him. You can't have a normal conversation with your dad without having a panic attack, and you two used to be inseparable. Can you have a normal conversation with anyone?"

I glare at the unconscious person on the other side of the room. "Jimmy sure has a big fucking mouth."

"To be fair, I interrogate him."

I turn round and hand him the half-gone cigarette. "I need to go. Have a good night."

But before I can stand, Xander catches my wrist. "Don't bail because we're having a serious conversation. You don't get off that easily." He smears both cigarettes against the wall and tosses them toward the wastebasket by the desk. "You take everything personally."

I glare. "You make everything personal. My life isn't on display for you to judge."

He releases my wrist and holds my hand again. "You never take chances. You never risk anything. The entire time you've been here, you hide in the shadows and hope nobody notices you. And it isn't because you're self-conscious or shy or think you're better than everybody. It's because you don't trust anyone—not even yourself." We're hip to hip, side to side. "If you trust yourself, you can do anything."

It takes a second to find my voice. "I think you've had too many therapy sessions, Xander."

His lips curl up into a smile. "You have no idea."

"I should really go." I pull away, and hesitantly, he releases me. "It's late, and I might be able to sleep now I've been dosed with alcohol." I push myself to my feet but fall back down.

"You should stay."

I turn to him in surprise. "Here? In this bed?" His meandering eyes meet mine, and I bite my lip. "You want me to stay the night with you."

He shakes his head. "I mean, I wouldn't argue." He quirks a smile. "I can sleep on the floor if you'd prefer. Just don't walk all the way back to your dad's. You've had too much to drink."

Falling back down on the bed made that quite clear, but I pull my keys from my pocket. "You know I have my own room across the hall, right?"

"Oh." He furrows his brow and looks at the door. "Right."

I clear my throat and look away. "Thanks, though—for the offer." I try to stand again, this time successfully, and turn to bid him goodnight.

He looks at me with dilated eyes. "Should I walk you?"

I rest a hand on the footboard to steady myself. I must be heady from the alcohol. There's nothing about him that makes any sense. "No, thanks." I grab my jacket from the mini-fridge and excuse myself.

Xander watches as I close the door, an odd dazed look on his face.

Twenty-Five

It's strange to be in this room again, considering how poorly my last attempt worked out. The room is the same: Full bed, beautifully organized decor, the Matisse painting, the alarm clock with bright-red numbers, the frame on the dresser. But this time, the circumstances are different. This time, I have Mo.

I brought the last of my things when I arrived this morning, far more hung over than I was willing to admit.

I pause at the foot of the bed. My stomach is unhappy, but it's the idea of being here, in this room, in this house, that causes me unease. It's getting dark outside, but I'm still unpacking.

The bed is covered in textbooks, notebooks, my laptop, sketchbooks, and an array of writing and drawing utensils. The clothes are in my backpack, though it's not like I need much for a week.

I lay my backpack on the dresser. The bottom drawers have extra blankets, but the other four are empty, and I dump the contents into one of the larger middle drawers and drop the backpack on the floor.

My reflection is tired—made worse by however much

whiskey I drank last night thanks to that idiot—and I remove my hair tie. The mass of corkscrew curls cascades past my shoulders, a halo of frizz poking out now it has freedom. I run my fingers through it.

On the mattress, my phone buzzes. I drop the hair tie on the dresser and return to the bed. *I'm safe back in Auburn,* Zane's message says when I open it. *How's your family stuff?*

Could be worse, I text back. After all, I could be downstairs with them.

I don't even bother to put the phone down. His response is prompt, per usual: *I hope it gets better. I miss you.*

So we're back to this.

I'm not sure what he's expecting from me—surely not reciprocation, even after my obscure display of affection last night. That was a bad idea.

Instead, I drop the phone and lean over the bag I packed this morning. A few last-minute items. Some extra pajamas, the book Mo gave me for Christmas, my note cards for history class, and the letter.

I brought it on a whim. Even now, it sits at the dark bottom of the bag, waiting. When I pull it out, it's more worn and pathetic than at Christmas. I don't know why I brought it back to Bradford or here to Dad's house. It doesn't mean anything anymore. It's a stupid piece of paper.

Still, I hold it in a tight grip, and my eyes scan the plaintext, seeking out the true meaning. The code is simple, but like all codes, only if you're looking for it.

Dear Dad,

I'm sorry. I don't know what I did wrong. Please come home. I miss you.

Mina

I can't believe how naive I was.

I cross the room to the dresser and flatten the paper on the hard surface. My eyes flit away, searching for anything else to look at instead of those scribbled words.

What they land on is worse—the picture frame, inside which is a photo I don't recognize. Mom got rid of most photos of Dad four months after the divorce went through, at the start of my sophomore year of high school, even the ones like this. The ones with me.

I lift the frame for a better look and lean against the dresser. I had to be eleven or twelve because that's my first pair of glasses, and there's Dad, kneeling beside me, an arm around my shoulder, grinning. He doesn't smile like that anymore. Hell, neither do I.

Was this picture here at Christmas? Has it been here the entire time? Are there others around the house I somehow missed? Did Imogene know? Are there photos of her somewhere?

A knock sounds on the door.

I jump, almost dropping the frame.

Imogene pokes her head in. "How're you doing?" She raises an eyebrow at the sight of me. "Are you going to do something with your hair? I could put it up."

I return the picture frame to the dresser and peek at my reflection again. "It definitely needs something." I offer her the hair tie.

"Sit down by the bed." She grabs some bobby pins from my toiletry bag, sits on the mattress behind me, and combs her fingers through my hair. Then, she pauses. "How do you want me to do this?"

I shrug. "I don't care. Something that doesn't take very

long."

She releases a short laugh and resumes her work. "I'll just do a quick updo now. We can moisturize the next couple days and braid it. You settled in? You've been in here a while now."

I glance around, making sure not to move my head. My view here is limited; I can see the door, one nightstand, and the edge of the dresser, but I know I'm nowhere near settled. "I guess I'm trying to figure out how."

"I know." Mo's voice is soft and understanding—or at least she's trying to be. "It'll get easier, you know. You have to keep trying." She pauses in the middle of flat-twisting around my crown. "I know you want to be here."

"You have more confidence in me than I deserve." I rest my chin on my forearm and close my eyes. "But that's one of my favorite things about you, Mo. You always believe in me no matter how stupidly I behave."

"It helps you don't tell me any of the stupid things you do." She lets out a short laugh. "Do you feel better?"

Right. Terrible hangover this morning.

I nod. "Thanks for making sure I ate something."

"Did your evening with Zane turn into getting drunk and having mad, passionate sex?"

I try to turn back, but she holds my head still and twists the thick hair into a bun, which she secures with a couple pins. Instead, I say, "Don't talk like that. You're a child."

Imogene snorts and switches to the other side of my head. "I'm sixteen, Billie. I'm not a child anymore." She doesn't give me the chance to respond. "I was teasing you… though I am curious."

I frown. "No, I didn't have mad, passionate sex—or any

kind of sex—last night. We didn't even drink."

Zane's actions said he wanted sex, but frankly, that part of the evening isn't the memory burned onto my brain. Somehow, talking to and drunkenly cuddling Xander left me feeling far more naked than Zane's attempts to unclothe me.

"Then why did you come back hung over this morning?" I try to protest, but she interrupts. "Don't lie to me, Billie. You were definitely hung over."

I hesitate. "Are you mad at me?"

She makes a short humming sound. "Mom isn't here to see or smell you." She shrugs. "Besides, drinking is a pretty normal part of college from what I understand."

"I wasn't drinking with Zane. I wasn't there that long."

"Who were you drinking with?"

I almost don't want to admit it, but I have nothing to hide. It's not a secret. I wasn't cheating. Nothing sexual even happened with Xander.

Still, something about the idea of me being alone and drinking with Xander feels strange, uncomfortable, even surreal.

I heave a long sigh. "I was with Xander. And Jimmy, though he was mostly unconscious."

Imogene places a hand on my shoulder. "Really?"

"Why do you say it like that? They needed someone to drive them back to the dorms 'cause they were drunk. It wasn't a big deal."

She leans closer. "I wasn't accusing you of anything. It's perfectly reasonable for you to drop everything to pick up your drunk best friend."

"Yes, perfectly reasonable."

She sits back and resumes twisting. "What's less reasonable is you getting drunk and staying the night with Xander while Jimmy's passed out. I am right in assuming that was after you got them back to their room, right?"

"I didn't stay the night."

At last, she wraps the second section of twisted hair around the bun and pushes in more bobby pins. "Oh, sure, of course you didn't." She releases me, and I turn around to look at her.

"Finally." I scoot farther away. "What took you so long?"

Her smile widens. "I've been done for ages. Even your afro doesn't take that long."

I scowl. "You wanted to interrogate me."

"I have to live vicariously since I'm away from home." She shrugs. "And you've got this whole secret love triangle thing going."

I freeze. "What the hell are you talking about?"

She stands and takes a few steps toward the door. "Now, come on, let's go downstairs."

I reach for one of my books. "Why, so you can vicariously study for my history class?"

Imogene takes hold of me before I can grab anything. "No, Billie. You don't have classes for a week. We're working on a puzzle, and you're joining us. You used to love puzzles." She leads me by the hand out the door and downstairs.

"I also used to be a little kid." But I follow her anyway. "Rennold assigned a lot of reading for the break."

"You can do that later. We don't often get to spend time together, the three of us."

We reach the bottom of the stairs, and Mo turns left to the dining room. There's a reason it isn't often, but I can't deny her this small pleasure.

In the dining room, we sit on the side opposite Dad, and Imogene starts examining the jigsaw pieces spread across the table. It's one of Charles Wysocki's all-American paintings. On the other side of the table, Dad is crouched over his section, expertly hooking together pieces. He looks up as we sit down.

For the first time since I started at Bradford, he genuinely looks happy. His normally worn, cool-umber face is now a warm sepia, years younger with a smile spread across its features.

"Should I put the kettle on?" Without receiving anything more than a nod, he disappears into the kitchen, humming as he walks.

Imogene turns to me with a smile. "I don't know how long it's been since I've been this happy," she says in a conspiratorial voice. "This isn't that bad, is it?"

Try as I might, I can't be mad at her.

"No, of course not."

"Now if only I could get you to smile too."

Xander's face, drunk and uncharacteristically kind, flashes before my eyes, and a jolt of unease passes through my body.

"I smile all the time." I turn to the puzzle.

The pumpkin patch in the foreground has barely been outlined. I sift through the pieces for any bits of orange to fit together. The table beneath is covered in dust, and I brush the fibers away as I work.

"What did you mean before?"

She doesn't look up. "When?"

257

"'Secret love triangle'—what does that mean?"

Imogene laughs. "Right. Sometimes I forget how out of touch with reality you are."

I shake my head. "It doesn't matter how out of touch I may or may not be, there's no reality in which I'm part of a love triangle. This isn't one of your books."

She laughs. "No, you're missing a few key elements."

"Like a love triangle?"

"You need to learn archery," she says matter-of-factly. "Then, halfway through, you discover the guys are werewolves or demons or brothers, and no matter how hard you try, you can't choose."

I sigh. "Can we have a serious conversation about this? Or are you going to remain aloof?"

Imogene laughs and locks eyes with me. "Okay, Billie. Seriously—" she stresses the word "—I specifically said 'secret' because you're unaware."

"Look, if this is about Zane. I don't know what you've heard from Jimmy, but—"

"He really likes you, and you don't even try. And it's kinda cute you met because he needed a tutor, so he knows you're smart and capable, and he's not intimidated." She hooks in another puzzle piece.

Dad returns with a steaming pot of raspberry green tea and three matching mugs from the bi-annual campus pottery sale. He passes the tea around before returning to his section of the puzzle.

Imogene continues after the pause. "And he should be intimidated. You're really smart, and you don't take crap from anyone."

My gaze shifts to our dad, who's pretending not to pay

attention. "I'm not that smart."

She laughs. "It's not like you to be modest, Billie. Being smart isn't a bad thing. Besides, Jimmy sent me a picture—he's cute."

I frown. "Why would he do that?"

"I asked him to. He sent me a link to his profile." She cocks her head. "I didn't think you'd be that interested in a frat boy, though, but close proximity and all that. How do you keep your professional and romantic lives separate? Tutoring him has to be weird now you're—I don't know, are you dating?"

Across the table, Dad stiffens.

"No, no." I drop the puzzle piece in my hand. "We're definitely not doing that."

Imogene pauses. "Are you embarrassed?"

"There's nothing to be embarrassed of."

"But Jimmy made it sound like you and Zane were—"

Dad looks up, his eyes calculating, and speaks in a quiet, steady voice. "Nelson?"

I freeze, my hand resting on the table edge, and stare at the two pieces I was about to connect.

"Zane Nelson." There's a finality to his words. "You're dating Zane Nelson."

"No, I just tutor him. We're not even friends."

Beside me, Imogene silently picks up her mug and takes a long drink.

"He wouldn't have gotten into my class without your tutelage last semester." Dad's voice is firm, accusatory.

I shrug. "That's what he paid me for."

"You have feelings for him."

I take a breath and lift my eyes to meet his. I can't deny

it. It's not even a question. This isn't a discussion.

"He's three years your senior and graduating in eight weeks. He won't stay if that's what you think. There's nothing here for him." He pauses before adding in a hushed tone, "He's not smart enough for you, Mina."

The tea, when I take a drink, is hot but no longer scalding, and I hold the mug close. "We're not together. There's nothing to be concerned about."

He returns his attention to the puzzle, and Imogene changes the subject.

Twenty-Six

"WHAT DO YOU WANT, MINA?"

I barely glance at the Jittery Bug's menu before requesting a latte. Imogene orders a glass of fresh-squeezed lemonade, and Dad pulls out his wallet.

"You don't have to pay for everything."

But he ignores me.

It doesn't matter. He's paid for everything we've eaten or seen or done in the past five days. Any offer to help is ignored.

Imogene and I settle into a booth, and Dad joins us after paying. The drinks arrive shortly.

"I can buy my own stuff." I swirl the tiny black straw through the foam and nudge a micro-braids behind my ear. Mo spent yesterday putting them in.

"You know there's an art gallery downtown." Dad glances at Imogene. "It's quite nice for a little town. They sometimes showcase Bradford students' artwork."

A smile lights up her face. "That sounds like a fantastic idea." She sends me a grin. "You been there, Billie? They probably can't keep you away."

I honestly didn't know it existed. I shake my head.

Surprise flashes across her face. "Really? You haven't gone to see your competition? You know, it'd be great to see what they're displaying in case you have the inclination—"

"I don't."

She frowns, confused by my short tone, but keeps her mouth shut.

"Dad," I say, eager to change the subject, "what are plans for lunch?"

He turns, suspicious. "You're hungry already?"

"Uh, yeah."

I've eaten more in the past five days than the previous month combined. Having every meal at my dad's house means I have to eat—to keep up appearances.

"Well, should we have a snack here before heading to the gallery? Then, we can do lunch afterward without feeling pressed for time." He smiles. "Shall I get a few pastries?"

I nod, and Imogene agrees. Dad goes to look at their baked goods.

Imogene turns to me as soon as he's gone. "What is your problem?"

"What do you mean?"

"You were glaring at me. Because I suggested you might be interested in displaying your artwork." She pauses and casts a glance toward Dad, waiting in line to order again. "Does he not know you draw? How can you keep it from him? I mean, really, how do you manage? You draw all the time."

"I don't draw that much. Not with all the schoolwork and math tutoring."

Dad reaches the register and begins his order.

"Billie, why would you hide that from him? He'd be

262

happy you're doing something that brings you joy." Imogene sips her lemonade and scoots closer. "Seriously, he wouldn't be upset you're not doing math twenty-four-seven. That's ridiculous."

I shake my head. "I'm not being ridiculous, Mo. I want to keep these things separate."

She sighs. "I know you're trying really hard, but hiding things from him isn't going to make this easier. You shouldn't keep secret such an important part of yourself."

"I'm not keeping it secret."

"No matter how you word it, you're hiding it from him."

Dad places a plate of five scones on the table. "Cinnamon, orange, blueberry, vanilla, and lemon. I wasn't sure which you'd like."

"Thanks." I grab the orange scone.

Imogene grabs one. "Tonight's the last part of *Pride & Prejudice*, so we have to eat dinner fast. It starts at 6:30."

I roll my eyes. "Not another night of Colin Firth. You know he's super old now, right?"

She laughs. "Yeah, well, he was beautiful when it was filmed."

Her smiles are infectious.

◆

Outside, it's already dark, but the overhead light brightens the bedroom. It's my last night here, but I've only just settled into the rhythm of things.

"Everything alright? How's staying at your dad's?" Jimmy asks.

Downstairs, Dad and Mo are preparing a fancy dinner

for our last meal together. Meanwhile, I'm up here.

I switch to the speaker and set the phone on the nightstand. "How's your trip?" I lie back on the bed with my Aristotle text for Honors, an uncapped green highlighter in my hand.

For a second, Jimmy doesn't say a thing. Then, he hums thoughtfully. "It's been eventful." Immediately, the excitement is apparent in his voice. "The beach is beautiful. I've never swum this much—not even in my parents' pool. Xander went scuba diving yesterday."

I press highlighter to paper to stress a paragraph and turn the page. "You mean you remember it? It hasn't been an endless stream of drunken shenanigans?"

Jimmy's laughter crackles through the speaker. "Honestly, no. We had drinks for the first time last night." He pauses, and I scan the page. "The first couple days, I didn't want to go near the stuff. Seriously, never let me drink that much again."

"That requires me to be there when you guys party." I dog-ear the page and close the book. "That seems unlikely."

"You wouldn't have to drink, but you should come out with us. Xander…" But he trails off.

I swallow. "There's a difference between having a glass of wine and getting trashed. Speaking of getting trashed, you said 'we.' Is Xander not drinking every night while it's legal and he doesn't have class in the morning?"

"He doesn't want to spoil the fun by being hung over."

I frown. That doesn't sound like Xander at all.

"What's going on there now, Billie?" On his side of the line, a sliding door closes. Liquid pours into a glass. Jimmy takes a drink.

I move Aristotle farther away and pick up the phone again. "Mo's flight is tomorrow afternoon, so they're cooking a big special dinner." I roll my eyes as I turn off the speaker. "At this point, I'm trying to survive the last twenty-four hours."

"I'm sure you're doing fine." But he pauses. "You are doing fine, right?"

"Yeah, I guess." My gaze settles on the crumpled sheets. "Oh, I discovered I got ripped off. Imogene has the better room." Not because of that stupid photograph. "It has the bigger bed. Hers is a queen, but this is only a full."

"Sneaky."

I laugh. "Not that it matters. Still way better than the shitty twins in the dorms."

He chuckles. "Have you heard from Zane?"

Right. He was too drunk to discuss my little lapse in judgment in Zane's bedroom. He still thinks the guy's mad at me.

"Uh, yeah. I'm not sure where we stand, but we're talking. He's texting me again."

"And that's, what, good?"

I guess.

For a moment, Jimmy doesn't speak. "I'm sorry it took me so long to call. We've been busy." He lets out a small chuckle. "I've been distracted."

"It's fine." Although, this is the longest time we've spent apart in years. "I've been busy too. There's a lot going on."

"Actually, Xander, uh, asked me how you recovered." His voice quivers. "Did something happen I don't know about?"

I sigh. When it comes to Xander, there's a lot of things Jimmy doesn't know about. That unfortunate drinking session is hardly the first secret. "Trust me, you didn't miss much. But you can tell him I'm fine if you must." To be fair, I'm impressed Xander remembers he got me drunk.

"He also wanted me to ask if you're having fun yet."

I scowl. His memory is better than I give him credit for. "If he wants to talk to me, put him on the fucking phone. Don't be a go-between."

Jimmy laughs. "That's exactly what I told him. He declined."

My jaw tightens, and I stand. "Is he there?"

There's a long pause on the other line, then Jimmy says, "He's getting out of the shower."

"Give him the phone. Now."

Jimmy groans, and for a minute, they bicker in the background. Finally, Jimmy returns, saying, "Here he is," and hands off the phone.

"What?" When Xander speaks, his voice is an irritated grumble, but he quickly relaxes. "Couldn't wait to talk to me till tomorrow?"

I pace the room. "Naturally. I miss you so much I desperately need to talk to you the second you're available. It doesn't matter if he had to drag you out of the shower by your hair."

"I knew you think about me naked."

I snort. "Really? That's all you glean from what I said?"

In the background, a door closes. His words are muffled. "To what do I owe the pleasure, Dixon? And can we make this quick? We do have plans."

"Listen, if you want to mock me, do it to my face—don't send Jimmy to do it for you."

"When was I mocking you?" He pauses, considering.

"Recently, I mean."

"You know exactly what I'm talking about, Xander. Don't be a dick through him because you won't pick up the phone to be a dick yourself."

For a moment, he's silent, and I stop beside the footboard. Then, he clears his throat. "You want me to call you?"

I lean against the bed. That's not exactly what I meant. "If it means you won't send veiled sexual comments through my best friend, I guess I could handle it."

Xander's laughter echoes through the earpiece. "I don't think I said anything sexual."

"This time."

"Fair enough." He releases a quiet laugh, and a mattress squeaks as he settles on a bed. "What are you doing right now?"

I shrug. "Waiting for dinner. We're having baked salmon. When is your flight tomorrow?"

He sighs. "Early morning. Six-hour flight, plus some layover in Miami and Philadelphia. We'll be back on campus by four, probably earlier."

Right around the time Imogene has to leave for the airport.

The mattress squeaks again, and his low voice sends a tremor through my body. "Aren't you going to ask what I'm doing right now? It would be the polite thing to do, since I asked you."

I slump back on the bed, feet brushing the floor, one arm stretched above my head. "I can use my imagination."

When I close my eyes, I can see him—naked and sweaty. He stands by the light switch, his cock hard even though he already came, and he studies me. He wants me again.

I release a shuddering sigh. Sometimes, my imagination works overtime.

Xander laughs. "I'm sure you can."

If he were here now, alone in this bedroom, would he want me again?

His amused tone turns somber. "You should've come with us. I know you had this thing with your sister, but it would've been nice." He lets out a humorless laugh. "Like you'd drop all your plans because I say so, though, right?"

I frown and move my arm to play with the drawstring on my pajama pants. "Are you drunk right now?"

He laughs again. This time, it sounds genuine. "Can't go out till after I've gotten off my ass and put on more than a towel."

"Oh." Heat rises to my cheeks, and I sit up. "Sorry, I didn't realize you were—you know, indisposed. I figured you already got dressed. It took so long for Jimmy to put you on. I'll let you go, and uh, I'll see you tomorrow, right? Right."

For a minute, his loud laughter is the only sound. "It's nice to know I can make you uncomfortable without trying." He chuckles one last time. "Anyway, I'll leave you with that particular mental image till tomorrow. Goodnight, Dixon. Try to get some sleep."

"Night, Xander."

When I hang up, I press the phone to my chest and collapse on the mattress. I am uncomfortably wet.

I probably should've said goodbye to Jimmy, but Xander is a fierce distraction. I can't tell whether he grates my nerves more now or at the beginning of the school year—because something is different.

Now, we're friends.

A knock echoes through the wood door, and Imogene pokes her head inside. "Hey, food's almost ready. You coming down?"

I force myself off the bed. "Yeah, no problem."

She must've been baking because she's wrapped in a flour-covered apron. "Come on." She links her arm through mine and leads the way to the dining room. "We roasted potatoes, and Dad made soup. It looks delicious."

Beneath the apron, she's wearing a flowing shirt and skinny jeans, and her thick blond hair is tied into Bantu knots. Aside from a spot of flour on her cheek, she doesn't look like she's been in the kitchen. She hangs the apron on a hook inside the kitchen, and we continue to the dining room.

The table is set, and the pot of soup sits on a trivet next to a vase of carnations, lilies, and baby's breath. Dad lays a platter of baked salmon fillet and a small bowl of mustard sauce from the kitchen. The roasted potatoes already sit on the other side of the flowers.

I take my regular seat, and Imogene joins me.

Dad too is dressed up, but I'm wearing my Marvel sweat-shirt and my flannel bottoms. To be fair, I'm not sure he's ever dressed down. Even during the past week, I've never seen him in pajamas.

He takes his seat across from us and dishes up. "What time is your flight tomorrow, Imogene?" He glances at Mo as he spoons potato cubes onto his plate.

"It's at 5:50. I'll get into Springfield around 10:30. There's a half-hour layover in Atlanta."

I take a couple potatoes and a small piece of fish. Only a small ladle of soup—it's green. "Vegetarian split pea," Mo whispers to me.

"Would it be alright if I drove you this time?" Dad's voice is tentative but not meek, and he tears off a piece of salmon and slips it in his mouth.

Imogene turns to me, and I shrug. It's not like Xander would want to drive us back to the airport the second he gets back to campus. That'd be idiotic—and with such an inconvenience, he'd want something in return. Excitement pulses through me at the thought, but I push it aside.

"That'd be wonderful." Imogene flashes him a smile. "That's very kind of you."

His dark skin turns a warm brown as he blushes.

The three of us driving to the airport—which would mean just me and Dad on the return. We'd finally be able to spend time alone together again.

I glance up and aimlessly stir my soup. "I'm not sure I can make the trip."

Mo turns to me. "What d'you mean?"

I swallow down a spoonful of the green puree and try not to grimace. "Classes start Monday. The dorms open again in the morning. I should be studying. And if Dad's going to take you, I don't have to worry about you making it to the airport."

Across the table, Dad nods. "Of course."

But Imogene frowns. "Oh, okay."

I quickly change the subject. "Have you talked to Mom?"

"Yeah." But her words lack their normal fervor. "She's spent most of her time with Charlie and Thea. I think they met her boyfriend too."

"Does he have a name?"

"Roberto. He's from Ecuador."

I return to my barren plate.

Imogene nudges my arm and whispers, "Are you sure you won't come with us?"

No. I want to go.

"Of course I'm sure." I shake my head. "I have so much to do."

Imogene returns to her food with a melancholy sigh.

Why must I continually sabotage myself?

Twenty-Seven

"YOU DON'T HAVE TO WALK ME BACK, YOU KNOW." I LOOK both ways before crossing the street. "You need to be ready for your flight."

Imogene slips her arm through my backpack strap and rushes to catch up. "I've been ready since this morning." She nudges my arm and smiles. "And Dad said he could pick me up at your dorm."

I laugh. "You want to see my room."

She stumbles over the uneven sidewalk and has to catch up again. "This is the first time I've never seen your bedroom."

We reach Finchley Avenue and cross toward campus. The sidewalk winds toward Lincoln Hall.

"It's nothing special, I promise."

"That doesn't matter." Imogene pokes my arm and scurries ahead, calling over her shoulder, "I want to see it. Accept that and move on."

I roll my eyes. "Fine, moving on."

When we reach a fork in the sidewalk, Imogene waits for me, and we turn down the left pathway. Her face is somber. "When will you see Zane again?"

"I don't know." I nudge a stick off the path. "He's probably already back on campus. We'll have class together Monday."

"With Dad, right?"

I nod. Definitely not looking forward to that.

"Does Dad really not like him? That was…intense the other day."

"It wasn't unexpected. Zane isn't—well, he's not exactly a critical thinker. There's a reason I wasn't going to tell Dad about him."

"Ever?"

I shrug.

Her face falls. "Then you can't be that serious about him." She's more invested in this than I realized.

"Why do you care?"

Imogene heaves a sigh, and Lincoln Hall looms ahead. "I want you to be happy, Billie."

"That doesn't mean I need a boyfriend."

"If you're not serious about Zane, why are you seeing him?" Her brow furrows. "You've never been one to date for no reason, and obviously, there are other equally attractive guys out there."

"What, your stupid love triangle theory?" I roll my eyes. "Besides, I don't know how serious I can be when we haven't had sex."

She's surprised. "You mean, you haven't…?"

We stop at the doors, and I scan my ID. I hold open the door for her, and we lock eyes as she passes. "To the left." I nod toward the stairwell. "Top floor."

We take the stairs two at a time, but her pursed lips and crinkled brow say she's preoccupied.

273

"What's wrong?"

Imogene forces a smile. "I can't believe I—I mean, that you—" She sighs and tries again. "You haven't had sex at all?"

We reach the landing for the second floor, and I stop cold. "What?"

She pauses a couple steps ahead and turns back with a sheepish smile. "Just curious?"

I purse my lips and push past her. "That's none of your business. That's incredibly private. Why would you even think of that?"

"Oh my God."

I glance back.

She hasn't moved.

Suddenly, I'm apprehensive. "What?"

"You're covering your ass." She bounds up the stairs after me, and we pass the third floor landing. "If you hadn't, you would've said no. Who is it?"

I avoid eye contact. "No one."

She giggles. "Would you rather I believe you're lying to me or that you're a virgin?"

We reach the fourth floor, and I turn down the hallway, pulling out my keys. Several doors are open, and at the end of the hallway, mine is too. Val's back, and she's in the room.

I pause, pocketing my keys again, and stop Imogene. "You can believe whatever you want, but for God's sake, keep your mouth shut."

She's too busy laughing to assent.

Inside the room, Val is unpacking. She smiles when I enter, but there's no greeting. Imogene raises an eyebrow at the exchange but doesn't press anything. We drop the bags on the bed, and I gesture around the room.

"This is where I live. It isn't much."

My sister examines every nook and cranny until her eyes land on the pile of sketchbooks on my desk. She lets out a short exclamation and dives for them. In a few seconds, she relaxes on my beanbag chair, three sketchbooks in her lap, another in her hands, and flips through the pages.

I roll my eyes. "There's nothing exciting in there, Mo." I take a seat on the bed and wait.

On the opposite side of the room, Val finishes unpacking and grabs her purse. She doesn't typically stay long while I'm in the room. She sends me another awkward smile before leaving.

Imogene flips through the pages of the first sketchbook, barely registering my roommate's departure. "You're getting better." She nods and turns another page, but then, her eyes flit around the room.

A smile spreads across her face. "Who is it? Do I know him? Is he cute? Was he any good?" She passes a few more pages before spinning the book round to show off my drawing of Zane from the beginning of the semester. "Is he cuter than this?" She looks at the image again before turning a skeptical eye on me. "Seriously, why haven't you slept with him?"

I collapse on the bed, groaning. "Honestly, Mo, what the fuck does it matter? Please don't live vicariously through that experience."

"It was bad then."

Not necessarily.

A few more pages turn, and she calls my name again. The picture she shows me is a sketch of Jimmy and Xander playing Mario Kart, and she raises an eyebrow. "Do I know him?" Her voice has an edge. She's not joking around anymore.

I shake my head and lie down again.

"Okay." She sighs. "Why aren't you coming to the airport? Seriously."

I clench my eyes shut. If it's not one thing, it's something else. "I told you before. I need to study. Classes start tomorrow."

"And I'm calling BS. I want you to come see me off, and you're chickening out because that means spending the return drive with Dad. Billie, why can't you give him a chance?"

I shift positions to see her again. "I want to, I do."

"Then what's the problem?"

Nothing.

Everything.

I close my eyes. I have to be honest.

It's me. I'm the problem.

"He's trying so hard. He wants to make things right with you, even after whatever the hell happened over Christmas break. And I know it's hard—you were the one most hurt when he left—but it's difficult for him too."

I know that. But it doesn't make this easier.

Imogene pulls out her phone. "Dad'll be out there in a few minutes. You sure you want to stay here?"

All at once, a flurry of knocks and bangs echoes through the room.

I bolt upright.

Jimmy and Xander, grins on their faces, burst into the room, ignoring any previous precedent, and start talking over each other. Until Jimmy notices Imogene sitting on the beanbag.

"Imogene." Jimmy's smile turns shy—they've always had a strained relationship. She stands and pulls him into a hug, and he wraps his arms around her, patting her back awkwardly.

Xander moves around the pair to join me on the bed. "I'm glad you're here. We have so much to tell you." He's tan again, his skin a rich golden beige like at the beginning of the school year, and he squints his eyes as he inspects my hair. "This is new." He nods to the auburn braids cascading over my shoulder.

"Mo did it."

He grins. "You should wear it like this more often. You look…" He pauses, and a small frown spreads across his features. "You look good."

I lean into him, ignoring the blush that rises to my cheeks, and smile.

He clears his throat. "Have you gone snorkeling before?"

"No, I haven't."

He scoots closer. "Then you'll come with us next time."

"'Next time'—you're going again?"

He nudges my arm. "Well, we're going somewhere, and you're coming with us—no arguments." His leg brushes mine, then retreats.

A small smile forms on my lips, and I fold my legs together so my knee rests against his thigh. "Do I—"

"Sorry to interrupt." Imogene stands beside the bed, a reluctant smile on her face. "Dad's waiting. I can't miss my flight."

I stand to give her a hug, and she holds me tight. "I'll see you in a couple months, Mo." She squeezes one last time before releasing me.

She waves a quick goodbye to Xander, then a one-armed hug for Jimmy, and she leaves.

Jimmy steals her seat. "What did you tell her?"

Xander rolls his eyes. "Nothing yet. Do you want to tell her about the reef? Or the girl at the bar who tried to take you up to her room?"

"That did not happen." Jimmy laughs. "Don't listen to him, Billie. He's exaggerating."

"That's normal." I sit down again—decidedly farther from Xander.

"It is not." Xander sits up, and a scowl forms on his face, but he brushes it aside. "Okay, fine, maybe a little."

My phone buzzes. The text is from Imogene.

I can't believe it. You slept with Xander. No wonder you're not serious about Zane.

I conceal the phone against my chest. What could've possibly given that away? I barely exchanged two sentences with him before she left.

Jimmy quirks an eyebrow. "Everything okay?"

"Uh, yeah, fine." I hide the screen and craft a short response: *How could you possibly know that?*

Mo's response is quick, but I can't look at it yet. I stand and move to the window. Below, Dad's car is pulling out of the parking lot onto Vallee.

"Is that Zane?" Jimmy asks, but I shake my head.

"You don't have to lie about it," Xander says. "If you want to keep your relationship from your only friends, you're obviously not very serious about it."

I cock my head. "What do you mean? You want to meet

him?"

He shrugs.

On the beanbag, Jimmy smiles. "That sounds like a great idea."

"No." It's a horrible idea.

I take a breath before looking at Mo's message: *Because you just confirmed it.*

Twenty-Eight

D R. L EWIS IS LATE AGAIN.

At five minutes past, he staggers into the classroom, bungling his laptop carrier, a binder, and a mountain of books. He barely manages to push it all onto the desk without dropping anything. This is protocol. He leans against the chair, his gray sweater-vest horribly out of place with the windows open for the first time in months, and he scans the room with an apologetic smile. "How was everyone's break? Anyone do anything exciting?"

I roll my eyes and sketch a small figure on the corner of my paper as a low chorus of responses floods the room. I couldn't care less what my classmates did over spring break.

A few minutes later, when Lewis launches into the subject matter, I erase my sketch and pay attention: "Since it's such a nice day out and I know you're dying to spend some time outside, we'll make this session short."

He pulls out a stack of papers and distributes them to the first row. "You turned in your research papers before break. Now we're going to look at our semester discussion from a different perspective. I mentioned a creative project last time, so let's talk about what that entails. Does everyone have a copy of the rubric?"

He glances around as the girl in front of me passes back my copy. "For this project," Dr. Lewis continues, "you will use your imagination and creativity to dissect our theme of truth. Like the research paper, you must choose a case study and form your thesis around that case—this time by creating something."

I scan the rubric. We'll be graded on content, whether we meet all the requirements, originality and creativity, and—ah, yes, the oral presentation.

Lewis takes a seat on the edge of the desk. "This creative project can be whatever media you like—as long as the focal point and thesis fit our subject matter. Think about things deeply as you analyze. Use your creativity to bring a new perspective to your project. We can discuss ideas together if you're struggling." He smiles. "You need to start now. This is in-depth and will require a great deal of focus. Then, you can enjoy the beautiful weather."

He sits at the desk and pulls out his planner, and I return my attention to the rubric.

The medium is obvious—Imogene was right, after all—and I've practiced long enough I can draw a comic pretty easily. Superheroes are often the embodiment of truth and justice. All I need is a character and a single-issue plot.

I'm one of the first students to discuss my project with Dr. Lewis.

◆

"How was your class?" Zane holds the door open, and he follows me inside the Jittery Bug. "Anything fun? That's

Honors, right?"

We stop at the end of the ordering line.

"We're starting a new project." I pull out my wallet.

"You hungry?" He peruses the menu posted on the wall behind the register. "I'm going to get a sandwich. You want anything?"

I shrug. "I was going to get a chai latte."

"Alright."

The line moves up, and Zane steps ahead of me to reach the register. "A chicken salad wrap with chips, a sixteen-ounce cup, and a chai latte."

I open my mouth to protest, but he's already handing over his card.

When we sit at a table, I fix him with a glare. "You didn't have to do that. I can pay for my own drink."

"Of course you can. I'm going to go grab my coffee." He shakes his empty cup in front of me before walking to the coffee station.

My eyes follow him, but I can't focus. Unease settles in my stomach, and I pick at my nails to quash it.

When he returns, Zane takes the seat next to me. "That's an interesting hairstyle."

I finger one of my braids, pulled back into a ponytail, but he isn't looking.

"Did you have a good break?"

As if he wasn't texting me the entire time.

A server drops off my chai latte, and I stir it with my pinky. "It was fine."

"I spent the week with my friends from back home. You know, we don't get to see each other often, so it's kinda weird now. We aren't as close as we used to be." He takes a long drink. "But yeah, we went to the city and saw a few games, checked out the Armory Show, a couple guys went to a concert."

I turn on him with wide, determined eyes. "You went to the Armory Show?"

He frowns. "Yeah, so?"

"The international art fair?"

He nods. "It wasn't really my thing. One of my friends wanted to go, so we went. It was crowded—and expensive." He shrugs. "I wasn't impressed."

A server delivers his sandwich and removes the number card, and Zane begins to eat.

I stare, but he doesn't notice. I would've killed to go to the Armory Show.

"Did things go alright with your dad and sister?" he asks between bites. "It wasn't too awkward?"

I sip at my drink. "It was the normal, expected amount of awkward."

He sends me an encouraging smile. "That's good. I'm glad things are settling down with your dad. I mean, he's super intense, but I guess I'll have to get used to that, right?" He lets out a small chuckle. "I want you to be happy, though."

Probably not a good time to mention my dad's minor freak-out over our potential relationship.

Zane sets down his sandwich and wipes his hands and face. "Seriously, Wilhelmina."

I frown. He hasn't called me that in a while.

"If there's anything I can help with, let me know. I know things are strained between you and your dad, and if you need to talk about it or anything…"

"Thanks, I guess. Things are fine, though. You don't need

to take care of me."

He tilts his head. "Well, I mean if there's any way I can help, let me know."

Uncertain, I can only stare. As tense as my relationship with my father is, Zane doesn't need to fix anything. He doesn't need to help.

All I can say is, "Okay."

Zane smiles and leaves his wrap behind to lean close. I glance around the shop before his lips make contact with mine in a simple, chaste kiss. Then, he returns to his food.

I cling to my mug and take a long drink.

I'm not used to his kisses—especially when they're more awkward than romantic. There's no hunger, no spark, no desire for more. The only thing I'm left wanting for is somewhere safe to hide.

When he's done, he wipes his face and hands on a brown paper napkin and turns his full attention to me. He abandons the napkin on the table next to his basket. "Billie, can I ask you something?"

"Sure." I take another sip.

He pries my hand away from the mug and links our fingers together with a smile. "I think it's safe to say this is a date."

I freeze. He's not going to ask for us to be official, is he?

"And we've been more open with each other." He rubs his thumb back and forth on the back of my hand. "I think it's time to take the next step."

I open my mouth, but he keeps going.

"I want to meet your friends."

His face and voice are completely serious—and if he were joking, this isn't something to joke about. This is his way of asking us to be official without voicing the question.

But I'm still not sure how I feel about him.

"Do you think that's a good idea?"

"Yes." Despite my skepticism, his determination doesn't waver. "We've been talking and seeing each other for a while now—"

"We have different definitions of 'seeing each other.'"

"—and we've only spent time just the two of us. We haven't introduced each other to our worlds, you know." He smiles. "I want you to meet my friends, come to our next party, get to know the guys—and I'd like to meet yours. I know you're not comfortable introducing me to your dad as your boyfriend. I thought it might be easier to meet your friends first. You're not that close with them anyway, right? What's the harm?"

I watch him for a moment.

It's rare to see him so calm and resolute. He obviously spent a lot of time deliberating this before bringing it to my attention. He must mean it to put this much effort into it.

Although I don't want to give in, I don't have a good reason to deny him. Jimmy and Xander already expressed interest in meeting him, and I can only imagine the surprised look on Xander's face when I actually bring around the would-be boyfriend.

"You can eat lunch with us in the cafeteria on Friday."

Twenty-Nine

WE SWIPE OUR CARDS AT THE FRONT DESK, AND ZANE TAKES
my hand as we enter the cafeteria. "Don't be nervous." He
squeezes. "I'm great with people. They'll love me."

His attempts to calm me aren't relaxing.

On the far side of the cafeteria, Jimmy and Xander sit at
our regular table with their suitemates, Connor and Blayne.
Despite seeing them often in our seminar class last semester
and in our hallway, I've barely spoken with them. They're
introverted like me, and our schedules don't mesh—they're
already gathering up their things to head to their noon class,
though Jimmy and Xander are only now sitting down.

"We should get food first." I lead the way to the buffet
lines, breaking contact.

I grab a plate, but none of the options look appealing.
Zane fills his and grabs a couple cups for our drinks while
I settle on some fries. He fills our cups, and I take in the
view of the cafeteria. At our table, Jimmy has spotted me
and smiles. Xander doesn't notice; he's eating a plateful of
fettuccine alfredo. Connor and Blayne are gone.

"You ready then?"

I turn back—Zane is standing beside me, balancing his

plate and two cups—and I nod.

In a moment, we stand at the edge of the table behind a pair of empty chairs, and I set my plate on the table and sling my bag over the back of the chair. "Hey, guys."

Zane takes the seat beside me.

Jimmy smiles.

Xander cocks an eyebrow. "Who're you?" As if he hasn't seen him before.

"Guys, this is Zane." I nod to each of them as I speak. "Zane, meet Jimmy and Xander."

Zane grins. "Nice to meet you."

Jimmy reaches over to shake his hand. "Yes, finally." He settles back into his seat. "We've heard a lot about you."

"All good, I hope." He laughs.

On the opposite side of the table, Xander releases a derisive snort and drives his fork into his fettuccine.

Jimmy forces his smile wider. "Of course."

"Then I'm a little out of my element." Zane snags one of my fries. "You've heard a lot about me, but I know practically nothing about you."

Xander raises an eyebrow—more for effect than out of surprise. "You mean Dixon hasn't told you all the down and dirty of what we do together?"

I lean forward to hide the blush creeping up my neck and face, then take a drink. Vanilla, cinnamon, the bite of carbonation—I set down the cup and cover my mouth with my arm to cough. Why the hell is there Coke in my cup?

"You okay?" Zane leans close, but I push him away as I recover.

I shove the cup farther away. "I'm fine."

Zane turns back to the guys. "You call her 'Dixon'?"

"Yeah." Xander stares him down, his hands resting on either side of his plate. "And?"

Beside me, Zane shrugs. "It's not particularly friendly," he says noncommittally. "What do you guys do together? She doesn't talk much about her life outside of classes. I'm taking her to her first party next week."

It's weird to hear people talk about you like you're not there.

"She goes to parties with us," Xander says.

Surreal.

"My apologies." But Zane doesn't sound sorry. "I meant her first frat party. Have you been to one of our house parties?"

Xander lifts an eyebrow. "Who are you?"

"Rho Lambda Nu. Best parties on campus."

With a scoff, Xander twists his fork in the middle of his pasta. "Can't say I've had the pleasure."

"Maybe you guys should join Billie when she comes next weekend." He leans back and rests his arm on the back of my chair. "Then you can see how the professionals do it."

Xander snorts. "I said I haven't had the pleasure. I didn't say I hadn't been."

"Mostly we study together." Jimmy's trying to alleviate the tension. "Play video games, watch anime, hang out. Billie always has her head in a sketchbook."

Zane turns to me in surprise. "I didn't know you could draw. Will you show me? I'd love to see."

I send Jimmy a glare. "It's private."

Beside me, Zane smiles. "Surely you can make an exception for me."

My mouth gapes.

"What about you, Zane?" Jimmy pokes at his plate. "What are you majoring in? Your plans after graduation?"

"I'm an Advertising major. I'll probably head back to New York for a while, but my plans aren't really set." He squeezes my shoulder. "There are plenty of reasons to stay nearby."

I lock eyes with Jimmy, who raises an eyebrow and tries to mouth something. I clear my throat. "Tell them—"

"New York isn't that nearby." Xander jabs his fork toward us. "It'd be a pretty big inconvenience to whatever you leave behind."

"I don't plan on leaving anything behind."

"If your plans aren't set, how do you know?" Xander cocks his head, brow creased. "Besides, have you talked to her about that? Because at this point, you're a senior trying to bang a freshman who doesn't even like you. What exactly do you want from her?" He returns to his food, letting the words hang in the air.

I push my plate away and grab the cup with its offending contents before walking away. I drop the cup off at the dish room window and return to the drink station for ice water. The liquid is cool and refreshing on my throat.

This was a terrible idea. What the hell is happening? I can barely get a word in—and when I can, I don't know what to say.

"Hey."

I look up to find Zane beside me. I didn't notice his arrival. "Hello."

"You look a little upset." Somehow, he isn't bothered by Xander's words. "Do you want to leave? We can try again later."

"No, it's fine." I let my eyes wander back toward the table, where Jimmy and Xander are having a heated discussion. "I don't know what I was expecting." But I definitely don't want to repeat it.

He pulls me into a one-armed hug and lays a kiss on my temple. "Don't let it bother you," he whispers in my ear. "I'd be pretty upset too if you brought some other guy around. He's jealous."

I step away. "Who, Xander?"

Zane shrugs, but the smile on his face is confirmation.

Obviously he doesn't know anything. Xander doesn't have any reason to be jealous. He doesn't have romantic feelings for me, and that sex was just sex. After all these months, we're barely friends.

But the word nags at me.

Zane pulls me into a long kiss while I'm trying to process. He wraps his arms around my waist, smiling against my lips, and I let him hold me to his chest. He nips at my lower lip, I open my mouth to him—and water splashes against my arm as the cup nearly slips from my fingers.

I pull back, tightening my grip on the cup rim, and step away. "We should get back." I nod toward the table.

For a moment there, I forgot we were in the middle of the cafeteria.

When we sit down, Zane lays his hand on my thigh and squeezes, but he isn't looking at me. "I don't know, I think she likes me plenty."

No one says anything. In fact, Xander won't look in our direction. He's too busy stabbing his pasta. Jimmy opens his mouth to say something, but no words come.

After a moment, Zane leans close. "I need to head back

to my apartment before my next class. Do you have time to come with?"

I'm not the only one ready to get out of this situation.

I nod, and he squeezes my thigh before gathering his stuff. "I'll catch up with you."

Zane throws his bag over his shoulder and picks up his plate and cup. "Alright, boys." He casts them a smile. "It was great to meet you, but I've got to run before class." He kisses the side of my head before departing.

Jimmy says a quick goodbye, but Xander's eyes don't leave his plate.

As soon as Zane is out of earshot, I lean over the table, gripping the edge with both hands. "What the hell is your problem?"

At last, Xander turns his attention away from me, his lips in a tight purse. "What are you talking about, Dixon? I've been nothing but cordial."

"You know exactly what I mean," I snap. "Just when we're finally becoming friends, you have to be a complete ass. You wanted me to bring him to meet you guys, didn't you? You should at least be friendly since it was your idea first."

Jimmy holds his hands up. "Guys, come on."

But Xander doesn't notice. "Were you listening to him? He's smug and conceited. How can you find that attractive?"

"Oh, like you're one to talk. You're the most conceited person I know."

"He's an idiot. He's only graduating because of you."

"He wasn't failing." On the tabletop, my knuckles are white. "He wanted to keep his GPA up."

"Fine—barely passing. What's the fucking difference?"

291

His words come out in a deep snarl. He's finally getting angry. "I know you have higher standards than that. Right, Jimmy?"

Jimmy lets out a nervous chuckle. "Nope, not going to be a part of this, guys."

Xander turns back to me. "I'm trying to help you. It's not my fault you have terrible taste in men."

I pull back, and my hands clench into fists. "No." My arms are shaking. "I don't want your help, Xander—and I don't need it. We're hardly good enough friends for that. And pulling out a yardstick to measure your dicks isn't helpful." The chair squeals against the floor as I step backward. "You know what would be helpful? If you'd stop acting jealous, stop pretending you care, and actually be a friend to me."

For a moment, Xander can only stare, but behind his blue eyes, his brain is calculating. "You think I'm jealous?"

I square my shoulders. I'm not backing down.

He breaks eye contact to take a drink, and I furrow my brow. He is the picture of calm. "You want me to stop pretending?" But there's a fire inside his perfectly articulated words. "Fine. But let's get one thing straight. I'm not jealous. Please get your head out of your ass, because if you're under the impression I slept with you for any reason other than to get off, you're wrong."

I turn away and shoulder my backpack. "Zane is waiting for me." I pick up my dishes and leave.

Zane is waiting outside the cafeteria doors, a small smile on his face. "You alright?" He pushes away from the wall to catch up as I march past him.

"I'm fine."

He rushes after me, and when his long legs reach me, he takes my hand. We stop, a few feet from the doors leaving the JW Student Center. "You sure? You look a little upset."

I shake my head, trying to ignore the sting in my eyes and the lump of emotions in my throat. "It's just Xander. He's an ass."

"Okay." Zane leads me by the hand out of the student center.

The walk back to his apartment is a blur. The weather turned cold this week, and a thin layer of snow dusts the ground between clumps of green grass.

Zane's apartment is no different than the last time I saw it. The living room is a small communal area with an attached kitchen, separated by a breakfast bar with two stools. To the left and right are hallways to the bedrooms and shared bathrooms; Zane's is on the left. There are no decorations or additional furnishings aside from the campus-provided furniture and appliances—and someone's flat-screen in the living room.

He sets my backpack and coat on one of the stools, and I poke around the TV, searching for something interesting. Something to distract myself. "Do you have any good games?" There's a small stack on the floor. Half the disks are out of their cases.

By contrast, Xander's video games are neatly organized and in perfect condition. The only scratches on the disks come from continual use—dedication, not abuse.

Not that it matters.

"I think we've got a few of the *Halo* games. Some *Call of Duty*. Have you played *Black Ops*?"

I purse my lips. "Can I have a glass of water?"

Zane steps into the kitchen and fills a glass with tap water and some ice from the freezer. "You sure everything's alright, Wilhelmina?" He hands me the glass over the breakfast bar.

I lean against a stool. "There's nothing to worry about." I take a sip and swallow down any remaining feelings about the argument in the cafeteria. It doesn't matter.

"I'd like it a lot better if I could believe you." He walks around the bar to stand beside me. "Do you have any other classes?"

"No, my eleven o'clock was the last one today."

He nods. "I have my fitness class, but it's not a big deal. We can stay here and talk if you want."

Talk. I'm not sure I'm in the right place to talk. That's what Jimmy's for. Not that I'm keen on discussing what just transpired with him yet.

"What movies do you have?"

He hesitates before glancing at the television. "Whatever's streaming. What do you want to watch?"

Anything really.

"I think they have a few Nicholas Sparks adaptations available."

I pull a face. Maybe not anything. "I was thinking more along the lines of *Akira*."

His furrowed brow gives me all the information I need. He's never heard of it.

"I should work on my Honors project." I place the water glass on the counter behind me. "I've been procrastinating."

Zane shakes his head. "You can do that later. None of your stuff's here, and you've got weeks before it's due."

I frown, staring at the glass. "It's important, and it'll take a lot of work to get it right. I shouldn't be wasting this time."

He pulls me into a hug and presses his face against my ear. "Staying with me isn't wasting time, Billie. Talk to me. What did Xander say when I left?"

"Don't worry about it." I nudge him away, but he holds his ground.

"I don't think he liked me much." He releases a chuckle. "Do you care?"

"No."

"Good." He drags my mouth to his for a kiss, his thick lips firm against mine, and I kiss him back. His hands hold my shoulders and play with the neckline of my shirt. He pulls back for a breath. "I hate to tell you this because I know you're friends, but he's kind of an asshole."

I almost laugh as he pulls my collar aside and kisses my collarbone. "I know that better than anyone."

He pauses. "Then why are you friends with him?" He kisses me on the mouth but retreats quickly.

"Jimmy."

He kisses me again.

Firm hands glide down to my hips, and his fingers slip beneath the gray fabric of my t-shirt. He searches my torso, hands sliding across my stomach, up my ribs, under the wired bra to tease my breasts. His lips break contact, and his gray eyes are dilated with desire. "Do you want me to help you forget?"

All at once, one hand moves to undo my bra clasp, and his mouth returns to mine, eager, needy, insatiable. The elastic snaps free, and he grabs me, one palm on each breast, squeezing, tweaking the nipples. All I can think to do is kiss him again.

He leans away to get the full view of me, and his hands

slide down and lift the shirt over my head. "You're beautiful." He slides my bra down my arms, and it joins my shirt on the floor.

It's hard to take him seriously when the only part of me he's looking at is my tits.

His hands touch every part of my bare skin, reverent, and I close my eyes. Wet, open-mouthed kisses trail along my shoulder, and his hands meander down to my waist and pop open the button of my jeans. The zipper is next, and then, the jeans themselves. He lifts me out of them and sets me on the open stool, my back pressing into the counter. Then, his hands are gone.

When my eyes flutter open, he has shed his own shirt. His bare chest is hairless, ghostly pale and lean, and his hands struggle with his belt. In a few seconds, his pants too are on the floor, and he nudges open my legs to step between them and kiss me again. I never noticed how tall he is—sitting on this stool, our faces are finally level. Beneath his silky green boxers, his erection presses against my underwear.

His hands find me again, tugging at my underwear, and he trails his lips along my jaw to my ear. "I want you." One hand slides between my ass and the cushion-top stool, guiding my underwear out of the way. He slips the cotton fabric down to the floor before nudging my legs open with his hips again. Chilly fingers drag along my thighs, close to my heat, and a rough thumb grazes my clit and pushes inside. "God, I want you."

The erection pressing against my leg already gave that away.

I hold him by the shoulders, trying to stay upright so

my back isn't forced against the counter, but he captures my lips in another kiss. His thumb pushes and nudges, and I gasp into his mouth as his nail scrapes against me, my own fingers digging into his shoulders. He presses closer.

His free hand reaches around and yanks out the tie holding up my hair, and the auburn micro-braids cascade onto the counter. He twists the hair around his fingers, and his chest pushes me harder against the counter. My forehead clenches in pain. He pulls out the hand between my legs and breaks the kiss to suck off his thumb. I imagine that's supposed to be seductive.

When he slips off his boxers, his erection nuzzles against me, teasing my entrance. He kisses me again, and I gasp as the erection tries to slip inside. I press a hand to his chest, and he pulls away.

In a moment, he's gone, stooping to grab his wallet from his jeans, and yanks out a condom. I blink, and he already has it on.

Zane crashes his mouth against mine in a hungry kiss. One hand kneads my breast, and the other positions himself before he plunges inside. I clench my eyes shut as he pulls back and thrusts, forcing his way deeper. My hands clamp down on his shoulders, holding so tightly it hurts, and he rams into me again and again, his face contorted, eyes half-lidded.

He releases my mouth and moves down toward my tits, kissing and biting my skin. Above my left breast, he stops to suck at my flesh. His teeth break the skin. He pushes me down on the counter and captures my nipple in a wet kiss.

I dig my fingers into his shoulder blades, refraining from voicing my discomfort, but the pain only encourages him.

His mouth nips and sucks desperately at the nipple. He pounds into me, harder, faster than before. My position halfway on the counter angles him deep enough it hurts. "God, you feel amazing," he mumbles against my breast, and he guides me by the hips to meet him thrust for thrust. I cling to him as his movements turn spastic, jerking, convulsing as he comes.

Zane rests against me, his forehead pressing on my sternum between my breasts, his hands clutching my hips, his dick still inside me, slowly losing its erection. He heaves, and his hot breath spreads across my abdomen.

He pulls away.

It's over.

He steps back, holding onto the top edge of the condom and disappears to clean up, and I stumble off the stool to find my clothes. My legs are shaking, but I need to get out of here.

When he returns, I'm half dressed, zipping up my jeans and slipping on my sneakers.

"You going somewhere? I thought we were going to watch a movie." He's still naked.

"I told you. I have to work on that project." I shake my head. "Do we need to do a study session this weekend? Or are you good?"

He tries to form words, but it takes a minute. "Uh, no, I don't think so."

I clasp my bra and pull on my shirt, then my hoody. "Then have a good weekend, I guess." I grab my backpack and pull it over my shoulders. The textbooks weigh down on the large tender section of my back. A bruise is already forming.

"You guess?"

I head for the door, and he doesn't prevent me. I pause, my hand on the knob, and turn to him with a forced smile. "I'll see you in class on Monday." I yank open the door and slip into the chilly spring air.

◆

Loud knuckles rap repeatedly against the door. "I know you're in there. Open the door, Billie."

I flip through my sketchbook on my bed again, trying to find something—anything—to work with. Finals are in six weeks, and I haven't made any progress on this stupid project. None of these sketches work. None of these characters fit the parameters of the assignment. None of it will work.

My phone is ringing again.

I could do anything for this—it wouldn't be difficult to stretch. But I don't want to do anything. I need this to make sense. It has to work. It has to fit. Nothing here fucking fits.

"I know you're in there, Billie. I can hear your phone ringing. Are you seriously hiding from me because of what Xander said?"

Weezer stops playing, and I push the phone farther away. I don't have time for this.

How the hell am I supposed to do this? I've never made a comic before. Sketching superheroes is vastly different from drawing the panels and forming a coherent storyline. I know nothing about story structure. Or character development. Or storytelling and writing at its basest form. I'm not remotely prepared for this.

Val heaves a sigh and pushes her chair away from the desk.

My phone starts to ring again.

I can't do this. I have no idea what I'm doing.

And worse—I have to do a fucking presentation over whatever bullshit comic I create. I have to justify what I create to a group of twenty-something students and the professor who's somehow my father's closest friend.

Oh, God, my father.

What the hell am I supposed to do now?

"Billie, answer the door, dammit."

Jimmy is relentless. I suppose I should cherish that. He cares—which is more than I can say for anyone else right now.

But I don't have time for this. I'm going to fail. I'm going to fail because I bit off more than I can chew. Because I don't have the ability to explain a project in front of so many people. Because I can't let anyone see these stupid drawings in the first place.

I'm an idiot.

The phone won't stop ringing.

Val groans and finally stands with an irritated huff. "You've got to be fucking kidding me." She slips on her shoes, grabs her jacket and purse, and heads for the door.

Don't let him in.

Val doesn't open the door wide enough for me to see his face, but she pushes past him and slams the door behind her. "Obviously, she doesn't want to talk to you." On the other side, her voice is muffled.

The phone stops. For a moment, it's silent.

I switch to a different sketchbook and sift through the

drawings inside.

This was a mistake. Obviously, I need to tell Dr. Lewis I can't do the project. There's no way I can do this. There's no way I can show anyone this. I'm terrified.

"Okay." At last, Jimmy's voice is calmer. "I know you're in there, so just listen. You know you don't have to hide from me—ever. I'll give you some time to sort out whatever you need to, and when you're ready, you can come talk to me."

When he's gone, I hug the sketchbook to my chest and close my aching eyes.

I need to get a hold on myself, dammit.

I take in a deep, shaky breath and look at the drawings again. I flip through a few more pages, focusing on my breathing as I look, until my eyes land on the drawing I did of Zane in Honors class.

I can still picture Imogene holding it up and asking me why I hadn't slept with him yet. I didn't have an answer for her, but on some level I knew, even then, it would be a mistake.

For being drawn from memory, the line work is decent, but his smile makes me queasy.

I rip the drawing from the sketchbook and tear it to pieces. That's the last thing I want to look at right now.

Thirty

Steam billows from the cup as he sets it on the coffee table in front of me. "Would you like anything else, Mina?"

I look up. "No, thanks."

Dad settles into the seat beside me and clasps his hands together. In the dark of the living room, his green sweater-vest blends in with the couch. "Is everything alright?" He edges closer.

The teacup is hot. The liquid burns my tongue, but I choke it down. Some sort of mint. "Everything's fine, Dad." I set the cup on the saucer again.

He nods, but we both know I'm lying. If everything were fine, I wouldn't be here.

"You've been here almost every night for the last two weeks. Maybe there's something you want to discuss with me?"

He's right, of course. Before spring break, I never visited two nights in a row.

"I thought you might be getting lonely since Mo left."

It's been three weeks since her return flight, but that hasn't affected his good mood. He smiles more than before. He's happy, though not as upbeat as while she was here.

Dad leans back. "How kind of you, Mina."

I force down a bitter laugh. That's hardly the first compliment I expected from his mouth. I don't remember the last time I did something kind.

"I have this morning's Sudoku if you'd like to take a look." Without waiting for a response, Dad rises to his feet and retrieves the bit of newspaper from the dining table. He saved it for me.

"Thanks." I accept the proffered paper, already folded into a small rectangle so only the Sudoku and word jumble are visible, and sort the numbers in my head.

No matter what, numbers make sense. In Sudoku, it's simple permutation. Even in the complex versions of the game—this one is a four-star puzzle—it's just a more advanced way to reason out the permutation. The answer is always concrete, and there's only one.

Nothing else makes this much sense.

At last, I take the pen off the table and fill out the squares, and Dad sits beside me again, hands clasped around his teacup. He sips patiently as I work.

"How is your Honors project going?"

I glance up from the almost-complete puzzle. "It's going."

In truth, I haven't gotten past my block. I have a general idea, but my execution is faulty. All I've managed to work on are a few character sketches—but I haven't decided on the character set list.

"You're making progress then? You have two and a half weeks until it's due, correct?"

Not that I need a reminder. I'm going to fail.

"Yes." I turn my attention back to the puzzle to fill in the final numbers. "My progress is sufficient for now. I'm caught up in all my other classes."

He nods. "Your execution has been excellent in my class, Mina."

I shift uneasily and place the completed Sudoku and pen on the coffee table. "Thank you."

"Are you still tutoring?"

Something must be off for him to blatantly ask me about Zane. Have his grades slipped that much?

"Uh, no." I clear my throat. "We've stopped doing the sessions."

He almost smiles, but he refrains.

Ignoring his texts and avoiding our usual location in the library doesn't mean Zane has left me alone, though. He sits beside me in Calc II, and I've never been so grateful for my father's no-talking rule.

Dad drains his teacup and sets it on the coffee table. "Would you like to help me cook dinner?" He turns toward the grandfather clock in the far corner to check the time. "It's nearly 6:30."

I follow him into the kitchen. "What are we having?"

"I have several large jalapeños that need eaten before they go bad. I thought I could use them for stuffed peppers."

I lean against the island as he kneels inside the fridge to pull out the peppers and a glass container of cooked brown rice. He places them on the counter and returns to grab a few other ingredients: a block of cheddar, mushrooms, half an onion, and an unopened package of grass-fed ground beef.

"Grab a cutting board?" He nods toward the bottom drawer on the island, and I retrieve a large wooden cutting board and place it on the counter between us.

Chopping knife in hand, he halves the jalapeños and removes the seeds. Then, he minces the onion and mushrooms.

I step closer. "How can I help?"

He nods toward the range. "There should be a pan out. Put it on medium high heat on one of the larger burners and pour in a tablespoon of olive oil."

At the stove, I move the large cast iron pan to the front burner and turn it on. Flames lick up the sides momentarily before receding as I turn it down to medium high. I pour the olive oil, located in a ribbed glass cruet next to the stove, into the pan.

"How do I know when it's ready?"

His piles of minced onion and mushroom are in a bowl now, and he's shredding the cheese now. He pauses to come to my side, bringing the bowl of veggies. "The oil will become less viscous. It's already starting to thin out. You can tell when you move the pan around."

I watch as he lifts the pan slightly off the burner and rotates it so the oil coats every inch. "Then, we add the veggies, right?"

He reaches across the stove and turns the oven to four hundred degrees. "Yes." He returns the pan to the burner and grabs a wooden spoon from the drawer to my right. "Stir them occasionally with this. You'll need to add more oil—the mushrooms absorb it quickly." And he returns to shredding cheese.

I empty the bowl of vegetables into the pan, and the oil sizzles at the contact.

As I stir them around, Dad sends me a smile. "How are your friends, Mina? I saw Xander at one of his classes. He has Statistics with Dr. Torres, and he was very polite." He brings over the bowl of cheese and the now-opened package of beef. "He mentioned he hasn't spoken to you in a while."

I focus on the vegetables. "I've been busy with schoolwork."

"Let's add the meat." He takes the wooden spoon and nudges the ground beef into the pan. The red meat browns on the bottom, and he breaks it into smaller pieces.

When he hands the spoon back, he smiles, then pushes the tray into the trash bin and washes his hands. Over the sound of the water, he says, "It sounds like you've been focusing on your schoolwork too much, Mina. You need to enjoy your time here too. There's more to college than classwork."

"But this is what matters most right now." I heave a sigh. "Classes are the most important thing."

Dad returns with a sad smile. "Yes, but what will matter five years from now? Getting your degree and having perfect grades aren't the same thing." He looks at the mixture on the stove-top and dumps in the rice, which softens as it collects moisture. "In a minute, we'll add the cheese and stick them in the oven."

He checks that the oven is up to temp and brings over the halved jalapeños.

"Dad," I say, staring at the steaming pan. I swallow the growing lump in my throat. "I don't know what I'm doing. Is this cooked enough?"

He nods and turns off the burner. "You're doing fine, Mina." He empties the shredded cheddar into the pan, and I fold the cheese into the mix. "If you need help, all you have to do is ask. That's why I'm here."

Together, we pile the mixture into each jalapeño and cover them with foil. Next, they go on a baking sheet in the oven.

◆

I take a seat on the couch and drop my backpack at my feet. My eyes stare out the enormous bay window.

My usual spot in the library has been taken—occupied most times by Zane, hoping to catch me. I haven't had the nerve to talk to him.

Instead, I now enjoy the solitude of the most secluded area of the library, the far back corner with an uncomfortable Victorian-style sofa and a side table with a fantastic view of the campus soccer field and tennis courts, most often chosen for make-out sessions. Not so often anymore; many couples have learned I've taken up residence now.

My pocket buzzes as I unzip my backpack and pull out my sketchbook. This stupid Honors project is the only thing I'm behind on.

I pull out the phone to check. Out of curiosity. It's not like I've been answering my calls much lately.

It's Jimmy again.

I hesitate, and the phone continues to vibrate in my hand. When it's about to stop, I slide my thumb across the screen and lift it to my ear. "Yes?"

For a moment, only silence. Then, "Oh."

I roll my eyes. "What?"

"I didn't expect you to answer. I thought I was leaving you another voice mail you'll never listen to."

I purse my lips and lean against the armrest. "I listen to

them."

"Fine." I picture him shrugging. "But you never respond, so that's basically the same thing. I've given you a lot of time, Billie."

"I'm not going to apologize."

He pauses. "That's not what I was going to suggest."

I frown. "Whatever you want to call it, I'm not doing it. I didn't do anything wrong; Xander did."

"I'm not denying that, Billie."

He heaves a sigh, and I tuck the phone between my ear and shoulder and flip open the sketchbook. I've drawn several sketches of characters—Superman, Batman, anyone that might be appropriate for the context—in an attempt to sort out my plans for the creative project, but I haven't gotten any further than that. A real idea for the project has yet to manifest.

"Can we at least talk in person?" Jimmy asks. "You're never around anymore. I barely see you, and it's getting ridiculous. Why won't you talk to me about this?"

"Don't exaggerate. I sleep in my room every night and go to all my classes."

"Yes, but the only reason I know you're not sleeping somewhere else is because your boyfriend tracked me down. You won't answer his calls or texts either."

Oh. I didn't expect that.

"What'd you tell him?" I hate the quiet desperation in my voice.

I flip the page, trying to focus on the drawings. I've drawn Batman plenty, but my experience with Superman is minimal. He's not one of my favorites, even if he is one of the best options for the project. But perhaps it's time to look elsewhere for options.

I begin to turn the page—and the sofa behind me jostles.

I spin round.

Jimmy, his phone to his ear, has a triumphant grin on his face. "I told him I didn't know where you were." He ends the call.

I let my own phone fall to the couch, and he takes the open seat. "Then how are you here?"

He sends me an amused look. "As if you were anywhere but the library, Billie. I just had to find you. I was hoping I'd be able to hear your phone ringing while I was searching, but you know, then, you answered." He turns to the bay window.

"Luck."

He shrugs. "Of course, asking your dad did help. Something tells me Zane hasn't thought of that."

I scowl. "You went to my dad. That's…"

"What I had to do to get you to talk to me." He looks back with a frown. "I was surprised to learn that while you're avoiding me and Xander and even Zane—and hell, pretty much everyone else—you aren't avoiding your dad. You spent Easter and your birthday with him. He said he's worried about you."

"I'm fine." I shake my head. "I've needed time to myself."

"How long do you need? Because it's going on three weeks now."

"No, it isn't."

He draws his lips into a thin line and levels me with a glare. "Yes, it is. I know I said I'd give you time, but I was expecting you to cave a hell of a lot sooner than this." He leans back and rests his phone on his leg. "You had sex—

what's the big deal? Surely you know my opinion of you wouldn't change because of that."

My fingers clench around the edges of my sketchbook, the wire spiral binding digging into my amber skin. "It wasn't just sex—it was so much worse. I really don't want to talk about it, Jimmy. I'm too…" My voice cracks, and I loath myself for that.

Jimmy considers me a moment. "Sex with Xander was that bad an experience?"

Right. We're talking about Xander.

I open my mouth, but no words come. Sex with Xander wasn't a bad experience. It still surprises me. I clear my throat. "No, it wasn't. He was…nice. I didn't expect him to be nice." And even the parts when he wasn't nice were nice.

"What were you expecting?"

Not the soft, deliberate touches. Not the potent kisses. Not any desire for me to orgasm, and not his willingness to repeat the act. Not the way I responded to it, my own arousal. Anything but that.

"I don't know. Ambivalence."

Jimmy laughs like he knows something I don't. "That seems incredibly unlikely." He quirks a mischievous smile. "You know, I tried asking Xander about it, but he wouldn't give me a straight answer. He said I'd have to ask you."

"No one was supposed to find out."

"Well, aside from whoever was paying attention to your spectacle in the cafeteria, no one else did." He shrugs, but I can't treat it lightly. "When did it happen?"

I push aside the sketchbook and lift my feet onto the couch, curling up. "That first Thursday after we got back from winter break. I was upset, and I went to find you, but you were in class."

Jimmy cocks an eyebrow. "And you found comfort in Xander's bed?"

"Not exactly." I groan. "Look, it was a stupid idea. I thought if I could get a little experience under my belt, maybe when it actually happened, I'd be prepared for it."

"What, sleeping with Xander doesn't count?"

"Of course it counts. I meant emotionally. Sex with Xander was…well, sex—and it didn't fucking prepare me for anything." I take a shaky breath.

Jimmy freezes, open-mouthed. "That's what you were talking about." Then, he shakes his head. "I shouldn't be surprised really, but part of me didn't think you'd sleep with Zane."

I lay my head on the armrest, sighing. "It was a mistake."

"That's why you're avoiding him."

For a moment, neither of us speaks. Honestly, I have no idea what to say. I don't know how to explain my stupidity or naiveté.

Jimmy shifts his weight. "You know, Zane wasn't what I expected. That whole lunch in the cafeteria was—well, I don't even know."

"Awful?" I suggest.

"Uncomfortable," he finally says. "I've been trying to figure out why you'd avoid me for two and a half weeks. It's not because you slept with Xander. What exactly happened with Zane?"

I close my eyes. That afternoon is the last thing I want to think about. "I don't want to talk about it." My voice sounds hollow even to me.

Jimmy pulls me into a hug, and I wrap my arms around

his torso. "We don't have to talk about it if you don't want to, Billie." He presses his cheek to the top of my head. "But no matter what, you know I've got your back."

I bury my face into his chest, the metal of my glasses digging into my nose. "I missed you."

"I'm across the hallway whenever you need to talk."

I pull away, trying to prevent the grimace from forming.

"You know, if you talk to Xander, you can come see me again."

Obviously, I'm unsuccessful.

I sigh. "He can't possibly want to talk to me. He made that abundantly clear. And I'm not looking on him too favorably either."

But Jimmy shakes his head in exasperation. "You're both so stubborn. It's not that difficult to walk into a room and say, 'I'm sorry.' Why can't you just admit—?"

"He was the one being an asshole."

Jimmy groans and slumps against the couch. "Okay, yes, but was his attitude toward Zane wholly unwarranted?"

No, of course not.

"Or are you more upset about what he said afterward?"

I turn back to the window, trying to sort my thoughts. He's right, of course. Xander's words were hurtful—intentionally so—but I don't know why it bothers me so much. We were barely friends, so why does it matter that the only reason he slept with me was for his own benefit? That was the premise from the beginning.

But he also had no reason to help me climax afterward.

Instead of answering, I say, "Why do I have to be the one to break the ice?"

"Because somehow—and I don't know how—he's more

stubborn than you."

My eyes narrow. "I resent that."

A small smile spreads across his face. "What, you resent you're not the more stubborn one? You're crazy."

I smile too.

"Can you at least talk to him?"

I heave a sigh. "Fine, I'll see what I can do."

He grins. "Thank you. He's been unbearable lately."

"Yeah, you better be thanking me." I swallow down any curiosity about how unbearable Xander's been in my absence—and why. "You owe me."

He doesn't and he knows it, but he says, "Yeah, alright. I'll make it up to you." With a deep breath, he pockets his phone as he stands. "You have to get back to your project, don't you? I'll leave you to it, Billie. See you later."

"Yeah, later."

He tightens his jacket, and he's gone as quickly as he appeared.

Thirty-One

THURSDAY EVENING, THE WORN DOOR TO ROOM 418 STARES me down. The dark layer of paint is chipping at the bottom edge, and the brass knob is darkened with use. There's no light shining from the crack under the door, but I know I saw him go in here an hour ago.

"Hey, Billie."

I glance to my left to see Felicia wave as she heads to dinner. She lives a couple doors down, but I barely know her. I send her a short wave and return my attention to the door. She's the third person to walk by in as many minutes.

With a sigh, I lift my hand to knock.

The room is dark, though. I must've missed him leaving. He's probably not here.

It is dinnertime, after all. Surely he's off eating with his friends—but despite being incredibly social and well-liked, Xander doesn't have genuine friends outside of Jimmy. Who would he eat with?

Finally, I let my knuckles rap against the wood.

For a long while, there's only silence, but when I turn away, searching for an excuse to give Jimmy, he unbolts the door and pries it open. He wedges his head between

314

the door and frame. "Yeah?" He's not wearing a shirt, the room's dark, and his head is covered with an unruly mop of black hair.

"Isn't it a little early to be in bed?"

His face transforms when he realizes it's me, and the blank look is replaced by his typical smirk. "I hear you're going to apologize, Dixon." He opens the door wider and steps into the hallway, shutting it behind him. "Out with it then."

I stumble back to maintain my personal space.

In front of me, he stands in only his boxers, covered with the cast of the Looney Tunes and possibly Michael Jordan, and a pair of holey socks. A shiny pink spot is transforming into a bruise at his collarbone, and there's a distinct bulge beneath his underwear.

I glance around the hallway, suddenly much emptier than a moment ago. Not that he checked first. How can he not care who sees him like this?

When at last my eyes trace back to his face, the smirk is wider. "Well?"

But I shake my head. "I'm not here to apologize."

Xander raises a skeptical eyebrow. "Then what do you want?"

I clear my throat, fiddling with the zipper on my jacket. "Can we talk somewhere a little more private?"

He laughs. "Trying to get me alone already, Dixon?" He reaches behind himself to open the door and steps inside. "Come on in."

I hesitate outside.

The room is dark, but he flips on the light switch and stoops to grab something from the floor before tossing it toward his bed. As I walk inside, he says, "Sorry." He doesn't sound sympathetic. "We'll have to cut things short, Stef."

He's not talking to me.

I don't recognize the girl or the name, but the smug look on Xander's face as he says, "Billie Dixon is going to apologize to me," doesn't faze her at all.

She scoffs. "Fine." She grabs the material he threw her way and pulls it over her head before climbing off the bed. She slips on a pair of red pumps and grabs her purse from the floor, and with nothing more than an irritated parting glance, she leaves.

Xander closes the door. "Where were we?" With a grin, he claps his hands together. "Right, you were about to apologize." He doesn't wait for a response; instead, he powers on his PlayStation and grabs the TV remote.

"Don't you want to put something on?" I ask in a tiny voice, huddling by the door.

"Why?" He doesn't look up. "You've already seen me naked. How's this worse?"

That's not the point.

"Besides, you know how much I enjoy watching you squirm." He plops down in front of the television and grabs one of the PlayStation controllers. "You wanna watch something?"

I inch forward to join him. "Are you even mad?"

He sends me an unimpressed, sidelong glance. "It has been weeks since you last looked at me, Dixon." On the screen, he flips through movie and show options, pausing every few seconds to read a summary before moving on. "I'm not sure I have anything to be angry about anyway."

He passes yet another show and begins one of the rows

again, and I roll my eyes. "Why don't you put *Gilmore Girls* on?"

"Hey." He turns to me with a glare. "Do you want me to be mad at you again?"

I let out a low laugh. "You're the one that offered to watch something but can't choose. I'm giving you an option."

Xander picks out an anime. The theme song starts. "I have plenty of options, thank you."

"Are we seriously watching this?"

"What? Don't you want to be the very best?"

"I think I'd rather apologize." I roll my eyes.

"I'm waiting."

I stare for a moment. "I thought you weren't angry."

"I'm not," he says with a shrug, "but I want to hear those words from your mouth."

"You want to gloat."

A wide grin spreads across his face. "Always."

I scowl. "I'm not going to apologize when you were the one in the wrong, Xander." I stretch my legs out and lean back on my hands, suddenly unsure. He was mean, yes, but I'm not sure how wrong he was—but I shake my head to rid myself of any thoughts of Zane. "I will, however, accept a truce."

He snorts. "You want to apologize without saying you're sorry."

"For Jimmy's sake."

Recognition lights up his eyes, and he sighs. "Fine, for Jimmy. But I want something in return."

On the television, the theme song finishes, and we watch as a concerned mother engulfs Ash in a hug.

"What could you possibly want in return for a mutual

truce?"

I shift my body to face him, but that's probably a mistake. I lean into him and watch the rise and fall of his chest. Beneath his boxers, the erection is mostly gone, but I could revive it with a touch. One arm stretches across the floor in my direction as he repositions his weight. His fingers brush my jeans, and I cannot repress the gasp at the contact. I pull my legs closer to my body.

When my eyes shift upward, he grins and twists onto his side. "You know, if you want something from me too, I'd be willing to compromise." His voice is low and gravelly, and a very small part of me—the part that doesn't think clearly—wouldn't mind taking him up on that offer.

I tighten my lips. "What do you want, Xander?"

He smirks. "I want to see your drawings."

I inhale sharply. Imogene is the only person who's seen them in years—not even Jimmy, and that's saying something. Even in high school, no one outside the two of them knew I drew in my spare time.

"No."

"Sorry, it's a deal breaker."

I shake my head. "No."

His grin widens, and he pokes my stomach. "What can I give you in return?" He waggles his eyebrows, and without refrain, his eyes trail down my body.

I swallow. I'm wearing jeans, a t-shirt, and my Converse, but I feel naked when he looks at me like that. "That's not funny." I shove him away.

His laughter says otherwise. "Oh, come on, Dixon. How do you expect to turn in an entire project based around your artwork if you can't even show me?"

Which might be a contributing factor to my poor progress on the project.

"I'm not ready for anyone to look at them."

Xander chuckles. "Obviously. Otherwise, I would've seen them already." He glances at the television, but I can't take my eyes off him. "You know I don't mind being the first to look. And you're doing a comic for your project, right? My input could be helpful."

I open my mouth to deny him again, but the words don't come.

He catches my gaze. "For Jimmy?" He doesn't even have the decency to wipe the smirk off his face.

I sigh. "You're incorrigible."

With a grin, he flicks me on the knee and leans back. "Oh, but you encourage me all the time, Dixon." His eyes meet mine, and he smiles. "Besides, maybe I can help you get over your paranoia about people seeing your work—you know, before you present it to your class."

I lie back and stare at the overhead light. It's a fair point, even if he's the one making it, and considering my chosen subject matter for the project, there's no one who knows how to execute it better than Xander.

On the TV, everyone, including Team Rocket, is tracking down the source of the sleep waves.

"Fine." My voice is uncontrollably bitter, and I don't take my eyes off the ceiling.

"Excellent." He grins like a maniac. "You have no idea how excited I am."

I close my eyes and yawn. "I can imagine."

For a moment, the television is the only sound, then he says, "You getting tired already? It's not even seven."

319

When I open my eyes, he's leaning over me curiously. He's too close. I scramble out from under him and crouch a couple feet away. My heart's racing. I cannot calm my breathing.

Confused, Xander sits back and watches me. "Are you okay? Normally I don't make you that nervous." His words are slow and quiet. Kind.

I take slow breaths to relax. "I'm fine." But I can't look at him anymore. "You surprised me, that's all."

"I can tell."

He stands, and I sneak a peek as he pulls something out of the mini-fridge. He settles down beside me, crossing his legs, and offers me a bottle of water.

"Thanks." I twist off the lid and take a drink.

"Come on." He takes my hand and scoots us closer to the TV.

On the screen, the team and Officer Jenny are taking Drowzee to the park to revive all the children who think they're Pokemon, and beside me, Xander wraps an arm around my shoulders and clasps his other hand around mine in his lap. "Pay close attention." He rubs his palm up and down my arm. "This is the episode where Misty catches Psyduck—if we're using 'catch' liberally."

I take another sip from the water bottle and twist the cap back on. "You say this like I didn't watch it when I was a kid." I rest my head on his bare shoulder. He's hot against my cheek. He smells like sweat and cigarettes, and I bite my lip.

Xander is holding me. Comforting me. I cannot make sense of it, but I do not want it to stop. I do not want him to stop.

320

Ash is fighting Team Rocket, but I close my eyes.

"You falling asleep, Dixon?" He tightens his grip and leans his cheek against my head.

I yawn again.

Thirty-Two

WHEN I TOLD XANDER TO MAKE SURE HE WAS FREE FRIDAY afternoon, his response was, "Sure, it's a date," with a snarky little laugh I didn't find funny.

I hoped the library would be mostly empty when we agreed to meet here, but I freeze at the top level. How could I be so stupid? It's been over a month, but Zane's sitting in the middle of the reading area, his calculus book propped open in front of him. As if he knows I'm coming.

I bolt down the stairs before he can see me and pull out my phone.

Xander answers after one ring. "I know, I know. I'm late." His lighter clicks a couple times; he needs a smoke before seeing me.

"You are, but that's not why I'm calling."

"I'm walking there now. I had to talk to Harding after class, which was a mistake because she talks really slowly and it takes forever."

"I'm not there anymore." I take the steps down to ground level and head back along the Lane. "Can we meet somewhere else?"

"Where? I'm walking from Gainor."

"Your car?"

Xander usually parks his Camaro in the lot off the Lane, close to the dorms. The car is easy to locate—most of the vehicles on campus are from this century—and by the time he reaches the parking lot, I'm leaning against the passenger door, eyes shut, trying to quell the panic.

"Too tired to wait up for me?"

I pop open an eye.

Chuckling, Xander's standing near the hood, cigarette in one hand, keys in the other.

I reach for the handle. "Unlock the doors."

He drops the cigarette to the concrete and smashes it before moving toward the red car.

Once inside, I sling my bag into the back seat and sit while he buckles himself in. That bit in the library was too close for comfort.

"You alright?" He shoves the key into the ignition, presses his foot on the clutch, and starts the engine, and then, he waits. It takes a second to realize he wants me to put on my seatbelt.

When the belt is in place, he shifts the car into gear, and I turn to him. "I'm exhausted, but it's not a problem."

"You getting sick?"

I shake my head. "I haven't been getting enough sleep." Not that that's anything new.

"We can do this later if you're too tired."

"I don't have time. Drive."

He glances in the rear-view mirror before slowly releasing the clutch and brake, and the car shakily backs out of the parking spot.

"As it is, I have to spend all weekend working on this. It's due in two weeks, and I've been procrastinating. I could

323

really use your help, Xander."

Halfway out of the parking spot, he steps on the brake and flashes me a grin. "Is that a fact? You flatter me." He twists the wheel and backs the rest of the way out. "You know I'm going to remind you of this moment for the rest of your life, right?"

"Oh, God." I turn to look out the window. "I'm going to have to deal with you that long?"

"At least the next couple years, right?" He shrugs and directs the car toward the lot exit.

"I suppose that's manageable."

My hands grip the edge of the seat as he zooms past parked cars, barely missing a backing-up Prius that stops as we pass. He stops when we reach the street. "Where am I going?"

I glance both ways. I hadn't thought about that. "Uh, the coffee shop?"

He turns left onto the Lane.

◆

Xander waits in line to order, and I slide into a booth at the back of the Jittery Bug. I set my backpack by my feet, pull the sketchbooks from my bag, and place them on the table. My hands interlace on top of them while I wait, and I suppress a yawn.

A couple minutes later, he sits beside me, holding two cups of bottomless coffee. "You like the Colombian one, right?" He slides one over and rifles through his jacket pocket. "And lots of half-and-half." He deposits six cups on the table next to my sketchbooks.

I roll my eyes. "That's a little overkill, but thanks, I guess." I reach for the coffee cup, remove the lid, and pour in a couple packages. "And my change?"

He laughs and stands up halfway to pull a five-dollar bill from his jeans pocket. "I was hoping you wouldn't notice that. I gave the rest as a tip." He shrugs, unapologetic, and sits down again.

In front of me, the sketchbooks wait, but Xander doesn't reach for them or even act curious.

I'm not ready, but this was the agreement—and what's more, he's right. Not that I'd say that out loud. My presentation is a week from Thursday, and there's no way I can make it through an entire presentation if I can't show my drawings to someone other than Imogene.

Once I stir in the half-and-half, I take a drink, then a deep breath, and push the first sketchbook over.

Xander moves his cup to the far side of the table and touches the front cover.

It's a simple Strathmore drawing pad, the image of a woman's face of the brown cover. Thick, toothy, 80-pound paper perfect for Conte crayons and pastels. The second sketchbook, sitting beneath my own fingertips, is Bristol paper—heavyweight but smooth for ink pens and drawing pencils.

I watch with bated breath as he flips open the cover, taking care not to bend or smudge anything. He scans the page, then moves to the next and the next until there aren't any more pages. He closes it neatly and slides it away before grabbing his coffee.

"Well?"

He swallows and sets his drink to the side again. "I don't

know what you're worried about, Dixon." He turns toward me, eyes focused on the sketchbook. "You're not bad."

I place my hand on the sketchbook to draw it closer, but he lays his fingers over mine to stop me. "What does that mean?" I try to pull it from under him.

With a laugh, Xander pushes me away and opens the sketchbook again, searching. "You like landscapes a lot." He points to a sketch I did of the green space in front of the library. "I guess they're cityscapes, right?" He doesn't wait for an answer; he shrugs and moves on. "You don't draw people often. But," he adds, holding back a snicker, "you do enjoy drawing my bedroom."

I roll my eyes. "Don't say it like that."

"I don't know what you mean." But he laughs as he flips a couple pages forward and points to the image I drew the first Thursday night of the semester. "You draw with lines a lot."

My eyebrows rise. "Really?"

"I mean, you put in a lot of straight, meticulous lines, but this one—they're more prominent, heavier, not so perfect." He looks up with a straight face. "Were you actually feeling emotions on this day, Dixon?"

I laugh and elbow him in the arm. "Don't be a dick about this. It's serious."

"Yes, but not nearly as serious as you're making it out to be." He grins and nudges me back. "You don't need to panic because someone's looking at these. They're good."

I look up. "Good?"

Xander smiles. A genuine, kind smile that I cannot resist returning. "Yes, they're good. I can see how much of yourself you put into them." He scoots closer to whisper conspiratorially, his breath on my face. "Do you wanna know which one is my favorite?"

I'm pretty sure I don't.

He flips to the back of the book, commenting on a couple drawings as he passes: "A few good ones of Jimmy writing an essay. You've got his hair down pat. But this one." He stops at the second to last page. "This one is the best."

I know exactly which one it is by his smug tone.

"I mean, it's not exactly naked," he says, nodding his head from side to side, "but it'll have to do. You must have all the NSFW drawings somewhere else." He grins, and I try not to laugh despite my flushed cheeks. "You saving them for later?" He glances at the Bristol pad under my hand. "You definitely have more than two sketchbooks."

"I'm not going to justify that with a response."

He laughs and looks back at the drawing of himself. "You could've said something and I probably would've stopped screaming at the game."

I smile. "That wouldn't have the same candor. Besides, there are only so many times I can draw the same room."

He nods to the Bristol pad. "What's in that one?"

"Mostly sketches I've done for the project, but I don't know where I'm going with it. Oh, and a few drawings from stock photos." I hand him the sketchbook, and he slides the first one back to me underneath.

He flips open the cover and leans over the pages, examining the work inside. The Bristol pad contains mostly portraits—comic book characters in the style of Greg Capullo and Jock, Batman and his villains, Superman and Lois Lane, and some of the X-Men. Some are pencil sketches, some inked.

"These are decent." He nods as he looks through the pages.

The drawings from stock photos are for practice. Hands and faces. A girl sitting in different positions. Heads at different angles. Somehow, three-quarters is always the hardest.

"It's difficult to put them in original positions. The best are ones where I had an image to study." I nod to an image of Jamie Madrox and Dr. MacTaggert. "It doesn't feel organic."

Xander turns the page again. "I imagine the cure for that's practice, right?"

"Yes, but I don't have time. I have thirteen days to finish this project, and I'm basically nowhere."

He shakes his head. "Not nowhere." He turns back to the previous image. "How in-depth does it need to be? A final version—colored and everything?"

I pull the rubric from my bag, and he leans over my shoulder to read it with me.

"Well," he says after a moment, "it doesn't specify. I'd bet if you have the storyline sound and all the drawings and text penciled in, you're fine. You certainly don't have time to color it now; don't stress about it."

How can he be so blasé about this? Sure, it's not his project, but if it were, he still wouldn't let it bother him.

"What've you been thinking about for the plot?"

Before I can respond, a server drops off a basket of food with a smile and an apology for the wait—they're short-staffed.

I frown. "You ordered food?"

"It's almost five o'clock—yeah, I ordered food." Xander scoots the sketchbook closer to me and examines his fish

328

and chips. A small cup of tartar sauce is situated between two tenders. "Do you want any?" He offers me a waffle fry.

The very idea of eating something right now turns my stomach.

"No."

He takes a bite, wipes his fingers on a napkin, and looks back to the drawing pad. "Where were we?"

I can't take my eyes off the food. "Uh, plot?"

"Right." He pauses to swallow and continues. "There's no way you're fitting all these characters into a single issue. They're not all from the same universe. What are you doing about that?" He dips the fish in the tartar sauce before taking another bite. It smells awful.

"Uh…" But I'm drawing a blank. "Characters?"

He clears his throat, and I lift my eyes to meet his. "What's the story about? Who are your characters? What's the plot?"

I scoot to the edge of the seat. "I'm sorry, I'm having trouble focusing."

"Tired?"

I rest my chin on my hand. "Maybe I am getting sick."

Xander casts a smile in my direction. "Well, if you pass out here, you don't get to sleep in my bed again."

Deep breath. I close my eyes. "Shut up." It comes out more harshly than intended.

He reaches out a hand to my forearm, but I pull away and rise from the booth. "I'll be right back."

The ladies' room is a single-toilet room with a small sink and a decorative display of potpourri. The dark rust-colored walls make the light less harsh, and I lean over the sink and splash cold water on my face.

329

What is wrong with me? There isn't time for this. We have two more weeks before finals. I can't afford to be sick.

Deep breaths.

I pat myself dry with a paper towel before returning to the booth.

"You okay?" Xander asks when I collapse in my seat.

I nod.

It's a lie. Even as a nod, it's a lie. We both know it, but he doesn't pry.

Thirty-Three

I PAUSE IN FRONT OF THE COOLERS IN THE DAIRY SECTION, considering the Simply half-gallon juices. Regular lemonade or with raspberry? I pull open the glass door to grab a bottle before turning away from the grocery section.

It's eight o'clock, and the small-town Walmart is nearly vacant. I pass clothing, electronics, toys, sporting gear, and turn left toward the front. Hygiene and self-care products are at the front by the pharmacy.

I follow the tile floor through the departments and stop at Health & Beauty. Which aisle is it? With feminine hygiene, pads, tampons? Or would it be with the condoms? How the fuck is this place organized anyway?

I walk through three short aisles before I locate them, next to the condoms and lube. I glance at the condoms, frowning—I don't even want to know how much Xander spends on that—before scanning the section on the left.

AccuClear, Clearblue, First Signal, e.p.t., First Response, the off-brand.

Does it really matter? It's just in case anyway. I'm so stressed, I'm sure it's nothing more than a bad cold. Maybe the flu considering the nausea.

I grab a two-pack off the shelf and head for the check-out. There's no line.

"Did you find everything you were looking for?" The woman behind the register smiles as she swipes the box and the lemonade past the scanner.

Okay, let's not make this more awkward than it already is.

I force a smile in return. "Yeah, thanks."

She slips the items in a bag, and I hand her a twenty-dollar bill. She pops open the drawer, counts out my change, and hands it to me, along with my receipt. "Thanks for coming in. Have a great night."

"You too." I shove the money and receipt in my pants pocket before heading for the exit. This is going to be a long night. I twist open the lemonade cap and tear off the protective seal before I leave the store.

◆

The room is empty when I get back. Val is probably out. It is a Saturday night after all.

The bottle of lemonade is half gone when I place it on my desk. I take the plastic sack into the bathroom with me. No sign of Prudence or Cynthia.

I sit on the toilet lid and tear open the box. Somewhere in here are instructions. The folded paper is wedged between one side of the box and the foil-wrapped sticks.

Let's see.

Store at room temperature. Do not freeze. Keep out of reach of children. Do not use if the foil wrapper is damaged. Do not use if past expiration date. Do not insert into vagina.

How many women stick pregnancy tests up their vaginas? Seriously. Apparently, enough to warrant a warning.

I read through the instructions and pull one of the sticks from the box. The test stick, when unwrapped, is off-white with two small windows and a capped end.

For a moment, I can only stare.

I can either pee on this for five seconds and hope I don't get urine all over it. Or I can pee in a cup and dip it for twenty seconds.

I frown. That seems like an odd time difference.

There aren't any cups in here, though.

I set the test on the tank and slip out of the room to grab one of the paper cups from the vanity. This will have to do. I flip up the toilet lid and double-check the door's locked before sitting down to pee. The cup fills quickly, and I pull it out to finish peeing in the bowl.

This is supposed to be over ninety-nine percent accurate. It better be.

Now count to twenty.

I cap the stick and set it on the toilet's tank, face up, and wait.

I dump the contents of the paper cup into the toilet bowl, close the lid again, and flush. Cup in trash. Sit down. Wait.

All I can do is wait.

I tap my foot against the tile floor as the toilet continues to run. I hate waiting.

I left my phone in the bedroom. How do I know when the two minutes are up? I'm not leaving it alone to check the time. Anyone could walk in. And I can't take it with me. It says it needs to stay flat with the windows facing upward for best accuracy. I want the accuracy. I guess I'm stuck in here.

At least this way, I'm the only one to see it.

I sit down, facing away. I can't look at it. I don't want to see yet. Not till it's time. Not till I'm sure it's negative. It has to be negative. There was a condom for God's sake. It can't be anything but negative.

I should've brought in the lemonade. My mouth is dry.

Or my phone. I could play games on my phone. And you know, check the time. I could've set a timer. Two minutes. Two unbelievably long minutes. Maybe with a timer it would be more bearable.

The toilet is still running. Jiggle the handle. A few seconds later, it stops.

But now the room is quiet.

It has to be two minutes by now.

I take a deep breath and twist to grab the stick from the back of the toilet, my hand covering the results window. I guess it's time.

Minus, minus, minus.

This needs to be negative.

I close my eyes and inch back my fingers enough to reveal the results. If I don't open my eyes, it can't be true. It's negative. It has to be negative.

Inhale. Exhale. Calm.

I force my eyes open. It's faint, but it's there—a thin vertical line crossing the thicker, darker horizontal one.

This can't be right. It's a mistake. The test's not a hundred percent accurate. Should I do it again? Wait until morning? Isn't the first pee of the day usually better because it's more concentrated? This cannot be true.

I clutch the test in my hand and exit the bathroom. I

have to get out of here. I can't breathe. I can't think. I need air. Get rid of the evidence first. How many plastic bags do I need to wrap this in to make it inconspicuous while I carry it to the dumpster?

Keys, phone, student ID. Shoes. I need shoes.

◆

Campus is bigger at night. It's half past nine, and it's dark, colder, stranger, oddly beautiful. The lights cast elusive shadows in each direction. They follow me, haunt me. I stumble over the uneven sidewalk along the Lane.

Few students are out right now—at least here. It's Saturday night. They're probably hanging out, drinking, partying, having sex. That's probably where Xander is, and maybe Jimmy too. They haven't asked me to join them when they go out yet, which almost surprises me, but I don't imagine I'm the best company right now.

A couple students exit Rutherford Hall as I pass, to-go cups from the Eyrie in their hands.

Past Rutherford, the Lane intersects with King Street. I barely glance either direction before crossing, despite the red light. On the other side are the science, business, and art buildings and several off-campus parking lots. Beyond that, upperclassmen housing.

The wind is cold. I forgot to grab a jacket.

I cross my arms and huddle down. I don't know where I'm going. There's nowhere to go. But I keep walking, my feet pounding against the pavement. I don't know what else to do.

The light of the moon illuminates everything. I pass

parked cars and empty parking spots, flowering trees, maintenance buildings, hedges and garden space by the sidewalk. They're all a blur. Nothing stands out. Nothing matters.

I don't know how this could possibly get worse.

I trip over a section of broken sidewalk and stumble to a halt. Finally, I look around. How far have I gone? There's the Gainor Business School, and next to me, the art building. On the right side of the street is the Stoddard Center for Physical Sciences. And past that is the upperclassmen housing.

Dammit.

Why am I here? Zane lives over there. His apartment is in one of the closest buildings to the science center. This is the path he walks to and from classes.

I spin round and retrace my steps. My feet stumble over the broken sidewalk, and I fall to my hands and knees. I can't do this.

"Billie?"

Shit.

Shit, shit, shit.

Don't look up. Don't make eye contact.

I struggle to my feet and wipe my hands on my jeans.

Zane stands in front of me, wearing a blue Bradford hoody with a stylized falcon, carrying a to-go box from the Eyrie. He says my name again, but I give him a wide berth. He watches, frowning, as I pass, but he isn't ready to let it go:

"Are you not going to talk to me until graduation? That'd be pretty convenient, wouldn't it? Avoid me until you don't have to anymore?"

I close my eyes. This is the worst timing.

"Seriously, Billie." Anger laces his voice, but I keep walking. "Are you going to ignore everything that makes you uncomfortable?"

I stop.

No. I can't do this.

"That's incredibly immature."

My jaw clenches. It's hardly his place to comment. My hands ball into fists, and I turn back. He's squishing the to-go box between his hands.

"You think I'm ignoring this? You think I have the luxury of ignoring this?"

He gives a one-shouldered shrug. "I don't see any other explanation for what you're doing."

I level him with a glare. "You don't know. You don't have any idea."

"How could I? You shut me out completely after we slept together. It's been five weeks. The sex couldn't have been that bad."

For a second, all I can do is stare. "Bad?" The word leaves an awful taste in my mouth. "What in the world could've possibly made you think this has anything to do with how bad the sex was?"

"Maybe the fact that you bolted out of there the second it was over." He shakes his head. "Didn't you want to?"

I don't have an answer for that. I don't know. But that's hardly the concern foremost on my mind.

"I should've known it was too soon." He looks down. "I tried to give you space, hoping you'd eventually come and talk to me, but you were never going to, were you?"

"No, I wasn't."

Zane's face twists with confusion. "What did I do

337

wrong?"

How can he even ask that? After everything, how can he think he did everything right?

"Are you serious?" My voice is raw with horror. This is too much.

He frowns. "Why are you angry? You said you weren't a virgin. Did you lie?"

"It doesn't matter. That—the sex—never should have happened. It was wrong. It was an awful, terrible decision, and I can't believe that I—that I let you do that."

A muscle twitches at his jaw. "Yeah, I get the picture, thanks."

"I really don't think you do, Zane. You have no idea what kind of impact your actions have."

He scoffs and looks away. "Yeah, well, as long as we're being honest, I have to level with you. The condom broke."

My eyes widen. "What do you mean, it broke?"

His eyes meet mine again. "When I pulled out, it was torn. Most of it was still there—I didn't notice till I was throwing it away." His words are bitter.

"How could you not let me know when this happened?"

"Tell me how I was supposed to do that. You were out the door so fast. Besides, it's not a big deal. Maybe a little got out. What's the harm?"

"'The harm.'" I cannot keep my voice steady. "'What's the harm?' How can you think there's no harm in a broken condom? What could possibly be going through your brain to make you think that's okay?"

Zane raises an eyebrow.

"Not every girl is on birth control, you asshole. If you had said something—anything—I could've done something about this, I could've fixed this."

He frowns. "Fixed what? What are you talking about?"

"Nothing that concerns you. This has nothing to do with you anymore."

"Wait," he says slowly, "are you—?"

"No, no. I cannot talk to you right now. I just can't." I turn away and stalk toward the dorms.

"That's nothing new," he yells after me. For a moment, he's silent, and I reach the intersection. "Dammit, Billie, I can help you."

No. No, you can't.

I cross King Street and break into a run. Anything to put more space between us.

Thirty-Four

THE CAFETERIA IS SURGING WITH ENERGY. IT'S BEEN WEEKS since I sat down at one of these tables. There wasn't much point in going when I wasn't talking to Xander and Jimmy. Because of the nausea, I'm eating less than ever.

My class got out early, so they aren't here yet. I have my booklet of Bristol paper, several pages of outlines, sketchbooks, and a spiral-bound notebook spread across half the circular table. I flip between pages, looking from my sketches to the outline, then down at the script, gel pen in hand to make corrections and notations.

There's so much work to be done, and I have a week. One week. To do all of this. I'm still trying to wrap my head around it.

"Making progress?"

I glance up.

Xander's already sitting next to me. How did I not notice their arrival?

"Slowly." I press my pen to the page again, leaning close.

"Have you gotten anything to eat?" Jimmy asks.

I shake my head, not bothering to look up. "I'm not hungry."

"Like always." Xander scoots closer and picks up one of the outline pages. "You settled on Multiple Man then?"

"It seems the most appropriate to the assignment." My shrug is a tiny jerk of the shoulder. "He's not one of the main X-Men, though. I had to do a lot of research."

Xander nods. "He's a good choice. Fitting, given what we talked about." He glances around the table. "It's going to be bigger, right?"

I roll my eyes. "This is the outline. What do you think?"

"Have you started any of the pages?" He reaches across me to grab the sketchbook to my left and flips open the booklet. Inside, there are a couple pages drawn in 2H pencil. He strains to look at the panels before turning his attention to me. "This is it?"

"So far." I snatch the book from him with a glare. "You can see it when I have more to show."

Xander smiles and presses against my arm for a better look at the script I'm editing. "I'll happily look at anything you want to show me, Dixon." There's an edge to his voice that says he isn't just talking about my artwork, and my stomach twists at the thought. "Why're you majoring in math? You should be doing this. If this is what you can do by yourself, can you imagine how much better you'd be with a teacher?"

A blush rises to my cheeks, and he offers a smile. My knees are weak, my breath shallow, and all I can do is beam like an idiot.

"Wow."

I jerk and turn. Xander does too.

On the opposite side of the table, Jimmy stands, staring at us.

My blush deepens. "What?" My voice is weak.

Jimmy tries to shrug it off, but he's obviously unsettled. "I guess I didn't believe it." His speech is slow. Then, he clears his throat. "When you told me she showed you her drawings, I mean."

Xander laughs. "Would I lie to you?"

Jimmy forces a laugh and diplomatically decides not to answer. Instead, he excuses himself to get food, and Xander returns to examining the script.

"Can I look at this?"

I push the papers toward him. "I'm going to grab a drink."

He's already immersed in the page.

With a deep breath, I walk to the drink station. The plastic cups, stacked in large bins beside the fountain machine, glisten with water; they must be fresh out of the dish room. I fill one and turn toward the table. Xander is engrossed in my work.

I survey the room as I walk. A pair of gray eyes stare back. I come to an abrupt stop.

Zane.

He's watching me.

My hand clenches around the cup. I don't want to look at him, but I can't move. I'm trapped by his eyes and the anger and confusion lingering beneath them. He knows. Of course he knows. He might not be very smart, but he isn't stupid either. He knows, and he's trying to tell me something. But I don't understand.

"You getting anything to eat?"

I break eye contact and turn to find Jimmy grabbing a cup, a plate of food in one hand. He smiles, but I can't return it.

I shouldn't have come here. This was a mistake. I didn't realize he'd be here. I didn't realize he'd be watching me. This is wrong, so wrong.

I return to our table, where Xander has moved on to the next page, and Jimmy follows. I take my seat, clutching the cup close to my chest. My panicked heart is pounding in my ears. Xander's saying something, but I can't hear him. Jimmy's face is worried. He's always worried. I can't do this. I shouldn't be here.

Xander looks up when I don't answer, and he pushes the papers aside, his smile fading. He pulls the cup from my grip. His eyes don't leave mine. He closes his hand around my fist; his skin is hot on my cold fingers.

"You're okay."

For a moment, I believe him.

I take a deep breath and force my body to relax. I stretch open my fist and twist my palm upward to meet his, our fingers intertwining. "Okay."

He draws my attention to the askew papers on the table. "I'm not sure what's going on here—what's this about multiple personalities and doppelgangers? What's diachronic personality?"

I swallow, trying to get my bearing. "Well, the whole thing has to do with personal identity and personal truth. With Jamie Madrox, his duplicates develop their own lives, right?" My voice is shaking, but Xander's hand holding mine keeps me steady.

He nods. "There are plenty of storylines where you aren't sure which Madrox is the original and which is the duplicate."

"Exactly." I shift closer to point out a section in the script. "And when he absorbs the duplicates, he gains all their memories too, but somehow, they can develop separate personalities. I guess what I'm trying to ask is, are they a part of him, or are they genuinely their own identities?"

"How's it end?" His free hand lifts the corner of the paper to glance at the page underneath.

"That's what I'm working on. It mostly examines different theories—non-circular, empirical theories and non-empirical, circular ones. It's not really meant to give you any answers."

"Right." He turns to me with a smile. "Most philosophy I've read is supposed to make you think and draw your own conclusions."

I send him a small smile in return.

"What are you doing tonight?"

I frown. I know what he's thinking. I shouldn't be alone. "I don't know. I'm done with classes. I don't have any plans after my—wait, what time is it?"

Xander lifts his wrist to read his watch. "Just after noon. You have somewhere to go?"

"Shit." I pull away and gather my papers and sketch-books into a pile. "I have to go. I have, uh—" I pause my rapid movements "—a prior engagement." I push everything inside my backpack, zip it shut, and sling it over my shoulder.

Across the table, Jimmy speaks again. I forgot he's here. "'Prior engagement'? That sounds serious."

I shake my head, not sure how to answer. "Something I have to do."

Xander catches my hand before I can walk away, and I

344

pause to look at him. "We've got a shift at the Eyrie tonight, but it's usually dead. We're going to take a bottle of vodka and pour it in the slushie machine. Come hang out with us."

I almost laugh at the stupidity of it. "I'll try."

♦

Inside Acker Medical Facility, the room is cold and vacant. I sit on the aqua-colored seat, fiddling with my thumbs, staring at the motivational posters. Their happy nature juxtaposes the cold, sterile setting. How comfortable do they think the posters make their patients?

A knock sounds on the door, and a brunette nurse pops her head into the room, smiling. "Hi. Miss Wilhelmina Dixon?"

I nod.

"Come with me."

I follow her into the back toward the exam rooms. We pause on the way to check my height and weight.

She sits me on the edge of an exam bed, a sheet of white paper pulled down from a roll at the top, and she settles into the swivel chair at the computer. "My name's Judy." She sends me another smile. "I have a few questions to ask you before Dr. Sinclair comes in."

"Okay."

She logs in and pulls up my chart. They probably haven't yet added in the information I filled out in the waiting room. She clicks around for a minute before offering me an apologetic smile. "Let's get started. When was your last menstrual period?"

I knew they would ask, but I don't have an answer.

"I don't keep track. It's never been regular. Two or three months ago."

She nods. "How long do they typically last?"

"Maybe five days."

"Is this your first pregnancy?"

"Yes."

She asks a few more questions before saying, "Alright, we'll give you a few minutes to change." She gestures to the gown sitting behind me. "Then, Dr. Sinclair will come in to talk and give you a physical. Since your LMP is uncertain, she'll bring in a transvaginal ultrasound if we have one available."

The nurse leaves with a smile, but my stomach is uneasy.

A few minutes after I change into the gown, Dr. Sinclair knocks and enters. "Hi, Wilhelmina. I'm Amelia Sinclair. It's lovely to meet you." She pushes a stray silver lock behind her ear and sits on the chair. "Are you nervous? It's okay to be nervous." She gestures me to lie back.

I feel sick.

She rolls closer as I drape a white towel across my legs and recline on the bed. She pulls out two metal extensions and asks me to place my feet in them and scoot closer to the bottom edge. "We're doing a simple pelvic exam right now." She wheels over a tray with an assortment of ominous-looking tools.

"This might feel a little chilly." She picks up a metal clamp. "We've warmed it up so it isn't too cold." She smiles before delving beneath the towel.

She lied. It's cold.

My muscles protest as they're pushed apart, and Dr. Sinclair's hand snakes out to grab a small long-handled brush. "This'll pinch a little."

That one isn't a lie.

The pinch makes me jump and feel cold all over. Her hand darts out to grab a similar brush, then another pinch.

She pulls back and puts away her tools. The clamp is removed slowly, and I shift uneasily, trying to feel normal again. The brushes are placed inside separate vials and snipped off.

"You may have a little bit of spotting after this." She moves my legs down and pushes in the footholds. "That's normal. Some women's cervixes are more sensitive." She removes her gloves, throws them away, and washes her hands before returning to do the breast exam with a fresh set of blue gloves.

When it's over, she steps out for a minute to check on the status of the ultrasound machine. The nurse Judy returns promptly.

"Do you need to use the restroom? We need to test your urine, and you need to have an empty bladder for the ultrasound."

Judy hands me a cup and escorts me down the hall to the bathroom a couple doors down. I sit on the toilet, read the directions posted on the wall, and try to pee without splattering everywhere. The capped sample goes in the cupboard by the door, and I wash my hands.

We return to the exam room, and I sit on the bed again.

Dr. Sinclair returns a few minutes later with the ultrasound machine on a rolling cart. She wheels it into the room and takes a minute to make sure it's on. As she works, she asks me a few questions.

"Have you been experiencing any symptoms yet?

347

Exhaustion, nausea, breast tenderness?"

"A little."

"Are you taking a prenatal vitamin?"

"No."

"You'll want to buy some right away." When the computer is ready, she washes her hands again before settling on the chair next to the machine. "Most likely, you're in the early stages. Symptoms will become more apparent in the next couple weeks." She smiles while pulling a glove onto her right hand. "Are you ready to meet your baby?"

No, not even remotely.

"Alright, Wilhelmina." But I can't look at her. "This is what we call a transvaginal ultrasound, which means we'll insert a probe inside your vagina to get a closer look at your uterus. This early on, we wouldn't be able to get a proper gestation date with the transabdominal ultrasound because the fetus is too small. This method allows for greater detail."

She retrieves a long probe attached via cord to the machine. "This is the probe. As you can see, it's not much wider than a tampon, and we'll cover it with jelly so it can move easily. You should feel some pressure like with the pelvic exam, and there will be some general discomfort while it's inside because we'll put it right next to your cervix. If you feel anything more than discomfort or pressure, let me know and we can stop."

I nod, staring at the probe in her hand. The off-white instrument hardly looks inviting, and the length is a bit daunting, though part of that must be a handle.

"Once the wand is inside, sound waves will bounce off your internal organs to give us a picture of your reproductive organs. We'll do a few measurements to see the gestation age and listen to the heartbeat."

She sets the probe down and rolls toward the bed to pull out the stirrups again. She guides each leg into the footrest and has me lie back like before.

"Are you ready?"

I inhale deeply and look down at my bent legs, covered by the towel once again. "Yes."

Dr. Sinclair moves back to the machine and pulls out a condom. Her hand movements are expert as she tears open the wrapper and unrolls the latex. From the edge of the cart, she grabs a bottle of lubricant and squeezes a dollop inside before inserting the wand. The condom is too big for it. More lube is applied to the outside before she rolls toward me and lifts the towel.

"You'll feel some pressure."

The probe squelches as she inserts it, and I try not to tense my muscles as it moves inward and bumps uncomfortably against my cervix.

On the screen, the program shows more than black now. Fuzzy swirls spread across the screen in shades of gray as she moves the wand to locate my uterus.

"Right here," she says a minute later, "these are your ovaries, and here in front of them is your uterus." She zooms in on the computer. "This over here is your placenta—" she points to a slightly darker part of the screen "—and here is the fetus."

I honestly don't know how she can understand the mesmerizing movements on the screen. It doesn't look like much of anything until she zooms in farther.

With her free hand, Dr. Sinclair measures the fetus from head to butt. Its parts are barely distinguishable. It's tiny.

349

But it's there.

While the computer does its calculations, she moves the wand to get a better look at the uterus, the gestation sac, and the ovaries again. "Everything here looks healthy. The fetus is approximately two centimeters long, which puts it at eight weeks and two days. Estimated due date is December Twenty-First."

"Wait, that doesn't make any sense."

It's barely been six weeks since Zane, and Xander was a month and a half before that. Eight weeks is wrong.

Dr. Sinclair pauses. "The most reliable measurement we have is the start of a woman's last menstrual period, but conception is usually two weeks after that. Because we don't have a reliable LMP, we measure based on the size of the fetus. Your ultrasound says conception most likely occurred six weeks and two days ago."

I nod and look away from the screen, and she returns to the machine.

"Heart rate looks to be around 165." She types a note in my files. "I'm going to take a few pictures of everything for your files, and then we're done."

On the bed, I shut my eyes and focus on my breathing as she moves the wand and clicks away at the computer.

After a couple minutes, she pulls the probe away gently. "Alright, that's everything, Wilhelmina." She cleans the end and readies the machine to leave the room before putting away the stirrups. "I'll get your photo printed and be right back. Go ahead and get dressed. There are paper towels on the counter if you need them. When I get back, we can discuss our next steps."

When she's gone, I sit up and examine the room. I'm wet

and sticky and overall uncomfortable. I need to scrub all of this away, but it won't fix anything.

I slip down, wipe myself off, and pull my clothes back on. After that, all I can do is wait.

Dr. Sinclair returns, once again knocking and waiting a moment before entering. In her hands, she holds a small photograph, which she offers to me.

"We have some bloodwork to run; I'll have Judy take you there when we're done." She studies me with a smile.

I clutch the photograph to my chest. I can't look at it yet.

"Now, there is one thing we need to discuss before you leave. Wilhelmina, your BMI is 16.4. You're underweight, which can make carrying a baby to full term difficult. You need to gain somewhere between thirty to forty pounds during your pregnancy to maintain a healthy prenatal weight. Make sure you're eating high-protein, high-fiber foods, and you should be snacking two or three times between meals." She pauses a moment for this to sink in.

All I can say is, "Okay."

"Do you have any questions? You'll want to schedule another appointment as you leave. We won't need to see you again for another month…"

But I stop listening. I cast my eyes downward to look at the photo.

The image is dark on white paper, but the shape of the fetus is unmistakable. The two-centimeter measurement is marked on it, and on the bottom is the gestation date and my full name.

Now there's proof.

Thirty-Five

IN THE SUNLIGHT, THE YELLOW PAINT OF MY FATHER'S HOUSE glows. The porch, as well as the rest of the residence, is clean and bare, aside from the rarely used rocking chair and a large Japanese peace lily. At the front, the columns are painted white to match the gutters and picket fence, and the wood flooring is sanded and stained a deep ochre.

I don't know how my dad has the time to keep this place maintained, and for the life of me, I've never paid so much attention to these details before. But I've also never spent twenty minutes standing here, wondering whether I should knock.

The front door is shut, but several windows are open. At some point, the chilly spring turned warm. I don't know when. I haven't been paying attention. I've had a lot on my mind.

At last, I rap my knuckles on the front door and turn away. I'm not ready to see his face.

His footsteps approach. Then, the door creaks open.

"Mina?" His voice quivers curiously.

I turn slowly, my eyes focused on the bent paper in my hands, long tangled strands of hair falling in my eyes. I didn't bother to put it up after showering.

"Come inside." He ushers me across the threshold. "You're always welcome here. You never have to knock."

He leads me to the dining room, where he has a stack of worksheets to grade and an enormous 1,500-piece puzzle of Neuschwanstein Castle in Germany, half done. The elegant Cinderella-esque fortress is steeped in a beautiful layer of winter snow—contrary to the picturesque spring that's taken over St. Clare.

I sit on the edge of my chair and clasp my hands together on my lap. Under the table, my palms cover the photograph. Not that he could see it anyway.

He sits across from me, concern etched on his face. "Is everything alright?"

No, definitely not.

I shake my head, but I can't look at him. I tested a dozen modes of explanation on the way over. I still don't know what to say.

He tries again. "Would you like anything to drink?" There is, after all, already a pot on the table.

I shake my head again.

Dad leans close, but the table blocks us. "Tell me what's wrong."

People claim pictures say a thousand words. I slide the photograph into his awaiting hands and drum my fingers on the table as he examines the ultrasound, silent. My stomach churns.

"I don't know what to do." Hopefully, my words can wake him from his temporary stupor. "I haven't told anyone. I don't know how I could explain this to Mom. I've only had the one appointment, but the doctor talks like I'm supposed to be happy about this...thing inside me."

I can't bring myself to say the word.

At last, his hazel eyes flicker to mine. "What do you want to do, Mina?"

I run a hand through my hair. A large section of cork-screw curls falls on the table. "I don't know. What am I supposed to do? I'm barely an adult."

He takes a long breath and walks around the table. "Don't think about what you're supposed to do." Dad takes the open chair beside me. "If you spend your whole life doing what others want, you'll never do anything for yourself. Trust me when I tell you this is one of those things you need to do because you want to." He squeezes my hand, a soft smile on his lips. "Your mother and I were quite young when we had you, and I'm afraid it was too soon for us."

I focus on our conjoined hands and force myself to keep talking. "I'm not ready to have a baby. I wouldn't have the faintest idea what to do with it. Where would I live? How could I possibly get my degree? How could I get a job? There's no way I could pay for childcare." I sigh. "What kind of life would it have without knowing its father?"

Dad hesitates before venturing to ask, "Who is the father?"

I don't want to say it out loud. The idea that Zane would father my child is hardly something I want to put in words, but Dad already knows.

"It was Zane Nelson."

I nod slightly. "It was a lapse in judgment. I don't know what I was thinking. It'll never happen again."

But he directs me to face him. "It's okay, Mina. Mistakes happen. They don't mean you've failed. They're learning experiences." He smiles, but it doesn't reach his eyes. "What have I been teaching you your entire life?"

I almost laugh. "You're using this moment for a lesson?"

He ignores the minor jibe. "Mathematics is based on logic, the logic of the world around us and how it all fits together. When you're working a problem but don't know the steps, you're going to get the wrong answer. But you can learn and try again, and you will get the correct answer."

"How do I know I missed something until I have the wrong answer, though?"

"You'll never have all the answers, Mina, no one does. That's why we have teachers and parents and friends—these are the people we learn from, rely on. You have good teachers and good friends here." He quirks a smile. "I won't make any guarantees about good parents, though."

I release a quiet laugh, and he studies me.

"For a long time, I've wanted to tell you…" He hesitates. "Everyone makes mistakes—and no one more so than myself, Mina. Your mother and I, we stayed together longer than we should have because I didn't want to leave you. When everything came to a head, I didn't think you'd forgive me. I miscalculated how hard that was on you."

"Dad…"

He pulls me into a hug, his face buried in my hair. "You need to know, no matter what you decide, I'll always love you. This is your decision—no one else's. And I'm not going away anytime soon."

Part of me doesn't believe him, but I let my arms wrap around him finally.

"There are a couple clinics in Burlington and Montpelier," I mumble into his flannel shirt. "Could you drive me?"

He kisses the top of my head. "Of course."

"I'll set up an appointment."

◆

"You're here!" Jimmy's face brightens when I enter the Eyrie. "And your hair's down." He stands behind the counter, flushed and giggling.

Yes, they're definitely drinking.

I look around. There's one student on the far side, watching Comedy Central while eating, but no one else is here.

I join Jimmy by the register and lean against the counter, one hand gripping the strap of my backpack. "Where's Xander?"

"In the back." Jimmy grins. "He's closing up and mopping."

I peer in the direction of the back room, curious. "Does he know how to hold a mop?"

He laughs. "You want a drink?"

"You guys are going to get in trouble for this." But I nod.

Jimmy slips over to the slushie machines by the pick-up counter, and I follow him into the back room. "Only if we get caught." He fills a to-go cup with the frozen pink drink, snaps on a lid, and slides it and a straw across the counter. "Raspberry lemonade."

I set my backpack on the floor. "And vodka?"

He smiles in confirmation.

I push in the straw and take a sip. Yep, definitely with vodka. I cringe at the cold and twist around to take in the expanse of the room.

All the chairs are flipped over on top of the tables, and

Xander is in the back with a mop, his black hair stuffed under a backwards cap. It's a strange sight. The few times I've seen him here, he's running the register and goofing off—not actually working.

He leans down and pushes the mop under one of the bigger tables, and I bite my lip.

Jimmy slides around beside me, his own slushie in his hand. "Is there a reason you're staring at Xander's ass?"

"What?" I turn to him with wide eyes. "I'm not. I'm just surprised to see him doing something for a change."

He takes a long slurp, but the smile he sends me—he doesn't believe me for a second. "You're feeling better than earlier. You were pretty upset at lunch."

I look down. "Yeah, I am. I had dinner with my dad."

"And that made you feel better?"

"It did." I smile. "We…had a nice time."

Jimmy grins.

Xander comes back toward the kitchen with the mop and rolling bucket in tow. He smiles when he spots me. "You made it. Let me put this away. I'll be right back." He wheels the bucket behind the counter to the kitchen and returns a few seconds later with the biggest smile. He leans across the counter toward us. "I was starting to wonder if you'd come."

I set my cup on the counter. "I said I'd try." I cross my arms atop the counter and rest my head on my forearm. My auburn hair sprawls down my back and arms. "And here I am. It's not a big deal."

"What's up with your hair?" Xander tugs on a corkscrew strand. "You haven't worn it natural in a while." He twists the hair loosely around his finger. "You look good. It looks

357

like sex hair."

I roll my eyes, but heat rises to my cheeks. "Would you behave? One of the benefits of having my hair up is preventing idiotic comments like that." Although, most of those stopped after my big blow-up in middle school.

"Behave?" He laughs and releases the hair. "Never."

Jimmy leans forward to get a better view of the front room. "Shit. Customer."

Xander moves toward the register. "I got it. I'm definitely the less conspicuous one."

When I turn to Jimmy, he laughs. His red face is a dead giveaway. "I've had two cups' worth," he admits in a quiet voice. "I think it's starting to really hit me."

I shake my head, laughing. "These are twenty-ounce cups."

"Yep."

"You shouldn't be operating a stove-top."

Jimmy grins. "I'm not. Right now."

Xander returns a second later and pulls his cup from a low shelf. "They got a drink and one of those pre-made sandwiches." He takes a drink, and Jimmy slides his empty cup across the counter with a pout. "No, I'm not giving you any more. You're drunk."

But Jimmy shakes his head. "You've had more than me."

"Unlike you, I can handle my alcohol."

Jimmy scowls and turns away.

"You're a bad influence." I can't help smiling.

He beams back and mimics my position, leaning against the counter across from me. "You don't seem to mind."

"You must be a bad influence on me too then."

Xander's smile widens, and he inches closer. "I'm okay

with that." He pokes at the strands of hair between us, and his eyes flit up to meet mine. "You're not working on your project tonight?"

I glance down at the backpack. "I brought my stuff, but I don't imagine I'll have much use for it here." My cup's contents are already half gone. "I probably shouldn't be drinking."

"Have you drawn any more?" He lifts his head curiously.

I laugh and kneel down to open my backpack. Jimmy shifts back toward the conversation, no longer pouting, as I lay my Bristol pad on the counter. "I worked on it a little when I got back from my dad's." I flip to a new page. "They're pretty rough."

Both Xander and Jimmy peer at the paper.

"Are you going to have time to ink it?" Xander asks.

"I hope so."

"These are really good, Billie." Jimmy reaches out a hesitant hand to rotate the drawing pad for a better view. He hasn't seen anything I've drawn since we were kids, when it didn't matter.

I nudge the book in his direction. "Look at the others." He takes the book in both hands and flips through the pages, and Xander's smiling at me again.

His smile is contagious, his eyes mesmerizing, and I take a long drink instead of figuring out what to say. The slushie is stronger than I anticipated; the vodka is mostly concealed by the citrus, but there's a biting aftertaste that reminds me it's alcoholic. I'm already feeling dizzy, getting overheated, having difficulty thinking—but maybe that's his smile.

I reach the bottom of my drink and slurp at the straw, and Xander takes the cup, our fingers brushing. "You want more?" I nod, and he turns away to refill the cup.

The Eyrie uniform is simple black slacks, a gray-blue t-shirt with the Bradford falcon and "The Eyrie" written in a simple sans serif font, a black cap, and of course, slip-resistant shoes. Xander's backwards cap looks ridiculous, and he has a dirty white dishcloth that swings as he walks tucked into a back pocket. He looks good in black.

He returns with my cup, and I accept it with a small, "Thanks."

Jimmy looks up from the drawing pad and clears his throat. "You've gotten a lot better since the last time you let me see your artwork, Billie," he says in a quiet voice as he slides the book back to me.

I frown. Something's bothering him.

"Thanks." I step closer and nudge him. "You know how big of a deal this is to me, right?"

"I do."

"Then you know how much I appreciate you saying that." I offer him my drink. "You wanna sneak some of my slushie since the big meanie refuses to give you more?"

Jimmy takes a drink and smiles. "It's not very sneaky if said meanie is watching. I'll get you in trouble." He rolls his eyes, laughing.

My eyes wander back to Xander, who has an amused smirk on his face. "I don't know, I'm not too worried about getting in trouble."

Something tells me being in trouble with Xander might not be so bad. In fact, I rather like the idea.

"Yeah," Jimmy says in a conspiratorial whisper, "he's got a soft spot for you."

I take my drink back and have a sip, and in the distance,

voices draw closer.

Xander steps back to check on the front room and nods Jimmy in his direction. "Hey, Jim, look who it is."

Jimmy walks around the counter with a sigh, until he catches a glimpse of the new customers. "Oh, shit." He rushes to the register.

From my vantage point, I can't see anything in the front room but the drink station, but Xander waves me to join him.

"I'm not supposed to be back here." I take a hesitant step over the threshold, but he rolls his eyes and drags me to the wall separating the front and back rooms, a spot where we can crouch together and inconspicuously spy.

"Hey." Jimmy's voice catches with excitement or maybe nervousness.

I can barely see short blond hair and press closer to Xander for a better view. Cynthia and beside her, Prudence. I can't decide whether to laugh or groan. That idiot still likes her, even after that spectacular rejection months ago—and he'll never see reason.

I grit my teeth and turn to Xander.

He's already looking at me, his eyebrows bunched together. "Are your tits bigger?"

"What?" I stumble backward, but I hit the wall before I'm out of reach. I swallow down the panic and force a sneer. "Of course not. How much have you had to drink?"

He frowns and continues to stare at my chest. "More than I thought. I swear they're bigger."

I shake my head, and he looks up with an apologetic smile. "I'm not going to ask the obvious question because I really think it's better if I don't know."

"What question?"

I hesitate. "How often you look that you think you can notice a subtle change."

He laughs and leans against the wall beside me. "Yeah, it's probably better if you don't ask."

But I want to ask. I want to hear him say it. I want to know if he means it. I want him to be closer, to press me against this wall, to kiss me—and when he's done all that, I want him naked. I want to hear that surprised little inhalation, and I want to cause that surprise when I take him into my mouth. I want him to touch me, to subdue the ache between my legs.

It's crazy. I'm crazy. It must be the hormones.

"Exactly." I push away from the wall and walk out from behind the counter. "Better if I don't."

Thirty-Six

"Okay." Xander matches his pace with mine. "Did you memorize your speech? Do you have your index cards at the ready?"

Sunlight streams through the leaves as we walk down the Lane toward Beecher Hall, through mottled shadows, past spring flowers, along the sidewalk. Xander's done with his classes for the day, but he insisted on escorting me to my Honors Seminar for this brilliant little pep talk—after spending the previous three nights helping me finish the project and write my speech.

I clutch the large binder to my chest. It's the only thing I brought with me. I'm trying not to panic.

"You've got all the pages in there, right? All the lettering is legible?"

My nod is minuscule.

"Alright, alright." He pumps his fist. "You've got this, Dixon. You worked your ass off, and it looks fantastic. I don't understand half the covered material, but you say the class will, so I'll take your word for it."

Beecher Hall looms above, and I hesitate at the end of the awning.

"Don't panic now." He takes my hand and drags me toward the building. "There's no time for second-guessing. This is your final. You can't fail."

Way to pile on the pressure, Xander. As if I'm not already dealing with enough.

"You've got to walk in there and own it." He yanks open the door and pulls me inside, only to pause because he doesn't know where the classroom is.

"Third floor." I nod toward the stairs.

"Oh, thank God." He turns on me in the middle of the foyer; other students have to maneuver around us. "I was worried you lost your voice on the way over." He shakes me by the shoulders. "You can't go mute now. You have to speak to give a presentation."

I frown. "I hate public speaking."

"You'll do fine," he says flippantly, and he leads the way upstairs.

We stop again on the third floor, this time beside the drinking fountain and restrooms, and Xander locks eyes with me.

"Alright, Dixon, you have to stay positive—and there's nothing to be negative about. The artwork is brilliant, and the story is pretty good too. Make sure when you walk in there, you're confident and relaxed, and everything will be fine. If you set your mind to it, you can do anything."

I shake my head. Ten feet behind him, the other students file into the room. "I can't do this."

"Of course you can. You know how they say you should picture everyone in the crowd naked?" Xander lets out a small laugh before turning serious again. "Really, though, imagine you're talking to me. Preferably without all the ridiculously snarky comments. Probably no cussing too. But explain it the way you told me."

I look over his shoulder toward the classroom. Almost everyone is inside, taking their seats. Dr. Lewis isn't here, but his office is down the hall. Xander's face is covered with an anxious smile, and I grab his wrist to read his watch.

Two minutes till.

"I should get in there."

He leans in, so close his nose brushes mine, and a small smirk plays on his lips. "Do you think I could sneak in and watch?"

My eyes narrow. "I'm going to take that as a sadistic desire to watch me fail."

Xander rolls his eyes and, with a grin, tugs on my frizzy ponytail. "Slay them."

Presentations have been a free-for-all—volunteer when you want to go, and if no one offers, Dr. Lewis picks someone at random. We've been doing presentations for the previous two class periods, and most students have already done theirs.

But I don't volunteer; I wait until the last minute.

I am the last person to rise from my seat and stand in front of the class. I lay the over-sized binder on the table and turn to the class.

Dr. Lewis sits at a desk in the back corner and nods.

I begin in a small voice. "For my creative project, I knew exactly what I wanted to do."

"Please speak up, Billie," Lewis calls out.

I blink a few times, picturing Xander's face in the front row, recalling his instructions, and try again. "This semester, we've focused on truth and how we as a country perceive truth. The medium I chose is a comic book, a single-issue story to discuss what is possibly one of the most important truths—the personal truth."

I pause a moment and prop up the binder, though the images inside are too small to see from the crowd. "The issue follows Jamie Madrox, who is a character in the Marvel universe known as Multiple Man. He is in the X-Men storylines, and his mutant ability is to make duplicates of himself. These duplicates can stay apart from him for as long as necessary and only return to him when they physically touch. Until then, they can form their own lives, their own personalities, their own identities, and when he absorbs them, he gains those memories and experiences.

"I use Jamie Madrox's character to explore what personal identity and personal truth can mean while examining a number of theories on the subject. I draw from a number of sources and concepts, including diachronic and episodic personalities, dissociative identity disorder, and Logi Gunnarsson's *Philosophy of Personal Identity and Multiple Personality*."

I shift anxiously and glance toward Dr. Lewis. "The issue is fifteen pages, plus a cover. I'd hate to read a section out loud. You miss so much without the images."

Lewis nods. "Unless there's anything else you want to say about it, I think it would be great for everyone to walk up and take a look."

I nod and step away, separating myself from the project, and several other students come take a look.

In the back, Dr. Lewis waits a few minutes before joining me, notebook in hand. "You can sit down, Billie, if you like."

I return to my seat, trying not to watch as my classmates flip through the pages of the binder.

When most students return to their chairs, Dr. Lewis addresses the class. "That concludes the presentations. Thank you, everyone, for sharing. Just a reminder, we're not meeting next week. I'm taking extra time to grade these so I can return them before summer break. If anyone is leaving campus before Wednesday, shoot me an email and I'll put yours on the top of the stack. I'll email each of you when I finish your project. You can pick them up during my office hours."

The last student returns to her seat, and Lewis adds, "That's all, folks. Have a great holiday."

Everyone else gets ready to head out. Prudence pauses at her desk to send me a smile and a thumbs-up.

When most others are gone, Dr. Lewis calls out my name. He spent the last minute looking at my binder on the table.

I join him at the front of the classroom, and he jumps right in. "This is quite a project, Billie." He flips through the comic, not even looking up. "This is your artwork? It's fantastic. I mean, obviously, there's always more to learn, but you have a certain style of precision in your drawings—it's very eye-catching. Have you declared your major yet?"

"Not officially."

My plan was double-majoring in Math and Computer Sciences, but my adviser wanted me to wait until the end of the year to fill out the paperwork.

Lewis smiles. "You should look into the art program, Billie. Have you tried painting before? Or figure drawing?

We have some talented professors here. I'd hate to see this wasted. You've obviously been learning from somewhere."

I shake my head. "It's been videos online, drawing from stock photos—nothing special." I shift my weight from foot to foot. "I've been considering it—taking an art class, I mean."

"Please do. With some proper training, you could really go somewhere with this. And I love the storyline—you've implemented our class discussions well. It's funny too."

The jokes were all Xander.

Lewis adds the binder to his stack of creative projects and gets ready to leave. "Please look into the drawing class. I'd love to see your work after a few sessions with Greg Steele or Felix Quigley. They're some of the best undergrad art professors in the state—and there's plenty of time to change your schedule before the fall semester."

"Okay," I say, not sure what else to do, and I follow him out of the room.

Most of Beecher Hall is empty by the time I reach the ground floor. I take the steps two at a time; I have to meet my dad at his house now.

But there, sitting atop the handrail at the base of the staircase, feet dangling, is Xander. He waited for me.

I can't stop smiling. "What are you doing here?"

He looks up with a grin. "Well? How'd it go?"

I lean against the rail beside him. "Not as bad as it could've gone." I look around. Seriously, no one else is here. "Did you stay here the whole time?"

Xander hops down. "I didn't have anything else to do."

That can't possibly be true. It's almost finals week. Even

Xander—with his miraculous ability to pass classes without holding a textbook more than once a semester—should be studying. Instead, he waited for me.

"You wanna get lunch?" He nods toward the door. "Late lunch."

I follow him out of the building, and we fall into step as we walk along the Lane.

"I can't."

Seriously, I can't. I haven't been allowed to eat for the last twenty-four hours.

"When are you going to eat anything?" He releases an exasperated sigh. "You're paler, and you've been eating less—which I didn't think possible."

"I'm alright."

He cocks his head. "You don't make a very convincing argument, Dixon."

When we reach the JW Student Center, we stop and face each other.

"You're not going to come inside and hang out, are you?" He nods toward the cafeteria.

I shake my head. "I wish I could, but I have something I need to do."

He pauses a moment, his eyebrows knitting together. "You're calmer than before. Did something happen?" He sighs. "What aren't you telling me?"

I force a small laugh. "There's a lot I'm not telling you."

"Will we see you tonight?"

"I don't know. I might be at my dad's late."

He frowns and steps closer. "I wish you told me what was going on." He reaches a hesitant hand to my cheek, then pulls me into a tight hug.

369

I hold him—the steady rise and fall of his chest calms me—and when he lets go, I smile. "Don't let Jimmy's worrying get to you. I'm…doing better, oddly enough."

I check my phone. I'm late.

"Sorry, I have to go."

"I know."

I can feel his eyes on me as I walk away.

Thirty-Seven

"ARE YOU READY?"

Brow creased, spindly fingers clutching the steering wheel, knuckles turning white, Dad looks more nervous than I feel.

The nearest clinic is located in the beautiful town of Burlington on the eastern shore of Lake Champlain. It's a college town like St. Clare but much bigger, and it's vibrant and scenic and pretty much everything Vermont is known for.

I haven't been able to focus on that, though. Despite the sunshine, the temperature's barely above fifty. I spent most of the trip with the window down, the cool wind blowing in my face.

"No turning back now." I unbuckle my seatbelt.

"Do you want me to come with you?"

I turn to him with an anxious smile, and he too removes his seatbelt.

Inside, the small building is tiled with checkered linoleum, and fluorescent lights glare down. A couple rows of chairs line the room, several occupied by other women nervously awaiting their turn.

On the right side is a nurses' station, where a young woman with a brilliant smile greets me. "Do you have an appointment?"

"Yes." I pull out my ID and insurance card.

She takes the cards from the countertop and finds my name in the system. "Alright, Wilhelmina." She shows off her green braces with another smile. "I need you to fill out a few forms." She grabs a nearby clipboard with documents already attached and highlights the pertinent parts. "Make sure you sign here, here, and here, and initial these two spots. You haven't eaten anything for the past twenty-four hours, right?"

"Yes."

That was an easy instruction to follow.

"Good. Once you're done with the form, bring it back to me, and the doctor will see you soon."

I take the clipboard to an open seat. My dad sits beside me.

A confidentiality form as well as a health history form. It doesn't take long to be tired of checking boxes. I fill out emergency contacts and allergy information, write out the number of school years I've completed. I don't know why my smoking habits or whether I'm adopted have anything to do with this, but theoretically these forms are important.

At the end of the five pages, I draw my final signature and return the forms. The nurse on duty accepts them. "It'll be a few minutes if you'll have a seat."

I sit down and glance around. The room almost feels like a regular doctor's office, even with the eerie silence. There are other girls, one as young as fourteen, some in their thirties, and I can't help but stare. One girl, no older than fifteen, sits in the corner, holding the hand of her boyfriend. I turn away to give them some semblance of privacy.

At last my name is called, and Dad gives me a small hug. "You'll be fine, Mina," he whispers in my ear before I pull away.

The staff is matter-of-fact. The nurse, who identifies herself as Leah with a short smile, explains the procedure quickly.

"This way, Miss Dixon." She leads through a couple hallways toward the exam rooms. "What we'll do for you is called dilation and curettage. It's an out-patient procedure that only takes about ten to fifteen minutes."

The exam room is tiny and brilliant white, completely sterile.

She hands me a folded gown. "Dilation means we widen the opening of your cervix so that we can insert a speculum, and after it's wide enough, the doctor will remove the contents of your uterus with a curette. Dr. Addams may need to suction out any remaining particles." She removes something from the desk. "Any cramping and spotting afterward is completely normal. Do you need to pee?"

It sounds simple.

She instructs me to change into the gown and leaves the room, adding only, "The doctor will be in shortly."

I slip on the gown and sit on the bed.

It takes the doctor ten minutes to arrive. I'm fiddling with the hangnail on my left index finger when he arrives. He knocks and steps inside to introduce himself.

"Hello, Miss Dixon." His voice is a deep baritone, and he doesn't make eye contact. "I'm Dr. Addams. Are you ready to get to work?"

The nurse Leah and the anesthesiologist enter the room behind him.

"Please lie back." Addams pulls out the stirrups from the foot of the table, and I spread my legs like the ultrasound. "We'll get you fixed up here in no time."

◆

I blink and blink again.

It's dark, but not too dark. A few small lights around the gray room. An aqua-colored blob. Must be a nurse—the blob is moving. A blurry bottle of water sits on the table next to my reclined chair.

"Miss Dixon."

I can barely move my head, my arm, let alone look at her.

"Let me open that for you." She moves closer, faster than I can follow, and twists open the water. I try to reach for it when she offers, but my hand barely lifts into the air. She places a straw inside the bottle and holds it to my mouth so I can take a drink, then she returns it to the table and moves on.

I stretch my fingers, my hands, and close my eyes again. My throat is dry, even after the water, and there's a fierce churning in my stomach. Nausea—from the procedure or the anesthesia?

My eyes flutter open again. Everything's blurry. Where are my glasses? On the table?

The aqua-colored blob returns, and she offers me water again. "You have to stay awake for twenty minutes before we can release you, Miss Dixon. Do you think you can manage that?"

I try to say something, but it comes out as a groan.

"Don't try to move too much. You have someone waiting for you, right? Your father?"

I barely manage a nod and take another drink.

"We'll let him know you're awake. After twenty minutes, you should be able to move more easily, and we can wheel you out to the pick-up."

I swallow. My mouth feels a little better. I blink and squint, trying to focus on the objects around me. Yes, my glasses are on the table next to the water bottle.

"If you're tired, you can close your eyes and sleep more. It's a normal side effect of the anesthesia." She pauses. "If you need to throw up, there's a bag on your left."

The nausea is mild at best, but it's there, under the surface.

"Would you like more to drink?"

◆

"Mina?"

My dad. I'm in the car now. They wheeled me out to his Buick. I don't know how long we've been driving. Everything blurs together.

"How are you feeling?"

Dad sits behind the wheel, wearing a worried expression, glancing between me and the road ahead, his foot barely touching the gas pedal.

It's highway. The blur of the road and trees is dizzying.

"Water?"

He grabs a bottle from the cup holder and pries it open

before handing it to me. I gulp down half the contents.

"Have you read the print-offs they sent with you?" He nods toward the dash, where the papers sit. "I looked over it before we left. It seems straightforward."

I shake my head. "We talked about the important stuff before they brought me out." I take a deep breath, then another drink. "There's a twenty-four-hour number to call if I have any severe symptoms. It should be on there."

"Yes, I saw that."

I push myself up as far as I can manage. "How long did it take?"

"I'm not sure. I don't think they told me right after finishing, but it was faster than I expected."

I reach for the papers and flip through them, but I can't focus. A few words stand out: *symptoms, discharge, tenderness, depression, infertility.* It's too much.

"We can look at everything together when we get back."

I push the papers away. I still feel sick. "I'm sorry." I take a few sips of water again, but it doesn't quell the nausea.

"For what?"

Leaning back, I clutch the bottle to my chest. "For everything. I haven't exactly been the perfect daughter."

Dad lets out a little chuckle. "I never would've expected that, Mina. Besides, I can't claim to be the perfect father. I spent the three years before you came here wallowing in self-pity, unable to work up the nerve to contact you. If anyone's a disappointment, it's me. I've deserved everything you said and more."

"No, you haven't." I sigh. "And certainly not this."

"'This'?" He glances my way, eyebrows raised.

"Yeah, you know, this." I motion toward my abdomen.

"I should've kept it, but I'm glad I didn't."

"Then that's what matters. It was your decision to make, Mina, and I wouldn't begrudge you that. Besides, I'm about as ready to be a grandparent as you are a parent."

I smile softly and grow a little braver. "Well, as long as we're being honest…"

He reaches over to turn up the AC. I didn't realize it was on. "You mean you keep secrets from me?" He turns to me with a smile.

I can't manage a laugh yet. "Dad, I'm not sure I'm cut out for this."

"For what?"

"I always wanted to be just like you. Even when I was mad at you and blamed you for everything. But we're different people."

"Yes, we are." He heaves a long sigh. "I never realized how young you were, Mina. I treated you like an adult, but you were fourteen—and far more vulnerable than I thought. But I need you to know you never did anything wrong. Ever. You were my light in the darkness. Your mother and I wouldn't have lasted as long if it weren't for you—and your sister."

Tears prick at the corners of my eyes, and my grip on the water bottle tightens. "You read my letter. How?"

He clears his throat. "You brought it to my house. It was in your bedroom when I cleaned after spring break."

How could I have missed it when I returned to the dorms?

"I'm ashamed of my actions, Mina. I should have talked to you." He sends me a small smile, then turns back to the road. "I wanted to take you with me, but we decided not to separate you and Imogene. I was too broken up to tell you, too upset for my own sake—and I squandered our last months before the move." His voice cracks. "How can you forgive me?"

How can he beg my forgiveness when I've been lying to him—to myself—for the last nine months? How can I utter a word of acceptance when I can't accept myself? I can't bear the thought of lying after all this. Not anymore.

"I don't want to do math anymore."

He looks to me in surprise at the sudden turn.

"I'm taking a drawing class in the fall—I added it to my schedule."

Dad nods. "Imogene said you love to draw, and I've noticed your sketchbooks many times throughout the year. I'm not surprised."

My brow furrows. "You're not?"

"Apparently, you're quite talented."

"Mo said that?"

"No, Xander did."

I frown. Since when do Xander and my dad talk?

"You don't have to choose between doing math and art. They're both a part of who you are, and all of you is special. Changing your major isn't going to change the way I feel about you."

I almost laugh. It sounds equally ridiculous when he says it as when Imogene made the stipulation over spring break. Perhaps I am a bit paranoid.

"As long as you're happy, so am I."

I take another drink of the water, smiling. "You won't tell Mom, will you?"

He laughs. "Honey, I haven't talked to your mother since

we first discussed your studying here. I don't think you have to worry about her hearing anything from me."

I nod.

"What about Zane Nelson?"

Obviously, we aren't talking about art anymore.

"He graduates in a week." I shake my head. "I'm not sure there's much point in talking to him about this."

"You may feel differently later. Obviously, it's your decision, but you may feel he deserves to know."

I scowl at the bottle in my hand. Zane deserves nothing from me—but Dad doesn't know the circumstances, he can only guess.

"Not right now, but eventually, you'll want to talk to someone."

I doubt that.

"How long until we get back to St. Clare?"

Dad glances at his odometer and does a quick calculation. "Another forty-five minutes."

I nod.

"If you like, you can stay the night at my house."

With a deep breath, I lean back and close my eyes. That would probably be best. I'm not ready to go back to the dorm, to face Xander or Jimmy, to spend another night with Val, even if those nights are numbered—and the numbers are now in the single digits.

No, I can think about all of this later. Dad's right. For now, I need to take care of myself.

Thirty-Eight

ON MY BED SITS MY BACKPACK, MY DUFFEL BAG, AND A SUIT-case, and I pile the remnants of my possessions inside.

The closet is empty. The wall is bare. The desk, for once, is no longer cluttered with textbooks and drawing pads. Even my sheets and pillow are folded and packed away.

Val's side of the room is equally vacant. Her bags are already in her car, and she reclines on her bare mattress, flipping through her phone, waiting.

I move my bags to the foot of my bed, where my beanbag chair is already waiting, and sit down too.

It's nearly two—our checkout time. Our RA should be here anytime to go over everything, to make sure we haven't broken or stolen anything.

The door is open, but he knocks when he arrives, clip-board in hand. Val and I stand to greet him. "Hey, ladies." David smiles. "Let's take a quick look around."

First, he peeks into the bathroom area to see we haven't made a huge mess since Prudence and Cynthia left yester-day. Then, he systematically examines the room, checking to see all drawers and closets are vacant and clean, the floor is swept, there aren't holes in the walls, the window's latched, no furniture has been removed or broken.

"Billie, I can't sign this—" David holds up his clipboard to demonstrate "—while your stuff is in here. Can you move it into the hallway?"

I take the bags out two at a time and pause outside the door.

On the other side of the hallway, a couple doors down, Jimmy and Xander are carrying stuff out of their room. Their checkout time's in an hour. Jimmy catches my eye and smiles, and I head back.

Inside, Val and David stand together as she signs the document. When she's done, she hands the clipboard back, and he offers it to me.

"All done then?" I accept it and sign my name at the bottom of the form.

"Yeah." David smiles, takes the clipboard, and tucks it under his arm. "When you leave, make sure to lock the door. Then, you can take your keys to Safety & Security before leaving. Have a good summer."

He leaves, and I exit the room again. My stuff's still there.

Val follows me out and pokes her head in one last time. Then, she shuts and locks the door. "Well," she says, turning to me, "goodbye, I guess. It's been...weird."

I frown, not sure how to respond. "Yeah. Have a good summer."

She forces a smile, and then, she's gone, walking down the hallway to the stairs.

I return my attention to my pile of stuff in the hallway. How am I supposed to move all this without a car?

"*Hey!*"

I look up. Xander's returning from outside, and I smile.

He pauses at his bedroom door, then approaches. "You need help? My car's parked in the loading zone on Vallee while we're, you know, loading. You can stick them in there." He nods down to my bags.

I tilt my head. "If you put both Jimmy's and my stuff in your car—along with yours—how are you supposed to fit? It's awfully nice of you to offer, but I'm not sure of the mechanics."

Xander rolls his eyes and stoops to grab the duffel bag, then the suitcase. "Quit complaining and come on, Dixon."

I laugh, slip the backpack over my shoulders, and hug the beanbag to my chest before following him to the elevator. "You don't have to do this," I say when we enter the small elevator car.

He presses the button for the ground floor. "No, I'll let you walk them all the way to your dad's house." He scoffs. "You'll have to wait for David to check us out, though."

The elevator passes the second floor.

"I, uh, can't. I'm going to drop off my key, and then, there's something I want to do."

He cocks an eyebrow but doesn't ask, and the elevator stops.

Xander leads the way out of Lincoln Hall, down the sidewalk to his Camaro. He opens up the passenger side, pops the seat forward, and shoves the bags in the back.

"There won't be room for you anyway." He takes the beanbag from me and pushes it in. When he turns back, his blue eyes catch mine, and hesitant fingers peel the backpack straps down my arms. "This too, right?"

I bite my lip. All I can do is nod.

He shuts the door when he's done and turns his attention

382

to me again. "When should we meet you at your dad's?"

"I'll be there by the time you're done with checkout."

"Alright."

"You are staying for dinner, right? You said you would."

A grin spreads across Xander's face, and he leans down and squeezes my shoulder. "Wouldn't miss it, Dixon." He releases me. I'm cold where he let go. "I've gotta get back." He nods toward Lincoln Hall.

"Yeah, I need to turn in my key. I'll see you around 3:30?"

He nods, and we part ways.

My phone buzzes as I leave the JW Student Center, having dropped off my key at Safety & Security, and I pull the device out as I walk down the Lane. A text from Imogene: *Checking on your ETA. When will you arrive in Springfield?*

I tap to respond, then move my finger up and tap on the phone-shaped symbol to call her. It rings twice before she picks up.

"Hey." She's excitable as always. "I wasn't expecting a response for like three hours—and even then, not a phone call."

I roll my eyes. "I'm not that desperate to avoid talking to you."

"Apparently." Imogene laughs. "I'm correct remembering you're coming back with Jimmy, right? We're not picking you up at the airport."

"Yeah." I direct my feet to the right of the Lane and past the library. "Charlie and Thea are driving up on Monday to pick us up at Dad's. We'll head out that afternoon, so we should get back, I don't know, sometime Wednesday."

Imogene grumbles. "Flying would be faster."

"Oh well." I shrug. "This is what happens when you have to take a bunch of stuff with you. Besides, you get to bug me all summer."

"Fine, fine." She chuckles. "Like you don't bug me too."

On the back side of Mercier, Beecher, and Stanley Halls, I stop. The area is a huge green space between the lesson halls and Finchley Avenue, and on the other side of the packed street is Bradford's large auditorium. The green space in between is filled with people—students in formal attire, many wearing their black robes and blue and silver Bradford cords, and their families. The graduation ceremony just finished.

"That's nice, Mo." I'm not paying attention anymore. "I have to go."

I barely recognize any of the senior class. I never interacted with more people than necessary. I never put myself out there or tried to make friends. But that also means I don't have to say goodbye.

Perhaps.

I walk along the edge of the green space toward Finchley Avenue, passing the crowds of boisterous graduates and family members. In three years, will I too stand here, relieved for it all to be over, ready to start the next adventure?

Halfway to the street, I see him.

He stands near one of Bradford's ancient trees, posing with a man who's probably his father. He has the same angular features, the same straight black hair, and the same smile. The woman with the camera must be his mother; she fidgets with excitement.

After the photos are over, he poses with a group of male

graduates. Probably other members of his frat. The friends I was supposed to meet the week after we had sex.

Just when I start walking again, heading for Finchley, ready to make a U-turn and walk to my dad's house, Zane sees me. Through the crowds, his cool gray eyes land on me, and I pause again.

I don't flinch. I don't cower. I don't panic.

After a moment, he pulls away from his parents and frat brothers and crosses the green space, his black robes billowing behind him. He stops a few feet away, black cap sitting to the side, and I stand straighter in an attempt to look him in the eyes.

He keeps his eyes on me, uncertain. "What are you doing here?"

I swallow. "I wanted to see you one last time."

Zane shakes his head. "No, I meant, shouldn't you be off campus already?"

Ah, that.

"I'm staying the weekend at my dad's before heading home." After everything, one weekend with my dad is hardly a big deal.

But Zane's eyebrows shoot up under his bangs, and he studies me. "You're different."

Perhaps a little.

"What'd you decide?"

I don't have to ask to know what he's talking about. "That's none of your business."

He purses his lips. "I can help you."

"No, you can't."

He removes his cap and runs a hand through his dark hair. "Then why the hell are you here? You made it pretty

385

clear you didn't want me anywhere near you. Did you ever like me? Or were you playing along because of how I felt about you?"

I frown. "I'm not convinced you ever felt much for me. Be honest with yourself. Is there anything that made you think this could work?"

His lips narrow into a thin line. "If you liked me enough, you wouldn't ask that question."

"You're hardly the person who should talk about genuine feelings. If you liked me enough, you wouldn't have imposed on me. You wouldn't have pressured me into a relationship I didn't want." I heave a sigh, but he only stares. "I don't pretend to know how you feel, but you just got your diploma. I have three more years here, and I then have to figure out the rest of my life. Would you have waited for me?"

He doesn't answer.

"A relationship without honesty isn't a relationship at all. We spent the last five months lying to each other. If you thought this was serious, you were fooling yourself—and worse, you were trying to fool me."

He stands silently, considering my words. "If that's all you have to say, why did you come here?"

I step closer to Finchley Avenue. "Like I said, I wanted to see you one last time. I'm here for me, not you, and now that I've seen you and talked to you, I never want to again."

Zane grits his teeth and turns toward the crowd. "I need to get back. Goodbye."

Thirty-Nine

"YOU'RE BURNING THEM."

Dad rotates the hot dogs with a pair of tongs, frowning. "This isn't exactly my area of expertise."

I smile at him over the smoke of the grill. "You don't barbecue often?"

"I bought the charcoal this morning, if that helps you figure it out."

"Really?" I chuckle. "I'm surprised you have a grill then."

He looks up and smiles, tongs held aloft. "It was a gift."

On the grill, the hot dogs sizzle, and grease drips down to the charcoal, inciting flames.

"Usually, if they're dripping that much, they're done. The charred parts are also a pretty good indicator." I lift the platter closer, and he looks at it, lips pursed. "What, do you want me to lay down a decorative romaine bed for them? Put the hot dogs on it, Dad."

His mouth tightens—he's trying not to laugh—and he removes the hot dogs two at a time. When the platter is full, he closes the lid and hangs his tongs on the side, not sure what to do next.

"I'll buy you a brush to clean it, but for now, let's put

387

these on the table."

At the edge of the porch, he has a folding card table set up with a tablecloth and a number of condiments. There are two stacks of paper plates and plastic cups and several bags of chips and buns. Charcoal isn't the only thing he bought at the store this morning.

I set the platter on the table.

"I made potato salad." Dad indicates the large bowl beside the platter.

I hold back my laugh. Of course he did.

"Do you think there's enough food?"

I roll my eyes. "Dad, it'll be fine. If they're still hungry, they can raid your fridge."

The intense crease on his forehead says he doesn't care for that idea. Probably because he doesn't want them to ruin his organization. And I think he's got a baked Brie in there he's saving.

"*Watch out!*"

We turn round in time to move out of the way as a soccer ball careens to the left of the card table, and I turn to the perpetrators with a glare. "Watch where you're kicking that thing, idiots," I yell. "You're going to hurt someone."

To be fair, most likely, Jimmy will hurt himself. He scratches the back of his head and sends me a sheepish smile, and behind him, Xander cracks up.

The ball is now nestled in a low spot by the privacy fence. "Food's ready."

The two approach, smiling and laughing, and Xander nudges me. "Bossy." His breath tickles my ear, sending a shiver through my body. There's no complaint in his tone.

I shove him, and he stumbles into Jimmy. "Get your

food, asshat."

Xander recovers and grabs a paper plate, then another. "You're eating too, right?" He offers me the second plate.

I accept it and wait for them to dish up. My dad stands to the side, waiting and observing quietly. When our eyes meet, he smiles.

Dad only has a couple outdoor chairs, plus the bench swing, and Jimmy takes the first one with no remorse. Xander sits on the grass in front of the chairs, and I settle down beside him, leaving the vacant seat for my dad.

I lie on my stomach, feet up in the air, and poke at the potato salad curiously. Red potatoes, mayonnaise, dill, red onion, hard-boiled egg, among other things. I smile and take a bite. Dad couldn't fathom having a meal of only pre-made foods.

"What're you laughing about?" Xander raises an eyebrow curiously.

"Nothing."

Dad takes the open seat, and for a moment, he doesn't know what to do. He eats his potato salad.

In the other chair, Jimmy takes a bite, and I flick the bottom of his sneaker. "You're dangerous."

He chokes down his food. "No, it's him!" He points his finger at Xander, who laughs. "Blame the professional who's a terrible teacher."

Xander rolls his eyes. "I wasn't that good a player."

Jimmy relaxes, laughing, and nudges him with his foot. "Look at you being humble. I'm so proud of you."

He snorts. "Fuck you."

I turn to him, frowning. "You play soccer?"

"Played. But seriously, Dixon, how do you still know so

little about me? I was center striker."

I have no idea what that means, but it sounds like an offensive position. Not that I can picture Xander playing defense.

"You're shrouded in mystery."

He chuckles. "Have to keep you guessing."

I snort. "Yeah, I'm still guessing how you passed your classes without studying."

My dad clears his throat. "Xander, when do you intend to leave? I don't have any more spare rooms, but there are a couple couches if you'd like to stay the night."

Xander looks up with a smile. "I appreciate the offer, but it's probably time I see my parents." He shrugs. "Besides, I prefer driving at night. No one else is on the roads."

Dad nods and continues to eat, but I frown at my plate. Xander didn't go home for a single break during the school year—anytime he left campus, he was with Jimmy; they've been inseparable. I'm far more used to his being around than I'll admit.

Xander leans over and flicks my shoulder. "There's a funny thing about eating. It requires you to put the food in your mouth."

I send him a challenging glare. "You just want to watch me eat this hot dog."

His eyebrows shoot up to his hairline, but he doesn't say anything. Jimmy, however, gags on a chip and coughs uncontrollably, his hand over his mouth. My dad rises to get him a drink of water.

My face flushes. That's not even remotely appropriate in front of my dad.

Jimmy accepts the water and takes a drink to calm his

fit, and I return to my food, finally picking it up and eating. Everyone else is almost done.

When they clean up, Xander retrieves the soccer ball from the fence line, and he and Jimmy continue kicking the ball around. Xander gives him pointers, but they don't help much. Dad moves to put away the leftovers and clean the table, and I stand to help him when I'm done.

"What can I do?"

"Don't worry about it." Dad piles the plates and trash with a frown. "I suppose the convenient thing about this is the easy cleanup."

"This is killing you, isn't it?" I take the trash from him and move toward the house to throw it away, calling over my shoulder. "Why don't we make a pot of tea?"

He follows me inside and places his stack of buns and chip bags on the island to decide where to put them. "I'll take care of it." He looks up as I close the lid on the trash can. "What time is your appointment on Monday?"

"Eleven-thirty." I shove the chips in a cabinet. "Jimmy's parents will be here around ten, and he wants to show them around town while they're here. They didn't have time back in August."

Dad's brow crinkles. "That's convenient timing."

I force a smile. "It took a little work to get him to think of it." I lean against the island with a shrug. "But yeah, I can head over to Acker without anyone prying."

"Do you want me to go with you?" He grabs the buns and sets them inside the fridge. "Moral support." He turns back to me, a small smile on his face.

"I'd appreciate that."

He crosses the space between us and wraps an arm

around my shoulders, and I pull him closer. "You'll be fine. It's a check-up to be sure."

"I know."

I don't want to let him go.

He presses a kiss to my temple and squeezes one last time. "Go back outside and relax. You already helped me cook. You don't need to clean up too."

Outside, I sit on the porch swing with a new sketchbook and a stick of vine charcoal. The swing sways from the movement, and I sketch out the backyard.

On the grass, Jimmy tries to kick the ball back to Xander, but it misses by a couple feet and hits the fence.

Xander laughs. "You're terrible at this." He turns back to grab the ball from where it landed. "Have you played any sports?"

I flip the page and press charcoal to paper again.

"Do Yu-Gi-Oh competitions count?"

Xander grins despite the pained look on his face. "No, they really don't." He raises the ball into the air and chucks it at Jimmy, who catches it against his chest with both arms. "You should take this with you. You need to practice—I'll test you when we're back."

I snort. It won't help.

I flip the page again, and Jimmy holds the ball aside as he rubs his chest.

Xander crosses the yard to him. "You'll first need to learn how to catch it."

Jimmy rolls his eyes. "Gee, thanks." He drops the ball on a lawn chair and grabs a drink. The plates, cups, and a couple bottles of soda are the only things left on the card table.

Xander laughs and catches sight of me.

I turn the page again.

A moment later, he sits next to me, and the bench swings back and forth. "What are you drawing?"

I pull the sketchbook to my chest. "Mind your own business."

He scoots closer, a salacious grin on his face. "Oh, come on, Dixon, I've already seen everything." He waggles his eyebrows, and I let him pry my fingers off and take the book from my hands. He flips through the drawings as quickly as I sketched them. "What are these?"

"Gesture drawings. You sketch the shape or the action instead of a detailed drawing. Good practice—especially when your subject matter won't stop moving."

When Xander looks up, he's grinning. "I could pose nude for you if you want. You can go into as much detail as you like."

I laugh and take the sketchbook back. "No, that sounds like a bad idea." For so many reasons. I wouldn't be able to trust myself.

He relaxes against the back. "Wouldn't be our first bad idea."

I close the sketchbook and pull my feet up onto the bench, leaning into him despite the heat rising to my cheeks at the thought of that Thursday night, of him naked by the light switch, of his hungry eyes studying my every inch. "How long's your drive?"

"Twenty-two, twenty-three hours." He stretches an arm along the back of the seat, and I look down at his vibrant Charmander shirt. One tiny movement, and he could pull me into his arms. "If I leave in the next hour, assuming gas and food breaks, I'll probably get back around this time tomorrow."

I wet my lips. "You're not going to sleep?"

"I will if I have to."

"Why are you rushing? You should sleep."

He laughs. "Says the insomniac. But trust me, I'm in no rush to go home. There won't exactly be a welcoming committee."

I send him a concerned frown. "You should stay. You can head out in the morning, fully rested."

Xander cocks an eyebrow. "Why would I do that?"

I never thought it would matter. I never thought Xander would matter. But the truth is, I don't want to miss him. Not yet.

My face breaks into a smile, and I nudge him. "Because I want you to."

A grin spreads across his face, and his arm slips around my shoulders, holding me to his chest. "Well, Dixon, you make a very convincing argument."

Acknowledgments

This book wouldn't be possible without the support of many. My husband, first and foremost, is my most trusted ally and staunchest supporter, and I am endlessly thankful for him. Thank you to my parents and sisters for being endlessly supportive. I am also indebted to my dear friends Samantha, Marissa, and Shane for alpha and beta reading and inspiring me, even before this story took shape. Thank you to Michelle, my talented editor. Thank you to Sarah for her enthusiasm and, of course, the fabulous artwork. Thank you to Rayona for her kindess and dedication. Thank you to my proofreaders and beta readers for your suggestions and kindness. And thank you to anyone who has ever listened to me blab or ramble about this book during its development. You don't realize how much your interest means to an aspiring writer.

D. L. Pitchford

A Note on the Author

D. L. Pitchford is a wife and mother of two,
living in Springfield, Missouri. She graduated
from Drury University with a Bachelor's in
English, Writing, and Fine Arts in 2013.

Learn more at:
www.DLPitchford.com

A Note on Reviews

If you enjoyed this book, please consider leaving a review on Amazon or Goodreads. Reviews are like food for new and aspiring authors. This is not an instance where you shouldn't feed the wildlife. Please feed the starving artists with your reviews.